*COULD SHE STOP HER DREAM
FROM BECOMING A NIGHTMARE?*

Amaya had a dream—to help the warrior
husband she loved and the proud Cheyenne
people live in peace as they had lived, in
harmony with nature and the eternal
rhythm of the seasons on the vast expanse
of the Great Plains.

But now that dream was dissolving in a sea
of bloodshed, as everywhere white settlers
broke through the fragile barriers of paper
treaties.

There was only one person now who could
save Amaya's dream, and the man and the
people who meant more to her than life
itself.

That person was Andrew Pierce, the white
man whom she had rejected once and had
to go to in desperation now . . . willing to
pay any price . . . and fearing what that
price might be. . . .

CHEYENNE DREAMS

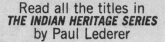

Read all the titles in
THE INDIAN HERITAGE SERIES
by Paul Lederer

(0451)

☐ **BOOK ONE: MANITOU'S DAUGHTERS**—Manitou was the god of the proud Oneidas, and these were the tribes' chosen daughters: Crenna, the strongest and wisest, who lost her position when she gave herself to the white man; Kala, beautiful and wanton, found her perfect match in the Englishman as ruthless as she; and Sachim, young and innocent, was ill-prepared for the tide of violence and terror that threatened to ravish their lands ... Proud women of a proud people—facing the white invaders of their land and their hearts ....   (117670—$2.95)

☐ **BOOK TWO: SHAWNEE DAWN**—William and Cara Van der Veghe were raised by their white father and Indian mother deep in the wilderness. But when the tide of white settlement crept closer, William and Cara had to choose sides on the frontier, he with the whites, she with the Shawnee. Brother and sister, bound together by blood, now facing each other over the flames of violence and vengeance .... (112000—$2.95)

☐ **BOOK THREE: SEMINOLE SKIES**—Shanna and her younger sister Lychma were fleeing the invading white men when they fell into even more feared hands—those of the ruthless Seminoles. But Shanna would not be broken, for she had the blood of a princess in her veins. Then she met the legendary warrior, Yui, the one man strong enough to save his people from white conquest—and to turn a woman's burning hate into flaming love ....   (122631—$2.95)

Prices higher in Canada.

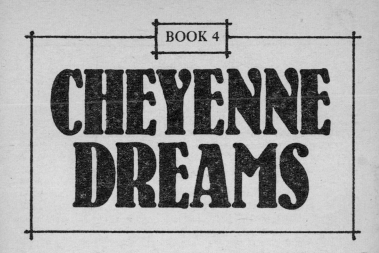

BOOK 4

CHEYENNE DREAMS

THE INDIAN HERITAGE SERIES

by
Paul Joseph Lederer

A SIGNET BOOK

NEW AMERICAN LIBRARY

PUBLISHER'S NOTE

This novel is a work of fiction. Names, characters, places, and
incidents either are the product of the author's imagination or are
used fictitiously, and any resemblance to actual persons, living or
dead, events, or locales is entirely coincidental.

SIGNET, SIGNET CLASSIC, MENTOR, PLUME, MERIDIAN
AND NAL BOOKS are published by New American Library,
1633 Broadway, New York, New York 10019

First Printing, July, 1985

1 2 3 4 5 6 7 8 9

PRINTED IN THE UNITED STATES OF AMERICA

PROLOGUE

HER MOTHER WAS Shanna, a Shawnee woman who had gone to live among the Seminole. Her father was Yui, a Seminole chief. She had been born alongside the long Trail of Tears where the wind from the east had pushed her father's people. She had been born there, in the dust, and her mother had died.

The Comanche warriors had taken her to their village to be wet-nursed and raised among them. She knew nothing of her past, of her parents. She knew nothing of the wind from the east, the wind which would continue to blow, to push the People before it like dry leaves.

Her name was Amaya, the Sky Maiden.

1

THE DAY WAS warm and the cicadas hummed in the silver-green willow brush along the quietly flowing Arkansas River. The women walked along the river gathering firewood, pausing from time to time to look northward expectantly, to listen for distant sounds, to scan the blue, puffball-filled skies for clouds of dust.

"Won't they ever come?" Amaya said. She stood with a bundle of driftwood in one arm, wiping her forehead with her sleeve. She was a lithe and limber girl, at that awkward and sometimes remarkably appealing age at the juncture of childhood and maturity, her fourteenth year. She wore knee-high boots of buffalo hide and a deerskin shirt. Her skirt was of two pieces of buckskin, falling to her ankles. Her hair, in the Comanche fashion, was cut squarely front and back, the part daubed with red paint. She had great dark, liquid eyes that stared out at the world in wonder, a high forehead, and delicately formed, gently hollowed cheekbones. The women around her were Comanche, their faces flatter, rounder than Amaya's, their legs much shorter. They did not find her beautiful, only different. She was beautiful, however, and growing more lovely each day—the men were well aware of it.

"What is this eagerness in you, Amaya?" Osa demanded chidingly. "Are you expecting a warrior to come from the north and take you away with him?"

Amaya smiled shyly. "I only want to see them. I have never seen the Cheyenne."

"Well, I have," old Masala said. "See these scars on my arm?" She pulled up the sleeve of her buckskin shirt and showed the two younger girls her scars of grief.

"The Cheyenne cut them there. They killed my husband and Weskath, my second oldest son. I don't know where their scalps are. I carry scars of grief because of the Cheyenne. Yes, I've seen them." Masala turned her head and spat.

The two girls glanced at each other and had to fight to suppress a fit of giggling. Not that there was anything funny about Masala's story. It was a tragic tale, really; but one had only to mention the Cheyenne and Masala began showing her scars.

"All of that is over, Mother Masala," Osa said to the older woman. "Now there will be peace between the Comanche and the Cheyenne."

"Perhaps," Masala grumbled. "Perhaps it is so. I do not even know where their scalps are." Still muttering, she wandered off up the river's edge, a small, bent rag bundle of a woman.

"She will never love the Cheyenne."

"Nor will Quahadi," Osa said as the two girls started walking toward the village which lay beyond the grassy rise. Quahadi was the war leader, the head of their band of Comanche. He was a dark, squat man who lived to make war. He had cunning eyes and his hair was always heavy with grease.

"Then why make peace?" Amaya asked.

"Quahadi makes peace for only one reason—to make more war," Osa said. Osa's father was one of Quahadi's lieutenants and she heard much of the war talk.

"I don't understand," Amaya complained.

"No?" The two stopped at the crest of the grassy rise, placing their bundles of wood down while they caught their breath. Below, the Comanche tipis stood along the Arkansas River's southern bank. Gray-green bluffs fronted the river. Tangled cottonwoods, some immense in size, crowded together in the hollows. There were exactly one hundred tipis standing in four wavering ranks. Quahadi's own tipi was the largest, painted completely red.

Smoke rose from a dozen cooking fires. Dogs yapped and raced back and forth through the camp, naked children at their heels. Beyond the camp, sequestered in the long sheltered valley, was the horse herd, more ponies than Amaya had ever seen together, more than she had dreamed existed. There were easily a thousand of them, perhaps more.

"What war does Quahadi mean to make, Osa?"

"He wishes to war with the white men. The Texans, as they call themselves. But he cannot make that war with the Cheyenne at his back. The Arrowpoint must be more than a river, it must be a barrier against the Cheyenne."

Amaya looked toward the river again, shallow at this time of year, broad and silver, undulating away. She still did not understand really, except to understand that Quahadi would have his war.

"The horses are for the Cheyenne?"

"Yes. Quahadi will make his giveaway to buy their peace." Osa laughed. "And the horses belong to his other enemies."

Amaya nodded. She had seen the black scars on the ponies where the Texans had burned their flesh to mark them. Quahadi was even now bringing more horses from the south. Still more stolen from the whites to give to the Cheyenne so that he might make war.

"You, Amaya! Hurry up with that wood, you lazy thing!"

The owner of the shrill voice stood at the base of the gradually sloping rise, hands on hips, the wind blowing the fringes of her buckskin skirt.

"I am coming, Beskath," Amaya called, waving a hand.

"Well, hurry up, then. We can't wait for you all day."

Beskath turned and strode away and Osa made a rude noise. "That for your sister Beskath."

Amaya laughed. "She doesn't mean anything. Mother says she acts like that because she is becoming a woman."

"I have been a woman for almost a year," Osa answered, "and I do not act like Beskath. Besides, she never acted politely toward you. Because you are not Comanche."

Amaya, who had been bent over picking up her wood, stiffened. "I *am* Comanche."

Osa's amiable face turned blank for a moment. Then she grinned. "All right, as you will. Beskath does not think so, anyway. And your mother is kind to blame Beskath's rudeness on her womanhood. It is all because of Quahadi, and everyone knows it."

"What do you mean?"

"You must know, Amaya."

Osa, laughing, had started off down the slope. Amaya had to hurry to catch up with her.

"No, wait. I don't know. What are you talking about?"

"You are making a joke now," the taller girl said to her friend. "You must know, Amaya. I think soon your family will have many new horses, too."

Amaya, juggling her wood, reached out and grabbed Osa's sleeve, turning her sharply. "What do you mean?" she asked a little breathlessly. "Say it right out."

"Quahadi wants you for a wife."

"Quahadi wants Beskath."

"Perhaps he did. Now he wants you. Do you not see his eyes comb you?"

"That is just his way of looking," Amaya said. Her hand fell away from Osa's sleeve. The wind lifted a strand of dark hair across her eyes and she brushed it away in annoyance. "Besides, I am not yet a woman." She said that with a touch of shame.

"But soon, soon. Quahadi will wait. He has patience where women are concerned—before he has married them," Osa said as a joke. She immediately regretted having said it. Quahadi's last wife had been divorced in shame after she fled the war chief. Quahadi had cut her nose off to seal the divorce. The woman's name had been Ha-hatha-ho, which means the Woman with Fiery Eyes, and she had been acknowledged to be the most beautiful woman in all the Comanche nation. She had displeased Quahadi somehow—it was said that he was very cruel with women he took to his bed—and then she had tried to run away. Now she followed along after the tribe. Sometimes she was seen in the dusk shadows stealing scraps of meat meant for the dogs, then running away before anyone could speak to her. She wore a rag across her face to cover her mutilation.

"You have much imagination, Osa," Amaya said lightly, but the thought, now that it had germinated, refused to leave her mind and she thought back to the occasions when Quahadi, wearing his finery, had visited their tipi to speak to Winona about marrying Beskath, to the moments when he had let his eyes drift to Amaya. She knew with sudden panic that there was something in what Osa said.

"Or perhaps I have too much imagination, too. Yes, that is it. I am only a silly girl." Amaya fell to speaking of other things as she and Osa walked the length of the great camp to place their firewood on the piles beside the cooking pots. There Amaya's mother worked and she went up to hold her hand for a moment.

Mother she was, though Amaya was not of her womb as was Beskath. The two of them, Winona and Amaya, were closer than blood. They had love as a bond.

The long summers, the hard winters, showed on Winona's face. Weather and hardship had cut long lines into her dark skin. She had lost a husband and four sons in war and now had only a brother and her two daughters.

She was stooped now, and had gray in her hair, yet when she smiled she was as beautiful as a winter dawn coloring the snowfields. The familiar lines of her face deepened and formed a welcome, unmistakable, warm and joyous.

"Hello, daughter," the old woman said as if she had not seen Amaya for many long days.

"Hello, Mother Winona. May I do some of your work for you?"

"There is nothing to do." Winona shrugged. "Everything is done. I do not like this iron pot, though," she confided. "Why do we have these white things? Why carry a pot around with us?"

"Only a wealthy people can afford these things."

"Yes, yes," Winona said, "and so we drag the iron kettle up here to show the Cheyenne that we are not poor. I like to cook in the old way, Amaya, in a kettle made of a buffalo's stomach. And when the pot is worn out, why, then"—she grinned with delight—"the pot can be eaten! And that is the best part of it all, is it not?"

"Yes, Mother Winona."

"Yes," the old woman said, distracted by another distant thought, "it is so."

Amaya watched the old woman stir the buffalo stew. Wild peas and chunks of *pomme blanche*, the Indian potato, floated in the dark gravy.

"You are still here, Amaya?" Winona said with surprise. "Why do you not go down to the river? Swim with the other maidens. There is little work to do now. Be young while you can."

"Yes, Mother Winona." She wanted to ask about Quahadi, wanted to know if he had spoken to Winona or Uncle Foxfoot about marriage, but somehow she could not bring herself to broach the subject. Osa was a foolish girl, after all, and she had just been chattering as she was liable to do about anything.

"Go along now," Winona urged. "The day is warm. Swim and cool yourself."

"Yes, Mother Winona."

Amaya again squeezed the old woman's hand. Then she turned and started off across the village. Glancing to the left, she saw her stepsister near the family lodge, watching her. Beskath, she thought, do not be angry with me. I do not want this mad war chief. I do not care for his gifts or for the status he would bring. *I do not want him.* She did not want any man. Winona often told her that soon she would have to marry, find a warrior to bring home the buffalo, but Amaya did not wish to think about it.

Uncle Foxfoot still rode on the hunts, although he was no longer young and his sight was bad. He still brought meat. Soon Beskath would marry Quahadi; then they would have all they needed. There was no young man Amaya favored. Her mind, her body, cried for none of them.

"Where are you going, Amaya?"

It was Crooked Arm, a youth of fourteen, who asked the question. Uninvited he fell in beside Amaya as she walked away from the camp, through the towering cottonwoods. Here and there children played in the shade, hiding from each other, pretending to be war parties lying in wait.

"To swim," Amaya said a little wearily.

"Then I will swim with you," the boy said eagerly. He was tall and very strong through the chest and shoulders. He was born into a warrior family, and if he had not been born with a twisted arm he would have been marked for leadership. As it was, he had become overly shy, not believing that he was tall and comely, giving too much significance to his slight abnormality, as youth does.

Amaya wished to be gentle with him, but she was in no mood for Crooked Arm's conversation. She wanted only to float in the liquid silver of the cool river, to watch the sun through the cottonwood trees, to dream for a time.

"I must swim alone. With the other women."

"We could go by ourselves downstream. I know a place."

"No. Not today."

"Quahadi," the youth said suddenly. The name was bitter in his mouth.

"What do you mean?" Amaya stopped and gripped his shoulders, ducking to look up into his eyes as he turned his face down. "Crooked Arm, what do you mean?"

"Everyone knows it," he said dejectedly.

"I know nothing. Today I have heard whispers, but I know nothing. Do they say that Quahadi wishes to take me for a wife?" she asked, looking intently at the boy.

"You have said it."

"Well, I will not have him!" Amaya said, her temper flashing. "He can have Beskath. She wants the war leader. I do not."

"You mean this," Crooked Arm said. He was very pleased. He took Amaya's hands and studied her face. Beautiful, she was beautiful, and just now quite angry. Her nose was too thin, he thought. Not at all like a Comanche's. Her skull was almost delicate, in fact. One saw in her face memories of distant lands. At times Crooked Arm almost thought ... But no, she could not have white blood in her.

Nor was she Comanche.

"I don't wish to talk about it any longer," Amaya said. The whole idea wearied her. She was tired of thinking, tired of Quahadi and thoughts of marriage, of Crooked Arm and his boyish proposals. "Please, I do not mean to be unkind, but I wish only to be alone, to cool myself in the river, Crooked Arm."

"Of course," the boy said, taking a step backward. He imagines it is his arm, Amaya thought. "I did not understand," he apologized. And then he was gone, shuttling through the shadows the great trees cast. Distantly a

Comanche boy imitated the call of a hunting hawk. The river beyond the trees murmured past. Amaya turned and walked on, glancing back only once toward the departing Crooked Arm, wondering at her own ability to cause him sorrow.

The oxbow of the river where the women had been swimming was deserted when Amaya reached it. The sun was sinking slowly, the shadows growing long, and it was cool along the shore. The air was alive with the hum of insects. Dragonflies, blue and orange, buzzed low above the surface of the Arrowpoint—or the Arkansas, as the whites who came to Bent's Fort upriver called it.

Robert Bent was a white who had married a Cheyenne. He had been on the river before most of the Indians had seen another white. He was widely respected and even honored. Amaya had been to his trading post, a high-walled adobe structure where the plains tribes met to trade among themselves and with the whites. There Arapaho and Comanche, Cheyenne and Gros Ventre, Kiowa and even Ute and Pawnee mingled and walked peaceably with one another. There one buffalo robe could be traded for three steel knives or for an iron kettle like the one Mother Winona used and disparaged; or a single pony could be traded for a smooth-bore rifle and a hundred rounds of ammunition. Thirty beaver pelts would bring a keg of magic rum or three pounds of white tobacco.

Amaya slipped from her dress and moccasins and into the dark silver of the river. Overhead, flights of doves circled before settling in the trees. The sun was very low. The tips of the cottonwoods still held light, forming a network of gold against the deep velvet sky.

The water was still warm from the day and it eddied around Amaya's body refreshingly. She ducked under the skin of the water and swam a little distance out toward the center of the river, then back to shore, where she climbed out and quickly dressed. The nights had been cool and they came on rapidly.

The cry went up suddenly, the shrill gleeful voices of children calling excitedly, and Amaya got to her feet. She stood frowning, looking toward the camp. Then she started that way, the cries in her ears still as the drums began to beat.

He was coming. Quahadi had returned.

Emerging from the trees, she stood at the perimeter of the camp, watching. The youths, the women, the old rushed to the south end of the settlement as the fires were prodded to life, more fuel added to set them blazing against the deep violet sky.

Amaya heard the horses above the shouting, above the snap and roar of the great fires. Horses, and many of them. She started that way, arms folded beneath her breasts, feet shuffling, eyes down. Someone ran by and touched her arm. She barely looked up to see that it had been Crooked Arm.

The noise of their hooves was very loud now. The earth shook beneath Amaya's feet. Quahadi had his war prizes running and she realized suddenly that he meant to run them through the camp. Others came to the same conclusion, and as the trampling hooves drew nearer, they pulled aside, old women shooing children out of the way.

There was nothing for a long while. They stood in the darkness listening to the drumming of the hooves, the sound mysterious in its way, like the pounding of a common heartbeat.

The warrior had his face and chest painted yellow. He burst into the circle of firelight, a cry of triumph spilling from his lips, ululating across the camp as he held his feather-decorated rifle high.

Behind him the wild-eyed many-headed thing appeared, bursting out of the darkness like one of the night's brooding creatures come alive. The horses were pressed together in a tight knot, their heads bobbing, their eyes fiery and frightened, showing white in the firelight, and on the flanks of the herd came the warriors of Quahadi, the supreme Comanche war chief, their bodies painted with their magic signs, their flesh glistening, their hair stiffened and daubed vermilion, their weapons held high as they drove their living coup through the heart of the camp.

A tipi was shouldered to the ground and then trampled over. Cooking pots were scattered, but no one cared. The children ran after the horse herd, screaming, cheering madly. The eyes of the old men glowed, the women beamed.

Amaya stood in the shadows of her tipi, watching. Quahadi finally made his grand appearance. On his spotted horse he looked tall, which he was not. Around his neck were his silver necklaces. His war paint of alternating yellow and black stripes streaked his face and torso. He came forward at a walk, his horse tossing its head. Quahadi looked into the shadows and seemed to see Amaya, but he went past, his pony lifting its heels high in that strutting gait the war chief had taught it.

"You leave him alone," the voice at Amaya's shoulder said, and she turned in surprise. "I won't have you looking at him like that, sister! Do you hear me?"

Beskath's breasts rose and fell beneath her linen shirt. Her fists were bunched at her side. For a moment Amaya thought she was going to be hit.

"I don't—"

"Don't look at him as if he were to be your husband. He is mine, Amaya! It is I who will live in the war chief's lodge . . . and if you forget your place . . ." The fury in her eyes finished the threat for her.

Before Amaya could respond, Beskath turned and stalked away, the single long braid down her back swaying angrily, like a snake that has been provoked.

"I don't want your man, sister," Amaya said to the darkness. "I don't want his hands on me, I don't want to feel the press of his body, I don't want to have to look into his scarred face or hear the words he growls around the mouthfuls of food he wolfs down. I hate him! Hate him!"

"Amaya?"

The girl turned slowly. She had been speaking out loud without realizing it. Mother Winona was there beside the tipi, her face curious, her eyes bright, her head cocked to one side like a watching squirrel.

"What is the trouble, Amaya?"

"Nothing, Mother Winona."

"Who is it you hate, girl?"

"No one." She felt Winona's finger beneath her chin, felt her lift gently.

"Everything is all right, then?"

"Yes, Mother Winona."

"Then go to the celebration. Our tribe is wealthy, very

wealthy. We have warm blankets and food for our bellies. What else could we need that we do not have?"

"Nothing, Mother Winona."

"No. Go on now and be with your young friends."

The girl turned and walked away, moving through the clutching shadows. Winona watched her until she could see nothing but a shapeless silhouette against the backdrop of the glowing red campfires; then she turned and went into her tipi. The old man would be wanting to eat.

The old man—her brother, Foxfoot. And when had he gotten old? She could recall him running the footraces against the Pawnee, beating their swiftest racer by many lengths. He had been fleet and straight, sinewy, always laughing, with even white teeth. When had he gotten old? When had Winona gotten old? The heavy burden of life seemed at times to be swiftly sliding away.

"I was waiting to eat," Foxfoot said from his bed.

"I was talking to Amaya, brother. She knows."

"Well, she must be told sometime. You should have told her before."

"I don't want to break her heart."

"Break her heart? In our time there was nothing saddening about marrying the wealthiest man in the nation, the boldest warrior."

"Amaya is different." The old woman was on her knees, spooning her brother's food into his earthen bowl.

"Different? It is only that she is young and still foolish," Foxfoot commented.

"Yes, perhaps."

"You have told Beskath, have you not, old woman?"

"No. Not yet. But I think she knows."

"You cannot do things this way, Winona. Why don't you tell these young women what has happened, that Quahadi has changed his mind and decided to take Amaya for his wife?"

"I don't know, brother. I am remiss."

"It is better to tell them soon."

"Yes," Winona agreed. It was better. As if that would solve anything. She had been happy for Beskath when Quahadi asked for her first daughter. Beskath was ambitious. She wanted to live in the war chief's lodge. Amaya obviously did not. But the war leader had changed his mind.

She knows, Winona thought. Someone has told her or she has guessed it by the look in Quahadi's eyes when he comes close. Winona had told Amaya: "We have food for our bellies, what more could we need?" But she knew. Winona had been young too. A woman dreams, and through her dreams a man must walk. He may be tall, a great hunter, a strong warrior, but always he is kind, knowing the ways of women, wishing to walk with one across the far hills, to lie down in the sun-warmed grass and be good to the foolish dreamer.

So it was not true that they needed nothing but food in their bellies. They needed dreams.

Quahadi, wealthy and strong, fitted Beskath's idea of what her man should be. She would have been a good wife to him. Quahadi would have had no cause to cut off her nose as he had done to that foolish Ha-hatha-ho.

Amaya was different. Winona had told Foxfoot it was so, and it was true. Different in many ways. Of course she was not Comanche, although no one knew what she was, but the difference went much deeper. Spirits lived in her at times, quiet, knowing spirits. One who was around Amaya much realized that. Ghosts lurked in her eyes. Friendly ghosts, infinitely sad ghosts, as if her blood held the memory of long-ago tragedy.

They had brought the baby to Winona all those years ago. Winona had her own daughter nursing then—not Beskath, but the little one that had died of the coughing disease. The baby the warriors brought was pathetically thin. It did not cry out. It only looked up at Winona with great dark eyes, and Winona's tears had welled up, love had flooded her heart, and she had taken the girl child to her breast to give it her own milk.

The dream had something to do with it, that long-ago dream which Winona had not understood and which she had mentioned to no one, not even her husband, because of the sadness it carried. In the dream Winona found herself old and alone. The milk in her body had long ago dried up. She sat alone in a blizzard, a constant storm which whitened and softened the world, which chilled her to the bone, freezing the very marrow. She sat alone, and beside her were two small cairns. How she knew, she could not have said, but Winona knew these were the graves of her girls. She was alone and she cried out to the sky, and the swirling snow suddenly stopped. The clouds fell away from the sky and from the void the small, softly glowing object fell. And as it fell it cried out, and Winona knew it for what it was—an infant falling from the stars.

She had awakened from the dream shaking. She first looked to her small, ill baby and found it alive but not strong. Then she had crossed the lodge to stroke the sleeping Beskath's dark hair, bending low to kiss her soft cheek.

"Only a dream, foolish thing," she had told herself; but she could not sleep again that night. In the morning the warriors had returned, and with them was the new-born baby. Winona had taken it and named it Amaya, the Sky Maiden, but she had never told anyone of the dream.

"Old woman, my bowl is empty," Foxfoot said, interrupting Winona's thoughts.

"Yes, brother." Winona sighed as she rose.

"You will tell the girl soon?"

"I will tell her, brother. Give me your bowl."

Amaya walked through the busy camp. The fires were very large; it was nearly as bright as day. The drums had begun again and Wolf Mountain had begun to sing, telling of his exploits and those of his father, of all the Comanche nation back to the beginning of time. To one side young boys with half-size bows were firing arrows at a target wheel. Ahead the dancing had begun in earnest and the people formed a snakelike procession which wove around and between the campfires.

"Amaya!"

Crooked Arm was between the tipis. He crooked a finger and inclined his head. There was eagerness in his eyes and Amaya realized that despite his pretensions, he was still a boy.

"What is it?" she whispered in return.

"Come on." He waved his arm with more urgency. "Quahadi is up there anyway." Amaya walked to where the youth stood and he broke into a grin. "I thought that would bring you to me. You *don't* like him, do you, Amaya?"

"No. I don't like him."

"I am glad. You and I will marry one day, of course," Crooked Arm said with ingenuous confidence.

"Yes, of course," Amaya echoed.

"Please do not mock me, Amaya. I am quite serious."

"I was only agreeing. What is it you wish?"

"There is something I have to show you. Follow along."

"But what is it?"

"I can't tell you. Just follow along. Please."

They walked together out of the camp, toward the south, away from the river. The sky was filmed over with milky stars. The drums followed them into the darkness.

"What is this, Crooked Arm? Where are we going?"

"You will see."

They slid down into a sandy coulee, a seasonal stream which fed the Arkansas but which was now dry, following that southward for a quarter of a mile, to find a large portion of the horse herd grazing silently on the dark plains.

"What is this?" Amaya hissed. Crooked Arm touched a finger to her lips and led the way down another small dry gully toward the low, folded hills to the southeast.

Now Amaya could see a brush arbor like the kind the women threw up to keep the sun from them as they worked. Poles had been set in the ground in a semicircle. Long boughs carelessly interwoven formed flimsy walls. There was a heavy log standing upright in the center of the arbor, a pole which appeared to have no use, since it was obviously not supporting the roof.

Again Crooked Arm cautioned Amaya to be quiet. Then he led the way toward the arbor, going to his belly once he was on the flat ground above the gully. They crept nearer, and Amaya could see the forms of two guards close to the arbor. Neither of them was recognizable in the near-darkness. One stood talking to the other, who sat legs crossed on the ground. Neither paid much attention to his work.

Crooked Arm had wriggled up beside the brush enclosure and Amaya could see him urging her with his eyes. In another moment she was beside him, sitting there in the night, smelling the fresh-cut willow and sumac the arbor was made from. Amaya looked questioningly at

Crooked Arm. What was this game he chose to play tonight?

In a moment he answered her question. Amaya saw him go to his stomach again and slowly, carefully part the interwoven brush near the ground. He looked a summons at Amaya and she scooted up beside him to look into the arbor. It was dark inside the enclosure, although bright starlight beamed down, and it was a long moment before Amaya's eyes had adjusted for her to see.

There were four men inside the arbor. They sat with their heads hanging, their hands behind their backs—tied there. Prisoners—but why was Quahadi keeping them way out here? Amaya looked more closely now. One of the prisoners had a big hat hanging down his back. It was decorated with silver thread. He had a dark, craggy face and a thin mustache. One saw many of these men near Santa Fe—he was a Mexican, part Indian, part Spanish. Two of the others were similarly Mexican.

The fourth was white.

Amaya bit at her lip. She found it hard to make out his features by starlight. But he was young, boyishly slender. He was dressed in blue overalls. He had to be a white corn grower. His hair was the color of cornsilk. There was blood on his forehead where a gash had been opened.

Amaya stared, fascinated, until Crooked Arm touched her shoulder, and together they slipped back through the darkness to the arroyo. They walked swiftly back toward the camp. Crooked Arm had broken off an arrowweed and he slashed at the trailside plants as they walked.

"Why does he have them out there?" Amaya asked.

"He hasn't made up his mind what to do with them yet," Crooked Arm guessed.

"Before, he has always—"

"Before, he has not been trying to make peace with the Cheyenne. What would the Cheyenne wish now? Perhaps he will present the prisoners to them to prove his prowess; perhaps he will kill them to prove his hatred of the whites. Perhaps he will let them go to demonstrate his benevolence. Who knows what Quahadi will do? He has not decided. He keeps them away from the camp so that there can be no talk among the council as to what should be done."

That was true, probably. The council seemed to have no power these days. It was Quahadi who spoke for the tribe. Only Quahadi. If he wished war, then there would be war as long as the warriors followed him. No council could stay war if the men wanted to fight. There were no freer people in all the world then the Comanche, none who loved war more. How often had that been said in Amaya's presence?

Amaya and Crooked Arm parted company at the edge of the camp. Crooked Arm, lifting a hand in farewell, ran off to join a group of boys who were playing the fire-toss game—a dangerous and lively game involving the throwing of burning brands.

Amaya stood watching the fires. Golden flames leapt high into the sky, the tongues of fire dancing higher than the tallest lodgepole. The dancing had stopped but the drumming went on. The drumming, and somewhere, the soft, rhythmic counterpoint of a flute.

"I am back."

The hand fell on Amaya's shoulder and she drew away, her mouth opening to cry out. The man beside her laughed harshly.

"Quahadi!"

"Amaya. I am back, little one. Back with many ponies."

His war paint was smeared. His body smelled of horse and exertion. His thick powerful shoulders were slightly hunched; his flat, scarred face was fire-glossed. Four eagle feathers were knotted in his heavy, well-oiled hair.

"I am happy that your raid was successful," Amaya said. She met his eyes, and then, unable to hold her gaze, looked away. Quahadi's hand rested on her shoulder and she felt her skin writhe beneath its touch.

"It is for you. I will give your uncle fifty ponies! What do you think of that?"

"It is generous," Amaya said numbly.

"Generous!" He laughed again, his hand kneading her shoulder, his thick thumb digging into the muscle there. "Yes, I am a generous man. Have they not told you? Has your mother not spoken to you yet?"

"Spoken to me . . ." And then all the doubt she had

nurtured and cherished was washed away. She knew as she had always known deep inside. All that Osa had said, that she and Beskath suspected was true. This man, this warrior, this terrible dark thing, wanted to marry her and take her to his lodge.

"My sister . . ." Amaya said futilely.

"She will find a suitor easily. Your family will have much wealth now. The young men will flock to Beskath's lodge."

"Yes. Of course."

His hand was touching her hair now and she twisted away uncomfortably. She moved away from him, but she was careful to do it under the pretense of simply shifting her position, as if her legs were weary. It would not do to anger this one. *Ask Ha-hatha-ho.* His hand again touched her hair and Amaya smiled tightly, falsely. One would always have to be careful not to give offense. Quahadi was a wolf, and when he was enraged, he snapped at all around him.

"I must go help Winona prepare my uncle's meal."

"Now? Now while we are celebrating the night? Let the old people prepare the meals, bring in the firewood, snore the night away. We are young."

"I promised her," Amaya said a little desperately. The hand in her hair tightened its grip. Quahadi's eyes met hers, seemed to bore into her skull and ferret out the lies. He let her go suddenly.

"All right, then. Go on and do your work. You are a good and faithful child, are you, Amaya? Good." He nodded his head, musing. "And you will be faithful and dutiful to me."

"Yes, Quahadi," she managed to answer.

"Yes. I think you will be. Go on your way now, girl. We will speak again. I will come for you soon."

She nearly ran from him as his hand dropped away, but she managed to control herself, to still the shuddering. But she could not quell the deep loathing inside, the roiling, bitter-tasting fear and mingled hatred.

Amaya walked across the camp, glancing across her shoulder once to see the squat war chief standing, fists on hips, watching her. The tipi was quiet. Mother Winona slept, or appeared to. Uncle Foxfoot was snoring loudly. The scent of his pipe, filled with harsh wild tobacco and herbs in a mixture called *kinnikinnick*, lingered in the air not unpleasantly. It was a part of the smell of home.

She slipped into her bed and lay there watching the stars float past above the smoke flap in the top of the tipi. Home—Uncle Foxfoot's *kinnikinnick*, Mother Winona's cooking, the constant scent of buffalo—buffalo hides, tanned and untanned, made into robes and caps and leggings and moccasins, trunks and parfleches. The tipi itself was buffalo. When they were little, Mother Winona had told them they were living inside a buffalo each time they raised the lodgepoles. Somehow that had been comforting as a child. The buffalo had meant home. Mother Winona, tender, her callused hands holding Amaya, brushing back the hair from her forehead. Now home would be no more. Amaya would leave the lodge and then there would be no home. There would be only Quahadi.

She rolled over in disgust, her arms flailing. She glowered at the darkness for a long while, pretending to be asleep when Beskath came in sometime later and crawled into her own bed.

She lay in the darkness and watched the bright, distant stars, wondering. And then she slept, but it was a terrible experience. She dreamed she was lost in a forest and it was dark. It was very dark and ground fog wove through the trees, and behind the trees faceless women watched, darting in and out, insubstantial as ghosts, whispering a warning song. Only once did she see a face clearly: it was Ha-hatha-ho—all of them were. They played some game Amaya did not understand and their song was an invitation to join them in it.

At last she slept without the torment of the dream, but it was a short sleep. At dawn a cry went up out in the camp. Amaya heard Beskath rise from her bed and rush to the flap of the tipi, raising it to peer out. Through the opening Amaya saw people rushing toward the river and she sat up sharply, her heart pounding.

"What is it?"

"Is it a war party?" Uncle Foxfoot asked almost hopefully. "Kiowa?"

"I don't know what it is," Beskath said in annoyance. "No—it is not a war party. You there, Osa, what is it?"

They heard Osa call back: "The Cheyenne. It is the Cheyenne. They have come."

For some reason, Amaya's heart continued to beat rapidly. She slid from her bed and tugged her moccasins on, looking at her family around her. Mother Winona, her long gray-streaked hair unbraided, sat placidly. Uncle Foxfoot sat rubbing his head. Amaya glanced at Beskath, who yawned behind her hand and walked to the fire to prod it to life. None of them felt the excitement. But it was there, beating in Amaya's pulse, lifting her emotions. She anticipated . . . What? The Cheyenne meant nothing to her. She knew she had none of their blood in her. She had come from the south, they said. From the people who had walked across the world, though no one knew which tribe. It was said that some of her people had tattoos, profuse and ornate, and since then Amaya had watched for tattooed people at gatherings like that at Bent's Fort. She had never seen any. The Cheyenne, she knew, did not indulge themselves in that way.

Then why was her blood stirring? She only knew it was, and she rushed out of the tipi to join the throng moving toward the river. The sun was on the Arrowpoint; the river glided past, golden and deep purple. Across the river, smoke rose from fifty tipis. The lodges of the Cheyenne were arranged in a precise circle. Amaya saw no one in the camp, although much of it was shielded by the cottonwoods growing dense and tall on the opposite bank.

"When did they come?"

"I heard nothing, saw nothing."

"Where are they? I see no one."

The sun rose above the trees, a red, flattened ball going slowly yellow, and still no one stirred in the Cheyenne camp. Then a dog yapped and the people seemed to relax a little. Life went on there after all; the Cheyenne were not spirits.

Little by little the people appeared in the camp across the river. Amaya could not see much of them, except to note that they seemed tall, that they wore their formal dress, bleached elkskin clothing decorated with many

beads. The men wore their war bonnets. No one carried
a weapon of any sort.

The Comanche drifted away one by one. There would
be a great feast; it was time to make preparations, to
dress, to bathe, to see to the costumes, to feed the children, to herd the horses nearer the camp.

"Well," Osa's familiar voice said, "do you see him?"

"Who?"

"Who?" Osa said teasingly. "The great warrior who
will take you away with him to his northern lodge."

When Amaya did not answer this banter, Osa knew.
She looked at the Sky Maiden and said, "Oh. Then you
have been told."

"I have been told."

"I'm sorry, Amaya. Well, there are worse fates than to
be betrothed to the wealthiest of men. You will have
other wives to help you with your work. You will never
go cold or hungry. Mother Winona will be kept in her old
age." Osa fell silent. The little speech was cheering no
one. Osa tried to imagine what it would be like to have to
marry Quahadi, and failed. Not that he would want her.
There was an advantage to being plain, she decided.

"How could I go?" Amaya said so quietly that at first
Osa did not realize she was speaking to her. "How could
I leave here? I am Comanche. No matter what they say."

"Yes, you are Comanche," Osa agreed. Amaya's expression was distant and calm.

"I am Comanche. And no man will come. No great
warrior."

"Come on!" Osa tugged at her friend's arm. "I was
just playing. Come with me! Let us see what is happening in the camp. Let us put on our own finery and
prepare to dance all day, to feast all night."

Still Amaya hesitated, and Osa had to tug at her, to
chide her, pleading and chattering as she moved them
off toward the village.

There everything was alive with activity. Men and
women rushed everywhere, some to bring the horses in,
others to butcher or prepare the meal for the evening
celebration—eight oxen brought all the way from the
home camp at Shinshin, the white river.

Beskath was already in her finery, her hair parted and

braided, turquoise beads around her neck, her lips reddened. Her feet were encased in those delicate beaded moccasins Quahadi had bought from the Crow woman for an entire bolt of calico cloth.

And now Beskath knew as well. It was in her eyes, in the dark glitter of them, the taut-standing tendons on her throat, the flaring of her nostrils, the pinched tightness around her mouth. It was more than a suspicion now, and the hatred had deepened as humiliation was heaped upon it. Her baby sister, not yet a woman, not even Comanche! To this thing she had lost her prized warrior, Quahadi.

"Get out of my way," Beskath said angrily.

"Sister—" Amaya began, but that was as far as Beskath let her get. She pushed Amaya aside and walked out of the tipi, her face masked with fury. *Take him,* she wanted to scream out, but she did nothing of the sort; she simply put her hand to her face and sat down cross-legged on her bed, looking at nothing.

Winona started to go to Sky Maiden, but did not. There was little comfort in anything she could say.

"There will be races soon," Foxfoot said. He too had put on a war bonnet. "I want to see the races. I want to see if the Cheyenne have a horse that can beat Long Skinner's paint pony."

"Do not bet all of your belongings on a horse race," Winona cautioned him. It wouldn't be the first time if Foxfoot fell prey to that temptation. He was a gambler like most of the Comanche men, only a little less lucky than some.

"I do what I must," Foxfoot said. "What shall I do? Fail to put faith in the pride of the Comanche? Let the Cheyenne brag?"

"Do what you must, then," Winona said a little irritably. After all, her brother had little left to wager. When he was gone, Mother Winona said to Amaya, "Dress now. Take what pleasures the day offers. Disregard the evil until it has shown its face."

"Evil, yes." Amaya shook her head heavily. "Evil is the word."

Winona turned away so that Amaya would not see her tears. "Dress. Listen—the drums have started. Cheyenne drums too! They haven't the skill of our men, have they?"

"No, Mother Winona."

"Dress, child. Dress and go out."

The camp was alive in the morning light. The world seemed to shimmer with excitement. The children were more active than ever, their games charged with energy. The men in their dress clothing seemed intoxicated, and not all of it was due to the opening of the rum barrels taken from the white traders.

Amaya walked through the camp, searching for a quiet island. She found none until she reached the river and walked away from the camp, eastward toward the folded hills. She glanced toward the bluffs and beyond, wondering about the prisoners still hidden there.

Then she stopped.

Looking across the sheen and glitter of the moving river, she saw the young man standing alone, as still and smooth and hard as a cedar carving, as polished and yet artless. He stood across the Arrowpoint, wearing only a breechclout and poised on the gray cottonwood branch which overhung the river. He stood with his arms raised, his hands together as if he would dive, cut through the silken surface of the river, dive deeply and skillfully, swimming to the bottom, where the cattails and reeds were rooted, where the darting finger-fish swam, the larger, sweet-meated speckled trout, where the eggs of future generations of fish and river crabs lay. Then he would surge to the surface and rise from the river in a fountain of white water, beads of moisture sliding from the bronze of his skin, his mouth opening in an exultant, gasping breath, settling slowly to stroke firmly, smoothly toward the bank, where he would lie and dry on the sandy beach.

But he did none of that. He stood, his arms overhead, his eyes closed, his lips murmuring muted words Amaya could not hear, and slowly she moved away, leaving the Cheyenne boy to his prayers.

She walked through the willows, feeling diminished, cheated. A stark memory of the dark, squat Quahadi forced itself upon her and she pushed it away angrily. The sunlight flickered through the yellow-green leaves

of the cottonwoods. There was a soft scent on the air,
like flowering sage, but more gentle, beckoning. Amaya
looked back toward the low-hanging branch where the
Cheyenne boy had been. He was gone. He was not in the
river; he hadn't completed his dive. It was a gesture
begun and never finished, a promise, a wish.

She hurried along the trail.

"Where are you going?" Crooked Arm had come from
the trees and stood beside her as Amaya leaned against
the trunk of a cottonwood, watching the river, which
was darkly shadowed here.

"Why? What does anyone care?" she demanded.

"I don't," Crooked Arm said with a shrug, although he
obviously did care. "Your family is looking for you.
Quahadi is looking for you."

"Let him look," she snapped.

"Don't be angry with me, Amaya, I have done you no
harm," Crooked Arm said dolefully. He sat down beside
the tree, tossing bits of bark and twigs into the water.

"I am not angry," Amaya said, softening.

"It is all true?" he asked, and she didn't have to ask
what he meant.

"It is true."

"But you don't have to marry Quahadi!"

"I don't have to marry anyone, but what can I do? Who
will support my mother and my uncle? Who will hunt
buffalo for me and for Beskath?"

"I will."

She didn't even answer. She looked into his eyes, those
soft boyish eyes. He would be a warrior, a hunter, but he
was not one yet.

"I do not have to marry him yet. Not for a little
while," Amaya said.

"Then there is time for some solution to be found.
Perhaps Quahadi will favor another. Perhaps he will go
back to Beskath."

"Perhaps." She asked him, "What do they want me
for?"

"Quahadi wants you to go with him to the feast."

"Me? For what?"

"He has no wife to serve."

"Still . . ."

"Among the Cheyenne, girls from the best families sometimes serve as maids of honor at the feasts. Perhaps Quahadi wishes to follow the custom of his guests."

"When has Quahadi cared about his guests' wishes?"

"Never before, but this is different. He needs peace badly. He cannot have the Cheyenne at his back as enemies."

They walked slowly back along the river. A jay followed them for a while, hopping from bough to bough, chattering madly. "Will there be a great war?" Amaya asked.

"Yes. There will be."

"I thought so."

"There will be much honor to be won," Crooked Arm said. "I will be old enough to fight this time."

"Yes."

"Perhaps I will grow wealthy," he said hopefully, but the girl who walked beside him did not answer. They were near the camp now, walking past the arbor where Quahadi's war shield hung to keep it away from the bad magic of menstruating women. The camp was just over the rise. There was no one around, but humming sounds of activity, swarming, milling sounds, filled the air.

"Amaya!" He grabbed her arm impulsively. She shook him off but turned to him. "Please listen to me," he said.

"What is it?" she said calmly.

"You hate Quahadi."

"I hate him."

"Then come with me. We can go away. We can live together." His eyes were wide, pleading. The drums had begun and they filled the silent seconds before Amaya answered.

"No. It is foolish. No one can live without the tribe."

"A man alone—"

"You are not a man."

Crooked Arm brushed that remark aside. "A man who can hunt can live anywhere. I can hunt."

"And when the enemies of the Comanche come, can you fight alone?"

"I would fight," he assured her.

"And when winter comes we would be cold together, and when a child was born you would birth it, you who do not know the rites. And since we have no horses, we would walk across the long prairie alone, trailing the buffalo."

"I have killed a buffalo. I did not need a horse, but only a wolfskin! Besides, I could steal horses like Quahadi himself." But the eagerness was dulling. He could see that Amaya thought him a boy in a man's savage world, and perhaps he was.

He had no argument against her convictions and duty. "The old must be provided for. Mother Winona must not go hungry. Uncle Foxfoot must not be cold in the winters. Will you take them with us, Crooked Arm? Will you do for them as well?"

He did not answer. He couldn't answer. He felt foolish and futile and small. She stepped to him and hugged him once, briefly, and then was gone, leaving her scent in his nostrils and an empty gnawing in his heart.

Osa found her before she reached her lodge. "Hurry, Amaya, it is time for the feast. Everyone has been looking for you. Quahadi is furious."

"Let him be," she said stoically.

"That is not funny. At least you are dressed. Come along, let us hurry." Osa practically ran with her to the big red tipi near the river, where Quahadi and his retinue of war chiefs, council leaders, shamans, and healers waited in the shade of the great trees. Everywhere people stood together talking; children raced along behind Amaya and Osa, taunting them.

"At last," Quahadi said when Amaya finally arrived. "Just stand beside me. I do not know what the Cheyenne will expect. Perhaps you will serve, perhaps nothing. We are waiting for Horn still."

Horn was the greatest of the Comanche medicine men, the one who had foretold the shower of stars in the year of Amaya's birth. He was very old and slow to speak, slow to move. Behind his eyes amusement danced. He knew them all; he was a silent bird knowing their follies, the savage innocence in them.

"Perhaps we should demand that they cross the river." This was Red Corn, a bull-like, much-scarred, much-honored subchief.

"No," Quahadi said, and Red Corn, folding his arms, shrugged. Amaya thought: He wants the peace desperately. What is wrong? One would think the war had already started. Quahadi was demeaning himself by crossing to the Cheyenne camp, begging for peace in fact.

Horn was coming now, slowly, leaning on the shoulder of the young woman, the sacred woman, who took care of him. He looked at all the people as he came, smiling at each, searching for Quahadi, or perhaps for some sign.

"Are you well, old man?" Quahadi said. His manners were only a formula, Amaya thought. Horn seemed to feel the same.

"I am only a man farther down the trail than you," Horn said. "We are all the same man."

Quahadi was impatient. "Yes, I know, old man. Are you willing to cross the river with me and bless this meeting with the Cheyenne wolves?"

"Quahadi . . ." Red Corn cautioned.

"Yes, I know," the war leader replied. He had let his hatred of the Cheyenne show through briefly. He turned again to Horn. "Are you willing to cross the river now?"

"Yes. Yes, Quahadi." The old man smiled and it was obvious that Quahadi didn't like it. There was nothing humorous about this. There was nothing at all humorous in Quahadi's world. The war chief glanced at Amaya, assuring himself that she was there, but it was the same look he gave to Red Corn, to his medicine man, to his chief lieutenant, Three Fingers, an accounting glance which inventoried his retinue.

"Now, then," Quahadi said. He had no weapons, none of them did, not the smallest belt knife, not a war club. He carried only the great feathered pipe made by his grandfather at the redstone quarry site in the land of the Sioux. He carried that and his tobacco sack, nothing else.

They walked to the river now, the river which ran shallow and warm, which would run away to the south and east a hundred generations on, which cared nothing for the pride and valor of man, which kissed their flesh and carried away a memory of their dust which would be lost somewhere across the ancient land.

The opposite bank was empty. There were only the trees waving gentle arms in the breeze, the sunlight falling like golden eyes against the ground, the mutter of the river, disturbed by the feet of the Comanche party as it slowly crossed to the northern bank.

Amaya's breath came tightly, her mouth was dry. They were the invaders now, entering an alien land. A land where nothing stirred, lived, breathed. They walked through the long grass and into the clearing and were suddenly among the Cheyenne nation.

Eighteen old chiefs stood in a row, their war bonnets shifting in the wind. Around their necks and across their chests were silver necklaces, elk teeth and turquoise, bear claws and vests of eagle bones. All of their finery was worn for display; the bold beadwork on their elkskins sketched tales of bravery and prowess.

They watched and Amaya felt their eyes, cool, measuring. The Comanche seemed suddenly short, their faces less handsome, their bodies less comely. She saw a young Cheyenne maiden, silver buckles in her hair, and Amaya turned her eyes away. These were a people . . . Then she forced herself to walk straighter, to stand taller. She was *Comanche*. The Cheyenne knew well that warriors and their women walked among them. They had tasted the bite of Comanche arrowheads, felt the war clubs of the southern horsemen.

Quahadi stopped before the high chief of the Cheyenne and offered his pipe. It all happened in slow motion, or so it seemed to Amaya. She saw the eyes of the old Cheyenne chief, peering out from the weather-cut face, saw Quahadi's implacable gaze, the answering smile, the faintest smile, on the face of the Cheyenne, the wind drifting their eagle feathers, the signs of many coup counted against the enemy, the enemy which had often been the Comanche.

The brown, strong hands of the Cheyenne reached out and took the pipe. A hand rested for a moment on Quahadi's shoulder, and Amaya, half-expecting a cheer of approbation, was stunned by the silent acceptance of the other Cheyenne; they were not hungry for peace.

They walked to the center of the camp. A great lodge had been constructed there, not of buffalo hides, but of brush, one end standing open like a great mouth. Low fires burned beyond the lodge where the peace council would be held. There were no children in sight, few women, perhaps an indication that the Cheyenne did not trust Quahadi totally whether he carried weapons or only his pipe.

All etiquette was observed. The men entered the lodge first, circling to the right, waiting for their hosts to invite them to sit. Amaya and the two other women, the wives of Red Corn and the sacred woman of Horn, went to the left as they entered, and stood silently.

The great chief of the Cheyenne, he who would speak for his own band as well as for the Hevataniu and the Omissis, the other Cheyenne bands which had griev-ances against the Comanche, seated himself and invited the visitors to join him.

Quahadi was seated first, cross-legged, facing his host. The other warriors sat then, and after them the women, their legs folded, heels beside them.

The pipe was then filled. This was Quahadi's duty and he did it dourly. In his eyes Amaya could still see the warrior and she was sure the Cheyenne could as well.

The *kinnikinnick* was of tobacco and bearberry. The tobacco was white-grown, brought from the southern lands, very dark and very sweet. When the pipe was filled it was passed to the Cheyenne chief whose name was High Top Mountain, and he lit it with a brand from the fire. The smoke rose sweetly. The Cheyenne drew on the pipe and his breath returned, visible now to the spirits as he prayed for peace and understanding between the people.

"Let no man break this peace before it has endured," he said, and in that was implicit warning. The peace, not yet concluded, was already perceived as fragile.

The pipe was given to Quahadi and he inhaled deeply, nodding his head, chanting a small prayer before hand-ing it to his left. Then the pipe went around the circle, passing from hand to hand, from Cheyenne to Comanche and back again.

High Top Mountain called for food then. To speak on an empty stomach was no good. At such times a man was irritable. The food was brought in by young and, Amaya thought, very beautiful girls. They were clearly not ser-vants or slaves, but as she had been told, maids of honor.

The meal was a silent affair, with the men exchanging secretive or boastful glances.

Despite the fact that this was a peace conference, that neither camp was allowed to carry a weapon, Amaya felt uncomfortable. The worst of it was, she felt that if there were treachery here it was her own people who were involved in it. The idea frightened her and she chased it away, shooing it like a ground-feeding dove. This was a time of peace, the dawn of a great peace.

And of a great war.

"Now, if I may give more presents . . ." Quahadi said suddenly. Amaya looked toward him anxiously. It seemed to pain Quahadi to be polite.

"If you have gifts, let them be given," High Top Mountain of the Cheyenne said.

"Red Corn," Quahadi said, extending an arm, and the subchief rose and went out of the lodge.

"Will you follow along?" Quahadi asked.

The Cheyenne shrugged and got to their feet. They towered over Quahadi, their war bonnets lending them the illusion of still greater height. High Top Mountain gestured with his hand and Quahadi led them out.

"Call your men," Quahadi said as they emerged from the lodge. Most of the Cheyenne stood or sat nearby awaiting word from the conference. They wished for peace, obviously, but were just as obviously uncertain that Quahadi had brought it to them.

Horn, leaning still on his silent, sacred woman, stood beside Amaya, chanting in a whisper. Amaya glanced at him and he nodded at the bundle resting near his feet. "What is that?" she asked, but the medicine man went on chanting and the sacred woman looked at Amaya as if she had violated his prayer.

Red Corn came into the village again, bringing with him three Comanche warriors, each of whom had a bundle of twigs. The Cheyenne men stirred a little and moved forward, anticipating what was to come. Perhaps it was good to make peace with the Comanche after all.

With an air of triumph, Quahadi moved to the old chief, High Top Mountain, and selected a specially marked stick from one of the bundles. He added a red stick and a yellow stick and then drew ten more, fifteen more from

the huge bundle, and placed them at the feet of the great
chief. The second Cheyenne council leader was similarly
treated, and the third. Meanwhile, the other Comanche
moved among the Cheyenne warriors, handing out two
sticks at a time, three, four, depending on the man's
rank. Youths of fourteen and fifteen were given a stick.
When the sticks were gone, Quahadi sent his men into
the woods to break off more, and these were handed out,
hundreds in all.

When he was done he raised his hand and someone
nearer the river relayed his signal. After a minute they
heard the sound like distant thunder. The earth rolled,
the trees shook; the Cheyenne turned toward the south
and shouted happily as the first of the great horse herd
splashed across the river, throwing up silver fans of
water from the bright face of the Arrowpoint. Comanche
warriors drove them, shrilling, waving blankets overhead, and the horses came on, a limitless number of
them it seemed, one for each stick that had been given.
They were of all colors: paint and gray; dapple; buckskin and rare spotted Nez Percé ponies; dun and bay;
white, pure black; sorrel and roan, heads held high,
tossing manes, sleek muscles working smoothly beneath
glossy hides.

They came until the camp overflowed with them, and
then the Cheyenne traded their sticks for the gift horses,
the warriors taking two or three at a time to join their
own horse herd, the great chiefs standing, waiting for
their special horses, the long-legged red horse, the racer,
the fleet little lineback dun, and the stocky, deep-chested
roan which had been represented by the specially marked
sticks.

Quahadi stood back watching with pride which bor-
dered on arrogance. If the Cheyenne had taken him for a
poor southern Indian, they knew better now. The Comanche war leader walked toward Amaya and she felt
herself cringe, felt her body stiffen and draw in to itself.
But it wasn't Amaya that Quahadi wanted then.

"I must have the bundle now," Quahadi said to the
medicine man.

"No."

Quahadi looked as if he had been slapped. There was

no one who could tell him no. No one, that is, but Horn.
The old man made a conciliatory gesture.

"Let the past stay buried, Quahadi."

"It is a generous gift."

"You stir old memories in that way," Horn said. "Old
memories which can not live side by side with the new
peace."

Quahadi was furious, Amaya knew. He showed it only
by a gradual darkening of his face, by the slight narrowing of his eyes. He was angry but he did not dare challenge Horn on this issue.

The chief stood a minute longer staring at Horn; then
he said, "Perhaps you are right," and spun away, walking to join High Top Mountain.

"What is in the bundle?" Amaya asked.

Horn did not answer, but the sacred woman who had
crouched to pick it up pulled back the corner of the
blanket long enough for Amaya to have a peek.

Scalps. Cheyenne scalps, fifty of them. Amaya looked
quickly at the Cheyenne chiefs across the clearing and
then at Horn, who smiled knowingly. The sacred woman
had tied the bundle tightly and now she was on her way
into the woods to circle back toward the Comanche camp
with the ill-advised gift.

The fires had been lighted and the Cheyenne had
begun a dance. The men moved past, their ankles and
wrists feathered, their bodies painted. The Comanche
women had moved over from across the river and now
the feasting began in earnest. Comanche children played
with Cheyenne. Hundreds of dogs yapped and ran and
fought through the camp. Horses still milled.

Amaya strode around the great circle of the Cheyenne
camp, watching, listening. Not everyone was in a festival
mood. She saw two high-ranking Cheyenne men standing beside a dozen gift horses, talking in low tones. She
could not hear what was said, but she saw one of the
men move to the flank of one of the ponies and let his
fingers trace the burned-on mark of the former white
owner. The Cheyenne looked at the brand and then to
his companion. He shook his head gravely. He wanted no
part of that horse. They moved among the horses slowly,
reading the signs on the horses as Amaya might read the

sign of a hunted doe in the river sand. What the lettering and crooked signs might mean, she did not know, but she knew this: to the Cheyenne they represented trouble.

The two men went away, shaking their heads, leaving the horses behind. Amaya walked past the ponies, her hand running along their sleek flanks. She patted the big roan's neck and pulled up a tuft of grass to feed it. From the camp a roar went up as a horse race began, but Amaya did not even look that way. She looked at the horses, at the crudely formed star on the roan's flank, and she wondered.

2

"THEY ARE GONE."

Osa had entered the tipi and taken hold of Amaya's shoulder; she had begun shaking her from a deep sleep, talking so excitedly that Amaya could make no sense of it.

"Who is gone?"

"Quahadi is enraged! He threatens to follow them and make war. The horses have been left behind. Every lodge struck and taken away in the dead of night, every dog is gone. The Cheyenne are gone!"

"I don't care, Osa. Go away for a little while. Where is Mother Winona?"

"Down at the river. Sit up. I tell you something is happening."

Amaya sat up. Her hair fell dark and sleek across her shoulders. It reached to her waist when it was loose, as it was now. Osa envied Amaya her hair, so soft and silken, not coarse and heavy like her own, like all of the women's hair. Amaya looked around the lodge. Nothing was happening despite Osa's alarm. Uncle Foxfoot sat dejectedly in the corner, shirtless, eating his morning meal.

"I lost my buffalo pony," he said when he caught Amaya's eyes on him. "In that horse race. Well, the Cheyenne rider cut the Comanche horse with his quirt. I saw it. Right across the eyes as they crossed the river. I lost my buffalo pony," he moaned.

"Get dressed and come out," Osa urged Amaya. "I'll braid your hair for you. Everyone's excited. No one knows what it means."

Amaya was beginning to wake up now, and the event took on import. "They are gone?"

"Every man, every woman and child." Osa was combing her hair with the porcupine brush. She tugged too hard and Amaya winced. "But they left the horses behind. What an insult. Quahadi wants to avenge the affront with weapons. The other chiefs are trying to talk him out of it."

"I don't understand. Everyone was happy. There was a feast, the giving of gifts. Why would the Cheyenne change their minds? Do they want war?"

"I don't know. No one knows. Everyone is talking about it," Osa answered, speaking rapidly. She tied the ends of Amaya's braids with lengths of rawhide.

"I wagered my buffalo pony," Uncle Foxfoot complained again. "Why didn't I listen to Winona? Who would have thought that fool Elk Forest would have let the Cheyenne quirt his horse? Why did he ride so near?"

The buffalo pony meant much, Amaya knew. They were the swiftest, the most enduring of the ponies, the most courageous, worth a hundred buffalo skins. They were a hunter's pride.

"You will find another, Uncle Foxfoot, and train it well."

"There will never be another like my little red pony," the old man said.

"Are you coming?" Osa said impatiently.

"Yes." Amaya kissed her uncle and went out with Osa. The camp was very busy, although no one seemed to be doing anything in particular.

Near the river people stood in their blankets—the morning was cool—and spoke quietly. The Cheyenne camp, as Osa had told her, was gone. They could see Comanche men and boys moving through the cottonwoods, bringing the gift horses home. The Cheyenne had left them all.

"I can't understand this," Amaya said. "Why did they go? What displeased them?"

"No one knows. Perhaps they knew about the scalps."

Amaya knew that was not so, but she didn't answer. The brands. That was it. The white brands on the gift horses. But why? There weren't a hundred whites within fifty miles, and most of them were at Bent's Fort, traders from the north with their Ojibwa "squaws," with their long black beards and strange tongue that even Bent did not speak.

Amaya stood and watched as the horses were herded together and driven across the river. The conversation around her was repetitive. No one knew a thing; there were only rumors.

And Amaya felt a great loss, an inexplicable loss, a deep regret. The Cheyenne were gone. The youth she had seen along the river had never completed his dive. He had stood poised in the sun, a physical promise never fulfilled. The day was empty, the sky blue, the long-running river silver and white, whispering past.

"I hate you." The words fell soundlessly from Beskath's lips.

She was concealed by the trees. Osa and Amaya were talking, Osa laughing in that childish way she had, her body buckling, Amaya standing watching, listening, haughty and cool. Amaya was a child. A greedy child, intruding into Beskath's life. She was not her mother's daughter, she was not even Comanche! She was not even a woman, was not beautiful. True, there were the outlines of beauty already, the face delicate and yet strong, the straight nose and flaring nostrils, slightly full under-lip, the wide, long-lashed eyes.

"I hate her," Beskath said again, and as she said the words, her hatred grew within her. It became a grasping, needful hate that reached a taloned fist into Beskath's throat and clutched at her, demanding satisfaction.

"Why are you standing here?"

Beskath turned to find Uncle Foxfoot hobbling toward her. The old man was leaning on a stick. He had a green striped blanket over his shoulders.

"Where should I be?" Beskath asked sharply.

"We are leaving. Everyone is leaving."

"What do you mean?"

"The camp is going to be folded. We are leaving. Quahadi has told me."

"We are going back to the Shinshin?"

"No. To a new camp toward the mountains—you ask many questions, girl." His eyes lifted and looked beyond Beskath's shoulder. "There is Amaya. I will tell her as well."

"I will tell her, Uncle Foxfoot," Beskath said. Her face flushed with sudden heat. An excitement was surging through her. The old man was looking at her oddly.

"Mother Winona needs help to take the lodge down."

"I will tell Amaya," Beskath said.

Amaya was looking at them now, and she lifted a hand. Uncle Foxfoot waved in answer. "Do not forget," he told Beskath.

"How could I forget, Uncle?"

The old Comanche grumbled something and went away, hobbling on his stick. Excitement hammered at Beskath's temples as she looked around the camp. There was no unusual activity. She was apparently among the first to know that the camp would be changed. The first to know that when they traveled south the new camp would be toward the mountains, far from the Shinshin. If she acted quickly . . .

Beskath saw Osa turn and walk away, leaving Amaya alone. Beskath had to calm herself, to take slow breaths to still her heart. Then she started down the little slope toward the river where her sister stood.

"Good morning, Beskath."

"Did you see Uncle Foxfoot?" Beskath demanded.

"Yes, I did, sister."

"He wants you to do something for him."

"Anything."

"His little red pony, his buffalo horse. Long Walker saw the horse in a coulee to the north."

"The Cheyenne won that horse."

"I know they won the horse," Beskath said impatiently. She glanced around her. There was still time. "The other horses were left behind, weren't they? The little red pony was left here as well. Long Walker couldn't bring it. He was leading a string of gift horses and couldn't stop to capture it—you know how wild that red pony can be." Beskath lied easily. The story built upon itself and took on the weight of truth. "Nothing could make Uncle Foxfoot so happy as to have that horse back."

"How far north?" Amaya asked, and Beskath's heart gave a little exultant skip.

"Two miles. There is a broken cottonwood tree and then a small creek. The horse is in the coulee beyond."

Amaya looked northward across the river, then turned
and met her sister's gaze, a gaze which was somehow
fierce and challenging.

"Now do what I've told you," Beskath said roughly.

"Yes, sister."

Beskath turned and walked away. That was done. Done,
and if camp was broken quickly, they would be gone
before Amaya could return. Her search would be a long
one, since the red pony was nowhere nearby at all, but
being led northward to the Cheyenne homeland. As much
as two or three hours Amaya would be searching, and
when she returned, the tribe would be gone.

"Beskath?" Winona came toward her daughter, her
old face somewhat anxious. "They say we must move,
and hastily. Quahadi is worried because of what the
Cheyenne did. Where is Amaya? I need her."

"She is with Osa and her family. I will help you,
Mother Winona."

"But Amaya—"

"Let me help," Beskath said, and she put an arm
through her mother's, turning her back toward their own
tipi as around them people began to pack hurriedly.
Beskath glanced back once, seeing nothing. Amaya had
already crossed the river and was setting out on her
fool's mission. Quickly, she silently urged the people
they passed. Quickly now. And if they moved quickly
enough, Amaya would never find them, not in the mountains. "Hurry, Mother," Beskath said, "hurry. We don't
want to be left behind."

Amaya trudged on. The land was empty once she was
away from the river and out onto the prairie. There was
nothing but the dry buffalo grass, the little clumps of
sage or greasewood, the occasional thicket of nopal cac-
tus. The tracks of the Cheyenne were everywhere near
the river, but back on the hard, sun-baked plains, there
was not even that. She might have been alone on the
earth, so vast was the land, so empty the long-running
skies.

The day was pleasant, the breeze cool and gusting.
Amaya walked on, looking for the broken cottonwood
which would be her landmark. She saw nothing like that

for miles, and it puzzled her. True, Beskath had gotten
the directions secondhand from Long Walker, but to
Amaya's people directions of that sort were critical. People were careful in their instructions.

She thought of the happiness of Uncle Foxfoot when
she would return with the red pony. His seamed face
would break into a vast grin. Amaya hoped her stepsister
had not been mistaken; there was no cottonwood anywhere, and she had not seen a creek.

She looked to the north, where the Cheyenne had
gone, wondering at their abrupt departure. She thought
of the Cheyenne youth poised to dive, of the strange
sense of loss she had felt when he had failed to complete
the act. . . . She walked on. The day was warm, and
Uncle Foxfoot must have his red pony.

"Hurry up, hurry up!" Quahadi shouted again. The
people were too slow in striking their tipis, too slow in
packing their horses and travois. He rode through the
camp on his spotted horse, urging them on. It had been
nearly an hour since the order had been given.

"You, Winona, are you ready?"

"Yes, yes," the old woman answered. "What is the
hurry? What is happening here?"

Quahadi didn't answer. He didn't have time to explain
it to an old woman. Red Corn arrived in a cloud of dust,
his horse rearing.

"Anything yet?"

"No, Quahadi."

"Damn them all."

"Are you sure we have something to worry about?"

"You saw the Cheyenne study the white brands. You
saw them leave. You saw the smoke from a fire two days
ago. They are coming, and the Cheyenne were told."

"They did not warn us." Red Corn was confused. He
could not believe a party of whites would follow them from
Texas over a few horses, but that seemed to be the case.
Red Corn had no fear of whites. He had never seen more
than fifty together at one time, and that was at Bent's
Fort, where the French and Americans came together.

Still, other people of the plains had fought the blue
soldiers and much blood had been let. Quahadi had al-

ways avoided the blue soldiers, because a dream had told him that a white bullet would kill him.

These men that followed were not soldiers. Red Corn knew who they must be—those Texans who were along the Plum Creek, who were wild as Comanche, who fought the Mexicans to the south.

"You should not have killed their children," Red Corn said. "They do not suffer that."

"Do you criticize me now! Get the people moving onto the trail. Toward the mountains. Once we are into the foothills, we will lay a trap for them!"

"Quahadi!" The scout came riding in on a lathered pony. Foam spewed from the horse's lips as the Comanche warrior dismounted on the run. "Fifty men. It is them." The hand lifted toward the low bluffs to the east.

"Red Corn, circle around with the Wolf clan. Call them to you. When they attack, strike hard from behind. Long Walker! Where is he?" Quahadi was in a fever of excitement. "All right—stop the people! I want no one on the trail now! No! Bunch them together, send the children into the trees."

He suddenly stopped speaking. They had all heard it quite clearly. A dozen rapid shots from the south; it had to be the Comanche scouts, Belly Wolf's group. They must be harassing the Texans. Or that was what he should be doing. Surely he wasn't fool enough to engage the whites.

"Quickly." Quahadi waved Red Corn away. "Down along the river. They'll try to come at us from either side. We'll be pushed into the river if we don't hold them back there."

Quahadi himself started southward. In the center of what had been the village, old Horn stood, and he had a prayer blanket raised. Quahadi nearly rode over him, his spotted horse creating clouds of dust. Women wailed at him, men shouted confused questions he did not stop to try to answer.

Another volley of rifle fire sounded, much nearer. As Quahadi reached the trees, he saw three of his warriors on foot, fleeing.

They couldn't be that near! They would have to be mad to charge a Comanche camp. "You, Crow Wing! Halt. Where are you going? Why are you running?"

The Texans burst from the trees, some of them firing two revolvers, riding with their reins in their teeth. They were dark, sun-marked men with huge floppy hats, wearing beards or sweeping mustaches, riding horses with stars branded onto their flanks; three of them wore bits of silver pinned to their shirts.

The man had a big red mustache, he had a patch over one eye. He wore a leather jacket and a dark blue shirt. In his hand was a blue steel revolver, and he lifted it slowly.

Quahadi saw all of that in a single fragment of a moment. He saw that and then saw the rose blossom at the dark muzzle of the gun, saw the tiny white blur in the heart of the black cloud of smoke. Then his face was smashed by a mule kick and he was blown back from his spotted pony to land on the hard earth and be trampled over by the war ponies of the Texans.

Quahadi lay and he looked up at the bellies of the horses, but he saw nothing.

The camp was vast confusion. The people had been running and now they were told to stop and fight, but they could not fight. They were in the open and the Texans were among them firing in all directions. They shot at everything that was Comanche, remembering their own dead, driven on by the shouting of their leaders. Winona saw one Texan with two arrows sticking out of his torso continue to fire with either hand, and his bullets cut a dreadful swath. Then she saw no more. Someone was screaming and she thought it might have been Beskath, but she could not be sure. She could be sure of nothing. Her head was filled with screaming and smoke and fire and distant thunder and cataracts of sound and air and water and diving green-winged black crows. Her face was pressed against the dusty earth and the blood ran slowly from between her lips.

Amaya's head came up. She knew the sounds of gunfire too well. But that could not be gunfire. There were too many reports, far too many. Hundreds of shots would have to be fired. The sharp, crackling sounds met her ears in an unending concatenation. Amaya looked toward the distant camp, smiling uncertainly at her own foolishness.

Certainly not gunfire.

And there was nothing else it could be. She stood stock-still against the empty plains for a long moment, then started that way, walking slowly at first, then more rapidly. As the shots continued, she broke into a run.

The Cheyenne. The Cheyenne have come back, and it is war. Quahadi had somehow offended them with his gifts. The Cheyenne were treacherous. They meant to make war all along. . . . She ran faster, her legs churning, her breast swollen with the pumping of her heart, her lungs fiery and dry, her arms working furiously.

The Cheyenne. And Quahadi has answered their arrogance with his own guns. Uncle Foxfoot will not get his red pony. I can do nothing to help the battle. Perhaps Mother is hurt. Perhaps she is frightened. . . . Her thoughts tumbled on wildly.

The shots had stopped. The long fusillades, the staccato snarl of the weapons, were suddenly still. Now there was only a report now and then, more methodical, less urgent. It was over. Another shot, unexpected, jarred against her nerves, the single sound somehow more disturbing than the constant rattle of minutes ago.

Now she could see the grove of trees, the river glinting in the sunlight as it wove its lazy way among them. A haze hung over the trees, a river fog rising. Yet there had been no river fog, and certainly couldn't be one at this time of the day.

Gunpowder, Amaya said to herself. She had halted again without meaning to. With surprise she discovered that she was simply standing, looking, watching the wind whip away the smoke. She started forward again, her throat constricted, her mouth dry, her eyes stinging.

The smoke was gone long before she reached the river, but something much more terrible remained. It was intangible at first, a tiny whispering in the leaves of the cottonwoods, a dark stain against a cloudless sky, a scent, a memory come alive, a foreboding.

She crossed the river, and the intangible resolved itself sickeningly, horrifyingly.

They were everywhere, driftwood along the riverbank, carelessly stacked cords near the cold fires, scattered litter crumpled and stained.

That morning they had been human beings.

The first body terrified her, the second caused her stomach to knot, to toss and discard its contents as she leaned against the tree. Then there was nothing left. She walked among them and there were so many that they had no meaning; death was common, to live was unique.

And only Amaya was alive. Amaya and a dog which howled distantly.

What had happened here? she thought. Something, but she could not understand what. There had been a people and a family and existence, and it was all gone. Something had gone wrong and the universe in some mad, perverse way had struck out, life striking against itself, life using its power of ending itself to destroy the world, the people, the way.

Something has gone wrong.

She saw Red Corn. There was a hole in his head where his eye should have been. He had been scalped. Two children lay near him, both dead. Amaya looked away.

She hurried on, seeing the burned packs, the dead horses, the savaged bodies. She found Beskath, her skirt lifted up over her hips, her hair in a wild tangle, her face smooth and soft, childlike as it had never been in life.

Not far away was Uncle Foxfoot, and beyond him, Mother Winona, her eyes open, her hands reaching out toward something distant, and Amaya buried her face in the hollow of her mother's shoulder, wishing for the first time that she was dead as well, that she had not been left alone to witness this, to abide and endure as the world went dark and the time of the wolves came.

Amaya wandered on, hardly knowing what she was seeing now. She knew their faces but her mind no longer accepted the reality of this slaughter. There lay dear funny Osa asleep in the dust, and not far from her, Crooked Arm, who would never be a warrior now, who would never go out with the men and be bold and count coup and return honored. Who would never marry.

"I am sorry, Crooked Arm."

The spoken words were grating. The day belonged to the silence of the time, the moaning of the wind in the trees, the babble of the Arrowpoint.

There were none of the enemy dead on the ground—they must have taken them away. But here and there was a rifle, a horse, a bit of cloth, enough so that Amaya knew it was the whites who had come, the men Quahadi had made his war on.

She sat down in the middle of the camp. She sat there and stared bleakly at the carnage. She should see to their funerals, but there were too many, just too many. She looked to the deep blue sky and saw the dark swarming things there and she turned her head and was sick again.

After that she could not stay. She wanted nothing from the camp, nothing of her own from the packs, nothing from the dead. She could not bring herself to take the food they carried. She could not take the water skins from their travois, broken and scattered.

She began to walk without knowing what direction she was taking, where she was going. The people were dead. Someone had come and taken the world away. There were no friends, no family, wise men, leaders, warriors, lovers, sisters. There would be no more celebrations, no common sorrow, no nights sleeping in the buffalo's belly.

She walked on, trudging across the river and onto the plains, away from the place of death. The long winds blew and the sky grew gradually dark as ranks of black clouds drifted over from the north.

The plains were limitless, as was her sorrow. Empty plains, empty heart. Catclaw grew around her, and sumac. A distant, too crimson stain of rosecrown brightened the gray-brown grass. She walked on, head down, the wind whipping away her tears.

At sundown it began to rain. The sky went to a confused burnt orange and deep purple as thunder shook the earth beneath her feet. Still Amaya trudged on, going nowhere. She followed a coulee away from the sunset. She was not hungry, not tired. The world was too large—one couldn't find the end of it, and that was what Amaya wanted, an end to things.

It was suddenly cold, so very cold. The rain hammered down out of an iron-gray sky. It was too dark to walk, but she refused to stop. She walked on until her feet suddenly went out from under her and she tumbled down into a small arroyo where icy runoff water ran. She landed hard on her hip and a jolt of pain ran up her spine.

"Stupid girl," she muttered, but when she tried to rise, she found she could not. There was no strength at all in her muscles. Her body, knotted with anxiety all day through, had just given up. It would go no farther.

"I will go on," Amaya said, but she didn't make the attempt to rise. There was nowhere to go. The rain had come and the world was dark. At such times there is no point in anything, in the living or the dying. The world contracts and the rain hems in the soul, leaving it small and childlike.

She sat with her head hanging, her hair in her face, legs spread, the water running past her, the rain slanting down from a lightning-slashed sky.

She sat and she felt the strange seeping warmth, the small ache, the fluttering of her stomach. I'm going to be sick, she thought, but she wasn't. The warmth spread across her belly and thighs, and Amaya laughed. She looked to the skies, the rain driving down against her upturned face, and she laughed. She laughed until her stomach hurt from laughing, until the laughter had turned to a hysterical sobbing which strangled itself off to a dreadful silence.

The rain was cold, harsh. The warmth still spread over her, seeping from her belly. She had become a woman.

She slept in the rain and the mud and rose stiffly to a clear day. The meadowlarks called in the distance. The sun was bright, dancing behind the shifting bulky clouds.

Amaya rolled to her feet and stood shakily, staring out at the world, stretching the stiffness from her body.

"I continue," she said in a hushed voice. "I continue." The world was gone, there were no more people, but she continued, and she must exist and discover what Destiny needed her for. She alone had survived and there had to be a reason for it or all of life was a mockery. To exist and be snuffed out again for no reason, making no progress whatsoever, generation on generation, was senseless.

"I am here to do," Amaya said. She had never thought that before, but as she spoke she realized that it must be

true. She was here to do something, something undefined, only hinted at, perhaps a simple task, a small act
performed in some small corner, but she was here for
that purpose.

The generations had brought her forth. People she did
not know, whose names she had never heard. Great chiefs,
perhaps, strong, noble women. They stirred only in her
blood, bringing her strength and resolve.

She would think no more of the slaughter, no more of
the death of the tribe, but only of the future. She would
forget all—except the hatred of the whites. That she
would carry and nurture and coddle. They destroyed. If
there was ever the chance, she would destroy them.

The earth was soft with the rain as Amaya moved
down into the coulee searching for her breakfast. She
sipped water from the creek in a cupped hand and
searched the tangle of brush along the sandy bluffs,
finding blackberries, and farther on, elk thistle, edible,
sustaining. With a stick she dug Indian potatoes from the
earth and stuffed them inside her blouse. These she
could eat raw as she walked.

As she walked where?

Southward were other Comanche bands. Fierce, no-
madic, with some of the warriors as savage and auto-
cratic as Quahadi. They were her people, the Comanche,
or had been. But she had been accepted in her own band
only marginally. There were those who scorned her because she was not of Comanche blood. Among a new
people, matters might be much worse. Southward—it
was a long, long way.

To the east the broad plains stretched, and from the
land beyond the plains came the whites, who destroyed
and pillaged. To the west were the badlands, and farther
on, the high mountains, the snowbound wilderness where
the Ute lived.

Northward lay the lands of the Cheyenne and Sioux.
She knew neither people. She would be a stranger among
them, and, as a Comanche, likely an unwelcome stranger.

"I must go home," Amaya said, and she started walking. She was walking, and the wind was on her face. She
glanced at the sun and wondered at herself. She was
walking homeward—to the north, to the land of the
Cheyenne.

She ate well. The land was ripe and wealthy with food for those who knew where to find it. Rose hips and milkweed buds became her staples. Here and there along the watercourses she found berries and wild persimmon. She grew lean from the lack of meat, but she lost no strength. Her moccasins wore out the second week and she considered making a bow and arrows, stalking the large buffalo herd which crept past her day after day, but she rejected the notion in the end and simply cut off the bottom of her skirt with a sharp-edged piece of flint. From the buckskin she made crude moccasins stitched together with the fringes that decorated the hem of her skirt.

She had not seen another human being, although twice she had found dead campfires, piles of bones. Someone had been following the buffalo herd south. White hunters or Indians, she could not say.

Everyone now wished to dishonor the sacred buffalo, the generous buffalo who sustained and provided. Her own tribe had killed six thousand buffalo the spring before. Six thousand hides traded for beads, for whiskey, for more guns to kill more buffalo. The whites were worse, or perhaps more efficient. The stacks of whitened bones littered the plains. The old Comanche, men like Horn, had decried the waste. They said that the buffalo was the Indian's manitou walking, that he must be respected and cherished.

Quahadi had laughed. "It has been this way forever. There is no end to the buffalo. My grandfather's grandfather set fire to the forest which was the plains to herd the wild game, to feed his tribe. In our time do we not drive the herds of buffalo over the high bluffs, killing more than we need? Didn't we last winter drive them onto the ice on the Shinshin River so that they might sink through into the water and freeze? Many were swept away, and we did not eat them. This is the same." He had patted his new rifle. "Life grows easier and the people want it so. You are old and foolish and confused by the mists of time which settle in your head, Horn."

Horn, shaking his head as if speaking to a mad child, had said, "They die, and if they die, we die," but Quahadi had listened no more.

Amaya passed still more bones. In other places the whites gathered the bones and ground them to make fertilizer. At times the herds were slaughtered for that purpose alone. And they did not follow the rites to ensure that more buffalo would come. They did not know the sacred ways. The hearts of the buffalo should be left behind, for in their hearts is the seed that will bring forth more buffalo. The whites did not know that; many Indians no longer believed it. They believed in their guns.

As had Quahadi.

Amaya made her bed of sumac boughs and grass up a small, shallow canyon. The sun sank and the rain began again as it had for day upon day. She had her cold lonely meal. Winter was rushing toward her, she knew, and she would not be able to sleep out for many more nights.

She lay there and tried to sleep, but failed. She stared at the stars which twinkled beyond the mist in her eyes. Where was she going? What sort of fool was she? What hope did she have that the Cheyenne might accept her? She had never so much as spoken to a Cheyenne. With a pang of panic she decided that she had made a terrible mistake. She should have been heading southward all this time, returning to the land of the Comanche. When winter came, she would be nearly helpless.

"Why?" she asked the empty sky, and it did not answer. "Why am I here and alone and lost in the night?"

It was as close as she had yet come to despair. From somewhere a calmness came, lifting her spirits higher. From some distant place reassurance settled like the voices of time, the memory of Being, the heart of existence, and Amaya slept.

". . . mile or two to the Platte."

Amaya sat up sharply and then pressed herself to the earth again hurriedly. Her heart clawed at her ribs, trying to fight its way out of her body. The voices and the language were unfamiliar, but certainly white. She lay there in the predawn, gray and cold, seeing nothing, hearing nothing again for a long while.

Amaya slid silently from her bed, her cheek against the damp earth as she worked her way downslope toward a deeper hollow cut into the bluff by years of runoff water. She dragged a hand behind her to scatter the boughs from which she had made her bed. Looking up, she could see the crown of grass on the bluff, see the wind shift it and flatten it. And then she saw the dark figures, erect and narrow, pasted against the dawn sky, and she froze.

She lay still in the mud of the hillside, peering up through her hair at the rim. There were two men there, white men. One was a blue soldier; the other wore buckskins and long hair.

"Long way to the next water even with the rain," the long-haired man was saying. Amaya could understand only one word, "water." It was a word she had learned at Bent's Fort long ago. A white word she and Osa had played with, liking the funny sound of it. She lay absolutely still, watching the blufftop.

Another man had appeared. He wore yellow stripes on his shirt sleeve. He was a big man with a fat belly and a red beard. He stood close behind the others but said nothing. He said nothing until his eyes, slowly sweeping the coulee bottom, struck Amaya. Then they widened and his arm came up sharply.

"Lieutenant!"

Amaya was to her feet and running wildly downslope as if the devils were behind her. She was into the willow brush along the coulee bottom, weaving through the thick undergrowth, feeling branches lash her face and hands. She slipped once and went down; crawling forward a little way, she stayed there against the sandy earth, watching behind her.

No one came. An hour passed and then another, and there was not so much as a sound.

Amaya still didn't dare move. She hardly allowed herself to breathe. It began to rain again and she watched it, her face against the sand. She watched a drop fall through the canopy of willow brush and pock the gray, soft earth. She saw a long-legged black beetle waddle away toward its dry shelter.

Distantly a small sound shrilled. A horse, she thought, but the noise was muffled and distorted by wind and weather. The raindrops fell and clung to the willows, gathering to form strings of jewels along the edges of the leaves. Amaya counted them one by one, not moving an inch as the minutes dragged by, accumulating into hours which hung heavily on her. Her shoulders ached, her thighs were stiff with the lack of movement. Still she refused to budge. They were out there—she could sense it. The whites were there and they would kill, and so she did not move. Since girlhood they had been taught that, she and Osa and Beskath—do not move. The eyes of men are made for hunting, and a hunter's eyes see movement. Study the wild things, watch them crouch and wait, running only when they know they have been seen.

A drop of cold water trickled down Amaya's neck. They had gone. Surely they must have gone by now. She lifted her head a fraction of an inch and instantly regretted it. Through the screen of brush she saw the tall, polished boots, saw the blue trousers above them. They had been striding away and now they halted. Had she been seen?

Amaya settled back against the earth, as silent as a leaf dropping in the forest. The boots turned toward her and started her way.

He does not see me, Amaya told herself. He could not.

In another moment she knew he did see her and panic overwhelmed her. She got to her feet and darted away, running through the tangle of brush, the blackthorn and willow tearing at her, clutching at her skirt with tiny fingers. She ran into the clearing and the tall man in buckskins stepped in front of her, his hand closing around her arm like an iron talon.

"Here she is!" he called out.

Amaya kicked at his shin and spat in his face and he backhanded her, spinning her head around, bringing the warm salty taste of blood to her mouth. Amaya sagged back. He still had hold of her arm, but if she could wriggle free . . .

"You just hold still, little girl," the man said in a soft drawl, "no one's intendin' to hurt you, but you'd better just stay put."

Amaya understood none of it. She was ready to strike out again, to try kicking him in the groin, clawing at his eyes with stiffened fingers, but the others were already nearly there, breaking through the brush to enter the clearing and stand panting, looking at her. She gave it up and stood glowering, the horny hand of the army scout pinching her upper arm, lifting her shoulder to her ear.

"Got her, did you, Pocono?"

"Yes, sir, I got her."

"Good." The man who now planted himself in front of Amaya was young, yet he seemed to be their leader. He wore silver bars stitched to his uniform shoulders. Around his neck was a yellow scarf. There were yellow stripes down the legs of his trousers. On his hat were crossed long knives. He had a small pink mouth, a freckled face which seemed very funny to Amaya, and eyes that were as green as grass. She hated him.

The third man, the red-bearded one with the stripes on his sleeve, looked at her closely, then turned his head and spat. "Not going to get much information out of this one, Lieutenant Pierce. She ain't Sioux."

"Cheyenne?"

"No, sir. What do you say, Poke?" the sergeant asked the scout.

"Not by her face. Not by her dress, neither. Thought we'd run into a Shoshoni by mistook at first, but she ain't that neither."

"What, then?" the lieutenant asked. He leaned forward to look into the young Indian's eyes and she spat at him. He withdrew quickly, muttering a boyish curse.

"She's a wild one, ain't she. And look at her feet, sir. Moccasins wore out complete. Cut off the bottom of her dress, she did, and a rough job of it. She's gaunted up. Walked a hell of a long way."

"Walking where? Yellow Knife—"

"Got nothin' to do with him, I don't reckon. No, we still ain't found us a Sioux. It's like Hart says, she's not Cheyenne nor Sioux. Got us a wild dog."

"Bitch," Sergeant Hart put in. The lieutenant didn't laugh. His education and background didn't allow for the abuse of women of any race.

"She don't 'speak,' do you reckon?" the scout asked.

"Give it a try," the officer said, and the scout asked Amaya questions in Mandan and Pawnee. There was no response.

"She don't understand it."

Hart disagreed. "She knew the Pawnee, Poke."

"Might have understood a word or two, but she don't speak," the man in buckskins guessed. "She's mighty young to know many tongues, though it's seldom you run across a full-grown Indian that knows only one language."

"Can you sign to her?" the lieutenant asked.

"No good. Asking for food or the way to the big river is about my limit. Why don't you call that Arik down."

"Tongue?"

"Yes, sir. Tongue, he'll know how to sign to her. He'll also maybe be able to tell us what she is."

The chatter went on around Amaya. She understood none of it. Once the white man in buckskins had asked her a funny question in the language of the Pawnee, the hated Pawnee, but Amaya had already made up her mind she would not try to answer their questions. They were white. They could even be the men who had killed her people. Except the horses they rode did not have the brands the raiders' horses had had. These men, all but the scout, rode bay horses of a uniform size. All of them had a black "US" stamped on their flanks. Still, they were whites and she would not speak.

After a time an Indian came trotting toward them up the river bottom. He was a shrunken thing, though not old. One eye was gone. His hair was braided on one side. Amaya did not know his tribe.

Tongue was an Arikara Indian. His people were a small tribe overrun by the Sioux for centuries. He hated the Sioux and so he scouted for the white army. Secretly he disliked the whites as well, but a small people, a small man, cannot fight everyone. He took the whites' money and did his work, and when there were Sioux to be scalped, he took their hair.

"Comanche," the Arikara said decisively.

"Comanche!"

"Not this far north."

"Yes," the Arikara said, his head bobbing. "See the beads? See the belt she wears? Yes, Comanche."

"Impossible," the sergeant said.

"Ain't likely," the scout said, "but Tongue probably knows. Me, I never did spend time down south, but I've spent plenty in Dakota and Colorado, in the high mountains, and I've never seen nothing looked like her."

"Maybe not Comanche long," the Arikara Indian said.

"What do you mean?" Lieutenant Pierce asked.

"Maybe not." The Arikara shook his head, stepping nearer to Amaya, who held her chin up proudly. Her hair might be tangled, her dress torn, her arms and legs scratched and skinned, but they would know she was not beaten.

"What is it, Tongue?"

"I think not Comanche."

"But you said she was!"

"Clothing, yes. Comanche clothes. Not her face." The Arikara rattled off three quick questions in the Comanche tongue. Amaya looked past him, into the distances where the white clouds bunched, refusing to answer. "Just another Comanche pig," the Arik said, and she threw herself at him, nearly tearing free of the scout's grip.

"Easy now!" the scout laughed. "What in hell'd you say to her?"

Tongue told them. "She is Comanche, but I do not think all Comanche blood."

"A slave?"

"Maybe. Maybe taken as a child. Comanche take many slaves, sometimes from Spanish people in Mexico."

"Yes." The young officer was studying Amaya more closely now. "I see what you mean. She doesn't look to be all Indian, does she?"

"Beg pardon, sir," Sergeant Hart broke in, "but what she is and what she ain't don't help us find Yellow Knife."

"I'm aware of that, Sergeant," the officer said a little stiffly.

"If she's been out here many days, it could be she's seen Yellow Knife's band," the scout said.

"Sign to her, will you, Tongue? Ask her if she's seen a Sioux war party."

The Arikara did so. Amaya's eyes watched him darkly, following the words his rapid fingers sketched. She understood. But she had seen no Sioux, and if she had she would not answer. She would tell the whites nothing. What would they do now? Kill all the Sioux as they had the Comanche?

"Stubborn," Pocono said.

The lieutenant looked at the scout. "Do you think she knows what he's asking?"

"Oh, yes, I think she knows right enough, sir. She just ain't talkin'."

"We're wastin' time," the sergeant said. The young officer ignored Hart.

"Ask her again," Pierce instructed the Arikara. "Tell her we will give her a reward. A pony and a new blanket—whatever you think might please her—if she tells us where the Sioux went."

Tongue tried again but it was obvious that the Comanche woman, if that was what she was, was not going to answer any inquiries.

"Sir"—Sergeant Hart was growing impatient—"don't you think we ought to be going?"

"Please restrain yourself, Hart," Pierce said, his Baltimore-accented voice assuming the tone of command. Ever since Hart's brother had been found among the dead at Horse Creek, the sergeant had lived with one purpose—to see the leader of the so-called Spotted Sioux, Yellow Knife, dead and his people crushed.

Hart was a good NCO who had gone a little wild-eyed with his hatred. From time to time he had to be spoken to. The colonel, John T. Hinshaw, was able to handle Hart. They spoke a common language. Hinshaw had lost a daughter and his son-in-law to the Sioux. Lieutenant Pierce had a harder time handling the bearded sergeant. Pierce was still young, very young, still new in the West. Even he wondered at times if the Indian method of promoting men through valor and proven wisdom wasn't far superior to the United States Army's system of providing leaders through university training. The men, some of whom had been in service for fifteen or twenty years, all knew more than the newly arrived Lieutenant Pierce about Indian fighting and life on the plains, and many of them resented taking orders from him.

"Just tryin' to point out that the man we're lookin' for is gettin' farther away, sir," Hart said, and he wasn't trying hard to hide his surly disposition.

"I am aware of that, Hart. Mr. Pocono, how far behind Yellow Knife would you estimate we are?"

"Two days still, sir. We haven't closed no ground. He's

movin' fast. No women, no kids, no travois. We ain't gonna close ground on him," the civilian scout replied.

"No," the young man mused. "I don't think so. We've only got another day out. The colonel wants us back no later than the tenth."

"You can't be talkin' about going in to Fort Laramie," the sergeant blurted out.

"Hart, if I am, the decision is mine, isn't it?"

"Yes, sir."

"Yes, I'm talking about going back to Laramie. We've been chasing Yellow Knife for ten days and we haven't gotten any closer. We're nearly out of supplies and the men are tired—"

"If the men knew," Hart interrupted, "that we had a chance of catching up to Yellow Knife—"

"We don't!" Pierce glanced at Pocono, who thrust out his lower lip and shook his head. There was no chance.

"Sir, if I could speak—" Hart began.

"You can't. Dammit, Hart, I've been bending for you since you asked to come on this patrol. As far as I'm concerned, it will be the last time you come out with me. And if you continue to press matters, I will have to present an unfavorable report on your conduct to the commanding officer."

"Yes, sir." Hart was submissive and sullen.

Andrew Pierce looked to the western skies, to Amaya and then to Pocono. "That's enough, Poke. We'll not find the son of a bitch this time."

"I think not, sir," the scout agreed. "What about her?" He inclined his head toward Amaya.

"I don't know. Think she's lost, wandering, a runaway?"

"No idea if she won't talk, sir."

"No, dammit, you're right." Pierce rubbed his forehead with a knuckle. "All right. We'll take her in to Laramie. Let the minister have her."

Hart looked away, his face immobile. He obviously didn't think much of that either. This Dr. Quill and his school for Indian orphans. It was a joke. An Indian couldn't learn anything—everyone knew that. Second, he couldn't become a Christian no matter what you forced on him. It wasn't in him. An Indian wasn't no more and no less than a dog when it came to having a soul, and that

Methodist minister, if he wasn't a fool for trying, was doomed to failure.

"There's not a lot of point in it, sir," Hart said.

"In what, Hart?"

"Taking her in, sir."

"No? What would you have me do with her, Sergeant Hart? Shoot her?"

Hart winced. "No, sir. Whatever the lieutenant says, sir. I meant nothing."

His sarcasm was transparent. Pierce responded sharply. "I am going to do what I think is right. We have a problem communicating, do we not, Sergeant? Perhaps the colonel can straighten things out. Pocono, if the woman can be escorted to a spare horse, then we can proceed."

"Back to Laramie, sir?"

"Back to Laramie."

"Yes, sir. She'll have to be tied, I expect. She doesn't seem all that eager to go to the Reverend Quill's Indian orphan school," Pocono said.

"Then tie her! She can't be wandering around out here anyway. Where in hell did she come from?"

"No tellin', and she won't talk."

"She's an army charge now." Pierce turned away. "There's been enough discussion about her, and about Yellow Knife. He's eluded us again. Perhaps the next patrol will have more luck."

Amaya thought the conversation would never end. Finally the whites disbanded and she was led to a waiting horse by the man in buckskins. The horse she recognized as an Indian war pony. Something had been cut out of the mane. A medicine bag, she decided. There were still traces of paint on the flanks of the horse, on its pale shoulder. And across the withers there was a darker stain, deep maroon.

There were forty men with the party. The main body of soldiers had held back on a low grassy knoll while the coulee was searched. Perhaps in case they were being led into an ambush; Amaya did not know and she did not care. She was a prisoner—that she understood. What they would do with her, why they had bothered to take her instead of simply killing her, she did not know.

She did not understand these strange-smelling, hairy-faced men. The young one with the spots on his face led them out at a slow pace, Amaya jouncing in the unfamiliar saddle someone had thrown over the Indian pony's back. Her hands were free but she had no reins to guide the horse. A lead line ran from the animal's hackamore to the saddle of the soldier ahead of her.

She could not run, for if she ran they would catch her. She sat and listened to the unfamiliar language. The men spoke in mutters, perhaps so that their boy leader wouldn't hear them. Now and then they looked at Amaya and laughed in a dirty way.

They rode east and at night they camped on the flats, building a cooking fire out of buffalo chips. They boiled their food and a strong drink they sipped out of tin cups. Some of the men rode out to act as sentries while the others ate, talking very loudly still so that Amaya, who had camped with a Comanche war party once, wondered how these white soldiers ever found the enemy. They made noise audible for miles, they built huge fires. But then they must have been successful—there was the dead Sioux's horse she rode.

"Want somethin' to eat?"

The man crouched down in front of her. He had a yellow mustache and a sunburned face. When he grinned he showed crooked teeth.

Amaya shook her head. "Leave her be, Hobbs!" someone yelled.

"She's gotta eat, don't she?" the man said over his shoulder. "Here." He placed the plate in her hands. "It ain't much, but you eat it."

"You'll kill her with that army grub," someone cracked.

Then the soldier went away and Amaya, who had been tethered with a length of rawhide, her ankle tied to a fallen gray cottonwood, sat down to try the food. She took a bite and made a face. Someone laughed again and she scowled, not sure what they were laughing at. Maybe they had given her food to make her sick. It tasted bad, but it was warm and in the end she ate it.

There was nothing then to do but lie down upon the hard earth and try to sleep. She curled up like a fox, watching the fire burn down, listening to the chatter of the white soldiers, smelling their tobacco.

"Here." There was someone over her and Amaya sat up in fright. It was the boy leader of the soldiers, the one with the grass-green eyes. In his hand was a blanket. "It's a cold night, you might want this."

He crouched down then and wrapped it around her shoulders, and Amaya felt her flesh crawl. To be touched by a white thing! It was disgusting; but he stood up quickly and then walked away. She was alone then but for the soldier who had been assigned to watch her as she slept, and he was across the clearing, paying little attention.

The stars coasted past overhead, and far away a coyote howled its mourning song. She lay awake a long while, trying to plot an escape. There had to be a way to untie the thong or cut it, to slip from the camp and make a getaway. If she could reach the big coulee they had passed that morning, she could hide . . . but that was a long way, and they would track her down before she could reach it.

She lay trying to think of a way, but exhaustion overtook her and she slept, the enemy all around her, the night growing cold and bitter.

They were up with the sun, and after another meal like the last, they rode on, north by east, deeper into Sioux country, away from the land of the Comanche, which already seemed incredibly distant. Amaya remembered the long red-sand deserts, the buttes and mesas, the dry alkali flats, the long Staked Plain of her homeland. Distant, it took on a raw beauty, a significance.

Around her now was land which was almost completely flat. There was grass, sometimes to a horse's knees, and many little streams wriggling across the plains, glinting silver. Here and there were clumps of scraggly cottonwood trees and along the wider creeks tangles of berries and willows, blackthorn and redbud.

From time to time they came upon a broad coulee where an army could have been hidden. These had to be taken by riding down the sandy bluffs in a storm of dust, then clambering up the far side, the men sweating, cursing, the horses whinnying. As they rode farther east, though, the coulees had been crossed many times and trails had been beaten down along their flanks.

Now for the first time Amaya began to see white dwellings. Made of logs or of sod cut from the breast of the good earth, they stood forlorn and isolated, windowless, leaning precariously. She saw men laboring behind mules, cutting at Mother Earth, saw ragged children with gawking eyes and outsize hats, with flyaway yellow hair and dark brooding expressions. She saw the women, gaunt, beaten, tragic, small and determined. They watched, hands on hips as the soldiers rode past, and sometimes they yelled things out—at her or at the soldiers, Amaya could not be sure.

She counted as many as twenty houses and it seemed too many and not enough at once. Too many to have upon the land and not enough to defend themselves. No wonder they had their army with them. She only wondered that there were so many warriors and so few farming to feed them.

The big river came into view that afternoon while the sun, low at their backs, reddened the long plains and streaked the Laramie with fire.

"The Laramie," they said, and she knew they meant the river. The horses pricked their ears and moved ahead more eagerly, as did the soldiers. Amaya was carried along by the flow of motion. She no longer controlled her own destiny.

She looked toward the river, beyond it toward the mountains which had begun to lift up from the plains. She did not know the names of the mountains, but they were very tall. To the west, even greater mountains reared their heads. The wind that moved down onto the plains was very cold, and Amaya's teeth chattered. To their right, and very distant, was another large river, the Platte they called it, and as they rode north, the two flanking rivers drew nearer together. Ahead they joined and at the river junction was the place called Laramie. Laramie, where a great log stockade had been built. A flag of three colors fluttered from a pole in the stockade. There were steamboats on the river, flat-bottomed, almost colorless it had been so long since they had been painted.

On the decks men stood and waved their hats at the cavalry contingent. From the small settlement near the fort, boys and dogs, some men, ran forth, and they followed the horse soldiers, cheering and shouting.

The green-eyed boy leader took his men across a sandy ford upriver and then they were in the shadow of the great log walls. Camped beside the fort were Indians, very poor-looking people, their tipis patched. Amaya recognized the Cheyenne among them and her heart leapt. But these were not true Cheyenne. They skulked as the cavalry rode past, their eyes going to the ground submissively. It was disgusting and she did not look at them or at the other Indians, whose names she did not know.

The gate was open and the soldiers rode in. Dust was thick in the air and the late sun colored it as it boiled up and slowly settled.

The fort was a perfect square, and three sides of it had buildings against the walls. Amaya couldn't guess at the many functions these rooms had. Men came out from some of them to watch through the dusk as the cavalry patrol came in.

A white woman with her fair hair wrapped into a tight knot started toward them as they got off from their horses. Beside her was an Indian girl in a blue dress. Amaya could only stare.

"Brought you one, Mizz Quill," the sergeant said.

"Oh, the poor thing." The woman with the dirty yellow hair placed a hand on Amaya's legs and squeezed. "What has she been through? Where did you find her?"

"Don't know where she come from. Just found her lost and wandering. Figured she was a case for you."

"You poor dear," the white woman said. "Don't you worry. We will take care of you. The Lord has sent you to us and we will not fail Him."

The sergeant had turned away. Amaya noticed that the boy who led the soldiers was also gone. One by one the men walked their horses away toward a paddock across the yard. Amaya was left with the white woman and her Indian girl.

"Get down now, dear," the yellow-haired lady said.

The words meant nothing to Amaya. The gestures she

understood but ignored. If the horse could make it to the main gate . . . Already the gate was closing as night came in.

"Sign to her, Little Dove, won't you. Tell her that everything is all right."

"Yes, Mrs. Quill. I will tell her."

The girl—a Sioux, Amaya thought—stepped forward and signed rapidly to her. "There is food. Get down from the horse and come inside the lodge of this woman. This is a school. A school"—the Sioux girl's dark eyes flickered—"and a prison for Indians."

Amaya slowly smiled as her eyes met Little Dove's and they understood one another. Amaya swung down from the war pony and it was led away by a soldier.

"I'm glad you've come to us, dear," the woman called Mrs. Quill said. "I know this is hard for you, but in the end life will be better. We have many things to offer you that you would never have had out there." She said "out there" with distaste. "You'll see. Books, music, clothing, the word of the Lord, the benefits only a white culture can bestow—all of that will be yours, dear. I promise you we mean you no harm."

Then Mrs. Quill took her arm and Amaya shoved her away roughly. For a moment the white woman's mouth tightened, her eyes went harsh and narrow; but she regained herself and smiled.

"Lead the new girl to the school, will you, Little Dove? She doesn't trust me yet, poor thing."

The Sioux girl touched Amaya's arm and signed for her to follow. Together then they walked toward a long log building which was set apart from the other structures. Behind it was a small garden where squash and corn grew. In the narrow windows smoky candlelight showed.

They walked up onto the porch and stood waiting while the white woman unlocked the door, and then they went in together. They walked through a narrow hallway and into a room which had carpets on the floor, a large wooden cross on the wall, and several faded chairs. There was a desk at one side of the room sitting on a raised platform, and at the desk sat the man.

He lifted his eyes as the women entered the room.

"I've brought a new friend, John," the woman said, and the man in black bobbed his head. He wore spectacles which reflected the light of his candle. He had been writing in a large book, his pen scratching away.

"So I see." He smiled, and his smile, like the white woman's, had no warmth in it. He stood, a lanky man with a long, almost cadaverous face. His cheeks were hollow, his chin scooped and jutting. His eyebrows over brown eyes were dark and fuzzy, his nose long and fleshless, his hands soft and clawlike at once.

"This is the Reverend Mr. Quill," the white woman said to Amaya. "He will be your teacher here, as I will be your teacher."

Amaya didn't understand. She thought the man's name was "Quill," since she had heard that several times, but she knew nothing beyond that. Nor did she care to. The whites came and they killed your people and they took you away. Then they put you in this place and asked you to be their friend. She turned away, glaring at the wall where the wooden cross hung.

"You'd better show her her room, Dorothy," the minister said. "She'll want to rest, to eat, and to bathe. There is time—for now she is frightened and small and alone."

"Yes, John. Little Dove, you may go back to your class."

The Sioux girl nodded and walked away, her moccasins quiet against the plank floor. A door closed and then Amaya was led down the hall again by the white woman.

"At first, things will seem strange," Dorothy Quill said. She guided Amaya by her arm down another corridor and past many closed doors. Somewhere distantly voices sang a song in a language quite unintelligible. "For tonight I'm afraid we'll have to shut you up by yourself, dear, but things will get easier each day for you. I do wish you could understand me—but that will come too. Here we are."

The white woman stopped and Amaya stopped. A door was opened and as Amaya stepped in, it was closed behind her. She spun around, but it was too late. The door was closed and a bolt thrown. Amaya put her shoulder to the heavy wood, but it would not move. Anxiously she looked around the tiny cubicle, seeing only a single high window the width of a small log high on the wall.

She walked like a wild thing around the room, touching the walls, trying the door for a second time and then a third. From across the fort came the sound of a bugle as the last flat red rays of sunlight died against the log walls of the room.

Amaya sagged onto the bed in the corner and sat there, hands clasped together. How had this happened? How had she come to this place? Who had decreed that her world should end, that everything familiar must be taken away?

She looked to the high window, seeing a star shine feebly through the haze caused by the soldiers' fires, by the river fog. And how long ago had she lain awake watching the same star through the smoke flap of her family's tipi? The same constant star, bright, distant, mocking.

Amaya threw herself back on the bed and lay, arms behind her head, staring at nothing. She had come to this place and now she must survive it. She knew nothing of it, nothing of the Quills or the soldiers, of the Indians kept here. She must learn, she must survive.

It was, after all, only a school. A place where the souls of Indians were scrubbed away. A training ground—and a prison. That was what Little Dove had told her. A prison, and freedom lay far distant, in that undefined wild place where there were no whites and no white schools, where the long grass blew and *he* rode his strutting buffalo pony. *He*—for Osa had been right all along. Amaya was waiting, she would always wait, for the warrior who would come and rescue her from this life, from this prison, from this way. And she watched the star through the high window, watched it fade and diffuse behind the mist, the mist which was not all river fog and smoke from white fires.

3

IN THE MORNING Mrs. Quill and two older Indian women came bringing a dark blue dress like the one Little Dove had worn. Amaya threw it down and refused to put it on, but they took her old dress away and then there was no choice but to wear the dress or stand naked.

She was led then to a large hall where girls of all ages sat at long benches. Before them were tin plates of food, and after they all bowed their heads and chanted, they ate.

Amaya saw Little Dove at the head of the table. The other girls, Sioux and Cheyenne for the most part, paid no attention to her. They kept their eyes turned down, and they ate rapidly and quietly while Mrs. Quill and the two Indian women watched over them.

After the meal they filed out in their dark dresses and went to a narrow, dark little room smelling of furniture oil, and girls washed with harsh soap.

The reverend came and stood up before them, his eyes small and glistening behind his rimless spectacles, his pale hands fluttering over them as he spoke. Amaya looked around her at the young faces, bored and absorbed, angry and placid, frightened and assured. It seemed that the younger girls were more comfortable here, more willing to accept Quill and his wife, their doctrine and their ways. Amaya saw one girl snickering behind her hand.

Later still they went out into the fresh air. It was a cool, breezy day. Little Dove and another girl came up to Amaya, greeting her in sign language and then in the Sioux tongue.

"Cold day. Now we must work. This is my friend Tantha, the Cheyenne."

"She doesn't understand you," Tantha said.

"Well, she'll have to learn. We must speak."

"Then teach her English. We'll all be speaking it soon enough."

"No!" Little Dove was suddenly rebellious. "I won't teach her English. Let them force it down her. Why should I do it for them?"

"All right," Tantha laughed. "Then don't. We'll sign and that will be that."

Mrs. Quill and the two big Indian women—Amaya found out later they were Osage—came out of the building and unlocked a toolshed. All of the girls were given tools and they filed out a side gate of the fort to the garden beside the river.

Amaya had a hoe in her hand. She did not like the feel of it. She did not like the dress she wore, nor this Mrs. Quill, nor the Osage women. But she worked, and as she worked she watched the river, the few boats that sailed along it, the settlement beyond the trees, the army sentry making his slow round atop the walls. She would not be here forever. They could make her farm, they could force her to chant to a white god, they could make her a slave, but they could not keep her. She looked at the other girls, at this Tantha, the Cheyenne whose face was twisted into a challenging sneer as she worked through the rows of corn, and Amaya knew she was not alone. She knew there were friends here.

The days became the same. Prayer, English lessons, garden work. On rainy days there was more prayer. Sometimes they sewed or tried knitting. Only the young girls who had been at the orphanage a very long time cared for that. Amaya and the older girls chafed under the routine.

"It is, after all, only a prison," Tantha said.

"Then," Amaya said quietly, "haven't you thought about escaping?"

"Often. Where would I go? I don't even know where my people are. And you—you have no place to go at all."

"You could not run far," Little Dove said. "The soldiers would bring you back."

"Coward," Tantha said. Little Dove just looked up from her sewing and smiled.

"I say what is true."

"Quiet," Amaya said, and instantly the two girls fell silent. The door to the sewing room stood open and now Amaya could see the narrow form of Dr. Quill filling the doorway. He moved around the room, speaking to the girls.

"That's very lovely, Mary . . . oh, and yours is coming along well too, Catherine . . ."

"Why does he have to use those Christian names?" Tantha hissed. Little Dove didn't answer, nor did Amaya. She could hear the footsteps of the minister drawing nearer, his shoe leather whispering against the clay tile floor. She could hear his breathing as well, asthmatic and shallow. She stiffened and bent even closer to her sewing.

"And how is your work coming, Emily?" he asked, and his hand was on Amaya's shoulder. He leaned over her back, speaking near her ear. His breath smelled like cloves. Emily, he called her, because to his ear it sounded near to her name.

"Very well, sir," Amaya answered, speaking haltingly. She did not want them to know how well she knew English already, how well she had been coached and rehearsed by Tantha and Little Dove. None of them allowed their teachers to know what apt students they were. It made the teachers less cautious when they spoke.

"Good." The flaccid long hand squeezed Amaya's shoulder and then slid away, and Amaya watched the black-coated figure shuffle toward the doorway. When she started to sew again, she found that the needle shook in her hand and she had to put her work down on her lap.

"Filth," she said, and it came out in the language of the Comanche. She looked at Tantha, shrugged, and got back to her sewing, jabbing her finger twice before she settled to her work and managed to get Quill out of her mind.

In the mornings Amaya went out by herself to draw water from the river for the girls to wash with, to cook their breakfasts with, to do their laundry. It was then, she thought, then that someone could make an escape.

She was alone. There was only the guard on the parapet to see her. A sleepy soldier who had been at his job all night and who couldn't care much about an Indian girl from the orphanage anyway. If she could slip into the willows and work her way upriver, it would be an hour before they knew she was gone. Why would they care anyway? What did they need with one more pagan soul to save?

These thoughts filled her mind as she went out one morning, the sun low and red, the willows standing before it stiff and black like iron palings. Doves began to rise against the sky. There was still a fog on the water, still a frost on the grass.

Amaya filled her first bucket and set it aside. Then she turned, still in a crouch, her eyes sparking. The soldier stood over her grinning.

"Hello, remember me?" It was the boy leader, the lieutenant who had commanded the patrol which had brought her to Laramie. "You know me, heh, girl?" he asked.

"I couldn't forget my captor," Amaya said, forgetting her vow to speak only imperfect English. "Nor do I wish to spend much time remembering him."

"Excellent," Lieutenant Pierce said, unperturbed. "The accent could use some work, but the rest is excellent. I'd be happy to teach you if you need some extra lessons."

"I need nothing from the army, Lieutenant."

"Look, call me Andy, will you? Andy Pierce."

"I need nothing from army soldiers," Amaya said defiantly.

"All right. I apologize for my pidgin English. But I didn't know you had learned so quickly, did I? How could I?" Andy Pierce crouched down beside her, watching as she filled a bucket for the second time. The first bucketful had been spilled when Pierce startled her.

"I need nothing," Amaya said, and she was aware that Pierce was watching her, studying her face, her figure, which had blossomed in that mysterious manner to womanhood.

"I feel responsible, you see," Pierce went on. He stood again and turned his back. "I brought you here—well, at the time I couldn't discuss it with you, could I? I just

knew you were alone out there and you looked sick, thin.
I thought the best thing to do was to bring you to the
Indian orphanage." There was no answer again. "My
God, are you going to go back into that dumb Indian
routine, Amaya!"

"You know my name."

"Of course I do."

"How do you know it?"

"I made it my business to find out."

"Yes." Amaya stood and shouldered the pole which
held her water buckets. "I have to go or there will be
trouble."

"Surely another five minutes ..." But Amaya was
already walking away from him, the buckets gently
swaying as her hips did. Pierce stood watching until,
angrily biting at his lip, he turned and stalked off.

"Where have you been!" The Osage woman menacingly waved the switch she always carried. Amaya didn't
bother to answer, nor did she flinch when the Osage
woman lashed at her with the weapon. She placed the
buckets on the floor and then walked out, leaving the big
woman to grumble in her own language. Walking quickly
to the dining hall, Amaya seated herself at the long table
next to Tantha. There was an empty spot on the bench
on Amaya's right hand.

"I thought you'd gone with her," Tantha said.

"What?"

"I thought you'd gone with Little Dove."

"What are you talking about?"

"She ran away. Early this morning. I thought you'd
gone too."

"But they'll catch her."

"Yes." Tantha shrugged. "I wanted to go. Would you
believe it—in the end I hadn't the courage."

"They'll only bring her back," Amaya said, and then
she fell silent as Mrs. Quill came in and the prayers
before breakfast began. Around Amaya there was rude
muttering and terrible jokes, some very dirty in different tongues as the girls pretended to pray. It was nothing
new, but on this morning Amaya couldn't smile. She was
gone. Little Dove, one of the trusted ones, had gone.

"They'll only bring her back," she had said, but perhaps not. Perhaps (even now) she was free, walking the long plains somewhere, her head thrown back, arms stretched out as she breathed in deeply, taking the air of freedom into her lungs. She would walk northward, follow the foothills until she reached the Niobrara River. Then she would be into Sioux country and her people would be there waiting for her. Little Dove had some family left, although her father and mother, her brothers, were all dead, killed by white soldiers. They would find her and there would be wailing, the flowing of tears, a celebration of love.

The tin plate was placed in front of Amaya and she sat, staring at the mush and salt pork.

After breakfast was over it was obvious that Little Dove's disappearance had been discovered. The girls were hurried off to their classroom and they sat there for nearly an hour in silence until Mrs. Quill arrived.

"Please, girls, take out your slates." There was a pause then, and a shifting of bodies as they scraped for their slateboards. "Now, suppose we begin our multiplication tables. Start with the threes, I think. Anna!" That was the name they had given Tantha. "Anna, please go out into the corridor. Dr. Quill wishes to speak to you."

Amaya's heart lifted its pace a little. Tantha looked at her and smiled and then went out. Amaya tried to do her times tables, but the resultant scrawl resembled nothing at all.

She knew her turn was coming and five minutes later when Tantha returned she was not at all surprised to have Mrs. Quill say, "Emily, please go out into the corridor."

She put her slate down and went out. The minister was there waiting, his cadaverous face especially pale, especially severe. Amaya went near to him, her head bowed. She could smell the cloves, the bay rum, all the disgusting sharp smells he carried with him.

"Yes, Quill," she muttered.

"Your friend is gone."

"My friend?"

"Little Dove."

"My friend Little Dove," Amaya repeated childishly.

"Yes." The hand reached out and gripped Amaya's

chin. The thumb pressed into it uncomfortably, but the reverend was smiling. "You are a clever girl, aren't you, Emily?"

"I do not know."

"Don't you? You do not like living here, do you? It's hard, isn't it?"

"I do not know."

"All right." Quill let go of her chin. His eyes were very bright behind his glasses. His hand twitched at his side. He moved nearer to Amaya and his thigh was suddenly pressed against hers. He moved away immediately, as if it had been accidental.

"I do not know what you want."

"Do you know where Little Dove is?"

"In her room."

"Damn you, girl," Quill said, flaring up suddenly, violently. "Don't play the fool with me."

"I do not know—"

"You know. You know too much, you and your Cheyenne friend. I won't have this! I won't have girls running away from this school. I've come here to teach you, to save you, to be your friend—I won't have you running off!"

"No. We cannot run away," Amaya said, and the fire which had blazed in Quill's eyes softened again. He moved closer to Amaya.

"I know you're a good girl," the man said. "I know you want to do what is necessary."

"What do you mean?" Amaya turned away and stood facing the wall. There was only the feeble light of a candle at the end of the corridor. She felt Quill's hand on her shoulder, felt it tremble. Then he pressed against her, his hands groping, and Amaya spun angrily away.

"Damn you, girl," Quill said, and there was savagery in his voice. He grabbed her by the arm and threw her against the wall. Then he was against her, his hands reaching for her breasts, his open mouth searching for hers.

The door opened suddenly and Mrs. Quill emerged. Quill leapt back, panting, and Amaya, frozen with anger and revulsion, stood against the wall, her dark eyes bitter.

"John," Mrs. Quill said through tight, puckered lips.

"They've found her. They're bringing her around now. If you wish to speak to her."

"Of course," Quill said, and his voice was perfectly calm. He strode toward his wife, whose face reflected nothing. Together then they closed the door behind them, and Amaya turned, sagging. She remained there, her forehead against the wall, her heart beating savagely. She jumped as someone touched her arm, but it was only Tantha.

"What is it?" Tantha asked.

"Nothing."

"Tell me, Amaya." Tantha turned her friend toward her, seeing the anger and frustration in her eyes.

"Very well." Shrugging her shoulders, Amaya did tell her. Tantha just shook her head.

"That dried-up old man?"

"Yes."

"The coyote. That's what all his chanting is about, is it?" Tantha, surprisingly, laughed.

"Don't tell anyone else, Tantha, please."

"Why not?" the older girl asked. "It would do everyone good to know, especially those who think he's such a good man."

"I don't want anyone to know."

"All right. Did you hear that they have Little Dove?" Amaya nodded her head, taking a slow deep breath. "She didn't get far, did she?"

"No one does."

"Others have tried it?"

"All the time. Now she must be punished, I suppose."

"What kind of punishment?" Amaya wanted to know. "Oh, no—not something dreadful."

"They'll whip her. Take off her dress and whip her with the reverend's belt. They like that, I think."

"We can't allow it, Tantha."

"No?" The older girl laughed again, harshly. "And how do we stop it."

"But they can't do that. All that they've said about forgiveness . . ."

"Yes, well, that's all for someone else. For their god, isn't it? They forgive with their mouths, Amaya, but never with their hearts."

"You two," the big Osage woman said, sticking her head into the hallway. "Come in here. We're going to sing from the book now."

Tantha made a rude sound, but they went in and took up their places. The Osage woman led them in song, and they sang loud, all of them, very loud indeed, but it wasn't enough to drown out the cadenced slapping of leather against flesh, the muffled screams of pain which came from a distant room.

When Amaya went out for water the next morning, he was there again and she turned angrily away. He followed her to the river anyway and watched as the buckets were filled.

"Have I done something to offend you?" Lieutenant Pierce asked.

"Yes. You were born white."

"And you are an Indian. But you can't be that foolish."

"What do you mean?"

"You can't blame an entire people for the crimes of a few."

"No."

"Well, then?"

"I simply have not yet met a white who could be trusted."

"You have the minister and his wife here. They feed you, clothe you, shelter . . . What's the matter?"

"Nothing." Amaya kept her face turned away. Her buckets were full but she made no effort to rise.

"Something is wrong. What is it?" His hand rested on her shoulder and was shrugged violently away.

"Nothing. I hate you."

"You hardly know me," Pierce laughed.

"I hate you. You are repulsive. You have those spots on your face and your eyes are absurd."

"Spots . . ." He touched his face questioningly and then burst out laughing. "My freckles, you mean? Are there so many?"

"They are repulsive."

"You've learned another new word, have you? Is everything going to be 'repulsive' now?"

"As long as I'm in the white world," she said caustically. "Please, now, go away and do not come back. I dislike you and dislike your attentions."

"Amaya, you should learn to trust. Many of us mean you no harm—some of us wish you well indeed. The minister—"

"Is a sadistic pig!" Amaya blurted out.

"What are you talking about? How can you say that?"

"Never mind. I can see you do not believe me. I don't care."

Pierce was puzzled. "It's just that I don't understand. Are those just words you plucked out of the air because you dislike him? How can you call him names? He works here for next to nothing, trying to take care of Indian orphans who have nowhere else to go. Some young women have left here quite well educated, ready to take on a profession."

"I said you would not understand."

"Understand what?" Pierce spread his hands in a gesture of futility.

"Never mind. What will you do? Report to him and see that I am whipped?"

"Whipped?" Pierce laughed and reached for her shoulder. Again she withdrew sharply from his touch, and he slowly lowered his hand. "No one is going to be whipped. What sorts of stories have the other girls been filling your mind with?"

"Never mind. You would not believe. Not even if you saw." Amaya picked up her heavy burden.

"I do want to believe you," Pierce said quietly. "If you need help, I want to help you."

"Yes. I believe *that*. You, a soldier!"

"Listen, Amaya, the army has nothing at all to do with Dr. Quill and his school except that we share the same facility. Do you understand that?"

"You are white," she said, and then she walked off, looking straight ahead, her back erect, her expression unreadable. Andy Pierce stood watching her for a long while until she slipped in through the side gate and entered Fort Laramie. Then he slammed his fist against his thigh, and turning away, ground his teeth together and stood watching the river.

*   *   *

"You are late again, you silly girl," the Osage woman said. "What is it? Have you got a soldier out in the bushes?"

Amaya placed the buckets on the floor without responding. She looked at the woman's bloated dark face and walked out. In the dining room Little Dove and Tantha sat together waiting for their meal. Little Dove's head was resting on her folded forearms while Tantha leaned low, speaking to her.

"Is she all right?" Amaya asked.

"Thirty lashes. Welts all over her back."

"Little Dove?" Amaya touched her hair gently and the pain-filled eyes turned up to her. "It will be all right."

"I will kill them," Little Dove said in a harsh whisper. "Kill them, do you hear me?"

"Don't talk like that."

"Why not?" she said shrilly. "Haven't I the right? Aren't they the enemy of my people?"

"Think what you like," Tantha said, "but don't speak of it. Amaya is right."

Little Dove stared at them a moment longer and then lowered her head again.

"We will get even," Tantha said. "I vow it. We will settle the score with this white man."

"Pierce!"

"Yes, sir." Andy Pierce wheeled toward the owner of the voice, Captain Charles Lord.

"Where in hell have you been? I've been looking for you."

"Something up?"

"Plenty. There's a meeting in the colonel's office at nine hundred hours and you will be there. If you see Lieutenant Staggs come limping back from town, you might tell him the same thing."

"Yes, sir." Pierce held back his smile with difficulty. Harry Staggs was the post hellraker—at least that was the way he saw himself. A hard-drinking womanizer, Staggs was barely twenty-two years old, baby-faced, and working on a physical disability.

Pierce continued on toward the base officers' quarters, where he changed into his dress tunic. Whatever it was that was up, it apparently was important. For the past week dignitaries from Washington had been arriving, high-ranking army officers from the War Department, Indian Affairs people, a representative from Agriculture and one from Interior.

Andy Pierce dusted off his newly shined boots and straightened his tunic. The door to the officers' quarters opened behind him, and in the mirror he saw Harry Staggs limp in, his uniform stained, his face unshaven.

"Get with it, Harry. Commander's call at nine hundred hours."

"I'm off-duty," Staggs groaned.

"No one's excused."

"What?"

"It's the big one, the one we've been waiting for."

"The big one? Nothing big happens at Laramie, Andy." Staggs sat down on his bunk and stared at his muddy feet. "I can't make it. I haven't got it in me. Tell them I'm sick."

"Uh-uh," Andy Pierce answered. "But if I were to tell the colonel that, you *would* be sick. You'd be resigning your commission as well."

"Not that bad an idea, actually," Staggs said, lifting his liquor-reddened eyes. "Then I could go back into Laramie and die in Belle Fox's arms."

"That just might happen too," Pierce laughed. Belle Fox was one of a handful of white women for hundreds of miles, and nearly the only accessible one.

"What's this about anyway, Andy?" Staggs asked as he changed his own tunic. "Any real idea?"

"No. None at all. I thought at first it was going to be an all-out push against Yellow Knife, but no new troops have arrived. The people from Agriculture and Interior certainly haven't come to plan a war for us."

"There's only one alternative answer, isn't there?" Staggs said unhappily. "I mean, it's absurd, but that must be the answer."

"What do you mean?"

"I mean peace, damn you! Peace with Yellow Knife, the whole damned Sioux and Cheyenne nations."

"Do you think so?" Pierce asked, his eyebrows drawing together.

"Of course." Staggs sat on his bed and then lay back, arms outflung. "Since I am a warrior, the war must end. It's my fate. Other men come home studded with medals. If Harry Staggs arrives on the plains, there will be peace."

He moaned and clowned for a time longer while Andy Pierce applied the finishing touches to his uniform and person. "You may be right, Harry," he said after a while. "Dammit all, you just may be right."

The office of Colonel J. T. Hinshaw wasn't large enough to hold all the military personnel and Washington dignitaries, the civilians who ranged from freighters and buckskin-clad scouts to sodbusters and merchants from Laramie. The meeting was held in the dining hall with Colonel Hinshaw, ill-at-ease apparently, standing at a jerry-built dais.

After a few introductions and inconsequential remarks, the colonel handed the meeting over to a civilian, James Dawes.

He was erect, graying, with soft eyes. Spare, lanky, he showed a military background in his bearing. He smiled at the assemblage and to a man they smiled back. That was the strength of James Dawes; everyone who met him trusted him. The unique quality of the man was that the trust was justified. He had been a soldier, and now he abhorred the waste of war. He had been harsh and abrupt but he had learned early that he gained nothing that way. He had seen tragedy and suffered rejection. He was perfectly suited for his job.

"Gentlemen, we have a chance to end war on the plains," he began. "For those of you who do not know me, I am with the Bureau of Indian Affairs. More exactly, I have been and still nominally am the agent in charge of the tribes of the Arkansas, Platte, and Kansas rivers—which is to say the Sioux, the Snake, and the Arapaho Indians.

"Those of you who have not lived at Fort Laramie may not be aware of it, but over the past spring alone we have witnessed fifty thousand and more white gold-seekers and homesteaders move through our area of responsibility. Fifty thousand, gentlemen! And in their wake, I am sorry to say, there has been devastation. Dead grass, slaughtered buffalo, cholera, and hunger. Nevertheless, the Sioux—with the notable exception of Yellow Knife—have remained quiet.

"However, the complaints of the Indians against the immigrant whites are growing more numerous. There is bad feeling growing out on the plains. There has already been warlike activity among the western Cheyenne, preparations for war if not actual aggressive behavior. Here and there bands of Sioux, especially the Spotted Sioux, strike back at what they feel are belligerent acts." He avoided deliberately accusing the army, Andy Pierce noted. "I will tell you this," Dawes went on, "we are walking the line between total war and a peace which may endure. We must make peace. If we do not, it is only a matter of time before the Sioux and the normally peaceful Cheyenne rise in anger over the white incursions—illegal and unauthorized incursions."

"What is this?" Harry Staggs asked in a whisper. "Love the noble red man? Hasn't this fellow ever seen Yellow Knife's work?"

Andy Pierce didn't answer. Whether or not Staggs wanted to hear James Dawes, he did.

"I took it upon myself," Dawes told them, "to go to Congress with a request that a conference be held, and I must say I am astonished and overwhelmingly gratified with the result. That is to say"—he looked up and smiled—"within the next few weeks we can expect members of Congress to arrive, representatives from the Bureau of Indian Affairs and delegates from the following tribes: the Sioux, the Crow, the Cheyenne, the Shoshoni, the Arapaho, and the Pawnee.

"The Comanche nation," Dawes said, "was invited, but they have refused to come north, telling me that there are too many horse thieves on the northern plains. Apparently they have had word of certain of our traders."

The tone was dry, light, but in the front row of the assembly sat Aaron Barclay, who had great expectations of making a huge profit from the coming peace conference. Barclay was the chief supplier of army matériel, and notorious for squeezing nickels. Dawes let his eyes flicker to Barclay, and the sutler scowled. Perhaps Dawes *had* heard about that deal with the southern Snake Indians. Barclay leaned forward and quite deliberately spat on the floor.

Outside, the day was dry, cool, a gusting wind blowing out of the north. After the meeting, Andy Pierce stood beside Staggs, watching James Dawes and a small party of visiting dignitaries cross the parade ground toward the Indian school.

"Well, what do you think?" Andy asked.

"Think?" Harry Staggs looked up from the shadow of his hat brim. "I think he's another fool dreaming a fool's dream. Peace? Who wants it really? Not the Indians, not the people of the United States."

Not Harry Staggs, Pierce thought but did not say. Harry wanted his medals and his whiskey and his women. And just what is it *you* want, Andy Pierce? he asked himself. He couldn't answer the question. He had joined the army and come West out of a vague need for adventure, a wish for something beyond the stilted life his Baltimore merchant family led. What he had wanted, expected, he couldn't have said. At twenty-five years of age, Andy Pierce had not yet managed to define himself. He watched James Dawes meet and introduce himself to the party of Easterners, men and women who had come to see what conditions were for the "tame" Indians of Laramie.

He watched Dawes and then glanced at Harry Staggs, seeing the contempt in his bleary eyes. Andy Pierce nodded, turned on his heel, and went toward the paddock, looking for his NCO, Sergeant Hart. He was conscious of a disturbing contrast between Staggs and Dawes, between the army and the Indian Bureau, and it troubled him. Not that Staggs was representative of the army officers Pierce knew, but it was true that for a group of men supposedly devoted to "keeping peace on the plains," as President Fillmore had defined their objective, there was a considerable amount of interest in provoking clashes rather than avoiding them.

Staggs had performed well at Clan Camp, on the Lodgepole, the month before. According to his commander's report, that is. What had actually happened was that Staggs had provoked a party of hunting Sioux until it became a war party. Then Staggs had had his battle.

Pierce found Sergeant Hart and set about scheduling a mounted drill, forgetting Staggs and Dawes and the coming peace conference for a time.

James Dawes could overhear them speaking in low voices before he reached the small party of men and women waiting at the door of the Indian orphan school. He recognized with a weary familiarity what they were talking about, and smiled to himself, wondering why in God's name people were still shocked by something that was becoming very common indeed. Dawes's own military career had been wrecked by the circumstances of his birth, but he no longer regretted that. He had found a niche in life with the BIA. Here he was doing something to solve the Indian "problem" that bullets could never do. Besides, at his point in life there was no sense in wasting energy on anger.

". . . from a very reliable source," the matron with her back to Dawes was saying. She wore mesh gloves and carried a similarly made reticule crammed full of religious pamphlets and notes taken on this Western tour. Her name was Hilda Grange, and her husband, unfortunately, was Secretary of the Interior. She had wangled this junket easily, attaching herself to Dawes's group as a method of promoting one of her many charities. She couldn't have had much trouble in arranging for her husband to let her come West without him.

"It's quite true, Mrs. Grange," Dawes said, and the woman's head snapped around. Her eyes were wide with surprise, her face powdered and pinched, her lips pursed in perpetual contempt.

"Why, Mr. Dawes, we were just talking about you."

"Yes," Dawes answered cheerfully. "Fine, talk away." To the others he said, "It's true that I am part Indian. On my grandmother's side."

Two of the women looked shocked. One man, Tom Heron, a minister, muttered, "How interesting."

"Oneida Indian," Dawes clarified. "An Iroquois tribe, you know."

"Oh," Heron said. "I thought you meant a Sioux or

some such. There's a vast difference between the Western and Eastern Indians."

"Yes," Dawes said, opening the door to the school,
bowing courteously to Mrs. Grange. "Quite a difference.
The Western Indian still exists. We haven't quite managed him yet, have we?"

Mrs. Grange started to answer, shut her mouth again,
and entered the school building. Inside they met the
sober, narrow Dr. Quill and his wife. They walked slowly
through the building, seeing the dormitory and the school-
room where three dozen Indian girls in neat blue dresses
sat with their hands folded on their desks, reciting their
lessons.

"Class!" Dr. Quill said, tapping on the lectern with a
pointer stick. "We have guests with us."

"Good morning," the girls chorused.

Mrs. Grange smiled with dry pleasure, gripping her
reticule with both hands as she whispered something to
the woman next to her. Dawes looked at the faces of the
students, trying to read their expressions. There were
none. They were simply programmed little beings, dolls
or pets or servants. He supposed the Quills were doing
the best they could. *Anyone* seriously trying to help the
Indian was praiseworthy in Dawes's view, although most
of what he had seen going on in his travels amounted to
trying to cram the American culture down the throats of
people unready for or opposed to it.

The class began to sing: "Isn't it a happy day this
morning . . ."

Dawes happened to be looking at a pretty young woman
who was not singing but just moving her lips. He had
noticed her because she was not Sioux. Nor was she
Cheyenne. He was pondering her derivation when he
followed her eyes to the ledge above the door, and so he
was one of the few who saw the severed head before it
fell.

There was probably a string tied on it, though Dawes
never saw one. He only saw the hog's head, and beneath
it, fanning herself with a pamphlet, Mrs. Grange. Dawes
took a step toward the woman, but it was too late.

"Isn't it a lovely day this morning . . ."

The hog's head fell, spattering blood on everyone beneath the sill. Mrs. Grange was hit directly by the pink leering head and she screamed. Not once, but a dozen, two dozen times, shrilly, repetitively, wiping at the blood on her dress while the hog's head rolled across the floor and stopped upright, glaring at them with tiny porcine eyes.

Quill was running toward them, his pointer stick waving madly through the air. The Indian girls all had straight faces. They looked directly ahead, their song trailing off.

"Jesus Christ!" Quill shouted, shocking Tom Heron more than a little blood could.

"Filthy! Filthy!" Mrs. Grange repeated endlessly, still wiping at her dress. She looked directly into Mrs. Quill's eyes, and for a moment Dawes thought she would spit right into the minister's wife's face.

Instead she spun on her heel and clattered out of the room, the other women on her heels, Tom Heron trailing after them a moment later. Dawes was alone with the Quills and the Indian orphans, and for a moment Quill seemed to forget Dawes was there.

"The dirty savages," he breathed. "I ought to . . ." His eyes snapped up to meet Dawes's, and he fell instantly silent.

"I hope there won't be any punishment," Dawes said. "It was only a prank."

"You don't understand," Quill said, shaking his head. "They were going to collect funds for us—to expand the school," he added hastily. "Now do you think Mrs. Grange is going to devote her time to this cause?"

Again Quill's eyes went to the girls, who sat, their hands folded on their desks, their hair all done the same—in two dark, heavy braids—their faces scrubbed and innocent. Quill muttered something unintelligible and stalked off. After a minute, Dawes went out himself.

He stood outside watching the activities of the army post, watching the skies where soft white clouds were drifting past.

He knew.

He had told Quill that it was only a prank, and it was true, but there was something more to it. The school was neat and modern and white. The girls were orderly, polite, well-trained. But there was something very dan-

gerous lurking beneath the surface. The hog's head had
been a symbol of it. Violence. Blood and violence, savagery and frustration, lived in that simple school building. They were perhaps making a few converts in the
orphan school, but they were making many more enemies. One day blood might flow again, and then it might
not be the blood of a slaughtered hog.

"Who had access to the kitchen! Who was there when
the hog was slaughtered!" Mrs. Quill had a leather strap
in her hand. She was in a rage. She walked up and down,
occasionally slapping it down violently on a desk, inches
from the folded hands. "Who did this! Someone will tell
me."

But no one would, and Mrs. Quill grew angrier. She
had suffered much out here. Living in a dirty hovel with
her idiot husband, waiting until he had convinced the
army to build the new school for him. And even now,
what did she have? She had two dresses, and one of
them was six years old. Her food was no better than that
the Indian girls ate. She was growing old and knew it;
there was nothing at all in her future, no simple luxury
to soften the burdens. Mrs. Grange had come with the
promise of funds. And now these savages, these filthy
little wenches, had driven her away.

She didn't mean to do it the first time. She only wanted
to frighten Little Dove—Little Dove, who was so much
trouble. Little Dove, who had run away, defying them.
The strap rose and fell, and instead of hitting the desk,
it lashed across Little Dove's hands, cutting a deep red
welt.

The Indian girl didn't cry out. She sat there expressionless, her eyes black and dancing. Dorothy Quill's
eyebrows arched menacingly. Her face was suffused with
blood. How dare the little imp challenge her in that
way? As if she hadn't felt that lash! She would feel the
next one, by God, and deservedly. The hand rose and the
lash fell and a red cut opened on Little Dove's cheek.
Still the Sioux girl was expressionless.

Amaya was the first one from her seat. Tantha was
only a step behind her. As Dorothy Quill lifted her arm

again, Amaya stepped between the minister's wife and Little Dove.

"No."

"Get out of the way, Emily. She did it! She did this to me!"

"I did it," Amaya said softly.

"She put the pig's head there. She ruined everything."

"Did you not hear me?" Amaya said. "I did it."

"You!" The woman's eyes had been round with passion; now they narrowed to mere slits. "You, Emily?"

"That is what I have said."

"Damn you, then, damn you!" Her hand lifted again, and again the strap fell, striking Amaya's shoulder this time. The pain was incredible. It was as if red-hot iron had touched her flesh beneath the blue dress. Amaya staggered back a step. Mrs. Quill came after her, pushing an empty chair aside to clatter against the floor.

"No!" Tantha blocked her way. When Mrs. Quill tried to shove the Cheyenne girl aside, Tantha grabbed her dress front and the two of them lost their balance, nearly falling. "I did it. Not Emily," Tantha said.

Mrs. Quill lifted her strap again, and then she realized it was no use. It was just no good. Let Dr. Quill mete out the punishment. He understood them. She did not. She understood nothing, not even her own anger at that moment, anger which had only wanted a target.

She slowly let the hand with the leather strap drop to her side, and then without speaking again she pushed past Tantha and Amaya and went out into the corridor, slamming the door shut.

The taunting voices followed her down the hallway.

"Isn't it a lovely day this morning . . ."

The song didn't last long. Little Dove took her hand away from her cheek and they saw the smear of blood there.

"Oh, no. Get something to put on it," Tantha said.

"Warm water and a cloth," Amaya called.

"It hurts," Little Dove said. "Almost as much as my back. He'll whip me again now."

"No he won't."

"Yes. And he makes me take my clothes off."

"He won't whip you."

"I want to run away. Why won't they let me run away?" Her head sagged onto her folded arms.

"He won't hurt you," Amaya said, stroking her friend's head.

"No. They won't dare to," Tantha said. "We've taught them a lesson. There will be no more beating the girls." She looked at Amaya for support, but she was silent. You did not teach people like the Quills a lesson. Apparently the girls had done them a deep hurt, and the Quills would remember. Their kind would have a long memory for slights. They would know how to carry a grudge.

It was a month before the first of the peace delegations arrived. In that month Mrs. Grange and her party had gone, Colonel J. T. Hinshaw had been promoted to brigadier general, James Dawes had begun writing his history of the Sioux nation, and Congress had repudiated its own intentions and sent word via Major General Charles C. Cooney as to what its policy would be in dealing with the plains tribes.

Dawes was in General Hinshaw's office when the word was given to him in the form of a hand-delivered letter from the BIA.

"No." Dawes lifted his eyes to General Cooney, a round, pink man with muttonchop whiskers and tiny dark eyes. "This is just not acceptable."

"Acceptable or not, that is the decision of the Congress of the United States and your superiors in the BIA," Cooney said sharply, in the tones of one used to command. "John—have you more of that brandy?"

Hinshaw said he did, and he poured as Dawes sat staring numbly at the letter. It was quite explicit. It was also utterly contrary to what he had been promised, to the alleged purpose of the great conference.

"I can't understand your displeasure," Hinshaw said. He was sipping his brandy, as he had been all morning. He was retiring within three weeks and his recent promotion had capped what he viewed as a distinguished career. His sole purpose in life now seemed to be to await his replacement's arrival.

"Sir," Dawes said, spreading exasperated hands, "this

is not at all what I promised to the Cheyenne and Sioux. This is not at all what the Bureau of Indian Affairs, and through them, Congress, promised me."

"Look here," Cooney said, "we all want peace. This will ensure peace indefinitely. It is the best thing for all concerned."

"It requires the Indian to live on a government reservation!" Dawes said hotly.

"Of course."

"To give up his freedom."

"He will be one hell of a lot better off on a reservation with food, medicine, and housing guaranteed by the United States," Cooney said, with an annoyed side glance at Hinshaw.

"General—"

"Do you have any idea how many savages die each year from lack of food and medicine? When winter's hard and the buffalo are gone, the young ones and the old pay a heavy price—*that* is what the men in Congress are thinking of."

"No they aren't," Dawes said, sagging back into his chair.

"Pardon me, sir?" Cooney said stonily.

"I say it isn't what they're thinking of, and you and I both know it. What they are thinking of is a military solution, keeping all potentially dangerous Indians grouped together in a small area where they can be watched and turned into harmless wards of the state."

"Which is—"

"Which is exactly the opposite of what I have promised the various tribes who are gathering here! They are autonomous nations—the Cheyenne, the Sioux, the Arapaho—and the government of the United States has an obligation to deal honorably with them. Would we consider holding citizens of a European country in camps?"

"Mr. Dawes is an idealist," Hinshaw said. Cooney had stronger words in mind, but he managed to keep them to himself. Dawes was, after all, only a civilian. He pretended to understand the situation out here, but obviously didn't.

General Cooney turned away. "All of us can only follow our instructions."

He heard the door slam behind him. Glancing across his shoulder, he saw that Dawes was gone. The two officers refilled their glasses. "I think," Cooney said finally, "that Mr. Dawes's superiors should be informed." They spent fifteen minutes then drafting a letter to the Bureau of Indian Affairs.

James Dawes stood outside, trying to cool off. The river rambled away to the southward, mirrorlike. In the near distance, cavalry soldiers drilled on horseback.

"Fools," he said, taking another slow, deep breath. They had managed to destroy the greatest hope for peace before it had even been tried. They had promised the Indian nations peace and now proposed to offer them enslavement. It must have sounded like a fine idea in Washington.

He shook his head again and started off at a brisk walk, trying to cool his temper. He headed out around the stockade, striding out, breathing deeply. He found the three girls beside the orphan school. The two of them standing next to the wall of the building helped hold a third girl up. When the dark-eyed face came up to glance at Dawes, he saw the cut on her smooth skin.

"Are you all right?" Dawes asked, stepping toward them. They withdrew from his hand, eyes flashing, lips drawing into thin lines. "What's happened?"

"No speak," one of the girls said.

"Come now," Dawes said a little angrily. "What has happened here? Will you tell me? You need the camp surgeon for that cut, by the look of it."

They turned away. They simply turned and walked away, their moccasined feet stirring up warm yellow dust, which drifted to James Dawes's nostrils. Anger flared up again, a different sort of anger, impotent, cold. They had turned away from him. Three young women who obviously needed help. But not from him. From no white man.

He recalled the other woman, the other beautiful woman who had once turned away from him, long ago, in a Florida prison. She had been his own cousin, the Seminole Shanna. She had not been able to trust him, and Dawes had experienced the same impotent frustration as she was taken away. They could not trust him—none of them. The world was divided by factors of race and it always would be.

Perhaps the generals see me for what I am, he thought bitterly. Maybe I am only a fool.

The following morning the Snake Indians began to arrive. There were three hundred in the first group drifting in from the west. They brought many horses with them, but the women walked behind in the dust. The old and the very young rode on travois dragged by the horses. Some of the children had wickerwork cages tied to the travois rails to keep them from falling off. They stayed off a distance from the fort, a mile or so, waiting patiently in the sun.

"Well?" General Cooney was pulling on his gauntlets. A corporal stood beside him holding the reins to his big gray horse. James Dawes looked at the officer and nodded.

"I'm ready. We'd better talk to them."

Cooney mounted slowly, heavily. His rotund frame was never meant for a saddle. He watched the lean, gray Dawes, disliking the man for what he was—a crybaby, one who cared more for the dirty Indian than he did for the safety of his own people. He wouldn't have taken Dawes with him now, but the only other man who spoke the language of the Snake Indians, a civilian scout, was gone with a patrol.

Dawes was the sort who would waste his time learning a half-dozen Plains tongues. Another wasted effort—the Indians were learning English at a rapid rate. There was no sense in using a dozen languages on the plains when one would soon dominate all.

The gates swung open and they rode out of the fort, an escort of two dozen men accompanying them. Cooney tried to appear stiff and warriorlike, not quite achieving it. Dawes was simply worried. He knew Iron Leg, the Snake war leader, very well, and it was only through Dawes's personal assurance that this gathering was for the good of his tribe that the Snake Indians had traveled this far.

"It is not that I don't trust the whites," Iron Leg had told Dawes, "but how will my young warriors hold them-

selves back from killing the Crow? We have many enemies there."

"It is a peace conference. No violence is allowed."

"Yes." Iron Leg had nodded. "That is easy to say, not
so easy to make happen."

"It is important, Iron Leg. Important to everyone living on the plains. War is ahead of us. Let us strangle it in
its cradle."

"Yes," Iron Leg had agreed. "Let us try that. Can it be
done, James Dawes?" the old warrior had asked.

"If not this time, then perhaps never," Dawes had
replied.

And now the bureaucrats in Washington had changed
the rules before the game had begun. They had already
demonstrated that the Indian nations were to be treated
as inferiors, not as equals. Dawes shivered a little, and
not all of it was from the cool wind off the north.

"Is it all right for us to ride in, sir?" Lieutenant Andy
Pierce asked.

"Pardon me?" Dawes smiled.

"We're all armed. Should we just ride in like this?"

Dawes glanced at General Cooney on his other side.
Cooney was concerned only with preserving some image
he had of himself as a great leader.

"You should ask your officer, Lieutenant Pierce."

Andy nodded. The answer was a good-enough one.
Dawes didn't like it, but that was the way it was going to
be. The Snake Indians still had not begun making camp.
They were wary, and rightly so. The cavalry contingent
rode slowly through their ranks, Cooney pompous and
showy.

Dark eyes looked up at Andy Pierce. He hadn't seen
Snake Indians before, knew nothing of them but that
they were Shoshoni stock and bitter enemies of the Sioux.
Andy felt his stomach tighten, and he had to wipe his
palms on his trouser legs to dry them. This was a new
situation for him. They were surrounded now by Indians, warriors, old men, shamans, women with blankets
like cowls over their heads.

There was a cry of welcome, and Dawes swung down
to walk to take the hand of a very old, weathered man

who wore his hair in a topknot and had an eagle-bone necklace and a full set of white elkskins. Iron Leg.

Andy glanced at the general, who didn't think much of the enthusiastic way the two men greeted each other. The situation, to the military mind, called for some restraint.

Dawes turned. "Please get down. Iron Leg is our guest."

"Dawes," Cooney said dryly, "get on with this. Show the Indian where his group is to camp."

"Sir, we can't approach things in that way."

"In what way, Dawes?"

"Just telling them where to camp, riding off. They are our *guests*. Here at our invitation. They've ridden hundreds of miles."

"All right," Cooney said with obvious irritation, "what do they want?"

"They wish to hold a feast, sir. It's their way. They want to eat, to smoke, to dance, to seal our friendship."

"Is this all really necessary . . . damn all! Are we going to go through this with each batch of redskins that shows up?"

Dawes had taken three steps toward the general, who remained mounted on that stocky gray horse. "We are, sir," Dawes said with some intensity, "if we are going to consummate any sort of agreement here. We are not going to insult them and then compel them to do our will, are we?" Cooney tried to interrupt, but Dawes went quickly on. "Even your superiors, General Cooney, will not suffer the situation to be put on an antagonistic footing. Even your superiors, sir, wish this conference to be productive. It will not be in any way productive to insult your guests."

Cooney had turned a vivid red. He knew the eyes of his men, of the Indians, were on him. He couldn't speak for a moment, and when he did, his voice was papery and thin.

"Let us then bow to their custom, Dawes," the general said, and it might have been a threat.

Dawes turned and spoke to the entire tribe, and their faces broke into smiles of relief. Somewhere in the farther ranks an Indian let out a whoop. Iron Leg shook

Dawes's hand again and waited while Cooney swung down to be introduced.

Then the feast began. There was dancing, the participants weirdly painted, moving sinuously to the thumping of drums and the shrill peep of whistles, the shaking of tortoiseshell rattles. And they ate. They ate venison and prairie chicken and buffalo tongue and something sweet with gooseberries and honey. They ate cakes and turtle eggs and the soldiers stuffed themselves until they thought they would pop, surprised at the variety of the fare, thinking the Indian subsisted on burned buffalo meat and water, perhaps.

James Dawes spoke seriously to Iron Leg. "Things are not as I told you," he said bluntly.

The old Snake Indian's eyes tightened slightly. "What do you mean, James Dawes?"

"My promises—what they told me I could promise—have been altered by the leaders of our people far away."

"No." Iron Leg was disgusted. He turned his face away and skyward briefly. The pink-cheeked general was watching them, eating slowly. He understood nothing they said, but still Iron Leg didn't like having him there. "What promises are changed?"

"They say . . ." Dawes was hardly able to keep his eyes on Iron Leg's. ". . . that they want the Indians to live here, near Fort Laramie."

The Snake laughed. "Here? This is not our home. What do they hunt here?" His arm described an arc. The land was empty. "We live along the big river."

"Perhaps," Dawes said a little desperately, "this can all be worked out. Perhaps the men from Washington, when they come, will understand that you do not want to live here."

"I will not live here!"

"No. They will have to be made to understand."

"What is he saying?" Cooney interrupted. Dawes didn't bother to answer him.

"We will go now," Iron Leg said.

"No. Please, give this a chance."

"A chance? We are here because you have invited us, James Dawes, because we do not wish to make war with the whites. Now you tell me the whites wish to make us prisoners on the land."

"Not prisoners—"

"When a man cannot ride where he chooses, when he cannot follow the herds, he is a prisoner. That is that, James Dawes, and you know it."

Dawes could only nod his head. He knew it. "Let me talk to the men from Washington," he pleaded. "Perhaps there is a mistake."

Dawes waited a long time before Iron Leg said, "All right. You talk to these men. Tell them this: I am gone if they wish to make my people slaves to their will. I will know, James Dawes. I will know if they have not changed their minds," he said, lifting his arm toward the fort, "and you will walk to the window and see that the Snake, Iron Leg, is gone. You shall see this. Talk to them. Tell them that the Snake wants peace. Tell them that the Snake wants his home on the big river, no one else's home."

Andy Pierce rode near to Dawes as they returned to the fort and he asked the BIA man what Iron Leg had said. Dawes told him in a monotone.

"Well?" Andy said. "And what chance is there that there has been a policy shift?"

"You are a government employee," Dawes said to the officer.

"Yes, but if this is going to be inflammatory ... what is the sense in this, sir? What sense in holding a peace conference to provoke the other side?"

Dawes didn't answer. He looked at Pierce and smiled, but there was very little humor in it.

The days became crowded with activity and people. A dozen tongues were spoken in the vicinity of the fort. Men came from the East in ruffled shirts and high hats, ladies on their arms. And from the West came the warriors of the plains, the foothills, and the high mountains, traditional enemies and timeless friends—Crow, Arikara, Sioux, Cheyenne, Shoshoni, and Arapaho.

And James Dawes was near to despair. There was no mistake—government policy as described by the Congress of the United States included disarming the Indians and compelling him to live on reservations near military posts.

"Everything I promised has become a lie," Dawes said.

"Yes," the senator agreed. "It is unfortunate."

"It is impossible."

"No. Only unfortunate," the senator, who was from New York, replied. "And not so unworkable as you believe. Four separate tribes have agreed to accept our terms."

"I can't believe it," Dawes said.

The man who stood in the corner, Edward Shell, answered, "It's true, James, and so you see, perhaps we do know a little about what we are doing."

Edward Shell was Dawes's BIA superior. "But, sir," Dawes said, "four clans out of the hundreds? Four who have been plied with whiskey and promises? While we have alienated the others?"

He was near the window. He could look out across the parade ground and see over the low stockade wall to where the camp of the Snake Indians had been. There was nothing there now, only an area of trampled grass. Iron Leg was gone.

"It is a start," the senator said. "The others will come around. It will become obvious to them that here they are cared for, given food, blankets, all they need—"

"As children are."

The senator stiffened. "It is a beginning," he repeated. "We all want peace. This is a step toward it. Those who have turned their backs on us and ridden away are those who have voted for war. And," he added, "I will be very much surprised if they do not have war."

"Edward . . ."

The BIA man was a politician too. He shook his head, sending eye signals to Dawes. There was no point at all in going up against the decision of the United States Congress on this matter. What was gained? You were in effect defying, or at least flaunting disrespect for, the law of the land. It was no better than those people down in the South who refused to accept the idea of centralized power, clinging to states' rights like some sort of religious icon. They were outnumbered in the houses of government; James Dawes was grossly outnumbered in the houses of policy.

Besides, he was part Indian and his ideas were obviously quite slanted.

Dawes stood at the window for a long while, watching the empty campsite, seeing a place where his promises had taken root in shallow soil and then been whipped away by the fierce wind of expansionism.

I should, he thought, resign. But what was the point in that? The machine of state rolled on, grinding opposition. One grain of sand could do nothing to slow it, but it needed to be there as an irritant, a reminder. And there was, after all, no other place to go, nowhere that his conscience could be of any use to the vast, sad history of the world.

Dawes walked through the reservation with Edward Shell, General Cooney, and three members of Congress, puffy, self-satisfied men who favored Virginia cigars. With them were Lieutenants Staggs and Pierce, Captain Charles Lord, and the Reverend John Quill.

They were there, those who had accepted the government's plan—two bands of Yankton Sioux, one of Ponca, and one of Pawnee Indians. Eyes lifted to the strolling men. The smell of green lumber was in the air, the taste of defeat.

They had been paid well, the chiefs of these people, to agree to resettlement on the Laramie Reservation. Did they understand what they had sold? Even Dawes wasn't sure. They had reached out for shiny trade goods and promised to stay a while on the white land. They would be fed here, and housed—did they understand that it was a forever promise?

"What's the difference?" Staggs asked Pierce. "They're here. They're under our eye. There's that many fewer out on the plains."

Pierce didn't answer. He had felt for some time that he was in the wrong place, or at least on the wrong side of things—and *he* was not part Indian like James Dawes, who seemed very weary, very bitter. He had already received a letter from the Washington bureau censuring him. He had the feeling that someone had complained behind his back, that he knew who, but there was no profit in knowing that.

"There will be a dozen barracks here," Cooney was saying, "and the chapel to the west. There is where the new school will be, Dr. Quill. A vast improvement, wouldn't you say?"

"Yes. A great improvement. It will ease conditions at the old school," Quill agreed rapidly.

"Yes?"

"The plan is to release the older girls to the trades and send the recalcitrant down to the reservation," the reverend explained.

"The recalcitrant?"

"We have some, sir," he told Cooney, "who refuse to adapt, or are incapable of it. The thought is that these souls would be happier among their own people."

James Dawes lifted his eyes. He thought that Quill was right. After seeing the strap marks on the young women, he believed that they would be happier anywhere than at the old orphan school. Briefly Dawes's eyes met those of Andy Pierce, who was obviously disheartened. Andy Pierce was more concerned with the young women at the orphan school than anyone would have realized; he felt a sudden sense of loss knowing that Amaya would be farther from him, that he had lost her, failed her, as Dawes had failed, had lost, the Snake Indians.

She would not be tamed, and so she was lost to him.

"All right, all right. Hurry up! One dress only. Emily, put that back. One pair of shoes."

Mrs. Quill walked past the row of beds, urging the girls to hurry. She thought, of course, that she was witnessing a punishment. She couldn't realize how happy they were to be going from the school—the three of them, Tantha, Amaya, and Little Dove. The three who caused most of the trouble.

"Put that back," Mrs. Quill snapped. "That's our soap, isn't it? What will you need soap for among the Indians? Don't you remember when you came here, Tantha? How filthy you were?"

Tantha remembered. She was filthy because she had

spent a week running and hiding from white soldiers
who had raided her tribe's hunting camp. She had never
forgotten that. A Cheyenne does not forget.

"Hurry up. We have use for the beds. Two nice Yankton
girls are coming up here. You will soon discover that this
was a reward, this school. Now you will be back among
your own people, and what will you do? Carry firewood
and buffalo dung."

And be free, Amaya thought. Not exactly free, perhaps, but free of Mrs. Quill and the reverend and their
endless chanting, free of the dresses and the white
language.

"There they are," Tantha said, and Amaya looked
around to see the young girls who would replace them.

"Be careful," they heard Little Dove say in the Sioux
tongue. "These people want your souls."

And then they went out, out into the bright day, each
of the three carrying only a burlap sack filled with small
possessions. Across the parade ground they could see the
"graduating class" from the orphan school in bonnets
and blue dresses going off to the white towns to look for
jobs.

"I would rather carry buffalo dung," Tantha said. "What
is left for them?"

She turned deliberately away, and Amaya, watching
the ceremony which the Reverend Quill supervised, shook
her head, feeling a great sadness. Tantha was right. Little Dove was right. They would steal your soul if you let
them.

"What it needs," Amaya said, still watching the gradu-
ation, "is a great bloody hog's head."

They were walked down to the reservation by an un-
armed soldier who seemed completely uninterested in
them and probably was. There was a barracks much like
the one they had just left. The only difference was that
women of all ages lived in it, women who had lost their
men.

Amaya placed her bag on the floor and stood looking
around. An old Pawnee woman with a seamed face and
white hair stared back.

"I'm going outside," Amaya announced.

"Wait and I'll go with you."

"No." She wanted to go alone, to walk among the refugees, to understand what was happening here. Why would a free people come to live under the white aegis? She found no immediate answer outside, where the people seemed to be doing nothing. Sitting waiting, crouched and wary, watching her as she passed, her head held high.

The leaders of the Pawnee band lived in large new tipis, but they would not for long. The hides must be fresh each year. The tipis would rot and fall from the poles and then the Indians would move into a wooden building.

"What are you looking at, girl?" someone challenged. The tongue was Sioux, the speaker a very tall boy of sixteen with a scar across the bridge of his nose and up through his eyebrow.

"Certainly not at you," she answered shortly, turning away. She had gotten three steps before the hand gripped her arm and spun her. Amaya yanked her arm away and stood glaring at the boy.

"What are you?"

She didn't answer. She just turned and started on again. He was beside her, not speaking either. At last, as they entered the big oaks where the communal cooking pots were, he said, "You're not Sioux or Pawnee. What are you doing here?"

"What am I doing here? I have no people and no home and so I have no choice."

"What do you mean?" The boy was angry suddenly.

"What are you doing here?" she repeated, mocking him.

He reached up and took a tiny twig from the oak tree. He stood snapping it, looking at Amaya's feet. "I don't know why we are here. It's a disgrace. Are you Ponca?"

"Comanche."

"Really? Last spring I killed two Comanche," he boasted. Amaya walked on again and he fell in beside her without an invitation. "My name is Black Oak." Amaya didn't respond to that. "What's your name?"

"My name," she replied quietly, "is Amaya."

"There are no Comanche here."

"I am here."

"You know what I mean. You are alone?"

"I am. The soldiers captured me and brought me here."

"That's not so bad," Black Oak said, hurling the rest of his twig away. "My uncle and the others of the council brought us here without a fight."

"Why?" Amaya turned her eyes to him finally, searching his face. "Why would anyone live here?"

"My uncle is Thunder Horse. He brought us here to become rich."

"You look rich!"

"Not me," the boy said angrily. "My uncle."

"And is he rich?"

"The whites gave him fifty horses and three rifles, twenty blankets, gallons of whiskey. He laughs at them. He thinks he has tricked them, gotten a good price for making a winter camp here."

"Doesn't Thunder Horse know that he can't go now?"

"He will go. He told the council that. 'Let us take their gifts and abide awhile. Then we shall go.' Otherwise the other council members would not have agreed."

"I think your uncle is a fool!" Amaya said harshly. She was immediately sorry, but she didn't seem to have offended Black Oak.

Quietly he said, "I agree with you. We cannot go. We have been sold for a barrel of whiskey."

"Have you told him this?"

"He laughs. He says he will go when he wants, when the whites have forgotten him." The boy shook his head. "My uncle, my father, my grandfather, were warriors. They have fought their battles and now they sit around the fires retelling tales of bravery. What do I have to tell?"

"Why don't you run away?" Amaya suggested.

"I have thought of it. I am waiting to see if my uncle leaves." He told her, "You speak my language well."

"My good friend is Sioux. She taught me. I also speak English and Cheyenne."

"I speak English," Black Oak said. "I learned it so that I can call the whites out of their houses at night. I will call them, saying, 'Come out here, white man, and I will give you horses,' and when they come, I will cut their throats."

Amaya laughed. Black Oak scowled deeply for a moment and then he shrugged and allowed his own mouth to turn up into a smile. "Well, perhaps I will do that."

Perhaps he would. The reservation was large, Amaya saw, but not so large as the windswept plains. A trading post was being built, run by a man named Aaron Barclay. There, too, Indians would receive their rations of food, have free blankets distributed, farm tools given—or so the plan went. The Indians, Amaya now knew, had no intention of staying here. The Americans believed they had solved the problem; the Indians were not cognizant of a problem. The whites thought they had a treaty; the Indians understood nothing so final as a perpetual treaty. Even if they had, a few chiefs could not ratify such a treaty for the entire nation. A few chiefs and war leaders were trying to become wealthy by using the whites; a few whites would try to become wealthy by using the Indians. Amaya had somehow come to an understanding of the vast gulf between these people, of the misunderstandings, the mutual arrogance, the chauvinism, the racism, the centuries of cultural divergence. She was young and should have found at least a fanciful solution to this, but she saw none.

What she saw ahead was unending contention, unending violence.

"It's a start at least," Edward Shell said, congratulating himself again. He and Dawes stood with Lieutenant Pierce on the low rise overlooking the new reservation. Shell had a cigar in his mouth, thumbs hooked in his vest. "We have made a start here, Dawes. You thought it couldn't be done, didn't you?"

"It hasn't been done," Dawes said brittlely. Shell didn't like that. He took the cigar from his mouth, watching, waiting for an explanation. "We are failing badly. This isn't a solution, it's a travesty. It's a badly acted play, and behind the scenes, entirely different dramas are being worked out. You cannot steal their culture and herd them together like livestock."

Shell put his cigar in his mouth and took an envelope from his inside coat pocket, handing it to Dawes. "Something for you. I've been holding it back. Now I see it's useless."

Dawes took the envelope, knowing. He glanced only briefly at the letter of dismissal inside, hardly surprised. He stood looking for a while longer at the reservation where tipis shouldered against log barracks, where smoke rose into the hazy sky and was drifted away by the long winds of the plains. Then he stuck out his hand to Lieutenant Andy Pierce, shook hands with the man, and walked away, striding down the grassy knoll.

"Fool," Pierce heard Shell say. "Damned fool."

The young officer turned his head away. It wasn't his place to say anything. He too felt he was in the company of fools, however; and the erect gray man who was walking away from them was not the greatest by far. Lieutenant Andy Pierce watched the smoke rise from the hundred tipis, rise and dissipate, as fragile and ephemeral as the peace which existed on the Laramie Reservation.

4

AMAYA LOOKED UP from her sewing. The fire in the iron stove kept going out and it was very cold. When the door opened and the young army officer stepped in, she could see the snow blowing fiercely outside. Winter had been long and the people were hungry.

Andy Pierce glanced around the room and then his eyes settled on Amaya. He came forward, noticing that as he did, her gaze shifted away.

"Amaya? Can I speak to you?"

"I do not wish to speak to you."

"It's not for myself," Pierce said. "It's for the people."

"These people?" Amaya smiled bitterly. "When has anything been done for them? Where is the food the generals and the men from the East promised?"

"Dammit, Amaya. That's what I want to talk to you about!"

"Why me?"

"Because you speak English!"

"All right." She put her sewing aside. Pierce had seen the anger flare up in her eyes, but now it had cooled. She was not so quick to anger anymore. She was maturing quickly, growing more beautiful, taller. And farther from him. The year on the reservation, the hard winter, had done nothing but confirm her bitterness.

"What is it?"

They were in the small storeroom off the sleeping quarters. The small storeroom which was empty, where there were no rats because there was nothing for them to eat. It was horribly cold in there, away from the weak stove. Andy's breath steamed out as he spoke.

"They've found out what happened to the supplies. A freighter in Julesburg was selling them off. Then he pretended to lose them to hostile Arapaho Indians on the trail. More supplies have been authorized, and they will be on the way soon."

"How soon?"

Pierce removed his hat and rubbed his head. "You know how these things take time, Amaya. The army—"

"A very long time."

"Some time, but you have to tell the people, assure them—"

"They are often assured."

"Listen, this isn't my fault. I've come here on my own because no one else seemed to think it was important to tell the Indians. I could get into trouble over this."

"Perhaps you would starve to death," she said cynically.

"Do you hate me?" he asked. He took a step toward her and looked into her liquid eyes. "Do you really hate me?"

"I do not think about you, Andy Pierce."

He put a hand on her shoulder, but she might as well have been a wooden figure. He could feel no softness there, none of the vibrancy he knew she concealed. His hand fell away.

"I'm leaving. Maybe that will make you happy," he said.

"It does not concern me."

She didn't ask where he was going or when or why. *It does not concern me.* But Amaya concerned him. He knew it was foolish, impossible, but he loved her and had loved her since he first saw her. "I'm going to resign my commission and go to work for the Bureau of Indian Affairs."

She shrugged, that was all, shrugged and turned away. Pierce wanted to reach out for her, to touch her again, but he couldn't bring himself to try.

"Do you hate me?"

She shrugged.

"It's not my fault that the supplies haven't come through. I'm only a soldier, Amaya!"

"The soldiers have plenty of food."

"Yes, but that's different. It comes from a different

source. They couldn't share it if they wanted to. It would be against regulations."

"I see." She continued to look at the wall of the store-room. She had her shoulders hunched, her arms crossed beneath her breasts.

"Barclay has some supplies at the trading post—won't he offer you credit?"

"He offers credit. Now the credit is gone. What can the people trade? They cannot hunt for hides or furs, not in the winter. The women make moccasins and beaded shirts, but who will buy them? This Aaron Barclay takes many shirts, many moccasins, for one sack of sugar, for one blanket or sack of corn flour."

"But, Amaya, the government will pay you all a stipend soon. You know what was promised."

"When?"

"Congress is not in session right now. Certain senators want to reevaluate—"

"Never mind. I thought there was an answer. There is never an answer to my questions. Who is governing us? Who is lying, who is making promises, who is supposed to feed us? Why do they promise things and not deliver them?"

"Don't get angry, Amaya."

"Angry? Do you think I am angry? I am nothing. One person, a Comanche, not one who has made a pact with your government. Not a warrior with hot blood. If you think I am angry, Andy Pierce, then you do not know real anger. It is out there"—her hand pointed beyond the walls—"and it is festering. To come to me and give me reassurances, to expect me to talk to others, to explain something I do not understand myself, reveals a vast ignorance, Andy Pierce."

He nodded his head. His eyes were fixed on her clean profile, her slim figure, wrapped now in a blanket. "You're right. Yes, I am ignorant. Amaya . . ." There was suddenly nothing left to say. How could he make promises when the promises made by generals and congressmen and high officials all fell to ashes or were bogged down in bureaucracy, slashed by senators a thousand miles away who were unconcerned with any of this great experiment, undercut by profiteers like Barclay and the freighter in Julesburg? They didn't have any business trying to manage nations within the nation. What was needed was peace, honorable and just. Yet if a man like Dawes could do nothing, what could he hope to accomplish?

He looked at Amaya, shook his head, and walked by her, clomping across the wooden floor of the barracks to the outside door, which he opened, stepping almost with relief into the cold embracing arms of the winter storm.

When the door to the base officers' quarters opened, Harry Staggs quickly corked the bottle of whiskey and dropped it into his footlocker.

"Well, damn you, Andy!" he said with a grin. "Scared the hell out of me." He reached for the bottle again. "Where've you been?"

Pierce walked across the room before he answered, his back to Staggs. "Down on the reservation."

Pierce was in his locker, cleaning it out, throwing his uniforms onto his bunk.

"What's up?"

"Nothing," Pierce answered. He could smell Staggs at his shoulder, smell the whiskey on his breath. Pierce continued to throw his equipment onto the bunk. Shaving gear, a box of personal effects.

"Andy? You're not leaving?"

"Yes. That's right."

"But why?"

"My time's up. I've resigned my commission, you know that."

"Yes, but . . ." Pierce brushed past Staggs. "I thought you were waiting until spring. Hell of a time to travel. What about the celebration we were planning, the going-away party?"

"You have it."

Staggs stumbled a little, but he made it to his bunk, where he sat, bottle dangling between his knees, watching Andy Pierce pack.

"What's the matter—that Indian girl kick you out?"

Staggs saw Pierce's back stiffen, saw him slowly turn, his face bloodless and hard. "Don't say that again."

"No. All right." Staggs's eyebrows lifted with surprise. "Take it easy." His mood shifted. "But seriously, friend. There's no boat downriver. No coaches. The snow's deep for a horse. Where are you going in such a hurry? You've never yet made the acquaintance of Belle Fox."

"That's something else you can have," Pierce answered. He had his revolver in his hand. He turned it over and then tossed it away to clatter on the floor in the corner.

Staggs shrugged and lay back on his bunk, bottle balanced on his chest. You never knew—he had taken Pierce for a steady man. Now look at him. Staggs closed his eyes, took a short sip of whiskey, and lay waiting for winter to end.

But there was no end to the winter. Not on the reservation, where still the supplies did not come. A delegation had gone to the new post commander, Major Charles Lord, and asked that they be fed or allowed to go hunt on their own. Lord explained that they could do neither. After the third visit he refused to see the Indian delegations anymore.

The snow fell and the days were as dark as night, the wind whining and moaning in the chinks of the Indian barracks. Amaya knelt by the bed looking into the pale face, nearly as pale as a white's, into the huge dark eyes.

"Do you want something? Sit up and have some tea."

Little Dove's hand only reached out and touched hers. She had not been well for a long while, this young Sioux. But it wasn't illness which was killing her.

Tantha had said it. "She wants her people. Her heart is empty. How can you live with an empty heart, live alone, sleep alone, wish alone?"

"She will not die," Amaya said angrily, and for days which turned into weeks she tried to coax life into Little Dove, keeping her warm, giving her the sycamore-bark tea they had, the corn soup made from old rotting ears they had discovered. But Tantha had been right. Little Dove did not wish to live. Winter was ending, bright spring edging onto the plains, welcoming the birds and herds of buffalo, but the small one did not see it. They placed her in a tree as her people would have, building a platform to lay her body on. Even that was ruined by the whites. Men came from Major Lord and said that what they had done was dirty. They took the body away and buried it.

There was still no food. The Indians were able to move around a little now that the snow was gone, and find roots and bulbs, but the people needed meat.

"Amaya?" It was Black Oak who found her as she collected acorns beneath the oaks. "My uncle would like you to come with us."

"To see the major again?" she asked scornfully.

"The trader, Aaron Barclay."

Amaya shook her head. "We have been to see him as well. The man has a hoard of food in the back of his store, and out here small ones are going hungry."

"Then it's worth talking to him again, isn't it? Even the major has said we have money due us from the government. We must have credit still with Barclay." He paused. "Do you know how beautiful you have become?"

"Was the winter so long?"

"Eternal. Amaya, soon—"

She turned around sharply, her woven basket cradled in the crook of her arm. "Let us go see this trader, Barclay."

Black Oak waited a moment before striding after her. They were side by side when they found Thunder Horse outside his tipi in his best elkskins, wearing a feathered bonnet. The man seemed much older, thinner, less confident.

"Good," he said as he saw Amaya. "You will help us. I am afraid the man does not understand what we want. I should learn their tongue, but what is the use? I shall be gone when the grass is long."

Amaya didn't answer. The old man still clung to the idea that he controlled his own destiny, but a look in his eyes revealed that he did not. Now his whiskey was gone, now he had handed away all the gifts the whites had given him, and he wanted to go, but he would not. Thunder Horse had come to this place to die, and brought his people with him.

Aaron Barclay was standing on the porch of his store talking to another white man when the Indians approached. Amaya saw him nudge the other man with his elbow, saw his mustached lip turn up into a smile, and she glanced at Black Oak, who had also seen it.

Thunder Horse spoke for the people, Amaya translating his words. "We are hungry," he said. "The government has promised us food, but it has not come. The government has promised us money, but that has not been paid either. You are a man who knows the ways of your government. You have given us credit before. Now we ask for a little more until our money comes."

"No more credit," Barclay said, tapping out his pipe.

"Before, you promised credit," Amaya said.

"That was before. Now it's cash only. You bring cash money or good furs and we'll talk."

"Wait," Amaya said. The man was turning away from them. Behind Amaya, nearer the camp, a baby cried out. "What are we to do, what are they to eat?"

"Spring's here." Barclay chuckled. "If they're hungry, let 'em eat grass."

Then he was gone and Thunder Horse asked anxiously, "What did he say, girl? What did he say, Amaya?"

"He said"—her eyes met those of Black Oak—"'If they are hungry, let them eat grass.'" The youth's face tightened and his eyes went cold. He looked to his uncle, waiting for a sign, waiting for the word that the Sioux would stand for no more humiliation, that they were leaving this white camp, burning the grass as they went.

There was no sign. Thunder Horse turned and slowly walked away. Black Oak started after him, lifting a hand. Then he saw that there was no point in it and he lowered the hand. He glanced once at Amaya and then sprinted off toward the trees along the river, running as fast as his legs would carry him, trying to burn away the anger inside with physical exertion. Black Oak ran until he could run no more. Then he stopped, stripped off his shirt, and dived into the river, deep into its cool depths. He came up wiping his long dark hair back. The anger was still there, the frustration. It could not be washed away.

He climbed out and lay on the bank, letting the sun dry him. His heart beat rapidly still, pumping rage through his arteries. After a while he dressed and started walking, wanting to walk away to the end of the earth, away from this filthy prison where men came to die.

"Hey, Black Oak!"

He looked up and saw three youths he knew slightly. Scatter Crow was the thick one with the bald spot on his skull where a horse's hoof had struck him during a race. The other Pawnee was Moon Eye, who had a white eyeball. The Sioux with them was Chochovan, the Fire Striker. Black Oak drifted toward them.

"Where are you going?"

"Nowhere. Where is there to go?"

"Nowhere. Were you at the trading post?"

"No, but I heard it. Barclay is dog vomit."

South of the post were a dozen small homesteads where white farmers grew corn and barley. They all seemed to have a hog or two, and several a cow. The Indian boys climbed through a split-rail fence and started across a newly plowed field, circling the neat little farmhouse which sat in the middle of it, smoke rising from the chimney.

"There's something I could use," the Fire Striker said.

Black Oak looked down at the straw beside their path. A dozen hen's eggs were scattered there, white, smooth, rare as jewels. They stopped. The sun was hot on Black Oak's back. The turned-over earth was rich in his nostrils.

"You'd better leave those alone, they belong to a white man," Scatter Crow said. The Fire Striker turned angrily, his face dark with rage.

"Do you think I am afraid of the whites?" the Sioux asked. "As all of the old ones are?" His foot went out and stepped on an egg, bursting it. Colorless liquid seeped out from beneath his moccasin. "I am not afraid of the whites," the Sioux said. "I will prove it by killing one."

Black Oak felt horror and fascination mingle in his heart. To struggle against the enemy, to fight, to strike back—these were his birthright. He had told himself he was brave, fearless, but the Fire Striker was displaying boldness he hadn't dreamed of.

"You talk. All Sioux talk," Scatter Crow said.

The Fire Striker pulled a long knife from his waistband, and Scatter Crow stepped back. The Sioux laughed.

"Not for you, Scatter Crow," and he started toward the little house.

"Wait . . ." Moon Eye said, but his voice broke off. A terrible excitement was rising in him as well. Black Oak knew it because he felt the same excitement. His knife was in his hand, although he didn't remember unsheathing it.

They walked in a dream. The day was a tangle of sounds, birdcalls, wind soughing, the whisper of moccasins, the far cry of a man. There was dust in the air, a blank blue sky bisected by smoke from the white cabin.

The Fire Striker pushed in the door to the house and went in. Black Oak saw the woman with yellow hair turn toward them, saw her mouth open, and then the Fire Striker plunged his knife blade into her throat and the blood was everywhere, spattering the wall as the woman sagged to the floor, her fingers painting parallel red lines on the pantry.

And then Black Oak was there as well, his knife rising and falling into the dead woman's breast. Her fingers, he saw, had been severed. She had a dark spot on her front tooth. There was a mole on her forehead.

The child in the corner screamed and Moon Eye grabbed it, slitting its throat. Then they were all stabbing the child. Blood was everywhere, warm and good and thrilling. Scatter Crow had taken fire from the cookfire and was touching it to the curtains, the tablecloth, the woman's dress.

"What in the hell! You filthy savages!"

The white man was in the doorway. He had a gun but in his panic and anger he tried to fire it without cocking it, and they stabbed him to death, Moon Eye taking his scalp, holding it high in bloody triumph. The house was burning furiously now, smoke creeping around them in heavy, strangling wreathes, and they rushed out of the door as the first red flames leapt into the sky.

They started back toward the reservation. They knew where they were going, although none of them mentioned it. Moon Eye looked with wonder at the scalp he carried. It was so easy to kill, to strike back, to defeat a white.

When they burst through the door of the trading post,

Aaron Barclay was alone, dusting his bottles with a feather duster. He turned, his eyes narrowing.

"You get on out of here, you little bastards," he said in English. "I got nothing for you. What's that?" He squinted at the dark object in Moon Eye's hand. "Little old pelt? Weasel? Can't give you nothing for that. Maybe a penny candy each. Toss it in the back—"

It wasn't a weasel pelt. Barclay had time to realize that before the four Indians were on him, tearing at him, stabbing him with their knives, and Barclay heard his own screams as he died.

They dragged him outside and laid him down on the earth. A crowd of Indians had rushed to the store to see what was happening. To the south smoke rose from the settler's house.

The Fire Striker turned toward the Indians, the young and the curious, and he spat on Barclay's face. Then he reached down and plucked a handful of grass. Remembering what Black Oak had told him Barclay had said, he stuffed it into the trader's mouth. "Let him eat grass," the Sioux said, and there was a sudden mad rush forward toward the store.

Inside, the shelving was torn down, bottles were broken, sacks of flour were ripped open. One woman had taken shaved bacon from a slab and began frying it on top of Barclay's iron stove.

Indians, men and women, young and old, ran from the store with their trophies—blankets, tinned food, salt, sugar, tobacco, whiskey—and as they emerged, more rushed in to see what was left to be had. By the time Amaya, drawn by the noise and activity, arrived, the store was on fire. All around it people danced and chanted. An old warrior rode his horse past furiously, narrowly missing her. A score or more young men drank heavily from the whiskey jugs. They were all armed with bright steel hatchets taken from the store.

"Thunder Horse!" Amaya found the old chief and took his arm. "Stop this now! Don't you see what will happen?"

But his exhilaration had given him back his warrior's pride, his love of excitement and fire and blood, and he said, "Go away, woman! This is the time of the warriors, do you not see?"

"What is it?" Tantha asked breathlessly. "I ran across the camp. I was bathing." Her hair was still wet from the river. Jewels of water were in her dark, full eyebrows.

"They've killed the storekeeper. Someone has set a white house on fire."

"Good," Tantha said with soft pleasure.

"Tantha, the soldiers will come. Soon. We are no match for them!"

"Yes," Tantha, brought back to her senses, said. "Yes, you are right. What is that!" They heard a volley of shots, and looking to the north, they could see that one of the wooden barracks, their barracks, was on fire. The uprising had spread like a summer wildfire. Everything that would burn was being torched. Everyone they saw had a weapon in his hand.

"Amaya, we must go!"

"What?"

"Go. Out of here. Far away."

"Where?"

"To my people. Now." Another volley sounded from across the reservation. They could see a contingent of cavalry riding toward them, splashing across the narrow creek through the smoke and dust toward the store, which continued to burn hotly.

"Now? We can't—"

"How can we not? Don't you see what is going to happen!"

Yes, yes, she could see, she could smell destruction in the air, the final collapse of an ill-conceived bastard solution to a deep problem. They started away across the reservation, moving at a run. They ran blindly on through the low black smoke that now curled across the camp and through the trees. They heard shots again, and again the cries of pain.

"Here," Tantha said urgently, and they ducked into the oak trees, concealing themselves in the vines that flourished there just as the cavalry contingent rode past. Their leader was the officer who had been Pierce's friend, the one called Staggs.

His eyes were dull and red. He had lost his hat. He had a revolver in either hand, and as they rode through the camp, Staggs fired both of them, cutting down women and children, men and dogs indiscriminately in what appeared to be blind panic.

Tantha screamed out a bitter curse before Amaya could silence her with a hand over her mouth, but in the rush of horses, the roar of guns, she was not heard. It was a minute before they could resume their run, a minute in which they saw horses riding down children, saw guns explode the faces of friends and allies, saw two white soldiers die with Sioux or Pawnee knives in them.

Amaya saw the smoke, the dust, the rush of horses, the colors clashing—blue and yellow, bronze, red, terrible crimson, copper. The sun was a glittering thing through the trees. Winking, mocking. She realized where they were suddenly. She could see the platform clearly—the platform where Little Dove had lain.

Amaya grabbed at Tantha and almost bodily lifted her from the concealment of the vines. Tantha's lip was turned back; her hands clenched and unclenched, showing bloody incarnadine where her nails had cut her palms; her stance and expression were savage, feral.

"Now. It will be too late!"

"If I could kill one. If I had a gun . . ." But she had no gun, and the thunder of the war continued, a thunder which they knew meant a storm of death, the end of this way, this mockery, this joke.

"Now, Tantha!"

"Yes." Amaya felt her muscles slacken. "Now we must go. Quickly."

They needed horses but there were none to be found. Maybe it was for the best. On horseback they would have been more visible. They started west and north along the river, keeping to the heavy willow brush, the blackthorn and blackberries which scratched at their faces, tore at their flesh. They traveled on, moving rapidly, trying to leave the roar of the guns, the smell of smoke and blood, the cries of the dying behind them. At dusk they heard a party of soldiers approaching and they burrowed into the deepest thicket they could find, hiding, cowering like rabbits.

Not this time, Amaya thought. They found me before, but not this time. I will not go with them. They will have to kill me.

The patrol rode slowly past and was lost in the orange dusk. They did not stir. The dew settled heavily along the river, and toward midnight a low fog rose out of the river, swathing the night in milky dampness. Until midnight and far beyond they could hear the distant shots.

People were dying. The program had gone wrong. The government had miscalculated in its attempt to help, in its insistence that only a body of special interest-oriented men elected by people who did not know them could solve the country's problems, could direct the destiny of races and nations.

"Are you sleeping?" Tantha asked, shaking Amaya's shoulder.

"No," she answered automatically, only half-sleeping as the contrast between what she had been told was the white government and reality ran through her mind. Freedom: perhaps long ago law-givers had known what that meant. Now they understood only compulsion; and like all governments, they had made it a crime to dispute their laws.

"It is best if we travel. Now. Let us put the miles between us and the reservation."

"Yes," Amaya agreed. She was weary, her body was half-asleep, but she knew they must walk on. It would not do to be taken prisoner again. Never again would she be a slave, a penned animal, a blank slate for the whites to write their laws upon.

The moon rose golden and full and they walked away from it, only now and then glancing back to see the smoky pennants drawn across the eastern skies by the distant fires of discontent. They could no longer hear the shots; all of that had passed into a dream. They walked on, trudging through the ankle-deep sand of the coulees, moving westward toward the high mountains, across the endless land haunted by the souls of a race—the spirits of ancient times, buffalo hunters, fishers, shamans, lovers, children born alive and squawling, women dying giving birth, men dying hunting in the winter herds for sustenance, long walkers, long runners, lacrosse players and deadly painted warriors, hide-scraping women and weirdly painted dancers, drummers and nose-flute players. The plains were alive with the ghosts, with the sounds of them, the cries, the thrumming, ringing, wailing, drumming. The two who walked the plains were only the survivors of lost races, the life sprung from the loins of freedom.

They walked to sunrise, away from the threatening east where the accusing, white, peering ball of dawn's sun would crest the long dark line of the horizon. They walked and then they halted.

"We must not be caught," Amaya said, holding back Tantha, and she nodded with exhaustion, with agreement. Not now—they must not be caught now. They did not want to be taken back, to see what had happened.

Again they crawled into the deepest tangle of brush and vines and berries along the narrow coulee and tried to sleep the heat of the day away. At sunset they moved on, seeing a fire to the south, which had to be that of an army patrol. They never looked back now, not daring to think of what had happened, not wanting to rejoin the past.

The country began to be stippled with oak trees. They rose up singly and in clusters from off the night plains like dark specters. An owl swooped low and shrieked at them from out of a starry sky. The moon lighted their way clearly and they walked on grimly, hardly speaking now, knowing how far their voices might carry.

Again they slept as dawn approached. On the third day they began to walk in the daylight, certain they had left the soldiers behind. They still moved warily, their eyes alert. There were other enemies besides the white soldiers on the plains.

"Arapaho," Tantha hissed.

The girls lay behind a hill rise, watching the small Indian camp below them, across the stream where they had hoped to drink. It was a hunting party, possibly even a raiding party. Three dozen men without their women, without travois or dogs or children or lodges. They had blankets and guns, nothing else. It wouldn't do for two young women to be found by them. The Arapaho could take slaves as well as the whites. They lay there watching, the sun hot on their backs, the scent of yellowing grass stubble in their nostrils. A red ant crawled across

Amaya's hand and she blew it away with a puff of breath.

At nightfall the Arapaho moved out and they went down to drink.

"Tantha."

"What is it?"

When the Cheyenne girl came, Amaya showed her the dead man. He was white. Stripped naked, he had been cut up slowly while he lived. The Arapaho weren't hunting. They were making war. The way they were riding, they would come upon the soldiers from Fort Laramie.

"Keep moving," Tantha said. That was all there was to do.

"How far to the land of the Cheyenne?"

Tantha looked at her in surprise. "All of this is the land of the Cheyenne!" Her arm described a grand circle.

"And the Sioux? The Arapaho?"

Tantha was genuinely disturbed by Amaya's suggestion. "They are on our land, that is all. They will leave when the Cheyenne return."

They walked on, moving more slowly now, believing that the danger was behind them. Amaya asked where the Cheyenne camps were.

"They are north now. North and east. Near the Powder River in the little hills where the cowardly Crow hide. It is the season to hunt on those grounds. When the weather grows hard and the grass fades, then the Cheyenne will ride south, and interlopers like these"—she made a gesture of distaste—"Arapaho, will scurry away."

"How long, then? How long must we walk?"

"Not long. A week. What do we care!" Tantha smiled and Amaya realized it was the first time she had seen her do so for a month, certainly since the trouble at the fort had begun. "We are free again. Don't you see!" She danced in a little circle, her arms waving in the air. Amaya smiled. *Free.* And for Tantha it was a going home. Her people lived, rode free and proud in the far reaches of the plains. What was it for Amaya, who had no people? She looked back in memory, trying to regain the persuasion that she belonged with the Cheyenne, that they would accept her, but she could find nothing to tie that conviction to. It had been a girl's dream, a foolish

idea born out of panic and shock after the massacre of
the Comanche. Now, with her head cleared, with more
maturity, she felt no ebullience about coming among the
Cheyenne, only a hope that things would not be as bad as
they had been.

"Will they make me a slave?"

"A slave? No, Amaya, of course not."

"Then what?"

"You will be my sister," Tantha said, and she stopped,
placing her hands on Amaya's shoulders as sundown
flared briefly crimson against the dark western skies.
"You will be Cheyenne. You will be a part of my family." And then for a moment they held each other, until
Tantha stepped back and said, "How silly you can be."

Yes. Silly and small and concerned. At long intervals
it all came back: she was alone on the earth without
family or people. There was no one to sing with her, no
one to mourn her passing. She was ashamed that Tantha
had seen some of her sadness. Tantha was a good friend.
They would be sisters. They made their beds half an
hour later beneath a great oak. Beds of grass and leaves,
and they lay down to sleep.

But sleep didn't come to Amaya. The stars flickered
beyond the network of dark branches, and the moon
stained the oak tree to pale silver. A wolf howled far
away and was joined by another. Something small rustled in the grass and scurried away. The night was still
after that, still and cool and very empty.

In the morning they were virtually surrounded by the
great herd. Amaya gradually awakened to the sound like
thunder rumbling distantly. The earth beneath her was
moving slightly, swaying in a way oddly comforting. The
smell was overpowering, damp and ancient. She sat up
abruptly, seeing Tantha crouched, holding her skirt around
her knees, dark eyes bright, watching a moving, groaning
sea of buffalo.

They could not see the end of the herd to the north,
nor the beginning of it to the south. They passed—*it,* for
it was a single thing made of thousands of elements—at a
slow grazing walk, clipping the long grass in a wide
swath as they moved southward, gigantic, primitive, dark,
stupid, sacred, endless, life-givers.

"It started just before daylight," Tantha told her. "I was afraid it was horses at first, but then I saw how many there were. A dark cloud moving low on the horizon. I got up to watch."

They watched together. It had been a long while since they had seen a buffalo herd making its ponderous way across the world. Their knoll was a sunbright yellow island against the current of dark bodies. Amaya watched the big bulls with massive woolly heads, dark-horned, empty-eyed, humped, the cows with trailing calves. She heard the grunt of them, the clacking of horns, the occasional bawl of surprise or pain, the constant lowing sound, the quieter murmuring which was the working of thousands of jaws devouring the life-giving grass.

"The Cheyenne will not be far behind," Tantha said, rising, stretching her arms. "The herds have gone from the northern hunting grounds. The people too will be coming south, following the buffalo, as they must."

Amaya's eyes lifted involuntarily to the north, trying to imagine the coming of the Cheyenne, trying to look through that veil which obscures the future. Nothing is as imagined; what use then was imagination?

The sounds of the guns brought her head around in panic. They were distant, from the south. There were hundreds of shots. The sound brought back the dreadful memory; the slaughter at the Comanche camp lived again briefly, horribly.

"White hunters," Tantha said, touching her shoulder.

They could see the puffs of smoke rising against the sky, see the herd plod on unconcerned while their numbers were cut down, while the leaders dropped to the earth.

"So far west?"

"They too will be gone when the Cheyenne return," Tantha said with bitter decisiveness.

The shots rang across the plains for most of the day. In late afternoon the end of the herd appeared and Tantha and Amaya started on again, walking across earth that was still warm from the passing of the buffalo.

The land began to rise slightly, to tilt, like a placid sea beginning to swell and crest. Farther west yet the great mountains began to loom against the sky like monuments to dead aeons. There was snow at their crests and it glittered red-gold and violet in the sundown light. There, in the Rocky Mountains, the Utes, a strange and secretive people, had their stronghold. It was no place to live. There were no flatlands and therefore no grazing herds of buffalo. They had to come into Cheyenne land to hunt, and they did that cautiously. Still there was constant friction between the tribes, Tantha said.

They slept on a rocky outcropping fifty feet up a sandy, nopal-cactus-studded slope, and in the morning they bathed in the pool at the base of the bluff. There icy water from the foothills collected in a limestone basin, swirled around, and frothed off to the lower levels.

They stripped off their dresses and dived into the pool, the water cutting to their bones with its chill, shocking nerves to life, awakening every fiber and cell. Later they lay on the shelf of stone, letting the sun dry them as the cool breeze moved across their naked bodies.

That was the day the Cheyenne came.

Again Amaya and Tantha were walking, now weaving their way among the low hills south and east of the Bighorn Mountains moving away from the Powder River, which they could see rambling away across the long, empty grasslands. A diving red-tailed hawk screeched as if he were a harbinger, a bringer of joyous news, and the two girls turned their heads to the north, seeing the dark gathering there.

Another herd, Amaya thought briefly, but instantly she knew she was wrong. There was no thunder in the air, nor in the ground, and there was color and motion and sound which no herd of buffalo could produce. The clicking of wooden travois runners, the yapping of dogs, the running of children on long lean legs, darting here and there, the steady plodding of the horses of burden, the mane-swirling, prancing, sideways, prideful motion of the spotted buffalo horses, the war ponies with their manes and tails clipped or tied up, the men with bonnets of eagle feathers shifting in the light northern breeze, the fringes of their buckskin or beaded elkskin shirts moving like nervously drumming fingers, and the chatter of old men and women, shrilling at the children, raised in happy song, retelling the tales of the hunt and the bloody, terrible tales of war, of young love and of the spirit lore, of dreadful Aktanowihio, the spirit of Below, of He and Bear and *tasoom*—the soul which travels the Hanging Road to the skies—of children chattering as they listened to the tales, the songs, or ignored them and ran their own races with Being, chasing the rabbits the passing party stirred from the grass, aiming narrow bows which propelled spindly, featherless arrows at their bobbing, weaving, white-tailed prey or running in pursuit of the dogs which tumbled and fought in the long grass, leaping and chasing the rabbits or the prairie dogs, bright-eyed and quick beneath their winter fat, indomitable in their stone mounds where they took shelter and whistled shrill taunts at the warrior dogs.

A nation had risen off of the plains and it came southward to embrace the two women who needed its shelter.

For an expectant, endless hour—or was it less?—they stood waiting, wanting to rush into the massed confusion of the tribe, which drifted southward apparently in obedience to some common will, some central mind, as the buffalo did. But here Amaya witnessed and sensed intelligence, pride, warmth, humor—all that separated man from the stolid, rambling buffalo.

They waited, and soon the first of the party began to drift or race or trot or plod past them. Old women with bundles on their backs, children with flying moccasined feet, shirtless, bronzed, and healthy, yellow dogs with pink, dangling tongues. Amaya stood and she watched, and then the cry of joy went up, thrilling her, tracing its galvanic course up her spine. A woman threw down her pack and rushed toward Tantha, a younger girl followed. A warrior on horseback halted in the midst of the tumble and froth of people around him and stared; his mouth hung open until he too shouted: "Tantha-cho-wihio!" which was her full name.

The horseman rode his tall gray pony toward them at a gallop, swinging down on the run, rushing to her. He threw his arms around her and lifted her high, spinning her around so that her feet and pigtails flew out. Tantha was laughing. The two women had arrived, and as Tantha was placed on her feet again, they all joined hands, hugged each other, leapt up and down with sheer joy.

Amaya stood apart, watching as if from a vast distance, feeling the vague embarrassment an outsider suffers, a touch of envy, and deep pleasure all at once. There would be no such homecoming for her, ever, and so she watched and imagined, trying to share Tantha's happiness.

The remainder of the tribe streamed past. Now and then someone would call out: "Welcome back," or "Where have you been?" and "Hello, Tantha." Two younger women detached themselves from the body of Indians and came to join Tantha. They were friends of hers. Tantha hugged them all, speaking rapidly, her face plastic and expressive, her hands describing events, her mouth opening wide in laughter once.

"And Amaya . . ." She looked past the shoulder of the man. "Where are you, Amaya, come here. This is my friend Amaya. From the school. She has come to be my sister." Tantha took Amaya's hand. "This is my mother, Amaya. Her name is Nalin, but you must call her Mother."

The older woman seemed puzzled. Her dark eyes peered out of a web of weather-cut lines. Her white hair, done in a single braid, ran across her breast. She wore a faded red woolen shirt and a buckskin skirt. A turquoise necklace encircled her throat. Amaya could not read the expression in her eyes. Her lips moved slightly in and out as she studied Amaya's face.

"It is good," Nalin said at last. Then she smiled, a beaming smile, and her arms stretched out to gather Amaya to her. "It is good to have a new daughter. What a fortunate woman I am today. I have found the daughter that was lost and been given another one to comfort my old age."

They walked southward then, Amaya carrying a part of Nalin's burden, talking to the people around them, telling the story of the Laramie confinement over and over to choruses of disapproval, tongue-clicking, anger.

They walked southward for another day and a half, moving parallel with the great buffalo herd ahead of them. "The buffalo," Tantha's father told them, "will halt at the big basin. Every year they halt at the big basin to drink water and fill their bellies with grass—to fill our bellies." He grinned, rubbing his own stomach. "Our camp, Amaya, is near there so that we may have our last hunt before the great herd drifts away."

"It is," Tantha told her, "a beautiful valley where we camp. We call it just Buffalo Camp, and there are many pines, a deep river, the mountains rising to the west." She lifted a hand and pointed southward. "There, you can see the peak that towers over our camp."

She could see the camp, and as they crested a low line of dark, bunched hills where much brush grew, she could see the river, deep and blue, winding away through the scattered cottonwoods and willow trees. To the west and south the hills rose higher, and there were many pines, some cedar and blue spruce crowded together, lifting into the clear blue sky. Here and there pockets of grass, small sheltered valleys, could be seen, and lower yet, a large valley, perhaps two miles long, where a smaller rill flowed, feeding the long grass.

"There they are," Tantha said, and looking to the east, Amaya too saw the great herd, a black, shifting pool staining the earth as the buffalo entered the vast basin across the river.

"And so it is good," Nalin said. "It is as it has been, and the People will survive."

Amaya watched the old woman curiously. It was not a prayer, not a chant, but the words were singsong, directed to no one. Her eyes were partly closed.

"It is her song from long ago," Tantha explained.

"A song she has learned?"

"No. Her song. Do you not know?" At Amaya's puzzled look, the Cheyenne girl went on. "Many Cheyenne have their own songs. The warriors have them, they have learned them from the spirits. An older woman, a married woman, can also search for the dreams."

"What dreams?"

Tantha's mouth turned up with surprise. "Why, the dreams which guide our lives, Amaya. How do we know what the spirits want? How do we know which is the right way? How do we know ourselves, our own *tasoom*: our souls? It must be through dreams, and so it is. My mother fasted for six days. She dragged herself into the hills and while she was there she slept at last and had her dream. The song is all she has told us of it. The song she has just spoken.''

Amaya didn't fully understand, nor did it concern her much. Ahead the first of the tribe was beginning to enter the long green valley, the valley which protected and, beautiful as it was, offered shelter and comfort. Amaya looked at it, seeing the beauty of the place, feeling still a desolation in her heart, and emptiness. She had come among the Cheyenne, followed the long trail to their camp, and they had taken her in. But she was not one of them; their home was not hers. She glanced at Tantha, animated, cheerful, shouting to a friend. Tantha was free, she was among her kind. Amaya turned her eyes toward the valley again and watched it through the mist.

They raised their tipi in the shelter of the tall pines. Tantha, Amaya, Mother Nalin, and Tantha's father, Horse Warrior, together they raised the tipi and arranged their camp. The pines were green and their scent sharp, pervasive. Red squirrels lived there, and jays. An eagle had its nest in a crag higher up the mountain behind the forest. There were a hundred tipis scattered across the valley and into the trees, and the camp was alive with the sounds of children and dogs, laughter and work.

The family still had many green buffalo hides with them, hides which needed to be scraped and cured, softened if they were to be used for clothing, made supple for moccasins or tanned with smoke to treat them for the construction of a watertight tipi.

The work was hard, but Amaya didn't mind. She and Tantha did most of the work, staking the hides, hair side down to the ground, fleshing the fat from them, finishing the job with a small sharp scraper. Some of the hides, Nalin wished to use to make winter garments. On these they left the hair. Those for other purposes were scraped clean. The hides were tanned with a fluid made of the buffalo's liver and fat, the skins softened by working the fluid into the hide, by the action of tirelessly pulling the hide back and forth over a taut rope or through the hole in a buffalo shoulder bone.

Neither of the girls had done this work for a long time,

and their fingers were raw with it at first. Neither cared. It was freedom to work, to be among their people, beneath the pines where the wind sang, to talk while they labored.

It was Nalin who generally told the tales, Nalin who taught Amaya as patiently as if she were a small child: "If you are to be one of us, then you must know the Cheyenne. You must think and sing like a Cheyenne, or you will always be an outsider. You must know us if you would love who we are."

And she would begin to tell her tales. "Long ago, Amaya, there were no buffalo, not large herds as you see now, and we had only geese and ducks, small things. It was hard for the Cheyenne people." Nalin's eyes were half-closed. She swayed slightly as she spoke, her fingers automatically working tanning fluid into a hide, softening it. Over her shoulder the sun glinted in the pines. "The people became so hungry that the chief of all the Cheyenne chose two brave young warriors to search all of the world for food and not to return if they did not find all the tribe needed.

"They searched the mountains and the far plains, these men whose names I do not know—they walked the earth for eight days without eating themselves. One morning when they were weak with hunger they saw a high peak loom out of a red sunrise, and they spoke together, deciding to go there to die. They had failed their tribe, you see, and could not return.

"They found a stream between themselves and the peak they had chosen to die upon, and as they tried to cross, a great water serpent took them in its horrible mouth and held them fast. Out of the side of the peak ahead of them rushed a man wearing a coyote skin and carrying a great knife as long as his arm. He dived into the river and swam to them, cutting off the serpent's head with his knife. Then he and his wife took the two young warriors to the peak. There the rocks opened before them by magic and in a secret room within the peak the old man and his wife fed the warriors and healed them of the serpent's bites.

"Now, the coyote man and his wife had a daughter with yellow hair, and since he and his wife were growing old, they asked the young men to take her for a sister or a wife so that she would not be alone when they died.

"One of the men, I do not know his name, agreed to marry Yellow-Haired Woman, and for their wedding gifts they were given great magic. The secret of growing corn and the promise that the buffalo would come like water flowing across the world. But the coyote man cautioned his daughter that she must never express any pity for the suffering of any animal or all that they had been given would be taken away.

"Now, the Cheyenne were filled with joy when the warriors came home with Yellow-Haired Woman, for afterward they were surrounded by many buffalo and much small game. All the meat the people needed, they had, all the hides and warm furs. But later some foolish boys dragged a buffalo calf into the camp and, throwing it down, tossed dirt into its eyes until it bawled in fright. Yellow-Haired Woman saw this and said, 'My poor little calf!'

"She knew right away that she had broken the law of her father, but nothing could be done about it. That day all the buffalo disappeared. Yellow-Haired Woman left in disgrace to return to her father and mother. Her husband and his friend went with her, carrying nothing but a bow and three arrows. They were never seen again." Nalin looked up. "Hand me the tanning-lotion pot, please, Amaya, daughter."

Amaya did so, taking a moment to look out across the cloud-shadowed grasslands where the buffalo now grazed. "But the buffalo came back, Nalin."

"Yes. All of our people have taken the Yellow-Haired Woman's vow. We love the buffalo, worship the spirit in him, give thanks to him, but we cannot feel sorry for him, for then our tribe would go hungry." She took the lotion from Amaya and got back to work.

The wind was fresh through the pines. A lone hawk darted against the sky. Amaya was content for the first time in a long while. The Cheyenne camp was good, the land was rich. Before winter came they would have much meat smoked, many hides and furs to keep them warm in their new tipis. She was content—but there was something wanting, something that darkened her heart like the shadows of the clouds. She had no idea what it was; the answer was lost in her girlhood.

Her eyes lifted constantly to the east, waiting, wondering.

Nalin was the best of company for her. Amaya learned much working with the older woman, for Nalin was a storehouse for tales and she loved to tell them. It made the work go easy to hear of Heammawihio, the Wise One Above, and Aktanowihio, the Wise One Below, and their thundering battles, of the *minio*, which were water monsters and lived in many lakes, hunting the unwary, of Thunder, the bird who might rescue a Cheyenne from the clutches of such a monster if called to in time. How to tell a fortune with the hide of a badger, how to use a cricket to point the way to a buffalo herd. She learned that a bull elk was great magic for a lonesome lover because of its ability to call the females to it, that a bear has organs good for healing the body and the spirit.

There were also motherly lectures on proper behavior. "A Cheyenne," Nalin said, "is not like other people we have heard of. A Cheyenne woman is virtuous and true. Do not go around unclothed or making foolish remarks which might embarrass your family which nurtured you. Be generous and friendly—these are good traits, good for the woman, good for her family, good for the tribe. We do not suffer a liar."

Amaya took it all to heart. She did her work, and sometimes more than her share. The summer days passed in peaceful progression. One day Nalin told her, "No work today. Not here."

The old woman was smiling. Amaya noticed she had her hair combed back and oiled.

"Why not?"

"Because it is time for the hunt. The shaman has said so, and so things must be done."

"What sorts of things?"

"You will see."

Tantha was also in her best dress, the one with elaborate beadwork and quill designs. Her hair too was newly washed, scented with yarrow. She wore her red-stone-bead necklace.

"It is *massaum*," Tantha said cheerfully.

"I don't understand."

"The great hunt festival. It happens only every few years. The entire tribe must witness it. Then later there will be feasting. Come on, hurry. Get dressed." Tantha pushed her playfully toward the tipi.

Amaya was uncomfortable already. While she worked, she felt a part of the tribe. At play she did not know what to do. There were men and women among the Cheyenne who did not like her because she was Comanche. People like the woman Small Eyes, who was a member of the Quillers Society and a powerful person in the tribe. Small Eyes complained that having a Comanche in the tribe broke the law. She had told the clan sachem, a warrior named Crooked Foot, that Amaya had taken some beads from her tent.

"Hurry, hurry, hurry!" Tantha urged. "Wear my good dress—last year's dress. The year before, really, isn't it? A good thing you're smaller than I am, Amaya. Hurry."

Tantha practically undressed her, turning her this way and that, tugging at her while Amaya protested.

"The *massaum* is being celebrated, the shaman Sun Hawk has declared it. And you look at me darkly."

"I'm sorry," Amaya said, trying to smile. She stood naked in the tipi while Tantha searched for the dress and beaded moccasins.

"How lovely you are, Amaya. You have to smile, though. Remember, Mother says be cheerful."

"I will."

"Yes, so I see," Tantha scolded. "A person would think you prefer work to play."

"Perhaps. Then I feel like I am helping. Then I feel Cheyenne."

"The Cheyenne play too," Tantha said, rising with the dress, examining it critically.

"Yes. I only want the others to accept me. I don't want it to be like it was among the whites."

"Like that! How can you say such a thing, Amaya? You are my sister, my mother's daughter."

"But I am not Cheyenne."

"You are referring to Small Eyes."

"Yes."

"She is a crazy woman. Not the same since the

Comanche killed her three sons. Was there not someone in the Comanche camp who hated the Cheyenne?"

Amaya answered thoughtfully. "Yes. Yes, there was."

"Women with grief as a last sustaining emotion. Without husbands or sons, they have only anger and grief. That is Small Eyes. It means nothing, the rancor of such. Crooked Foot decided that her claim was baseless."

"And that will only make her angrier."

"It does not matter. Shall we spend our lives worrying about such as Small Eyes—except to pity them?"

"No." Amaya smiled and touched Tantha's shoulder. "You are a good friend, a good sister. Thank you."

When they went to the long valley for the start of the *massaum*, they were not alone. The tall young warrior with the scar on his cheek had joined them. He was called Stalking the Wolf and he had known Tantha since childhood. They had hung side by side in their cradleboards, suspended from the tree branches as their mothers washed their garments in the streams. They had suckled together and played naked. Stalking the Wolf had a finger missing on his left hand—he had done that to himself when he found out the whites had taken Tantha. They had had to restrain him to keep him from going to Fort Laramie himself to try to free his childhood friend.

Now there was more than friendship in it. They walked together, shoulders and hips occasionally touching, while Amaya strode behind, through the pines and down the long rocky slopes to the creek where the lone cottonwood tree stood, where the People waited, the shaman, Sun Hawk, chanting a song beneath the bright skies.

The sounds of drums and flutes became louder, shriller, as they approached. Men of the Contrary Society ran backward across the sandy flats. Their deity was the spirit Thunder, and to please him, they did everything the opposite of what others did. "Hello" meant "goodbye" to a Contrary Society member. They walked backward, rode their horses facing the tail, held their bows reversed, and courted grandmothers. They rejoiced in celebrations and painting themselves wildly. Amaya saw one man half yellow, half white, another black from the waist up, red from the waist down. One had eyes painted on his shoulder blades, his hair combed down over his face.

The men of the warrior societies were across the river on their war ponies, brave, fierce, silent; they too wore paint on this day. These were the heart of the Cheyenne strength, the men in war bonnets, their lances and war axes decorated with the scalps of their defeated enemies, their paint signaling their intent, their loyalty. A man with a red handprint on his face, meaning "I drink my enemies' blood," rode past solemnly, paying no attention to the mocking, leaping Contrary Society members.

The shaman was not an old man, as Amaya had expected. He was perhaps forty, round and smooth. But his eyes were deeply set, looking into distances perhaps.

"This is the feast of *massaum*," he told them, "the animal dance which must be done. The earth feeds us, the animals of the earth clothe us and feed us. We cannot take from the earth without giving back. We cannot take from existence without offering it its due. To do so, to live, flourish, pass away without thought for the future, for our past, our people's present, is a sin. We gather to honor the earth and its thousand spirits, to pray and offer our promises to the Life in the earth so that all the trees and the grass and fruits and animals may thrive and grow strong and thereby feed us."

The naked warrior came forward then. His head had been shaved. He carried a great glistening ax. His body was bronze-gold in the sunlight. There was a hush among the gathered Cheyenne. Amaya could hear the creek whispering in its bed. The sun was warm. Insects hummed lazily around her face. Glancing down, she saw that Stalking the Wolf and Tantha were holding hands.

The man without hair raised his ax to the sky, letting the highly polished blade reflect the sunlight. He moved then to a narrow cottonwood tree which grew beside the river. White, cottony seed clusters clung to the branches, some drifting away in the breeze. The leaves of the tree were bright yellow-green. The shaman, Sun Hawk, raised his hands and spoke to the sky.

The ax was swung at the tree, halting short of the bark. Again it swung, three times in all, before the formula allowed the cold, honed steel to strike the mottled tree. It bit deeply, the sound of the ax burying itself in wood clear and sharp.

Instantly fifty women rushed toward the tree, all of them carrying small hatchets or knives. They began to hack away at the tree in a bedlam of motion and noise, their chanting eerie, high-pitched, whining like the wind in the winter lodges.

It was a wonder no one's hands were cut. The tree fell in a matter of moments, and the women, Mother Nalin among them, scattered as it fell.

Now warriors rode across the rill and leather ropes were thrown around the tree, knotted there by the shaman and his assistants, and the horsemen moved off toward the village, dragging the tree behind them. A special lodge, double the normal size, had been built there, and within it the cottonwood tree was erected by the men of the warrior societies.

Amaya was carried along by a throng, the heat of their bodies, the scent of them close and somehow comforting. They rushed in a mass toward the village, following the cottonwood tree. The Contrary hunters whooped and cheered, leaping high, shouting that the ceremony was over.

Women carrying sacred buffalo skulls, some oddly painted, crimson and ocher with black circles around the eyes, wound their way toward the medicine lodge. There they had to make three false starts and then enter, praising the buffalo as they went, singing a shrill and ancient song, a blood-thrilling, ringing song, a wind chant, a cry as plaintive and timeless as the cry of a wolf at the winter moon.

And there was Amaya, watching as the shaman performed his rites, painting a buffalo skin according to a precise sequence, first the left forefoot, then the right, then the right hip across to the left shoulder until all the propitious markings had been formed.

Meanwhile the singing went on, like the shrilling of a hive or the pained nickering of wild horses as they went down before the hunters. There was fire leaping against the bright sky; children yelled and chanted nonsense words, trying to ape their elders.

Then from the medicine lodge the mock animals came,

moving across the clearing to the accompanying shrieks and shouts of approbation. Men in buffalo hides, horns on their heads, or in elkskins, cougar hides, fox, bear, coyote, blackbird—the skins of all the clans and all of the creatures which sustain. They growled, raised mock claws, scratched at the earth, pawed, and stampeded wildly as if in panic, like the animals they represented. Among them now came Contrary Society hunters hunting them, singing to them as the sounds of chanting rose from the gathered hundreds, praise to the buffalo, to the grass which sustained them, to the rain and Thunder, to the earth mother, to all of life and all creation which flew, crawled, raced free across the plains, wandered, hunted, killed, and was in turn hunted and killed, as it was meant to be.

The skies grew dim and sunset began to settle, and still the dancing, the chanting, the singing went on. Still gifts were offered to the buffalo spirit in the medicine lodge. It would go on, Amaya knew, for three days, possibly for five. Then it would be the time to hunt the buffalo, to decimate him so that the People might live. His spirit then would be fully appeased, then it would be fitting that the life-giver die so that others could survive the long winter of the plains.

The feasting and singing went on. Night fell and the flames danced skyward, casting a glow visible for miles. The faces of the people Amaya saw were bright with the fire, bright with the pleasures of the feast. She saw Tantha and Stalking the Wolf, and they beckoned to her as she crossed the camp, but she shook her head. It was their time to be together, not hers.

She walked toward the family tipi, still hearing the drums throbbing in her ears, her skull, seeming to pulse in her blood vessels. Still the sky was bright with fire. No one was at home. Nalin and Horse Warrior would be dancing, eating, sharing their tribal heritage, celebrating their blood ties. They would have welcomed Amaya, and she knew that; the night was more welcoming.

As she climbed through the pines, the stars grew brighter and the drums fainter. The pine needles were soft and springy underfoot. The trunks of the great trees were like the torsos of giant warriors looming out of the darkness. The moon rose pale and round, softly glossing the plains where the buffalo milled, where the world stood empty and naked and ripe with its goodness.

Amaya climbed on, seeing the horned owl cut a flapping silhouette against the startled face of the moon. She climbed a little rocky ledge and sat there, her legs dangling, watching the world, the constant, ever-changing earth. The shadows moved beneath the pines, crossed and pooled as the moon rose higher. The trees yawned and stretched in the night breeze. Beyond the trees was the great village where they had gathered together to praise nature and its spirits. Amaya's worship was a solitary night prayer. The night cooled as the hours passed, and a dew began to settle before Amaya rose and walked back toward the village, hearing them still—those she needed to be a part of, wanted to be with and yet was not, seemingly could never be.

She went into the empty tipi on the slopes of the pine hill and went to sleep.

"Amaya!" Tantha hissed into her ear, shook her, and Amaya opened one eye to the darkness of the early hours.
"Yes."

"The hunt. It is to be now. Turn out and bring your best knife, your best scraper."

Amaya sat up and nodded. Her hair was loose, to her waist, where it was gathered with a rawhide tie. Mother Nalin, looking fresh after a long night's celebration, was already up, hunched over a small fire, heating strips of venison for them to gnaw on as they went.

Horse Warrior was wearing only a breechclout, feathers knotted into his gray hair. His body and face were painted garishly. There was red on each of his arms from the elbow down, on his chest a red serpent struggling with a dark arrowhead. His face was bisected diagonally, red and white with a single black dot in the center of his forehead.

He had his quiver and rosewood bow in his hand. "I must go now, woman," he said to his wife, who only nodded. He strode out, proud as a warrior on this morning, despite his age. The women understood his pride, his manner. A man going to hunt, to fight the enemy, was distracted. He fed and protected the family, the tribe, the children who could not hunt, could not run if an enemy came.

"I must hurry as well, all of us," Mother Nalin said anxiously. "They will be waiting. Bring your knives, hurry, Amaya. The little sack with the scrapers. Water, Tantha."

It was not Amaya's first hunt, but it was her first with the Cheyenne. Outside it was cool, misty. "Whose kill do I see to?"

"Wanilak's. He is a good hunter. His wife was crushed by a falling rock and died." Nalin looked into the heart of the village. "There he is. You see, with the yellow face. Go and he will show you his arrows. I will do Horse Warrior's kill; and Tantha, Stalking the Wolf's."

"Already?" Amaya teased her adopted sister.

"Perhaps soon there will be more than that. Maybe I will do more than prepare his hides." Then she laughed and turned away, hiding her face. It was a solemn occasion not fit for humor.

Amaya with her bag of tools hurried through the camp, dodging hunters and their women, dogs and prancing buffalo ponies which were deliberately left half-tamed.

She nearly ran into Small Eyes.

The older woman turned. In her hand was a long-handled bone scraping tool. Her tiny dark eyes glistened in her broad face.

"What are you sneaking around here for? I don't want you around me, Comanche woman."

"I am sorry, Small Eyes."

"How dare you call me by that name? How dare you speak to me at all, Comanche woman."

Several of the older women laughed at Small Eyes' taunting. Amaya looked into their faces, bowed slightly, and turned away, hurrying on toward her hunter, hearing their mocking chatter. She was mad, of course. Not on all subjects, but on the subject of Comanche, certainly. Like Masala, the Comanche who had hated the Cheyenne, who had cut scars of grief into her body. There was an irony to this, but Amaya could not enjoy it. The Comanche, some of them, had hated her because she was not of their people; the Cheyenne, a few of them, hated her because she was Comanche.

It was not worth dwelling on. She found Wanilak, a stony-faced man of middle age, narrow and sinewy. He showed her his arrows; two bands of black and one of red were painted around the shafts.

"You will know these, girl?"

"I will know them," she promised.

"I will use only them. Not a musket gun like some of these so-called hunters. What good is a musket gun? Even if you make a killing shot, why, a man has to stop and reload the white weapon. It takes many minutes. I can put ten arrows in the buffalo, all properly placed, behind the last rib, where they will deflate the lung, before this man with the musket gun has fired a second time."

Amaya listened respectfully. Apparently musket guns were one of Wanilak's obsessions. Or he was jealous of the men who did have the thunder guns. Amaya wasn't sure which.

The sky was growing gray now, and above the plains a thin band of crimson edged with the purest gold lined out along the horizon. The hunting party began to surge forward across the dewy grass toward the big basin. Nalin had moved nearby without Amaya's awareness. She heard the old woman singing under her breath, "And so it is good. It is as it has been and the People will survive."

It was not a long walk, but Amaya's heart was racing by the time they reached the low knolls overlooking the great depression which was black with the bodies of the rising buffalo. The hunters were only now mounting their prized buffalo ponies, which had been painted as well, medicine bags woven into their manes, animals so valued that they were kept in the tipis when raiders were around. They were the life of the tribe. There were several buffalo near at hand, wandering far up the slopes of the knoll to graze. The wind did not carry the scent of the Cheyenne to them and so they were utterly unaware of danger. Amaya saw one shaggy, mammoth bull which weighed as much as two ponies and was a head taller than she at the shoulder. It seemed to look at her with dull, tiny eyes, but see nothing.

Below, the vast sea of animals began to shift and stir with dawn. They got to their feet bawling and shoving, grunting in their massive, maned throats.

The men wore only breechclouts in the chill of morning. Their paint was vivid, their faces stark in silhouette, their bodies lean and competent. There was no speaking now. As noiseless as ghosts, they used sign talk to assign the areas of hunt. The buffalo ponies, which would stand for no other restraint, had only a rawhide hackamore tied around their lower jaw with two half-hitches. They would be guided more by the hunters' knee pressure, by their own instinct to run with a herd, than anything else. Many of the warriors had sawed-off flintlock muskets; others sat with their chokecherrywood bows, bound with sinew, decorated with feathers. A bare foot hooked under the buffalo horse's foreleg was the hunter's only grip; his hands had to be free.

The sun was red now, damp and macerated against the paling eastern sky. The ground fog still crept across the basin, working its way among the buffalo herd like fateful fingers touching those which must die.

The hunt leader lifted his arm and the horsemen moved down the grassy slope.

The horses began to move among the herd. There was a moment when the buffalo seemed to almost accept their presence, to accept the death the hunters promised. Then—perhaps because an arrow was fired, perhaps not—the head of the herd came up, and it began to run. There was no lagging, no hesitation. The entire herd had one mind at that time, and without warning it began to move, millions of pounds of ponderous life, meat and sinew, bone and cutting hooves, blood, great hearts, and shaggy summer-thinned hides.

The Cheyenne were among them and now there was no need for silence. Whoops of joy of the hunting animal were raised to the sky and the dark horsemen pursued the darker beasts across the red face of the rising sun. The women, with chanting and shrilling, cries of joy, holiday delight, moved down toward the basin. A lone lame calf bawled and struggled forward after the bulk of the herd. They paid no more attention to it than Yellow-Haired Woman should have. It was a poor crippled thing ill-suited for life and so it would not live long.

The first of the herd began to fall. They saw a huge bull with a dozen arrows in it dance and snort and charge a nimble buffalo horse while the hunter fired again, trying for the vital spot behind the ribs.

The hunters with guns had begun to take their single shots. They rode beside the fleeing buffalo and placed the muzzles of their weapons nearly to the hide of them and fired, black smoke rolling skyward. There were loud cries of success, moans following a missed shot or the misfiring of a flintlock.

In some quarters the game had turned. Men on horses fled the thundering herd. Others were trapped in the heart of the black crushing storm of living flesh. One brave went down as Amaya watched, his hands flung high, his mouth gaping open in shocked surprise. His cry, if there was one, was lost in the drumming of hooves, as loud as a summer storm rattling its way across the land.

She tried to watch Wanilak, lost him briefly in the dusty tumult, and then saw him again. A cow buffalo had briefly separated itself from the herd and Wanilak was beside it, arrows in his teeth, face intent, hair flying. Amaya saw him draw his notched arrow to the head and let it fly. It hit the quarry squarely behind the last rib, and Amaya saw the cow stagger and run on. Wanilak lifted his hands exultantly and then rode toward his next fleeing target.

She moved in the wake of the herd, toward the downed cow, which was rolling frantically now, bawling and roaring before falling suddenly silent, its heart stilled.

Amaya reached the cow a minute later. She knelt, opened her sack of tools, and removed her skinning knife. The heat of the buffalo cow was palpable, the scent of it, of death and animal confusion. The sun was growing hot as well. Amaya rose and turned toward the animal.

"What are you doing!"

Small Eyes was there, in her hand her long-bladed skinning knife.

"This is Wanilak's animal."

"It is my husband's," Small Eyes said. Her voice was very calm, her eyes excited, primal. The thrill of the hunt, of the kill, seemed to have taken over her.

"I saw Wanilak kill it."

"Where is his arrow!"

But there was none. The buffalo cow had rolled and broken off the shafts of the arrows. There was only the dark reddish-brown hide, the darker streaks of blood, the froth on the heavy lips, the dead eyes.

"I saw Wanilak kill it," Amaya repeated.

"Go away, Comanche whore."

Amaya stiffened. She stared into the face of Small Eyes, seeing not logic, reason, but the hatred of an animal, the need to claw, to destroy.

"This is Wanilak's animal," Amaya said again.

Amaya bent to her task, but Small Eyes hurled herself at her and Amaya was knocked back against the dead cow, her knife flying free, her breath driven from her body, her heart beginning to race as she knew with her senses if not with her mind that Small Eyes had come to kill her.

Amaya rolled away, and lifting her skirt, tucked it into her waistband to stand waiting for Small Eyes.

"Run, Comanche. I will kill you."

Amaya didn't answer. Beyond somewhere, the buffalo herd ran on, in confused circles, and the hunt continued, the shouts of the men, the pounding of the hooves, the explosion of muzzle-loaders, the swift flight of deadly arrows. Amaya excluded it all from her vision, her thoughts.

The woman Small Eyes was coming nearer.

"If you die, who will care?" the Cheyenne woman said. "I am Cheyenne, you are a Comanche bitch. I will tell them what happened. You tried to kill me for telling everyone that you took my beads."

"Small Eyes, this is madness."

Amaya wasn't looking at the woman's face now, but only at the hand which held the long skinning knife.

"Not madness. Destiny. Each time a Comanche dies, it is destiny."

She lunged then, the knife sweeping up toward Amaya's

bowels. She leapt back, tripped and fell, and Small Eyes stood over her, blotting out the sun.

The knife in her hand glinted. There was a matching light in her eyes, her tiny malevolent eyes. The smell of the dead buffalo, its warmth, was near. The grass was rich and bright green. Small Eyes looked briefly to the sky, her head thrown back as if in exultation. Then she came at Amaya, the knife arcing toward her breast.

Amaya saw the bulky form of the horse, the blue arm reaching down toward them as if from the sky itself, and then Small Eyes was scooped up and spun away. She kicked out angrily and shrieked as Amaya scrambled to her feet, backing away. The hunter on the tall gray horse reached out and took the knife from Small Eyes before he let her go.

Other people were coming toward them now. Nalin and Wanilak on his spotted horse. Small Eyes stood, her narrow, rounded shoulders rising and falling with emotion, watching Amaya. The warrior spoke.

"Go home, Small Eyes. It is done."

"No. This is my man's kill, Indigo."

"Yes?" Indigo slid from his horse's back, lifting one leg over its head, sliding agilely to the ground. He was very tall, erect, his chest deep, his muscles like twisted cable. He was painted a deep blue from his bare feet to his neck. His face was unpainted. It was a strong face, youthful, deeply bronzed, well-hewn as if from fine dark wood. His hair was knotted loosely to one side. Azure and white beads were tied into his scalp lock. Three eagle feathers shifted in the wind.

"What is it?" Wanilak arrived panting. His buffalo horse danced away nervously as he got to the ground.

"Small Eyes wishes to claim this cow," Indigo said. He was smiling faintly. He said nothing about the attempted killing, perhaps knowing that it would lead to nothing but further antagonism.

"That is my cow," Wanilak said with certainty. "I saw this spot on her flank."

"Lies!" Small Eyes shouted. The hunter looked at her with curiosity. There was something wrong with Small Eyes, perhaps. She would call Wanilak a liar over this? Perhaps she had to believe it to justify her own actions.

"I do not lie," Wanilak said without emotion. "Everyone knows that."

Indigo had taken his knife, and behind the last rib he had begun to dig. Now he raised out of his crouch and handed the arrowhead he had removed to Small Eyes.

"It is Wanilak's."

"Then I have made a mistake." Small Eyes shrugged as if it were all of no importance. She turned and walked away, brushing past Nalin and several other women.

"I am losing the herd," Wanilak muttered. "Then what shall I chew on this winter?" He went after his horse, and the women drifted away to get to their work.

Amaya looked at the tall man. He smiled at her. She turned away and got to the buffalo, beginning to skin its massive frame. When she glanced up, he was still there. She could see his blue leg and then his chest, rising and falling gently. She looked at his face and saw the sun directly behind his head, forming a glowing aureole. Rays of sunlight fanned out from behind his dark silhouette. He stood unmoving, arms folded.

"The herd," she said, turning her face down again. "It will get away from you, too."

"Then it will return."

"It may not return."

"Then I shall follow it."

"You may not be able to catch it."

"Then I shall wait for another."

Amaya laughed. She turned and got back on her heels. "If I do not do my work, then I shall be failing Wanilak."

"Work, then. I wish to see if a Comanche woman can work with the skill of a Cheyenne."

Amaya's mouth tightened. She brushed a strand of hair away from her eyes. Her throat was a little dry, her words a little abrasive when she asked, "Do you despise the Comanche as well?"

Indigo shrugged. "When they are my enemy, I fight them. Otherwise I do not consider them."

"You just wish to consider me. To hold me up to scorn. Go away. I can't work when you watch me."

"I must watch you. I told you, I must see how the Comanche woman follows the buffalo hunt. I am a man who takes many buffalo. I am a man who brings many furs. I am a man who will find fish beneath the ice when no one else can. I am that kind of man."

"Yes."

"And so I must watch you. You will have much work to do when I take you to my lodge."

5

HIS NAME WAS Indigo and he was a son of Gray Feather, one of the forty-four council chiefs of the Cheyenne nation. He was strong and handsome. He had been to war many times already and had always proven himself. He was polite and upright, acting with dignity yet ready to laugh at a good joke.

This was what Tantha told Amaya, told her constantly, excitedly. "He wants to marry you. I know he does. Since the buffalo hunt he waits near the creek, hoping that you might walk by. He asks Nalin about you. At night I have seen him on the big rock across the clearing, watching from beneath the trees, watching you, Amaya, when we work."

"Perhaps," Amaya said.

"Perhaps! That is what you say? But you must want to marry him."

"Why?"

"Why, because he is a man any woman would want."

"You, perhaps?"

"Me? I have my Stalking the Wolf. Very soon marriage gifts will come to this lodge from him—he has promised me this. I want no other man." She smiled. "No, I don't wish for Indigo."

"Then why would I?"

Tantha gave up in exasperation. She slapped her hips and then raised imploring hands to the sky. "Is it . . . because you are Comanche?" she asked, her eyebrows drawing together.

Amaya didn't answer. "I must go out," she said instead, and then she ducked out of the tipi and started walking very quickly through the pine woods, her hair loose, her head down. She walked until she came to the high rock where she often sat, and there she paused, looking down across the valley.

Is it because I am Comanche?

She didn't know. Perhaps. Not that she didn't like having Indigo's attention. She too had seen him watching her, perhaps hoping for a word or a smile. What did she know of this man? Tantha's praise meant nothing. Amaya felt that she would have praised any man who came near her. Tantha seemed to want Amaya to marry, to become a part of the tribe in that way, to find a place through Indigo's position, to become *Cheyenne* through him. It could not happen that way. She could not find her soul, her place, regain the feeling that she belonged on this vast and dreary earth by the simple act of marrying a man.

It was not enough.

She did not know if anything was enough. Moons faded and went to red and fell away into the cradle of the mountains. The night came and the stars chattered silently in the empty sky. The sun rose and the world was bright and ripe, sweet-scented. Life was given, taken. A moment's breath became eternity and then there was the long walk away from the world they knew. And nothing at all had been accomplished.

It was not enough.

She felt the voices of the ages in her blood, the prodding of ancient, undefined ambitions, the needs of the generations and of the generations to come. In her heart at night they cried out and urged her onward. But they did not say what was to come. Still it was real. She felt the tug of need beyond knowledge. And that was what she did not feel about Indigo. He wanted to come to her as a man and take her as a woman.

Neither was that enough.

It wasn't enough that her body was tempted by his, that he was a fine proud thing walking the earth, a creature perfectly attuned to his time, to his place; it wasn't enough that others wanted him. If he could only understand a part of that . . . but she scarcely understood it herself. She only knew that the heart alone knew the secret ways.

She sat and waited and watched and thought, but she learned nothing from the empty day. When she returned home, Tantha showed her the horn ring she was wearing.

"Look, Amaya! Do you know what that means? Stalking the Wolf has made his promise to our family. This is his gift of his heart." The ring, of polished buffalo horn, was lovingly made. Tantha, lost in quiet thought for a moment, smiled down at the hand which wore the ring.

Amaya smiled in empathy. "And so you will marry."

"As soon as Stalking the Wolf can bring horses for Horse Warrior. He does not wish me to be purchased cheaply, my man. This he has told me. But he has given me his heart," she said, looking again at the ring, "and so I can wait."

"And I will lose a sister."

"I will go away to his lodge, but you won't lose me. Not ever." Tantha hugged her and then stepped back. She started to sing, "Isn't it a lovely day this morning . . ." and they both burst out laughing. Still Amaya did not laugh long. The English song had brought back a host of memories, and more, a knowledge, a deep knowledge that she had not finished with the whites but had only tasted their bitter waters for the first time.

Tantha was too happy to think such thoughts. The two girls went out riding, galloping across the long grassy basin, and when they and the horses were tired, they swam in the lazy, sun-warmed river while cicadas sang in the willows and frogs chorused in the cattails and the sun coasted homeward.

The horses were at the family's tipi when they reached home. They rode through the camp at the sundown hour, smelling the cooking fires, the meat juices dripping onto the coals, the softer scents of the village settling for the night.

"Look!" Tantha cried out and sat up straight on the back of her pinto pony. Around the family lodge were a dozen ponies tied to the towering pine trees. Horse Warrior was outside, walking among them. He looked up as the women approached.

"Father," Tantha said breathlessly. "So many?"

Horse Warrior was confused for a minute. Then he understood. "Stalking the Wolf did not bring these, Tantha. It was Indigo who came with a purchase price for Amaya."

Tantha managed to smile as she turned to Amaya. "Good—you see! We shall both be wed soon."

"Is this my price?" Amaya said almost to herself. "Ten horses."

"What is the matter? I don't understand," Tantha said.

"Nothing. It is nothing. Please tell Indigo to come and get his horses."

Then Amaya led their own two horses off to rub them down and turn them out to graze with the rest of the Cheyenne herd. When she got home it was dusk. The horses were gone. Inside the tipi the family ate silently.

When Amaya had joined them, Mother Nalin said, "Sometimes when a warrior is refused he does not return." Nalin didn't look at Amaya. She pretended the conversation was a general one. Perhaps it was, at first.

"Those were fine horses," Horse Warrior said wistfully. He did not look at Amaya either.

Amaya looked at Tantha, but Tantha had given up trying to convince her sister to marry.

"Sometimes a man gets older and his eyesight is not so good," Horse Warrior said. "Then he wishes that his daughters may marry good young men who will help him in his old age."

"And sometimes," Nalin put in rather sharply, "one who is not so old complains about the loss of some horses. Tantha will have a husband soon to help an old man."

"Yes. Yes, so." Horse Warrior smiled faintly. His dark eyes were hidden in the shadow of his brow. "Sometimes, they say, an old man can talk too much. I do not want my daughter to be unhappy." His hand reached across the fire ring and touched Amaya's. "My daughter who has brought joy to me since she was sent to live with us. I had no daughter and I thought I never would again. Then, a great miracle occurred. My daughter who had been stolen away returned, and with her was another young woman, one who laughed and danced and worked diligently and wished to be a faithful daughter to me. You are right—what do I need with more horses than one?"

Amaya stood and went around the fire ring to hug Horse Warrior, who patted her hands. "Do you wish me to marry, Father?"

"I wish you to marry, yes. But not to please me. I wish you to marry to be happy and have babies to crawl across your lodge and suckle at your breasts and give you their new life. But not for me—no. Then you would hate me the rest of your days."

"I would not hate you ever, nor Mother, nor Tantha. We are a family, are we not?"

"Yes," the old man said, "we are a family."

In the morning the horses had returned. There were more of them this time, twenty in all, and beside the tipi was a beaded blanket and a well-made beaded saddle. There was a musket rifle with silver nails in the stock, a sack of powder, and one of musket balls. Three new blankets, white Hudson's Bay blankets like those sold at Bent's Fort, and a new skinning knife in a beaded sheath. Horse Warrior looked at the gifts and then at Amaya, his eyes eager yet ashamed of the eagerness.

"Amaya . . ." He turned to Tantha. "Go down into the camp and find Indigo and tell him to take back his gifts." Then, with a small sigh, Horse Warrior replaced the shiny steel knife and went into his tipi.

In the days that followed, Tantha and Amaya were together much. They worked, preparing for the winter to come. They did not speak of marriage. Stalking the Wolf, who had gone to seek horses, had not come back. He had started for the land of the Ute with three other young men, meaning to take Ute horses for prizes and give them to Horse Warrior for the marriage price. It had to be that way. Tantha would have married him with no price at all being paid, but Stalking the Wolf was a man with a warrior's pride. He would find the horses.

Now he had been gone for a week. The days had gotten colder, the clouds building day by day above the northern plains. It was time to move the camp again, to head toward the winter shelter. And Stalking the Wolf had not returned.

"Look," Tantha said. She was on her knees beside Amaya. They were washing the family's cloth garments in the waters of the creek. "There goes old Small Eyes."

Amaya looked up, following the woman for a way with her eyes. "She is a sad thing," she commented.

"Has she bothered you?"

"No more."

"Stay away from her anyway. She has a long memory, and a hateful one."

Amaya had begun to answer when they heard the shouts. Looking up, they saw people running toward the oaks, splashing across the creek. Then they saw the incoming riders, two of them, one of them slumped across the withers of his roan horse.

"Stalking the Wolf!" Tantha leapt up, her hands going to her mouth for a moment before she too was running, her eyes wide, her arms flailing, nearly stumbling as she crossed the stream. Amaya was beside her, her own heart racing, lifting with fear.

They had Stalking the Wolf off his horse now and were placing him on the ground. Someone was seeing to the wound, which appeared to be low on his side. It seemed very bad. There was blood everywhere.

Tantha was there beside him and he saw her. His hand stretched out to touch her hair. "A blanket . . . I'm cold."

"Get a blanket!" Tantha shouted.

"Someone has gone. It is all right. He'll be all right."

That was very optimistic, Amaya thought. Stalking the Wolf was pale, very pale, his lips blue, his eyes clouded. The other young warrior was not injured. He was telling everyone what had happened.

"We rode the Horn River looking for the Ute camp. Stalking the Wolf and me, Storm Eye and River Bear. The Ute camp was empty. They had finished their hunt early this year and gone back to their mountain home. We thought about following them there, but Stalking the Wolf said that was very dangerous. We rode on, looking for a small band of Ute who might have stayed behind—we had seen their sign in the river sand.

"Instead we found the whites."

"Whites! On the Horn?"

"Just so, hunters. Men in buckskins. We watched them for a day and a night. Then we decided to take their horses. We slipped their tether at night and started away with their ponies, but one of the whites knew the Indian ways. He had a rope tied onto his foot from his horse. He shouted and leapt up, waking the others.

"Their guns spoke many times, too many times to count. Storm Eye and River Bear died there—" A woman's voice shrilled a wail of mourning, interrupting the warrior's story. When her relatives had led her away, comforting her, he finished briefly. "Stalking the Wolf was shot. Only once, but it is bad, as you see. The whites chased me, but I lost them along the Fire Creek, bringing Stalking the Wolf with me."

They had brought another blanket to the spot where Stalking the Wolf lay, and they lifted him gently, placing him on it. He groaned and Amaya saw Tantha flinch as if she herself had suffered the pain.

Four warriors picked up the corners of the blanket, and they started across the creek again, Tantha with them; Amaya and dozens of other villagers followed them. Indigo was there and he glanced at Amaya, but he was concerned with other matters just now.

"If there are whites on the Horn," an older warrior was telling him, "they must be driven off, Indigo."

"They will be attended to," Indigo said a little grimly.

They were entering the village now. Nalin had come down the hill slope. "What has happened, Amaya?"

Briefly she told her, and Nalin went ahead to try catching up with Tantha. At Stalking the Wolf's tipi Amaya halted. The warriors who had carried him in soon returned to stand among the milling throng. The healing woman went in with her powders and yellow moss to help the wound. Once Amaya heard Tantha say quite distinctly, "No, and if you mention the horses again, Stalking the Wolf, my love, I shall leave and we will never marry!"

There were warriors going to and from the council tent now. Indigo had entered the tent and had not come back. There would have to be a retaliation against the whites, although if they were wise, they would be even now riding as quickly as possible eastward.

The old man with the blanket around his shoulders and the erect carriage of a much younger warrior stopped beside Amaya. When she glanced at him, the old man asked, "How is he?"

"I do not know. Conscious and alert."

"He is young. He will heal." He paused, deliberately looking at Amaya, her face, her breasts, her hips. "I am Gray Feather. I am Indigo's father. I wanted to see what you looked like, woman who makes my son mad."

Amaya respected age and Gray Feather's position as council chief; still she was angered. "And what do I look like?" she asked tartly.

"Like a woman good for childbearing, good for making my son happy, good for comforting me in my age, like a woman who has a good mind, a good heart. A woman sad and longing, but not knowing what it is she longs for."

The old man rested a hand briefly on Amaya's shoulder and then went away, moving slowly down the slope toward the council lodge, leaving Amaya slightly stunned, puzzled.

It was an hour before Tantha came out. She saw Amaya and stepped to her, hugging her. "He will live. They say he will live, Amaya."

"Then the world is bright."

"Yes," Tantha said, and she laughed harshly, softly. That mood passed. "I will get my things. I am moving here to watch my warrior until he grows well. I will not leave him." Her voice was defiant, as if Amaya had been trying to talk her out of staying.

"I'll get your things for you, sister."

Nalin must have read her daughter's mind. Tantha's clothes were ready when Amaya reached the lodge. "How is he?" Mother Nalin asked.

"Tantha says better."

"I will pray for him so that the spirits don't enter his body through the wound."

"And so shall I," Amaya said. "Stalking the Wolf is a good warrior, a strong man. He will not walk the Hanging Road for a long while."

"Not until he has made many grandchildren," Nalin said, brightening.

"Not until then."

Outside it was growing dark, the skies above the dark ranks of pines coloring deep crimson and purple. Indigo waited in the heavy shadows beside the path. He startled her and she stepped back quickly.

"What is it?" Amaya asked.

"Why won't you accept my gifts?"

"Haven't you other things to do on this evening?"

"Yes. I am riding after the white hunters."

"Then you must make yourself ready." Amaya started past him and his hand went to her arm, holding her back. He gripped both of her elbows tightly and stood looking down into her eyes, his face determined.

"I must marry you."

Amaya shook him off, and he stepped back, amusement and disbelief both on his handsome face.

"Don't you like me even a little?"

"I must go . . ." He held her again as she started away. "Please let me go," she said without looking at him. There was a minute when she thought he would not, and then the hand loosened its grip and she was free. When she glanced back, he was gone, vanished into the trees. Amaya hurried down the slope toward Stalking the Wolf's tipi, feeling an undeniable and inexplicable ache in her heart. Angrily she rushed on.

Tantha was sitting beside Stalking the Wolf, who slept, his face peaceful and young in the dim firelight. His father and his aunt sat silently on the other side of the tipi as Amaya entered. Tantha seemed not to notice her. She sat gripping his hand, touching the horn ring he wore on his finger. His heart. That was all he had to give, all he needed to give. A warm mist stung Amaya's eyes and she managed to trick herself into blaming it on the smoke from the fire. After leaving Tantha's things, she went out into the night and walked slowly home beneath the stars. Sometime later she heard the war party ride out of the camp and she rolled over in her blankets to stare at nothing, her hand clenched so tightly that it cramped and her fingernails bit at her palm.

There was nothing heard of the war party for three days. The Cheyenne spoke of little else. Amaya did not even want to think about it, but she did. She thought

about them, about the tall man in the night, the words of
Gray Feather, who seemed to see inside of her: "A woman
sad and longing, but not knowing what it is she longs
for."

Was it because she was afraid to empty her heart, to
give of it? All of her days had been clouded with a fear
that she was not as others, that they would reject her . . .
and what if that weren't so at all? It was a new thought,
a somehow terrifying one, a joyous one. It was too new
and too strong to deal with and so she refused to think
any longer. She worked; there was much to do, with
Tantha busy at Stalking the Wolf's tipi.

One night there was a shower of stars across the sky.
It was the night weeping, silver tears falling earthward.
The next morning the horses were around the tipi once
again.

"Oh, no," Amaya said when she saw them. There were
five of them, and Horse Warrior, grinning, was moving
among them.

"What is it, daughter?"

"Must we send them back again?"

"These are not for you, child. They are for Tantha."

"Tantha . . ."

"Yes. The war party has returned. These are the white
horses which Stalking the Wolf had captured and then
lost. The warriors brought them home and now they
have been given to me. And now"—he beamed—"we
shall have a new son in the family."

Amaya threw her arms impulsively around Horse Warrior and hugged him tightly. And so, it had come for
Tantha, the time she had waited for, the time Stalking
the Wolf had nearly given his life for. "Was it Indigo?"
she asked without looking at Horse Warrior. "Was it
Indigo who brought them?"

"You are asking if Indigo has returned safely, daughter?" When Amaya would not answer, the old man said,
"Yes, it was Indigo who brought the horses."

Amaya had started away before he added, "And something I was to give to you only if you asked after him."

Horse Warrior pressed it into her hand, and when she
looked down she saw the horn ring there. Only that.
Only the horn ring. Only his heart.

"What do I tell him now if he should return, Amaya? Shall I send him away?"

"Tell him ... that I will take him for my husband, Father. Tell him that he has said what a maiden needs to hear."

It snowed the following week for the first time. On the day of Amaya's wedding the skies were gray and the earth damp with snowmelt. Smoke rose from the tipis and the Cheyenne were beginning to wear their winter clothing, leggings with the hair side out, buffalo coats and furs.

Amaya, dressed in her finest white elkskins, her hair pinned with tortoiseshell combs, walked down the long hill to the new lodge, the lodge Indigo had built for her. There she was met by his female relatives, his sister, Moon and Stars, his aunt, Where the Waters Flow, and his old grandmother, a toothless thing who didn't seem to fully understand what was going on at times. Amaya was taken into the lodge and the women praised her beauty, her dress, her manners. They sat together on a new blanket and the women brought gifts to Amaya. Dresses and shawls, rings, bracelets, leggings, moccasins, baskets and bowls. Then, chattering happily, they dressed Amaya again in these new clothes, braiding her hair, painting red spots on her cheeks.

When they were through grooming her, Indigo arrived with his friends. They remained outside the tipi, calling for Amaya. Emerging, she was led back to Horse Warrior's tipi and Indigo was welcomed inside.

She watched him, thinking how proud and handsome he looked in his finery. He spoke easily with Horse Warrior, as if Amaya were not there, as if this were not the day of their wedding, and she worried until his hand covered hers and touched the horn ring she wore now.

"You are my woman, my wife," he said in front of everyone. "I protect you. I give to you. I am your father's son and the father of the children we will have. We are always to be together, and let there be no shame between us."

When they went out again, half the village was there. Tantha stood beside Stalking the Wolf, who leaned heav-

ily against her. Stalking the Wolf had similarly taken
Tantha for his wife three days before. Nalin was there,
looking a little bewildered. She whispered to Amaya,
"Go and find happiness. I know this man brings it to
you, child."

There was a feast with much singing which lasted
until midnight. Gray Feather was in high spirits and
kept saying to Amaya, "And so I am to have a grandson
by spring hunt."

Amaya watched and listened. The night was a whirling,
dazzling thing. She wondered suddenly what had happened. How had she been swept away by events? There
were moments when panic, blind and cold, set in and
she wanted to leap up and run away, crying that it had
all been a mistake, an impulsive error.

But Indigo was beside her and he knew. "It is right,"
he said quietly. "You have your doubts, and you must,
but it is right. I shall be a husband for all of your life. I
will never let you regret the moment."

Their wedding lodge was deep in the forest. There
were no eyes but those of the stars peering through the
branches of the dark pines, no voices but the singing of
the crickets, the whispering of the wind spirits in the
trees, and Indigo carried her in. He placed her on a bed
of pine boughs and furs and she sat looking up at him,
wondering at the moment, half-regretful, half-joyous. She
felt from moment to moment fear, excitement, unease,
eager anticipation.

"Shall I start the fire for us?" Indigo asked, and she
nodded. She watched him crouch down and strike flint
to steel, breathe the fire to life and sit back, watching.
"Amaya," he said, "I do not wish to force you to do
anything."

"You are my husband."

He smiled. He stood before the fire for a minute, then
crossed to the blanket which hung across the entrance-
way. He lowered that and slowly began to undress. When
he reached the bed, towering over Amaya, he saw that
she too was naked, lying beneath a blanket of fox furs,
her eyes bright, her dark hair loose and silky, high-
lighted by the fire. Indigo could not read her eyes—he
was not familiar with women, but only with weapons

and horses, with war and sports—but he understood her smile as she lifted the corner of the blanket and he went to her.

Amaya lay still, letting him stroke her hair, kiss her shoulder. She felt his breath against her flesh, the warm, solid nearness of him. Something stirred within her, welling up like the beginning of tears. It was a deep and vast tenderness toward this man whom she hardly knew, this man who had chosen her and given her the ring, given his heart.

She looked at his face, boyish in the soft glow of the fire, and she kissed his forehead, drawing him to her breast. Indigo was uncertain and then eager, shy and then bold. His hands were strong against Amaya's body, searching her, moving across her thighs, her abdomen, with a sort of wondering touch. He watched her face as he touched her, asking approval, and she smiled again, reaching up to kiss his mouth, to cling to him.

Amaya felt the blood stir in her body, felt a small, distant ache in her loins, and the nearness of his body, the weight of him against her, was good. It was a beginning. It was, she suddenly realized, also the end of another life, of all she had known to now, and for that she cried.

Indigo didn't understand. "I have hurt you?"

"No." She kissed him again. She kissed him until her lips ached and her mouth was dry, until her arms were weary of holding him so tight, clinging to him while the night spun away into tomorrow.

They did not go down to the camp again for a week. They walked the high mountains and swam in the icy pool they found there, slept naked in the grass among the few remaining wildflowers, which drooped now with the weight of time, the knowledge that winter was coming on.

There was nothing Indigo did not tell her: his boyhood experiences, his first battle, his wishes, the way his heart beat when he was beside her. Nothing, that is, but his dream. He would not tell her that.

They lay in the grass. Amaya was dressed but barefoot. Indigo was on his stomach, naked. She tickled his back with a long blade of drying grass. When she tickled him the muscles of his back rippled beneath his dark skin. They could hear the hissing of the small waterfall which fed the pool, hear the burbling of the stream which ran away down through the deep red fern. In the shelter of the trees there was no wind, and though the day was cool, they were warm. Amaya bent low, her hair draping itself over Indigo's back, and she kissed him on the knuckles of his spine.

"Tell me your dream, Indigo," she said. She lay beside him on her side and looked up into his thoughtful eyes. "Is it against a law to tell me?"

"No." He met her gaze, kissed her forehead, and shrugged slightly. "I just don't like to talk about it. It is nothing."

"It is to you."

"To me, yes. It is important. A dream is something that you can return to, grasp again, take strength from. It is truth because it comes from beyond the mind. It comes from Manitou and is the truth of the breathing universe."

"Then share it with me. You are my husband. We are close and growing closer. We are closer than I believed I could ever be with you, with any man, with any living thing."

"You mean that, Amaya?"

"I mean that. I want to know everything, to touch you in your hidden places, Indigo, as you are driven to touch me."

"All right." He told her then: "In my dream I spoke to the eagle and he took me high into the air, far above the mountains, which were purple and white with snow. I was not afraid because the eagle said: 'This is your land. You will live and prosper.' Then I was not in the eagle's talons, but on the back of a turtle, swimming a deep sea, but I was not afraid. The turtle said, 'This is your sea. You will live and prosper.'

"Then I stood on a mountain and I saw a snowstorm falling from out of a cold sky. It froze me to the bone. My eyes were like ice, but still I was drawn to look up. I was alone and I cried out to the sky and the swirling snow suddenly stopped. The clouds parted, and through the parting clouds a small, softly glowing object fell. An infant falling from the stars. And I ran to where it was falling and caught it and it became a woman, beautiful, radiant ... yes," he said, looking away, "it was you, Amaya. And we walked a way together."

Indigo was silent for a long while, watching the wind ruffle the grass across the mountain meadow, the clouds scudding past the jagged peak to the west.

"Then I came to the mountains again and I was alone. The great snake with the hairy face emerged from the rocks and it roared at me from a throat like a cavern in time. 'Indigo,' it said, 'look behind you,' and I did and the woman was there, and with her hundreds of people, some my own children—I don't know how I knew this— and all content. And the snake said, 'Do not pass this way or I will kill them all and waste their seed.' I told it we had to pass that way. Then the snake challenged me: 'Kill me, then, Indigo.' I found a long stick like a war lance beside the road and I pushed it through the snake's eye and it began to laugh. To bleed and die and laugh at once. 'Now you have killed them, Indigo. Now you have finished your people.'

"When I looked back, they were dead. My people. There were only a few wandering away from me in tattered clothes, and when I stretched out a hand to them, they ignored it, and when I called, they walked away."

Amaya asked, "The woman too?"

He shook his head. "I saw her no more."

They were silent then for a long while. Then Indigo told Amaya, "I can never kill a snake. It is forbidden me."

"By the dream."

"The dream which is the truth. As you are the truth for me," he said, and rolled her over on her back, pinning her to the ground, looking into her teasing eyes, his hunger for her, his love, growing with each pulse of his body.

They swam in the pool, which had grown very cold, and then lay together again. The sun was nearly over the mountains, which were deep purple, shadows gathering in their hollows and valleys, feathering the high ridges as the sky darkened into streamers of color. The ledge of rock held the heat long after the sun had gone and night had come on.

"You never have spoken to me of the battle with the whites. The men who shot Stalking the Wolf."

"It was nothing to speak of," he said. "They were not warriors."

"I would like to know," she said. He was a man not used to speaking, a sign of deep loneliness, Amaya thought. She was determined to enter his life, to be beside his raw, beating heart, for his life had become hers.

"They had already crossed the Horn and were riding away. There was no proper battle. We chased them until one of their horses broke his leg. Then we were met by gunfire. They were good men, but they missed with their shots. We did not miss with ours." He shrugged it away, though Amaya knew he must have ridden into the face of death, perhaps heard the bullets whisper promises of mortality in his ears as they whined past.

"They should not have come into our land," Indigo said in the darkness. She rested her hand on his thigh, and Indigo's hand covered hers. "If the Ute come, then they will pay the price of death. If the whites come, they will pay. If they are Pawnee or Crow or Arapaho, they must stay away from our land. They must not take our horses or kill the buffalo which belong to the Cheyenne. That is the way it has to be. I wish to kill no man; my people, however, must survive."

It was a long speech, delivered tensely, with much passion, and it surprised Amaya, who had not thought of survival as warfare. That was a warrior's way of thinking. To her it had always seemed trouble could be avoided, that they could back away from it, but now she did not know. Where would they go? Into the mountains where the Ute lived? Into the sea?

He wondered, "You have been with the whites. Will they come?"

"I don't know. I cannot understand them. There is a council far away which knows nothing about the war, and they make the decisions. The soldiers will follow any law blindly. They would ride off a mountainside to please the council or their great chief. There are others who come to make friends—if you will do as they say and be like them and speak their tongue and pray to their gods." Her voice softened. "I think there are also good men among them. A very few. But I do not know what they want, Indigo. When I saw them they wished for the Sioux, the Cheyenne, the Arapaho, the Snake, the Arikara to live inside a fence so that the white men would not have to fight them. Then the white men would come and give them meat and blankets."

Indigo laughed out loud. "I know you are making this up. What Cheyenne would live like that? What Sioux?"

"It happened. Yes, Tantha and I were there. The Indians came in and gave their weapons to the whites and sat down to drink whiskey."

Indigo could not even answer. He was angry, confused. Such a thing could not happen. He knew the people of the plains. Why would they give away their weapons and eat the white man's meat? How could they hunt if they were fenced in? How were grievances settled if not with weapons? A man *was* the earth and the sky and the waters that flowed, the quiet lakes, the great herds, his horse, his freedom.

"Never us," he swore, and Amaya echoed him. And the possibility was so distant and incredible that they laughed about it as they lay together on the rocky ledge, clinging to the way of man and the dream of the Cheyenne.

Their days alone were over. The nights had grown cold and the clouds which drifted in from the north had begun to grumble and growl with menace. They came down from the wedding lodge in the mountains carrying their bundles of clothes and essentials.

As they approached the camp, people nodded and pointed and a few cheered. A Contrary Society man named Turtle danced along in front of them. Old women laughed toothlessly and children scampered before them, calling to people in tipis.

"I can hardly look at them," Amaya said.

"Hold your head up. Be proud, Amaya. I am."

Tantha was coming toward them, and behind her, leaning on a stick, was Stalking the Wolf. Tantha ran to Amaya and hugged her, whispering, "It won't last long. We had the same thing yesterday when we came home.

It means only that they love us, that they know soon there will be new Cheyenne children in the camp."

At Indigo's new tipi his relatives waited and at the forefront was Gray Feather. Indigo stepped forward to embrace his father and to lead Amaya before his eyes as if she were a strange, gentle creature he had found.

"Yes," Gray Feather said, laughing softly. "I knew this would be—did I not tell you that, Amaya? Yes, I knew it. It came in a dream. And now you must tell me—will I have a grandson soon?"

"Perhaps," she answered. "We shall see. Perhaps when the new grass comes."

"Yes," the council chief said, "I think so. It is good. We do not live only so we may die. We live to continue life, and that is what has been done."

There were only a few days more then. A few days in the big-basin camp when Amaya and Tantha whispered together and laughed, while they slept with their men and the nights grew colder.

One morning Indigo said, "It is the day. We will go to the winter camp along the Horn."

Outside it was gray and white and the earth was a deep, damp color. The tipis were being stripped to bare poles. The cottonwood trees along the river were barren and crooked. The horses were being brought in from the long valley.

It was a clear, cold day when the Cheyenne moved southward. Indigo rode his big gray horse and Amaya the blue roan he had given her. The pretty, friendly pony with soft blue eyes and a long white mane. She called it Drifting Sky and loved it as a part of Indigo.

The people lined out across the plains, following the river southward. Their breath rose in steamy clouds. The horses, long-haired and eager to be moving, tossed their heads and pranced grandly along the trail, especially the half-wild buffalo horses.

The earth seemed to have slowed, to have stilled as the weather cooled, the grass going brown and brittle.

They traveled on. After the first day it rained for three days in a row, a hard-driving rain which cut into the earth and turned the river into a frothing rush. With blankets over their heads they continued on. Behind the rain would come snow, and they wanted to make their winter camp before it came.

They met the Sioux on the fourth day, near the Na-Hoi by the Little Valley Hills. Amaya was riding beside Indigo near the head of the party when they saw the Sioux come cautiously out of the brakes. They were not a large party, but they were at least as large as the Cheyenne group.

"Kalatha Sioux," Indigo said. "Spotted Sioux."

Amaya halted her horse as Indigo did. The band of Sioux emerged slowly from the brushy area along the coulee. They looked ragged, rain-sodden. As they neared the Cheyenne, Amaya saw that there were wounded men among them, several being pulled on travois behind Sioux horses. There was old paint on some of the horses. Amaya glanced at Indigo.

"They have been warring." It was an odd time of the year for it, and it didn't seem that the Spotted Sioux had fared too well. Indigo held his hand up as the Sioux passed through the drizzle of the rain. The Sioux and the Cheyenne had warred, but they had more often been allies. It profited nothing for the two most powerful plains tribes to war. The horse had changed things. It was too easy to make war, and when it became too easy, too many died.

Amaya saw the scowling, scarred man guide his horse toward Indigo and Gray Feather, who had come up to sit his horse beside Amaya. The Sioux who rode up to them had a name hated by some, revered by others. He was a warrior and a brave one, but too reckless.

"It is good to see you, Yellow Knife."

"Good to see you, Gray Feather. Good to see your son." The black eyes flickered across them. Yellow Knife had a blanket around his shoulders, but no shirt beneath it. Amaya saw why. A portion of his bandaged wounds showed in the gap where he clutched the blanket.

"You are well, Yellow Knife?"

"It is nothing. A battle won," he said, although the eyes seemed to belie his words. The Sioux straggled silently past still. The Cheyenne had halted in a body. Amaya could hear the wind speaking in the brush along the coulee.

"Arapaho dogs?" Indigo asked finally.

"Whites, Indigo. We have fought the white soldiers."

Indigo sucked in his breath. What were the white soldiers doing this far west? Yellow Knife told him, "They were pursuing me, from the fort at the big river."

"This far?"

"They wanted my blood, and so they came. You see, my people are not fat for the winter. We are going to be with Red Cloud on the Lodgepole."

"The soldiers," Amaya asked impulsively, "they are ahead of us?"

"A day ahead if they have not turned back."

"This does not concern us," Gray Feather said.

"The whites think there is only one Indian—the one they pursue. Do you understand me? Cheyenne and Sioux." Yellow Knife wrapped one finger around another. "The same to the blue soldiers." He put a hand on Gray Feather's. "I am sorry I brought them to you. Come with us to Red Cloud's camp if you like."

"Run? For what? We have many warriors."

"They have many guns." Yellow Knife shrugged. "Be careful. The man who leads these soldiers is mad, I think."

"No one will find us in the rain," Gray Feather said. "If they do, then there will be a fight."

There had always been fights, always war, but Gray Feather's wars of honor, of simple defense, were things of the past. He didn't understand it, but it was so. This was a different time. The ways of the centuries would have to be changed, changed radically. This was what Amaya thought, at least.

"He wants us fenced up or driven into the sea," Amaya told Indigo again, bitterly.

"The white man?"

"Yes."

"It will not be done. There are more Sioux, more Cheyenne, than white warriors."

"No, Indigo. No there are not. They told me in their school. There is a city to the east which has five hundred thousand white people living in it."

Indigo laughed out loud. The idea was preposterous.

"They were lying to you, trying to scare the Indian girls."

"Perhaps. But we do not want to make war."

"No. I will not make war, the council will not call for war. Unless they will it."

"By coming on your land."

"Yes. By coming on our land. By taking a drop of Cheyenne blood. By killing a Cheyenne buffalo. By cutting their long grooves into the breast of Mother Earth."

He lifted his eyes then and looked across the empty, rain-subdued land. He seemed to see his vision out there somewhere, somewhere beyond sight.

"You know my dream. I cannot be defeated." he said with confidence.

"You cannot be defeated," she said, and she leaned across to him as the horses plodded on. She leaned to him and his arm went around her, briefly holding her. They rode after that in silence across the cold, rain-soaked land.

They sent out riders to look for the white soldiers, and a party of scouts under Stalking the Wolf found them. They reported to Gray Feather. "They are lost, looking around in confusion for Yellow Knife along the great coulee," Stalking the Wolf reported. "They have lost his sign—and he had five hundred in his party! The rain has washed his tracks away. The soldiers stand and look at each other in the rain. They have yellow rainblankets—you can see them for many miles."

"How many soldiers?"

Stalking the Wolf laughed again. "Twenty. And what if they find Yellow Knife? They are lucky the Spotted Sioux have their women with them."

Amaya listened, not sharing Stalking the Wolf's amusement. Maybe the blue soldiers were few, but they must have done something right. They had inflicted casualties on the Spotted Sioux. Yellow Knife, a hunted man for years now, had turned his back on the river and was riding north.

Gray Feather also looked worried. And Indigo. "If they cross the river," Indigo said, "we must kill them."

"No." It was Gray Feather who spoke. His lined face was concerned, but composed. "I do not think so, my son. We have much to lose by joining Yellow Knife's battle. Nothing to lose by letting them cross our land. They will kill no buffalo."

"Our law—"

"Our law was made before the white soldiers came," Gray Feather said. "Do not argue against me, Indigo."

"No. I will not argue."

They rode on in the direction of the winter camp, not looking toward the river beyond the hills. The river where the white armies were. Sun Hawk had gotten down from his pony and as they rode past, they could see the shaman, shirtless, chanting a prayer which the thin tendril of smoke carried to the clouded skies.

6

WINTER BROUGHT ITS own peace. The snow fell day after day, and the river was fringed with icicles. The lake beyond the spruce trees was frozen solid. The oak trees stood like black iron against the background of white. The skies would froth and mutter, explode with lightning, and the wind would blow. Then suddenly the clouds would clear away and the sky would become bright, deep, endless. Then the Cheyenne would emerge from their winter lodges to hunt and to play, to be reborn.

The children played on the lake, sledding on frozen skins, laughing, shrieking as the tolerant elders watched. Tracks, deeply cut in the new snow, zigzagged across the hills where hunters had walked.

Amaya wore fur-lined boots, a fur-lined skirt, and a new buckskin jacket Mother Nalin had given her. Indigo held her hand as they strode through the deep spruce woods, the air clean and cold in their lungs, the snow knee-deep in the clearings, spotty beneath the trees. When he stopped, he looked at his wife. He looked and then he looked again. "I love you with all my heart, wife."

"I have waited too long to tell you?" Amaya asked. She was momentarily downcast and then she smiled and threw herself into his arms.

"Yes, little one. Too long. I see why you needed the new jacket. Soon all of your clothes will be too small. I will set all of my family to work."

"Sun Hawk says it will be a boy. A warrior like his father."

"A better man, I hope," Indigo said, momentarily thoughtful, perhaps seeing the end of his time as he saw the beginning of his child's. The child which was cradled soft and warm within the womb of Amaya. The child which could not walk, speak, or even be seen but which was nevertheless a bond of love. They went on in contented silence.

At the crest of the hill, Stalking the Wolf's brother, Hands on His Face, had built an eagle pit. They could see the bloody meat on the snow, the boughs across the pit.

"Look," Indigo said, pointing. "There is an eagle. And a big one."

He was very big, circling against the brilliant winter sky. His wingspan was greater than Indigo's reach. It caught the rising currents and spiraled high into the blueness above the trees. They withdrew into the spruce forest and watched patiently as the golden eagle soared and searched, its eyes watching for a white winter hare or a weasel against the winter snow. Then it would fall like a stone and tear the prey with its awful talons, talons like knives which could sink into the back of a buffalo calf and carry it away.

Indigo touched Amaya's hand and she saw the eagle begin its descent. It swooped low uncertainly, rose to glide across the serrated tips of the spruce trees, then came in again still unsure, its native cunning struggling with the need for meat.

The eagle dropped to the pit, talons reaching for the fresh meat. Hands on His Face's arms shot out, his hands gripping the eagle's legs above the talons. There was a mad flurry of motion, the flutter of the great wings beating, the maddened shriek of the eagle, and a brief moment when it seemed that Hands on His Face would be lifted from the pit by the efforts of the great bird. Lifted and carried high into the winter sky.

But Amaya saw the knife, saw it flash in the sunlight and tear at the eagle's heart as its terrible beak had ripped at its own kill, and the eagle lay still, nothing more than a bag of feathers against the snow, its life leaking out crimson and warm.

They ran to the pit, where Hands on His Face, shaken, ebullient, was climbing out. There was blood on his face, on his hands. The eagle's talon had raked his cheek. He looked up at them as they approached. "Ai! Look at this one, Indigo. Many feathers."

They admired it suitably. Many feathers for their lances and for their hair, many whistles made from the bones of the wing, many underfeathers to be used for cloaks and baby blankets. It had been a noble bird, killed in the only acceptable way, by a brave warrior acting alone.

Hands on His Face apologized to the spirit of the eagle for having killed it, "But my people need the feathers from your great wings, from your magnificent tail. We shall carry them proudly, and from now until I die I shall tell how great an eagle you were." That done, Hands on His Face grinned broadly, picked up the eagle by its feet, and headed off down the winter slope, half-sliding, half-running toward the village.

Amaya had a new admirer and he had begun to follow them. He moved when they moved and hid when they stopped or glanced his way. Except he hid in the open, crouching against the snow as if he were behind a tree. His name was Laughing Nose, an impossible name for an honored member of the Contrary Society.

"What have you done to cause him to be so devoted to you?" Indigo asked.

"Nothing that I know of." She glanced to the side and Laughing Nose halted his backward-walking motion to freeze in a parody of concealment. Amaya laughed out loud. "Perhaps he hates me."

"Yes?" Indigo's eyebrow lifted.

"If he loved me, would he not throw stones at me?"

Indigo smiled. "Perhaps. But even a Contrary must have serious moments."

The snows came again and the winter extended itself, growing bitter and blustery, frigid once more. No one ventured out. It was a quiet time for Amaya, snug in the bed of furs, lying with her man, learning one another, feeling the new life within her grow.

But the spring returned and the People came from their winter lodges to stretch their arms and look to the brightening sky, to rub their bellies and think about the buffalo that would be returning.

A Sioux named Short Leg came through their camp with all of the news. The Oglalas under their chief

Crazy Horse had fought a battle in the dead of winter with the white soldiers. The Sioux had won. The whites, who had been encroaching on sacred ground despite warning, were driven back.

"They did not return?" Amaya asked. The Sioux cousin was eating as he spoke. He swallowed now and shook his head.

"There were not enough of them."

"More will come next time."

"No." Short Leg shook his head. "I have been to Chalmers' Camp." Amaya knew the camp to be a trading post farther down the Horn where much dealing in furs and guns was done. "And they told me what is happening. There is a war in the east. A vast war. All of the whites are fighting."

"All of them?"

"Brother against brother. Perhaps they will kill each other. All of them. No soldiers will be coming west to avenge their dead brothers. The Sioux are victorious."

Amaya was dubious, but the news was good anyway. The white armies had stopped, turned back to fight their own kind. There was bad news on the heels of the good. It was old news by now, but Amaya had not heard. She was sorry she had to be told now.

"At Fort Laramie the reservation is empty. They haven't got enough soldiers to watch their prisoners. Too bad this did not happen before the rebellion."

"My wife was there," Indigo told Short Leg.

"So?" The Sioux looked up with curiosity. "I thought no one had escaped. Fifty men were hung. Some others were just saved by the white president."

"Fifty . . ."

"Yes. All who touched a gun. It was one reason for Crazy Horse's war. Some of those who died were Sioux."

"Thunder Horse?" Amaya asked.

"Yes. And his son. His son was one of the warriors who began it, wasn't he?"

"Yes." Yes, Black Oak was one who had begun it.

"Over an egg. All over an egg," the Sioux said. And yet it wasn't over an egg or the lack of supplies, the broken promises, it was over freedom, freedom taken away from a people who had to be free to live.

They stayed another two weeks in the winter camp and then the scouts began to come in with word that the buffalo were moving north. It was time the Cheyenne too moved, and so the camp was packed again. The mountains fell away as they traveled out onto the long plains, in the buffaloes' shadows. Amaya walked rather than rode. It was far more comfortable, and it had been a long while since they had had the chance to stretch their legs, to stride out and breathe the clean air in deeply. She and Tantha walked together and talked and laughed at each other's increasingly rounded bellies.

The spring was easy, the buffalo plentiful. The world belonged to the Cheyenne who hunted and played and loved and rode their horses madly, laughing, shouting, dancing at the festivals. Then summer came, and with it the time for Amaya's child approached.

"Two." It was Sun Hawk, the shaman, who told her that. "There will be two children, Amaya. I saw a falling star last night and it split into two fragments, one half falling north, one half falling to the south. Then I asked who was meant and they answered: the wife of the warrior Indigo."

Indigo was growing increasingly nervous, protective, almost insufferably helpful. He carried wood, brought water, even did the cooking. At other times a Cheyenne warrior would scorn such work as unmanly, but during the last month they helped willingly. Indigo was overwhelming with his attentions, however.

"Go away for a time, Indigo," Amaya said as she watched him fuss with her blankets.

"Go where?"

"Hunt. Go for a long ride. Fish."

"I do not care for that. Not now." He continued to fuss around the lodge and Amaya fell silent, resisting the urge to drive him off with a stick. She was angry for a while and then a smile softened her mouth. To think that he cared like that.

"Come to me, Indigo."

"I have work."

"Come to me," she said, stretching out her arms, and he went to lie with her, to whisper and caress and place his ear to her swollen belly where new life beat.

Amaya dreamed of a falling star that night, except within the stars she could see young faces, shining, frightened faces. The stars fell away and disappeared and when Amaya awakened in the dead of the night, hearing the crickets around the camp, the humming of insects, it was with a sense of loss and of uneasiness.

"Foolish thing," she scolded herself. Sun Hawk's story had managed to frighten her somehow. There was an omen implicit in it, an omen which was an evil, lurking thing.

Amaya rose each morning before sunrise and walked. That is when the baby grows, Mother Nalin had told her, and so it is then that it needs its mother to exercise. She walked through the soft haze of predawn, following the river through the oaks. A mile downstream and a mile back, reaching camp again just as the rising sun painted the river orange and shifting gold. She was careful not to look at anyone with a bad eye or anyone with an affliction; nor did she look at snakes or spiders if it could be helped—Nalin had told her that to do so might mark the baby.

The days grew longer as she grew heavier. Her ankles hurt as she walked, and in the mornings it became harder to roll out of bed and begin her walk. Tantha seemed to be having an easier time of it.

"But then, you have twins in your womb," Tantha said. "Sun Hawk has told us."

"Is he never wrong?"

Tantha only shrugged. "Our daughters shall be great friends, Amaya, as we are."

"Does Stalking the Wolf not want a son?"

"Yes"—she frowned in thought—"but I want a daughter now. There is time still. Time for him to have many sons. And I shall give him many."

"You still love him so?"

"I love him more than my life, Amaya. It is not good to love so deeply, they say, but I do love him that way."

It was in the dead of night that Amaya awoke and knew it was time. Her belly, so large, so taut, had stretched until it could stretch no farther. Now it had to expel the grown seed within it.

"Indigo."

"Yes."

"Go to Mother Nalin. Tell her to come here."

"Are you ill?" he began to ask. Then suddenly he understood. He started naked for the flap of the tipi and came back hurriedly for a blanket. His face was composed as always, but his eyes had his boyish uncertainty in them.

He turned and left hurriedly. Amaya saw briefly a sky crowded with stars and then the flap closed again and she rose to prepare herself.

Mother Nalin came quickly with Indigo's old aunt, Where the Waters Flow. Sun Hawk had been awakened as well and he waited just outside the tipi, singing his prayers, shaking his rattle as Indigo, wearing only his blanket, watched worriedly.

Tantha had arrived, her hair loosely knotted, her own belly distended beneath the blanket she wore. She glanced at Indigo and went inside the tipi.

Gray Feather and Horse Warrior squatted beneath the nearby oak and smoked a pipe together, awaiting the arrival of their grandson or granddaughter. A sharply defined crescent moon rose above the plains as if summoned by Sun Hawk's chanting.

Indigo was too distracted to notice Laughing Nose. The Contrary stood rigidly looking at the tipi, his long, fully arched nose painted a crimson hue, his eyes staring with deep interest.

"What is it? Oh, it's you. Did you want to know about Amaya? It's just begun."

"I do not care about the woman," the Contrary warrior answered.

"No. I know that."

"May I go?"

"Yes. Whatever you want," Indigo answered impatiently. He knew that Laughing Nose meant "May I stay?" when he asked his question. Indigo was in no mood for dealing with the ways of a Contrary just now. Laughing Nose sensed that and was silent. Inside the tipi a woman cried out briefly in pain and then was silent. Indigo closed his eyes tightly and clenched his fists, turning half away.

Amaya had been led to a bed of straw, and there she

knelt, firmly grasping an upright pole which had been placed in the floor for that purpose. Her forehead was beaded with perspiration. The chanting of Sun Hawk filled her head. She could hear nothing else. She opened her eyes and looked down at her hands clutching the pole so tightly that the knuckles were like white bone. She could see a moccasined foot and then feel a hand stroking her hair.

"It will soon be over, soon over," Mother Nalin said gently, and Amaya believed her. Briefly, until the next clutching wave of pain took hold of her belly and she bowed her head to the pole, wanting the night to end, wanting an end to pain.

Tantha was there. She spoke quietly in her ear, saying something, kissing her face as the pain continued, as the older woman did something behind her, as Nalin told her, "Push, push," so many times that it seemed as insistent as Sun Hawk's singing, as the whirring of his rattle. And she pushed but nothing happened except that it hurt more. She pushed again and thought she cried out, and she was ashamed that she had.

Then the incredible happened. There was a weight within her, a weight she could not expel, a weight which fought against her will, brought tears to her eyes, sent pain through her womb, up her spine, down her trembling thighs—and then it was out. Something incredible had happened and Amaya gasped, nearly laughing, nearly choking on a sob.

"It is born? It is alive?" she asked, her constricted throat and swollen tongue forming the words with the greatest difficulty.

"Alive, yes." It was Tantha who answered. "And well."

"A girl?"

A new pain had begun. She could feel Mother Nalin's knowing hands. "Again, Amaya. Again, daughter. There is another one. The shaman knew. The shaman knew."

The entire incredible process had to be repeated. Amaya bowed her head in frustration, then set her jaw and began, finding it easier, but only slightly easier, the second time. Her entire body trembled, ached. She pushed as Mother Nalin exhorted her, rested when they allowed it, sagged against the pole, wished that it would end, prayed that it would.

"That is it. Take the sack. Yes."

Something else was done, something that seemed suddenly remote from Amaya, and then incredibly she heard the sound of crying, the crying of two infants, and she looked across her bare shoulder, peering through the veil of her own hair, the tears of her pain.

"It is done?" she managed to ask.

No one answered. They laid her back and someone was cleaning her. Then there was a wriggling, a warmth that her body knew already. Her breasts ached with milk which was ready to flow, to nourish, to continue life.

The infant's head rolled instinctively from side to side, searching, and its tiny fist pawed at Amaya's breast until it found a place to suckle. Tantha was kneeling beside Amaya now, in her arms another bundle.

"And this one may be hungry too, Amaya. How good she is. Look at her. She does not cry."

"Girls. Both girls?" Amaya asked through the heavy veil of exhaustion.

"Both girls," Tantha replied.

"I thought so." She yawned. The second baby was placed next to her. The rattle and singing had stopped outside. It was still and dark. Moonlight peered briefly through the tent flap.

"Brush my hair a little, Tantha, before he comes to see his babies."

Tantha took up the porcupine-quill brush and gently smoothed her dark hair, wiping the perspiration from her damp forehead. The older women were finishing the necessary tasks. The placenta was placed into a rawhide bag. Later it would be taken out of camp to hang in a tree. To bury it, the Cheyenne thought, might cause the death of a child. A powder made of decayed cottonwood pulp and the dry spores of puffball fungus had been dusted over the new babies to keep them dry. They had also been greased with animal fat so that their new skin could protect itself from rashes.

There was only one more ritual to be performed, and that would be done much later. When the umbilical cords had dried and fallen off, they would be sewn into a decorated buckskin bag, shaped like a turtle or a lizard, with totem emblems on it. The bag would then be worn around the child's neck to ensure a long life.

"Is she sleeping?" Mother Nalin asked.

Amaya's eyes opened. "Not yet. Not until Indigo has come."

Nalin kissed her forehead, peeked at the babies, who slept deeply now, exhausted by their own ordeals. "I will bring your husband," Nalin said, rising heavily.

Tantha followed her out. It was a time for the man and his wife to be alone. Where the Waters Flow had already gone to take the good news to the two grandfathers, who had waited as impatiently as Indigo, who now came up to Mother Nalin.

"It is all good?" He took her hands anxiously.

"All good. She wants to see you."

Laughing Nose was standing in the shadow of the tree and when Indigo went into the tent he turned and slowly walked away. "Good night," Gray Feather told him.

"Good morning. Two boys. That is very bad, very bad!" Then the Contrary walked away—backward—into his own strange world.

Amaya opened her eyes to see her man. His eyes were deeply tender, old and young at once, loving. "May I see?" he asked, and at her nod he turned back the blankets, studying their tiny unformed faces by the moonlight. With a nod of satisfaction he kissed each, causing them to stir a little. Then he kissed his wife, with amazing gentleness. Amaya fell asleep in the middle of the kiss and Indigo went out into the starry, moon-bright night. The woman slept, the children slept, and so he walked a long way out onto the plains before he threw back his head and cried out his joy to the skies.

Their names were Akton and Hevatha, pretty dark-eyed, happy babies. Hevatha was called Moksiis by her grandparents, the common nickname which meant "pot-belly." Akton was a more serious child and such familiarity never seemed to suit her even as a toddler. They grew strong, playing, learning to hunt, to work, to fish, to be Cheyenne. In their third year the son Indigo had waited for was born. He came the night a shadow passed over the moon and so his grandfather Gray Feather named him Dark Moon. He was a serious little fellow with flyaway dark hair. He would cling to Indigo's back given the slightest chance and ride proudly wherever his father chose to walk.

"There is," Amaya whispered to her husband one night as the sounds of the children breathing softly in their sleep filled the tipi, "no other life. None better. No time I would choose over this."

"No man?" he asked teasingly.

"No man, my Indigo."

But when he looked at her there were tears standing in her eyes and he was puzzled, not understanding this woman's ways. He held her close to give her comfort against know-not-what.

In Amaya's fifth Cheyenne summer the white men came again.

"There were twenty of them. More perhaps," the young warrior Mountain Wolf said. He sketched their position in the dirt with a crooked stick as Indigo, Amaya, Gray Feather, and Stalking the Wolf crowded around him.

"Toward the Black Hills?"

"Yes."

"Are the Sioux aware of this?"

"Yes. Yellow Knife knows. He hasn't got his strength anymore, however. He watches them and turns his back."

The bullet he had taken years ago had lodged in his lung and the chief of the Spotted Sioux no longer was the warlike thing he had once been.

Indigo said, "We can't allow this."

"What are they doing?"

"I cannot tell. They are not hunting. They peer through a little glass and then pound a stick into the earth."

"Thank you." Gray Feather turned away, glancing at his son. Mountain Wolf, who had not eaten in two days, went off toward his stew pot.

"How can they dare to come this far?" the old Cheyenne chief asked. "The white war in the east is over. Does that mean the soldiers will return in force?"

"It cannot be allowed," Indigo said. "They must be driven out. Now. Today."

Amaya looked at him with distress. She understood, but these had been peaceful years and she had wanted them to be unending, knowing all the while that war hung over them, that it always would.

"No," Gray Feather said. "There must be a council, Indigo. All of the Cheyenne must council. It gains us nothing to kill these white men."

"It will prevent more from coming."

"No, I do not think so. I shall ask for a council." Shaking his head wearily, the old man walked away. Amaya watched him, struck by the rapid aging. He was white-haired now, very stooped, and his hands were unsteady. Indigo watched his father, thinking his own thoughts.

"I think we must fight," he said almost apologetically. Amaya only took his arm and looked into the distances.

There was a scream and a puff of dust and little bronze legs churning, chubby hands uplifted, and then Indigo, laughing, caught his son by the wrists and swung him up on his back. Dark Moon squealed with delight and Indigo went running off, a great man with a bit of the child in his heart.

"Amaya? You will work with us today?"

Tantha was there, in her hands a sack for gathering and a stick for digging potatoes. With her were her two sons, small, quick, appealing.

"Yes, of course. Are we going now? Let me call my daughters."

Akton and Hevatha were playing by the river. Now they came running. All work was play to them. They got to be with the older women and hear the tales the Cheyenne had told their children since time began.

Every able woman in the tribe started out toward the hills with their gathering sacks and their sticks, singing as they went, the children running between their legs, clinging to their skirts, spotted pups running after them. The hills were dry and the sky blue.

"Look," Tantha said, "the woman who will not forget."

Amaya had seen Small Eyes earlier, seen her glare. The woman was shrinking into madness. She was smaller now, or so it seemed, with flaccid breasts and deep glowing eyes. Madness. Amaya heard her say quite clearly: "I had children but the Comanche killed them before they could grow."

"Small Eyes . . ." But there was nothing to say to her madness. Amaya shook her head, biting her lip with regret and anger.

"Old crow," Tantha spat. But when she saw Amaya's furrowed brow, she said, "She means nothing. She has been talking for years."

"That doesn't mean she would not hurt the children," Amaya said.

"Hurt the children!" Tantha halted in her tracks and stared at Amaya. "You worry about nothing, Amaya. Small Eyes is only a discontented thing."

"A mad thing."

"You are suffering a mother's worries. The woman is old and bitter. Her only pleasure is to bring unhappiness to others. Pay no attention to her jabbering."

Amaya said she wouldn't, but she couldn't get it out of her mind that easily. This hatred had been festering in Small Eyes for years. There was no real basis for it, but that meant nothing. It was as real to her as madness allowed.

They worked then, and sang, scattered across the hills which still smelled of buffalo, digging the *pomme blanche* from the dark earth while the children tugged at each other or tumbled down the hills or tried to work beside their mothers. It was late for gathering Indian potatoes—they were best in the spring—but there were plenty, all of them of good size, three or four times as large as a hen's egg. They could be eaten raw (and many were as the women worked), placed in soups and stews, or dried in the sun for winter storage.

They worked along one hillside and then in unison seemed to realize they had done enough for the day, that it was hot and the tribe was not suffering from want.

It was Tantha who began it.

"While we work, the lazy men sleep in the village."

"Our warriors! Protecting us!"

"Warriors? The enemy of the Cheyenne could walk in here and slaughter us all, take our furs and our horses, and no Cheyenne warrior would so much as wake up!"

Akton and Hevatha were staring at their mother, wondering how she could speak against their brave father. Hadn't she told them how brave Indigo was? But the older children had seen the game before and they shrilled with wild delight as the women started back toward the camp, carrying or dragging their heavy sacks full of roots.

"Send out a scout," Amaya called, and Akton, who was now starting to understand, ran ahead, falling once before she reached the crest of the hill. Other children beat her to the rise and called back.

"The enemy camp is just ahead, warriors!"

"Be brave," Tantha told the women. She walked backward before them, holding up her hands. "We are facing our lazy enemies, but we are not afraid because we have superior weapons. We have great hearts. Take no prisoners, Cheyenne women!"

At the crest of the hill they paused, breathing heavily, placing their sacks down.

"What do we do now, war leader?" Tantha asked.

Amaya told them all, "Prepare for battle. The enemy will pay a dear price. Set up a bulwark here. Defend yourselves. Let the cowardly depart."

With much laughing the women set their potatoes in a row before them as a defense while others collected sticks and buffalo chips in their skirts, bringing them to the crest of the hill where Amaya and Tantha, like two war leaders, surveyed the camp across the river where a few warriors had come out to watch.

"And now," Tantha said, "let them attack if they have the spirit for it." She let out a challenging war cry and the men in the village jeered in return. Indigo emerged from the tipi and they saw Stalking the Wolf point toward the hillrise.

Amaya cried out, "Cowardly Cheyenne warriors. We have come to defeat you. You cannot stand against us. Flee! Run away or enter the fight."

There was an answering war whoop from the river camp and they saw Stalking the Wolf race for a horse. It was a poor swaybacked thing, a packhorse spavined and half-blind. Other men charged across the river on foot. Indigo was there, carrying a ridiculous shield, a rawhide bag which he held before his face as he let out a long war cry.

"If you want your share of this food we worked for, then earn it in battle, you men!"

While the older or more sedate villagers watched, the men charged the hill, Stalking the Wolf and Laughing Nose leading the attack. Amaya and Tantha began to hurl buffalo chips at Stalking the Wolf, who charged recklessly up the slope—as recklessly as his half-lame horse would permit. The buffalo chips began to pelt him now and he fell from the horse heavily. The women cheered and shifted their aim.

Laughing Nose, coming backward up the hill, was an easier target. An energetically thrown stick rapped the back of his skull and he started running back toward the river without having looked their way.

Indigo was leading a wedge of warriors up the hill and the buffalo chips began to hail down on them. They all had odd shields to try to protect themselves but the women hurled all the ammunition they had on the braves' heads until every last one of them retreated, waving frantic, mock-frightened arms in the air. A vast cheer went up from the women and they danced around hugging each other. "Now you will stay alert, you lazy things," Tantha called after them.

"Mother."

Amaya turned just as Havatha slumped to the ground. There was blood trickling down her face. Amaya cried out and scooped her up, parting her hair to find the cut. There was an inch-long gash above her left ear and blood still flowed freely. Amaya placed a cloth on it and held the child while the women gathered around with concern.

"A stick must have hit her."

"Was someone throwing rocks?"

"Too bad, poor thing. It was an accident. We should have sent the children home."

But Amaya, holding the silent, trembling little girl, saw only the incredible cruelty on one face, the malicious glee in the deep eyes. She felt her stomach turn, her muscles knot with blind rage.

"I will kill her!" She started to her feet. Tantha held her back.

"Please, Amaya."

"Did you see her face? Small Eyes enjoyed it. She would have been pleased if they were dead, both my girls and Dark Moon as well."

"She is a hateful thing, but that doesn't mean she is responsible, Amaya."

"She threw a rock at Hevatha."

"Perhaps!" Tantha said strongly. "Perhaps it was after all an accident. An accident which the mad one enjoyed."

Amaya had gotten control of herself again. Hevatha stood looking up, her arms outstretched. She would not cry. Cheyenne children were taught never to cry. That could locate the tribe for an enemy. Amaya picked her up and held her closely, kissing her sun-warmed, childishly fragrant hair, swaying a little. Tantha's hand fell away, and the women around them began to disperse, to collect the potatoes.

It was late now, the sun rolling toward the mountains. Indigo was on the near side of the river, hands on hips, watching with concern. On his neck was Dark Moon.

"What is it?" he asked Amaya, and she told him. He frowned deeply, his face a mask of anger. "You are not sure?"

"No one could be sure in that crowd, but I am sure in my heart."

"That is not enough." They started across the river, which was only to mid-calf now. Indigo had picked up Akton as well. Her little brother pulled at her hair out of jealousy. "We will have to watch the children, that is all."

"Speak to your father."

"To have the woman banished? No. What would become of her? Where would she go?"

"What will become of our children?" Amaya said hotly, but at the same moment she knew that Indigo was right. She could still feel compassion for Small Eyes, the woman she hated more than anyone else in the world—except the whites.

"There will be a great council. Gray Feather told me today. All of the clans have agreed. The forty council chiefs and the four principal chiefs will meet on the Lodgepole, at the cottonwood island, in one week. We are leaving soon, all of the People."

"It must be," Amaya said. She looked up at her husband, smiled, and said, "I will begin to bundle our possessions."

The girls were put to bed. Dark Moon was crawling around restlessly. Amaya stood outside and watched the stars. It had been a mock battle, a game, a way for the women to relax after a hard day's work and extract a little revenge on the men. Only a game. Yet blood had been drawn. Her daughter had been hurt.

There would be a council meeting. The whites were coming into the land of the Cheyenne again. Something had to be done. And what if it was war? Would there one day be another battle, another army, not so innocuous as theirs attacking the camp? Another daughter or son injured, more blood? It disturbed her. She grew tired of thinking and was grateful when Indigo slipped out to stand beside her.

"They sleep."

"Walk with me," she said, and they started slowly toward the river, which was almost blocked out by the hundred tipis of their camp. They passed the Quillers Society tent where the fine handiwork of the Cheyenne was done by these women of Cheyenne aristocracy, said good evening to Crooked Foot, and then were at the river, walking slowly, arm in arm, toward the trees beyond. It was night and not at all warm, but the huge rattlesnake lay coiled in the riverside path, its body poised, ready to strike. It was as thick as Indigo's forearm. It was also silent. A freak of nature or a very old, very sick snake, one which was shedding its skin—they did not know, but it was a bad omen. Indigo stood perfectly still, waiting for the snake to decide what it was going to do. He could not kill it, Amaya knew; his dream forbade it. Indigo could not be defeated, nor his people moved from their land. That was the promise of his dream. To kill a snake was to break that pact.

They waited silently, watching, and after a minute the snake slithered away, making tiny scuttling noises in the leaves beneath the river trees as it continued on toward its own serpent destiny.

"At least," Amaya said in a laughing whisper, "it did not have a hairy face."

"No!" Indigo laughed. The snake in his dream had had

hair on its face, as Amaya remembered. They were alone now beneath the trees and Indigo drew her to him.

"As if we are young lovers," Amaya whispered.

"We are young. We are lovers," Indigo said. Amaya's fingers were on his shoulders. Her eyes caught the starlight through the trees and reflected it back warmly. He kissed her and held her tightly for a long while, one hand between her shoulder blades, the other at the base of her spine, pressing her to him. He seemed to tremble slightly and Amaya couldn't imagine why unless somehow the old snake had worried him. Was there more to his dream than she knew?

She pushed all of her concerns away. War and dreams of war were not for this starlit night. It was cool but she and Indigo went through the trees to the river. They stripped off their clothes and dived into the dark, quick current, to emerge, wipe back their hair, and stand together, clinging to each other beneath the starry sky while the river rushed past them like time flowing away.

In the morning the tribe rose with the orange dawn. Amaya and Indigo took down their tipi, rolled the hides, and tied them onto the poles which were used as travois. These were tied on behind the black horse, the stocky little one with the deep chest and the white ear, and there, in a small wicker cage, a protesting Dark Moon would ride. He wished to be with his father, he complained. Amaya quieted him. "If you're good you shall ride with me later."

The girls were old enough to ride the little dun pony. They were as alike as a reflection in a quiet mountain pool. Hevatha, the lively, laughing one, guided the pony while the silent one, Akton, rode behind her, small arms around her sister's waist.

"Are we ready, then?" Indigo asked. The leaders of the party were already crossing the river. The day was bright with only a distant coven of white clouds on the northern horizon. The grass was high against the horses' hocks, the meadowlarks flashed away on stubby wings, their yellow bellies as bright as flowers; wild timothy lay across the land, and black-eyed susans. There was purple aster in the hollows and mushrooms of many hues sprouting along the sandy bottoms. Antelope dashed away, but they had nothing to fear. The Cheyenne were not hunting.

There were hills now around them, rising off the plains to be sheared by the running water, forming hundreds of tiny plateaus where sage and gramma grass, cottonwood trees and sumac flourished. They frequently saw mule deer and twice cougar on the prowl.

On the second day they camped near the fountainhead where the basaltic cliffs to the west pointed the way to the stark purple Rockies. The Lodgepole was two days distant. They had seen smoke that evening, smoke that indicated another Cheyenne camp.

Mother Nalin was anxious for the great congress on Cottonwood Island. "I have a cousin who married a man of the Omissis clan. I have not seen her for twenty years. Her name is Fawn. Slender and beautiful—oh, the young men all wanted her. She married a warrior called Great Heart. But there was another young man called High Top Mountain who used to sing outside my cousin's lodge all night for weeks and weeks. Now he is one of the four great chiefs."

"Yes," Amaya said, "I know."

She recalled High Top Mountain from the camp on the Arrowpoint. He had been the Cheyenne leader who met with the Comanche, who stole away in the middle of the night to avoid the coming battle. That memory brought back a rush of other memories. The guns crackling, Osa lying dead on the ground, the blood painting the earth dark. Mother Nalin said something to her but she didn't hear it. Amaya touched the older woman's arm and said, "I'm sure your cousin will be happy to see you."

She called the girls to her then and they went to find Tantha. She was just beginning the evening meal. Her two sons squatted nearby, watching hungrily.

"Amaya. What is it, sister?"

"We are going to wash in the river. Come with us."

Tantha hesitated, then put her spoon aside. She stood, wiping her hands on her skirt. "Yes. Boys, let's go to the river and wash."

They didn't look eager to go down to the river with the women and girls. They had spent the day pretending to hunt, chasing rabbits with stick bows and arrows. At a river ford they had daubed mud onto their faces, pretending it was war paint. Nevertheless they went along, and in a minute they were talking to Akton and Hevatha—or rather teasing them, pushing them when they thought no one was looking, pulling their hair.

They walked a long way from the camp, following one of the winding streams which cut through the maze of hills and broken bluffs. The evening was cool, the sky clear. Frogs chorused in the willows and fish broke the surface of the shallow stream, snapping at the insects lying there. The bluffs were painted a deep violet by the dying sun. It was still and empty.

"Here, then?" They had found a quiet pool, nearly encircled by a horseshoe of willows and cattails. A sandy island projected into the pool. Amaya nodded.

"In, children, into the water. Akton, wash your hair."

She stood watching them for a minute, liking the roundness of their youthful bodies, the play of the gilded water around them. "I will watch them if you would like to swim," she told Tantha.

"Go first, Amaya, if you want to."

"It doesn't matter. Go ahead."

"Spank those boys if they aren't good for you," Tantha said with a sternness which was only half-felt. She touched Amaya's shoulder briefly, then went away toward the other side of the willows, undoing her hair as she went.

It was still. Tantha moved through the willows, hearing the frogs and crickets, the cicadas fall silent at her approach. She looked to the bluff ahead, liking the deep violet and black shadows which alternated along its rough face. Distantly a crow winged against the deep velvet sky.

She came to the river's edge and stepped from her dress, hooking her moccasins off with her thumbs. Then she stood a moment, arms outstretched, breathing in slowly, deeply, enjoying the sensation of being alive, of being in her own body. Her hair was soft against her narrow back. The faint breeze was pleasant as it moved against her body. She stepped toward the creek, but a slight sound at her back brought her head around sharply.

There were two of them there. White men with long

beards and guns in their hands, wearing tall boots and faded shirts, wide hats.

"What do we have here, now?" one of them said.

"Go away, men," Tantha said in her school English. She picked up her dress and held it against her breasts, backing toward the water.

"She speaks, does she?" The taller of the men laughed. He had a red beard and eyes that seemed to look in two different directions. They walked toward Tantha and she backed up again until her heel touched the water.

"Just hold it there, woman. We won't hurt you. You want plenty wampum lay with white warrior?"

Tantha dived for the water, hearing a yelp behind her. She was into the shallow water, paddling away blindly, when the hand locked around her ankle and dragged her back. She kicked at his bearded face, screamed with all of her might. The man laughed, and pulled her up onto the beach.

"Hold my weapon, will you, Lou?" the red beard said. Then he laughed again. Tantha tried to slam her knee up between his legs as he got down, pressing his weight against her, but he turned aside. She clawed at his eyes, drawing blood from his cheek.

"Damn you, you little bitch," he snarled. She saw his knotted fist rise and saw it fall. It snapped her head around and filled her brain with fire. She tried to struggle, but she couldn't move. The blow had numbed her body so that she could only lie and stare, hearing the laughing as the fist rose again, and again was driven into her face. Then Tantha heard nothing at all.

Amaya's head came up. She hissed at the children, "Get out of the water. Get back to the camp! If you see anyone, hide in the bushes."

"What is it, Mother?"

Amaya didn't answer Hevatha's question. The other children took her hands and pulled her out of the pool, not stopping to inquire what had happened, but doing what they had always been taught to do—obey on a moment's notice. Who knew when the Ute or the Arikara might come? The children rushed off through the willows without waiting to dress.

Amaya watched them for a bare second, then started toward the other fork of the creek. A scream sounded again and then was broken off abruptly. Amaya halted, crouched, picked up a long jagged branch from the sandy earth, and hurried on, her heart hammering, her breath shallow, heated, her eyes wide and determined.

She saw the flash of color, faded red cotton, through the brush. Then she saw the other man, rocking against the ground in a motion inexplicable until Amaya saw the still form of Tantha beneath him.

She might have screamed out in her anger—she was not sure. She burst from the brush and ran past the man who was watching, a rifle in either hand. Amaya's arms swung up violently, and clenched in them was the jagged willow branch. The man with the red beard turned his eyes to Amaya so that his face was visible as the pointed end of the stick with all of Amaya's strength behind it drove into his belly, tearing at entrails and organs. Blood flowed from his mouth and as the red-bearded man tried to scream, it strangled his voice. He rolled away and Amaya tried to stab him again, but the stick was embedded too deeply and she could not extract it.

From behind her there was another shout. She spun as the white man came forward. "God, Tom!" he was saying. "Tom!" Then his eyes went to Amaya and he lifted a pistol from his holster. "You murdering slut savage," he said, and his voice was level despite the frantic dancing light in his cold eyes.

"Who is the savage!" Amaya spat back in English. "Who is a murderer!"

The man halted his motion, frozen momentarily by the shock of hearing perfect English from yet another Cheyenne squaw. It made Amaya somehow less a thing to be used, to be killed without compunction, more of a woman, a human being.

That conviction didn't last. The white man could see that his partner was dead, that the other woman, if not dead, was badly hurt. He was alone in enemy territory and what had seemed like a little fun had turned into a nightmare. He had to kill the other woman now. If he didn't, she was going to tell her people what had happened and then it would all be up.

Slowly he put the pistol away and drew a long knife from his belt. He wanted to do it quietly. If she didn't run . . .

He thought no more in this life of anything. The arrow struck in the middle of his back, entering beside the spine, passing cleanly through two ribs to strike heart and lungs with the force of a bow designed to kill a bull buffalo. The arrowhead was protruding from his chest when the bearded man looked hazily at Amaya and toppled forward on his face, to lie twitching on the sand. Amaya didn't even see him fall. She was already to Tantha, trying to slap life into her face, trying to urge her lungs to take in air.

Laughing Nose came forward, his bow in his hand. He had held the bow properly this time; this time he had not been contrary. Even now, however, he managed to utter, "The white man lives."

"Laughing Nose. Please, please, help me carry her to the village!"

The Contrary nodded, put his bow over his shoulder, and scooped up Tantha. Amaya placed her dress over her inert body and started off, leading the way. They were nearly to the village before a party composed of Stalking the Wolf, Hands on His Face, and Crooked Foot appeared on the run. The children had taken a long while getting home.

"What happened?" Stalking the Wolf was badly shaken, enraged, a little frightened. Briefly Amaya told him as they rushed on toward the village.

"Are there more whites? Hands on His Face! Take a dozen men on horseback, scout ahead," Stalking the Wolf shouted, and his brother took off at a run through the trees around the camp, Crooked Foot behind him a length.

"How could this happen? Who were they?" Stalking the Wolf kept asking. "It was only a blow to the face. Do you see a wound? Was it only a blow to the face?" Then in a fury he threw his bow away and it went whistling through the air before striking an oak tree and snapping in half.

Indigo had arrived now, and Mother Nalin, her hands

to her mouth. Laughing Nose was grim, his devotion to his society set aside for the time being. When they reached Stalking the Wolf's lodge the Contrary took her inside and placed her gently on a bed. Mother Nalin was beside her, cooing, mopping her brow gently. Tantha's eyes seemed to flicker a little; then there was nothing. Amaya spun and went outside, too angry to speak, to see.

"Amaya. Amaya." Someone was tugging at her skirt.

She looked down at the two dark, earnest faces of Tantha's sons. "Is our mother sick? Is our mother hurt?" And then the smaller one asked, "Is she dead?" and Amaya felt her heart swell and turn over. She rested a hand on each boy's head.

"She is ill. She must rest now and get well. Come stay in my lodge and eat with us. Indigo will tell you stories of the Great Bear and of the long hunts in the land of the firefall."

The older boy was eager, but the little one hung back. Amaya turned them, taking their hands. "Come. Your mother says to go with me. Go with me, then."

They had taken half a dozen steps only when the horrible deep-voiced cry filled the air, echoing through the camp so that every head turned toward the tipi of Stalking the Wolf, and Amaya knew and so she hurried the boys on, ignoring their questions.

In the morning Tantha was placed on a litter in the branches of a huge black oak tree, her best quilt under her, her finest beaded dress on her body. With her, too, clenched in her small hand, was the horn ring Stalking the Wolf had worn. He could wear the ring no longer. In sorrow he had taken his knife and removed that finger, slashing his face when he had finished that, until it was a mask of blood. All night long he had moaned and sung his death song, and the sons of Tantha sat awake, staring at the empty sky.

"And if I had gone first it would have been me," Amaya said. "If I had bathed first—"

"It does no good to think like that. Today your children might have no mother. Would you have it that way?" Indigo asked.

"She was my sister," Amaya said.

"Yes."

A sister not by blood, but by choice. A girl who had come to Amaya and said, "Please be my sister, live with my people and share my blanket." There would never be another like her.

The scouts under Hands on His Face had ridden in to report that there were no more whites in the area. These two had apparently been looking for yellow dust. The Cheyenne party had found their camp and two sacks of the stuff hidden in their bedrolls. Indigo sent out other scouts. Nothing like this would be allowed to happen again.

They traveled on their way, but not before the short ceremony, held beneath the oaks, where the wind whipped the fallen leaves around their legs.

"My sons," Stalking the Wolf told them, "must have new names from this day." The two boys stood there trying to be brave, to look taller than their years. "I call them, therefore, Hatchet and Remembers Long. So shall I call them; so shall you call them."

Akton, who was nearly five, clung to her mother's skirt, listening to the tall man with the newly scarred face, looking at the little boys beside him. Something sad and terrible was happening, but she did not quite understand it.

Camp was broken silently except for the yapping of the dogs. Then silently they trailed southward toward the great council camp.

The next day found them within sight of the Lodgepole and the long cottonwood-covered island which the river flowed past, bright and silver. There were many lodges on the far side of the river, many along the near bank. On the island itself was only the single great yellow tipi, the medicine lodge where the council was to be held among the ten Cheyenne bands. As Amaya and Indigo led their people down off the grassy hills toward the encampment, other Cheyenne came out to meet them, Hevataniu and Omissis, Fox Cheyenne from the far north. There was welcome on their faces—the People were one again—but there was little joy. It was not a time for it.

As soon as the camp had been made, Gray Fox dressed in his ceremonial finery—beaded elkskin shirt, war bonnet trailing eagle feathers down his back. He carried his tomahawk pipe carved of red stone from the sacred quarry.

Indigo had dressed as well, braiding his hair, knotting feathers and ermine into his hair, wearing his silver-and-turquoise necklace. "The civil chiefs, the forty-four, must decide what is to be done," Indigo had explained, "but the war leaders must have their say too."

"And what will you say, war leader?"

"I will say we must drive out any white that crosses the Horn, Amaya."

"And begin a war."

"They have begun it." He took her shoulders a little roughly. "You hate the white man."

"I love our people. I do not want war."

Indigo shrugged and turned away. "Perhaps there will be none. Gray Feather feels as you do, that there is no real threat. That it is pointless to declare war against these few whites."

"Are you so eager to war?" she asked.

"I am anxious for my people." He turned away from her, but his back was expressive. "A few whites. A handful. It took only two of them to murder Tantha."

"Utes might have done the same."

"Then I would vote for war upon the Ute."

Amaya fell silent. She walked to him, rested her head on his back, and put her arms around his waist, holding him tightly. "I only want what is best for our people. I think peace is. The old chiefs will know best."

"Do you want to go with us?" Indigo asked. He turned, taking her hands. "Serve? You said you have been present at a council meeting before ..."

"Long ago, Indigo!"

"Then serve. You are Gray Feather's daughter-in-law. No one will object. Come and listen to what is said."

"All right. I will. It's not too late?"

"I'll go and find out. Why should you not come?"

Amaya was already changing her dress, frantically digging through her pack for her good dress—the one which Tantha had given her to celebrate *massaum*. Dark Moon was playing with a tiny bow and arrow, shooting at straw dolls. He made small hissing sounds with his breath. She heard him whisper, "Dead white man. Other dead white man," and she stopped, staring at the child. He knew already. If this child's vote could be counted, it would be war. War for the sake of Tantha.

The girls were playing somewhere. There were many games going on across the vast camp. She could see a group of older boys, perhaps a hundred of them, the future warriors, playing "knock him from his horse," a rough, bone-breaking game meant to inure them to pain and the fear of battle. Indigo was not in sight, nor Gray Feather.

She did see the small, furtive figure of a woman scuttling away, a woman who must have been just standing, watching her tipi. Amaya softly breathed an oath. Would Small Eyes never forget her empty hatred?

Indigo was returning now, walking swiftly but unhurriedly, a man of dignity, careful to maintain decorum among the assembled Cheyenne. He was, after all, the war leader of his people. No shame must fall on him.

"Finished dressing?"

"Almost."

"They can use another woman. Please hurry."

Amaya paused a moment, looking toward the place where she had last seen Small Eyes. "I want someone to watch Dark Moon."

"Mother Nalin has taken the girls to swim. I can ask Laughing Nose."

"Will he do it?"

"He is fond of the boy, he would 'refuse' in an instant."

Amaya smiled, but concern erased the expression quickly. Something had to be done about this situation. She couldn't go through the rest of her days with this threat hanging over her children. Still in her heart she was sure that it was Small Eyes who had hurt Hevatha, and she was convinced that the old woman would do it again, given the chance.

Now she finished dressing, putting silver buckles in her hair, changing to her best moccasins. When she was finished, Indigo was back with Laughing Nose, who after a little contrary banter settled down to play with Dark Moon. The man seemed to be at home with a child of that age.

"Hurry, please," Indigo said again.

"I've never seen you this anxious."

"I must know," was all Indigo said. "I must know if it will be war."

7

THEY CROSSED TO the island on a raft which was decorated with flowering shrubs, like a tiny floating garden. There were no clouds in the sky, not a whisper of wind. The drums from within the depths of the cottonwood forest were muted, constant. There Sun Hawk and the other shamans made their magic and asked that the leaders of the nation be brought to the proper decision. The great yellow lodge was in the center of the island, in a clearing surrounded by huge twisted trees. A chief of the Omissis, his war bonnet trailing the ground, came forward to make them welcome.

The drums stopped and their heads turned automatically toward the grove where the shamans were.

"So," Gray Feather said. "They are finished with their work. Let us begin ours."

Inside the vast lodge it was dim and silent. The great chiefs and great warriors sat together smoking the ritual pipe. The scent of *kinnikinick* was in the air, and the softer scents of tanned elkskin, yarrow soap, bear oil, of iron and of pine, of buffalo and of the centuries.

Amaya moved among the men, serving them. Their eyes, she noticed, were all very sober. Their mood was dark. Perhaps she was imagining it; perhaps her own fears were coloring her perceptions.

High Top Mountain was near Gray Feather. These two supreme chiefs watched Amaya, Gray Feather with pride, High Top Mountain with puzzlement until his eyes lit, his lips parted, and he turned to whisper something to Gray Feather, who nodded. He had remembered her, remembered the Comanche girl from long ago.

Amaya withdrew to sit to one side while the council members spoke. "The land is wide," one of the supreme chiefs said. He was narrow, his chest sunken now, but his head was held high. His eyes were bright. "We have shared it with the Sioux. We have given even the dirty Arikara and the Shoshoni permission to hunt our lands, to cross to the mountains. Why should we behave differently with the whites? Let them pass through to wherever it is they go beside the far sea. Let them take meat if they wish. I do not understand why certain of you wish to make war. What is the cause of it? I have seen but three white men in all my life. I do not wish to shed blood because a man is hungry and takes one of my buffalo to eat."

No one responded directly. There was a small muttering from one side of the tent, however. Looking that way, Amaya saw a young war leader with a face like a hatchet, eyes like flint. He wore paint on his face, the only man there who did. Anger crimped his narrow lips.

It was Gray Feather's turn to speak. "I agree with my friend Long Sky Dreaming. What is there to gain by war? Some of my people do not agree with me. The reason is this: white men came and attacked a young woman of my tribe. It was deplorable. It was a cause of much sadness. People cried and sang mourning songs among the lodges. There was a crime, a horrible crime. The whites that did it are dead. That was justice. To kill those who have done nothing is not justice—"

"All whites are your enemy! Any white would do the same thing. It will be another woman next time, and another!" The young warrior Amaya had noticed earlier had sprung to his feet. There was nothing more discourteous than to interrupt a high chief as he spoke, but this war leader with the painted face had done it. It was as if he was forced to do so by the anger in his heart. Around him the other war leaders gestured for silence or scowled in disgust.

"Sit, Sand Fox, or leave the council to your fathers."

Sand Fox sat disgustedly. Amaya watched him for a minute longer, seeing the clenching of the muscles at the joint of his jaw, the fiercely glowing eyes, the throbbing of a pulse in the great vein which snaked across his broad forehead. He would, if he were allowed, ride the war trail at this moment, killing everything white he saw. Amaya had not seen such hatred for a long while, since she left the Laramie Reservation, where hatred such as Sand Fox's had erupted into bloody rebellion.

Gray Feather was nearly finished with his interrupted speech. "If these white men persist in coming, if they try to stay on our land and build their houses, then they must be removed. But as Long Sky Dreaming has said, the land is wide. Let them pass through."

High Top Mountain of the Hevataniu felt differently. "I do not like war. I wish to live in peace and hunt the buffalo and watch my grandchildren at play in the long grass. I like to watch the dove fly low across the morning sky and hear the mockery of a green-winged crow as it swoops low above my camp. I like quiet forests where a man meets the many spirits, and quick-running rivers where the *minios* speak in their laughing tongues. No, I do not like war. How many battles have I seen? How many has my brother Long Sky Dreaming seen? My brother Gray Feather? Too many. There was glory in our battles, and the pride in our blood urged us to make war. Some young men died." His face grew thoughtful, his eyes briefly remote. "Some very strong young men died. Yet when the battles were ended, we had spoken with words unmistakable to our enemy: the Cheyenne live upon this grass. They will not be offended or pushed or insulted.

"Now it is time to speak again, to other people. To these white men." The old man leaned slightly forward, pointing a finger at one warrior and then another. "White men have come into our land and they have come to slaughter the buffalo, not to feed their bellies, to make their lodges, but to skin them and take the hides away, to leave good meat stinking on the plains. This I have seen.

"They have come, and when they have seen a Cheyenne alone who was hunting and was not painted for war, they have killed him as they would a coyote. This I have seen."

Sand Fox was leaning forward intently as he listened to High Top Mountain's words, like a dog straining against a rope, waiting to be cut loose, to attack, to tear and snap and rend.

The last principal chief had not yet spoken. He was a man of middle years with a hawk nose, lines around his mouth and across his forehead; a patch of hair was missing from his scalp. Three fingers had been sawed from his left hand. His name was Blue Heron. His voice was surprisingly mild, almost meek.

"I have listened to my brothers. I have listened to my people. An unjust war is a wrong thing. But when a man comes uninvited into my lodge, I must ask him to leave. When he comes onto my land and disgraces himself by ruining what he finds there, he must be told to go away. If he will not go, he must be driven. Blue Heron has spoken."

It was a short speech, softly delivered. It was a vote for war, which left the Cheyenne's principal chiefs evenly divided, with Gray Feather and Long Sky Dreaming casting their votes for peace. The debate now would be a long one, with the war leaders of each clan, the forty of them including Indigo, having the right to speak and perhaps influence the principal chiefs.

"Please, my woman," High Top Mountain said, "bring to us more to drink."

Amaya started to rise. She had gotten into a half-crouch when the flap of the council lodge was thrown open. The light behind the man was brilliant, throwing him into silhouette. Amaya knew instantly who it was. He had two children with him and he came forward as again the murmurs rose. The interruption was beyond rudeness; it was nearly mad. But then, Stalking the Wolf was nearly mad with his grief.

"I am a good man," he said by the way of apology. "I obey the laws." He looked around as if in some confusion. He had fresh war paint on his face, new blood seeping through it where he had cut himself again in protest, in grief. "Here are my sons, Cheyenne warriors. They have no mother today because a white man has come upon our land. Here I stand. I have no wife to comfort me in the night and to help me with my burdens. I am a good man. I obey the laws. The law must let me kill many whites in revenge. If it does not, the law is wrong. My horse stands without. His tail is tied. My medicine bag is knotted into his mane. Let me go. I am ready to ride them down and take their hair!"

The lodge erupted with sound and motion. Sand Fox leapt to his feet, yelling, "Yes! Let us go or we will go on our own! This warrior brother is right. And what of Lonesome Owl, who had a child taken from him? What of Lame Elk, who was shot by a passing white soldier?" The man was breathing harshly, his chest rising and falling, his eyes bright beneath the bony shelf of his brow. Amaya looked at Indigo, expecting something from him, something to stop this, but what? Indigo himself wanted war, as she knew. She looked to the principal chiefs, but two of them had already spoken of war. Gray Feather looked to be wavering. The ancient Long Sky Dreaming appeared disinterested. He had been asked for his opinion and he had given it; he had no interest in defending it against odds like these.

Opinion, the urge to war, grew like a prairie fire. Stalking the Wolf's dramatic entrance had sparked it, Sand Fox's fiery impetuosity fueled it. Now as the war chiefs spoke in disorganized unison, their voices fanned the flames.

There was no stopping it. Amaya stood looking right, then left. Slowly the war leaders remembered who they were, where they were, and they sat again, regaining comportment. They spoke again with measured words, discussing matters calmly. But now they spoke of war, only of war, of how it should be conducted, of who would lead, of when and where and how many. How many whites must be killed before vengeance was exacted.

There was no longer any desire for tea, for food. Amaya slipped out of the tipi and stood in the fresh air. The cottonwoods around and above her rustled furiously in the rising wind, as if the excitement had stirred them too. She started walking, her eyes down, her mouth set grimly.

She could see the vast camp through a gap in the willows. They had many warriors, over a thousand, perhaps twice that number. More than all the soldiers at Laramie, many more. The Sioux were also warring—if Red Cloud and Crazy Horse continued to have their way—and the whites would have no chance. They would have to pull back and leave the land they were encroaching upon. That was what Amaya's logic told her; her heart was heavy with doubt and something near to remorse—as if the dying that would come was somehow her fault, as if something should have been done to halt it. A brief, painful image of young Hevatha, her head bloodied, presented itself and Amaya felt almost physical distress. But the warriors were many. No soldier could come near this camp, near her home.

She halted abruptly. The round little man with the small eyes and the eagle necklace around his neck, his bare chest painted red and black, was suddenly there, as if he had popped out of the ground or fallen magically from the sky. There was a turtle-shell rattle in his hand, a bearskin belt around his waist.

"Good day, Sun Hawk," Amaya said to the shaman. His body, she saw, still glistened with perspiration from his dancing.

"It is war."

"How did you know?"

"I know. I know. Did I not dance, did I not fast and pray? Did I not dream?"

"It is war, but is war what is good?" Amaya asked.

"War is what must be. I do not know what the spirits think is good. I only know what Manitou sees. War is what he sees. War is what must be."

"But you—do you favor it?"

The little man's eyes unfocused, looked inward or far distant briefly, and then returned to Amaya. What *did* Sun Hawk see? What was his dream? Was it like Indigo's, a dream of invincibility?

"I do not favor it or deplore it. I only fear it," the shaman said. "I fear life. I fear death."

"You," she said in amazement. "You who know the spirits, who know the way to the Hanging Road, who know the *tasoom*! You fear life and death alike?"

"I know," Sun Hawk said. "I know too much, I see too much. I walk too many trails." He backed away from her now, vanishing into the trees. "I fear. The dreamer knows, but the price for knowledge is fear." And then he was gone, leaving Amaya alone and bewildered.

The war drums beat the night long. The war fires shot flames into the night skies, fires visible for mile upon mile. The men danced to exhaustion. Amaya lay awake trying to comfort the restless children.

"Something is pulling at my blankets," Akton said crossly, rolling over again, thrashing around.

"It is only the *mistai*, isn't it, Mother?" Hevatha said with a girlish squeak in her voice, a tiny suppressed laugh which annoyed the very serious Akton. "Creeping, crawling *mistai*."

"Don't talk that way," Akton snapped. "You know it makes me frightened."

"Quiet now," Amaya said, putting her hand on her little "Moksiis," rubbing her fat little belly. "If there were any little ghosts here, they are gone now. Besides, Hevatha, you know the *mistai* hurt no one. They may tug your blankets free while you sleep, or toss pine cones at us as we walk in the forest, but they mean no harm."

"I didn't say they meant harm. It was Akton who was scared."

"Then you mustn't tease Akton."

"Akton was born without a smile," Hevatha said a little grumpily. She rolled over in her own blankets and was asleep in moments. Amaya stroked her other daughter's head until she too slept. Across the bed, wrapped up in Indigo's blankets, Dark Moon snored childishly. It was good to have them near her. Good to know that they were sound and warm and well-nourished and happy.

Outside, the drums still beat.

Indigo slept barely an hour. He was prodded awake by his war spirits, the urging of his blood. He sat upright, his hair hanging in one long braid across his shoulder. He was naked to the waist. It was dark and misty in the tipi. Still a few golden embers burned in the fire ring.

He looked to his left and saw her sleeping there, so lovely, proud, and desirable. He stretched out a hand but did not touch Amaya's fine dark hair. He did not want to wake her. The stirring beside Indigo caused him to look to his right. There slept the little warrior. The young man with the chubby cheeks and wide, eager eyes. The one who always watched his father and imitated his walk, his speech. Indigo rubbed his son's head and slipped from the bed, hearing the night birds chorus in the cottonwoods on the island.

He picked up his war bag and his sack of food, parched corn, pemmican, jerky, and stepped outside into the massed gray of predawn. The air was damp, solid, and other warriors moved like ghosts through the murkiness. Indigo started toward the shaman's tent. Sun Hawk was waiting.

"Indigo. Is it a day for war?"

"That is what I have come to ask you," Indigo replied, and Sun Hawk gestured to him.

Behind his tipi was a badger, fierce and angry. Its claws tore at the earth around it. It snapped at the pole to which it was tethered. Sun Hawk was incredibly quick for a man of his bulk. His knife flashed; the badger died. Sun Hawk opened the belly, removed the entrails quickly, and stepped back. Steam rose from the badger's body.

"Now," the shaman said, and Indigo stepped forward to look into the cavity in the badger's body. It was good. Indigo saw himself with white hair, withered and ancient. He would live a long while yet. This war would not take his life.

"The omen is good," Indigo said, and the shaman stepped to the badger himself, apologizing to the beast which had to die so that Indigo might have his fortune prophesied.

"Not the bloody face, you are sure?" Sun Hawk asked before Indigo left. Sometimes a warrior saw his face reflected in the blood of the badger. The face would have no scalp. The face would be masked by blood.

"No. Why do you question me?"

"I only wanted to know, Indigo." Sometimes a man would pretend he had not seen the death mask. He would want to make his war so badly that nothing, not even a true portent, could dissuade him from it.

When the badger had been buried, Indigo was taken to a sweat lodge. There was still time before dawn to prepare the soul, and Indigo meant to be as strong as possible on this morning. He was taken inside the sweat lodge, which was made of bent boughs with buffalo robes laid over it. There was a fire burning in the center of the dark lodge. Indigo and Sun Hawk stripped off their clothes and hunched down near the fire. Sun Hawk began to chant.

He chanted and his prayers were for victory, for strength, for the life of the tribe and its war leader, Indigo. A pot of water rested beside Sun Hawk, and at intervals he threw water onto the hot stones. The fire hissed, steam rose. Now and then a rock cracked loudly from the sudden change in temperature. And the shaman chanted.

Indigo rocked back and forth, breathing in deeply. The steam was scented with the branches of laurel laid up in the fire. Healing, strength-giving laurel.

His head began to fill with images, with battle sounds. He looked once toward the clan shaman but could see nothing for the steam. Indigo's body was slick with perspiration now. He could barely breathe. He slowed his lungs, closed his eyes again, and listened, hearing the songs of Sun Hawk, the thundering of war horses as they raced nearer, and the final awful explosion as war flame, crimson and yellow, washed through his skull and he saw his enemy's face before him. He saw his enemy's face go to blood and bone and then his hands were raised high.

"Do not do me harm. Do not do me harm."

The snake had come again and it spoke to Indigo from the depths of his remembered dream.

"Do not do me harm. Do not do me harm."

And Indigo turned away from the snake, shaking his head violently to clear away the images of fire and war which now began to trouble him. He opened his eyes and saw that the flap to the medicine lodge was open. The fire was out, the steam dissipating. Cool air drifted in from the morning outside. Sun Hawk stood naked, watching the war leader.

"It was good?" the shaman inquired.

"It too was good," Indigo said, and he rose shakily, drinking water from the pot at his feet.

There was still no light in the eastern sky. Indigo stood on the low knoll where he could see the tips of the Cheyenne tents, above the ground fog, conical, familiar, like toy boats drifting away on a foggy river.

Now he began to make ready for war, painting himself with the indigo from his war bag. The color had been given to him in his dream and he alone, so far as he knew, used it among the Cheyenne. Most favored the red of their enemies' blood, the yellow of the sun.

He began at his ankles and worked his way up, coloring his warrior's body to a deep blue. That done, he knotted his hair and tied his weasel's fur into it, and then his feathers after offering them to the sky, speaking a brief prayer. He saw to his weapons—a musket with a sawed-off barrel and many brass studs driven decoratively into the stock. The heads of the shiny nails formed a snake to remind Indigo of his dream. He also had his two bows—two in case one should be lost or broken—and two dozen arrows, all painted the same indigo color. He examined his arrow feathers critically, looked down the shafts although he knew they were perfectly straight, examined the sinew strings of his bows. Satisfied at last, he placed the arrows and bows into an elkskin quiver, and with musket in hand, war paint from his feet to his neck, his feathers and ornaments, his talismans in his hair, he walked to where the war ponies had been gathered the night before.

There stood the big gray. Its mane had been braided, its tail tied up with rawhide. On its flank was a blue handprint; around its neck a snake was painted. From his war bag Indigo took his medicine sack. Inside was his magic, his personal medicine. The talons of a hawk, the scalp of a Crow warrior, the blue stone found in the brook the morning of his dream. This magic was not shared. No warrior knew what another carried in his medicine sack. He tied the sack to the gray horse's mane.

Indigo heard a small sound and turned.

Stalking the Wolf was looking toward the east, his eyes seeming to see nothing. In his hand was his steel war ax, his hand clenching the shaft so tightly that it was bloodless.

"So. It is a morning for battle," Indigo said.

Stalking the Wolf looked to his war leader with surprise. "I did not see you come. You are silent as the wind this morning." He looked again to the east and answered finally, "It is a morning for battle. Each morning will be good for fighting." His expression was haunted. Stalking the Wolf could be seen walking the village at night, as if looking for Tantha.

"No matter how many you kill, she will not come back."

"I must kill them!" he said almost desperately. "And then"—he shrugged—"they must kill me so that I may walk the Hanging Road to where my Tantha is."

"Hatchet and Remembers Long need a father."

"I need my Tantha."

"Who has the boys now?"

"Mother Nalin. She will raise them."

"You will raise them, you must. Tantha would want it." Indigo realized that nothing he could say would mean anything to Stalking the Wolf. He had already departed the world to live in his own special place.

Slowly the warriors had gathered. Hands on His Face, Crooked Foot, old Horse Warrior, were there, all looking grim. Their horses had been seen to and now they stood waiting. Indigo too looked east now, and as the first light of morning touched the gray of the skies with silver and then a flush of pale rose, he felt the thrill sweep over the gathered warriors. He felt their hearts beat with his, felt their common blood stir.

"Let us travel to the meeting place," Indigo said, and they led their horses toward the river, splashing across through the water and low fog. The cottonwood island was silent, empty as they passed it and emerged on the far bank. There the massed Cheyenne waited, the warriors of the ten tribes. Indigo looked at the hundreds and felt a little ashamed. All of these men going to make war on a pitiful few whites!

A few men were mounted, chiefly Sand Fox, who waited with immense impatience, riding back and forth among the men, calling to them, stirring them up. Sand Fox, whose blood was liquid fire, molten emotion searing his heart as it pumped through his body, driving him to fervor, lighting his eyes, urging him to quench the flames with the blood of his enemies.

Indigo's band was the last to arrive. Now Indigo went to report to Sand Fox, who had been voted chief war leader, possibly because of his unconcealed eagerness for this war.

"We are ready."

Sand Fox put a meaningless hand on Indigo's shoulder and looked past him toward the river. Behind him the warriors were beginning to mount their ponies, sensing the order to come, and when it was given, a cheer went up. A whooping, yapping cheer unheard anywhere in the world but on these plains. It was a sound Indigo had not heard for a time, a nearly chilling sound. He turned the gray pony back toward his band.

The sky in the east turned fiery red. A long strand of gold limned the horizon. The few low, sheer clouds were touched with crimson. Sand Fox raised his arm and then lowered it, and the warriors of the Cheyenne nation surged forward, the shrill cries growing louder, merging with the drumming of the thousand horses' hooves.

They ran their ponies for a mile and then slowed to a walk, bunching together in their own clans, sending a dozen scouts out ahead. The morning was warm. The land was alive. Buffalo plowed their way through the deep grass. The Cheyenne ignored them. The few clouds of early morning had congealed into floating puffballs. Their shadows played tag across the rolling grassland. The wind lifted their ponies' manes and tails, shifted their feathers, flattened the grass so that it showed silver in the winking sunlight.

The scout returned at noon. His name was Hawk Shows and he was a Hevataniu. They saw him racing with the wind across the flats, flagging his horse with his hand, waving to Sand Fox, who halted his party to wait. Indigo heeled his gray horse and started that way, reaching Sand Fox's side just before the scout. Stalking the Wolf followed.

"They are still there," Hawk Shows said, panting a little, leaning forward across the withers of his spotted pony, the one with the yellow circle on his forehead. "Down along the river. Six houses, perhaps. I saw twelve good horses. They will have guns."

"The men?" Indigo asked.

"In the field where they plant their corn. Not far from the houses, but beyond the trees."

Sand Fox's eyes were alive with fierce joy. He turned on his war pony's back and studied his army, spread out for nearly a mile across the plains, waiting in groups, watching.

"Me," Stalking the Wolf said pleadingly. He knew that Sand Fox was going to choose one band to attack the settlers. There was little honor in the horde he commanded overrunning the handful of whites. There were tactical problems as well. So many men in such a small area might end up wounding each other. "Me," Stalking the Wolf said again. "Whoever goes, I must be there. My heart wants blood, Sand Fox."

Sand Fox put his hand over Stalking the Wolf's, nodding his agreement. "Your band then, Indigo."

"It is good," Indigo said.

"Leave none alive."

"If there are children—"

"No captives. That is how it must be."

Indigo's eyes met Sand Fox's and then shuttled away. The man carried a canker in his heart. Stalking the Wolf's agony Indigo could understand, but what spirit was it that gnawed at Sand Fox's entrails?

"No captives."

Indigo and Stalking the Wolf rode back to the clan. They gathered around as their war leader gave them their instructions. Stalking the Wolf's party from the south, through the willows along the river. Hands on His Face from the east, up the narrow coulee there. Two houses flanked it. One was beneath the oaks. Nothing must be left standing. Do not carry off the chickens or anything living. They would ride far on this journey. If it was white, kill it.

"Now?" Stalking the Wolf asked, and Indigo nodded. "Let me stay with you. Runs Long will take my band." Indigo agreed, and Stalking the Wolf went to consult with his lieutenant. Indigo saw Runs Long lead the force out toward the south. The main Cheyenne force scattered across the land had dismounted and crouched now, or lay holding their ponies' tethers, passing time. Later they would war. Later there would be time for all of them to count coup.

Indigo waited until his flanking parties had been gone

half an hour; then he started forward with his force of seventy men. He looked at them, feeling pride, a kinship, a joy—he was one with the flowing movement of the horses, the painted, intent faces, the painted copper bodies straining forward, leaning toward the battleground as if to hurry the event, with the gleaming steel weapons, the black iron of the muskets, the timeless bows and arrows, the war lances and hide shields. He was a warrior and now was the time he lived for, for this time and others like it—yet there was a small, prodding uneasiness in the back of his mind, an insistent pain so distant as to be almost unreal. It was, he decided, a knowledge that those before them had no chance at all, that they were not warriors, but corn planters, men in overalls with hardworking wives baking their white bread in the kitchens . . . with small children.

Indigo forced these feelings aside. They should not have built their houses on Cheyenne land, they should not have planted their corn in Cheyenne soil; if they loved these women and these children, they should not have brought them to die in the land of the Cheyenne.

He reined up and swung down from his horse, dropping the hackamore to run forward in a crouch, to press himself to the ground at the hillrise and peer down into the valley, to see if all was as Hawk Shows had described it.

Smoke rose from the stone chimneys of three of the houses. They lay as Indigo had been told. Looking to the south, he could see nothing of Runs Long's flanking force. Toward the coulee to the east he saw the sun glint on a silver ornament. Indigo scowled. Many lives could be lost because of the conceit of the man who wore that bright decoration. He would be warned later.

Stalking the Wolf had bellied up beside Indigo. Indigo could smell the eagerness about the man, a metallic, primitive scent.

Indigo placed a cautioning hand on his friend's shoulder. Stalking the Wolf seemed hardly aware of it. He looked intently into the valley, his eyes bright, the tendons on his copper neck standing taut, the arteries there pulsing strongly.

The two men slipped back from the rim of the hillrise,

moving in a crouch toward their ponies. Sliding onto the sun-warmed back of the gray pony, Indigo primed his musket and nodded to those around him. Slowly they moved forward, this time mounted, in a picket line. Indigo rode alone to the forefront, once more to the hillrise. Below they would be watching for him, waiting for his signal, and now he gave it. His arm dropped and from the south a shrill cry rose and wavered and fell away, to be replaced by a constant chorus of wild cheers. A dozen horses burst into view and from the coulee other Cheyenne appeared.

Indigo was riding his own horse down the slope, seeing Crooked Foot to his right, Stalking the Wolf to his left from the corners of his eyes. He had his musket in his hand, his bow beneath his left knee, quiver on his back. Across the stream, beyond the oaks, Indigo saw a white farmer turn, rifle in hand. He saw the puff of smoke, heard the report of the weapon, saw that it was a miss. Then the warriors were upon him, riding past, striking him. Indigo saw the farmer fall.

To the south a woman fled a Cheyenne brave. She was caught by the hair and dragged into the trees. Indigo's horse splashed across the stream. A gun was fired from one of the cabins. Crooked Foot's horse whickered wildly, bowed its head, and tumbled, throwing its rider. Indigo saw the splash of crimson on its chest, saw Crooked Foot leap free.

The cabin to the right was on fire. To Indigo's left a dozen shots sounded. He heard a cry of fear or of pain. A man, a very young man with yellow hair and without shoes, was running toward the oak trees. Stalking the Wolf shrilled exultantly and urged his horse on, veering toward the running white, who looked across his shoulder, his young face very pale, twisted with anguish, with the knowledge of coming death.

Indigo leapt from his pony and kicked at the door of the house in front of him. A shot from inside caused him to leap aside. Old Horse Warrior was standing beside Indigo, and the two men looked at each other in momentary confusion. There were no more shots and so Indigo kicked the door in.

A white woman lay twisted against the floor, one side

of her head blown away. The big pistol lay near her hand. Smoke still hung in the air. Horse Warrior took her scalp, which was long and red.

Indigo went outside the house and watched as three young men with flint, steel, and straw started setting fire to this house as well. Shots still rang to the south, and Indigo swung aboard the gray horse to ride that way. Stalking the Wolf had returned, waving a pale scalp in the air. There was blood on his face, blood on his hands, and he reveled in it.

Indigo saw them suddenly. They were very small, one boy and one girl, both with hair like cornsilk. They ran into the willow brush and he watched them go.

Stalking the Wolf yelped and leapt from his horse, rushing forward. Indigo was already on the ground. He hooked his arm around Stalking the Wolf's waist and slowed his rush.

"White children!" Stalking the Wolf said breathlessly.

"No."

"I saw them, Indigo!"

"You saw nothing. You saw nothing, Stalking the Wolf. Do you understand me?"

"Sand Fox—"

"There is nothing there," he repeated. Slowly Stalking the Wolf's muscles relaxed. His chest, rising and falling at a furious rate, stilled. His expression as he turned dark eyes to Indigo was unreadable.

"All right." Stalking the Wolf pushed away from his war leader. "It is as you say." Then he went to his horse and swung up onto its back in one smooth, expressive motion. He kneed the war pony and thundered off toward the burning houses.

Indigo looked at the willow brush for one moment, then followed. He passed a dead dog, half a dozen chickens with their necks wrung, the body of a fat man, its scalp peeled off. Smoke was heavy in the air. Someone had begun dancing wildly through it, like a ghostly dancer in a winter fog.

"It is done," Horse Warrior said to his son-in-law.

"Yes. It is done." Indigo called out to his men. The houses, all six of them, were in flames. Even as Indigo swung his horse westward, the roof of one collapsed and sparks gouted into the sky. They saw nothing alive as they rode to the hillrise where Sand Fox waited.

The war chief's eyes were hungry for news. Indigo told him, "They are all dead, Sand Fox. You see that their houses burn. Every animal, every living thing white is dead."

"You are sure?" The smoldering eyes met Indigo's.

"I have said it," Indigo said in annoyance. And when he turned away, Stalking the Wolf was watching him with eyes not so very different from Sand Fox's.

They rode southward until nightfall, then made their camp in three different groups along the river. Their fires burned briefly in the sunset and then were extinguished. If there were soldiers in the area, they would have seen the smoke and they would pursue the Cheyenne. If there were soldiers pursuing this army, their fate was already written.

Daybreak brought a fiery sunrise quickly smothered by stalking gray clouds from out of the north, rumbling, blustering things filled with thunder and spiked lightning. Sand Fox planned to cross the river and sweep the country to the east for fifty miles or so before returning to the home camp near Cottonwood Island.

None of the war leaders objected. They had come to fight; all wanted a taste of blood and fire as Indigo's group had had. It was already raining when they crossed the river—again remaining in three different groups separated by a mile or so, for defensive purposes. Riders were sent from group to group with any messages.

It was nearly noon, the rain falling breezily from a dark sky, when Sand Fox's rider found Indigo.

"White soldiers," he reported. "Two miles ahead, drifting toward the river. Perhaps they know, perhaps not."

"How many?"

"Fifty."

"A large patrol," Indigo murmured.

"Sand Fox wants you to remain along the river, to cut off a retreat to the west."

"Very unlikely," Indigo said under his breath, but he understood Sand Fox's reasoning. His warriors had had their battle; now the others must be first into the fray. Indigo would have far preferred fighting the armed soldiers to raiding the homesteaders, but he had been given no choice. Now his force was to serve merely as reserves.

"Indigo?" Stalking the Wolf was beside his war leader, his face eager, rain-damp, narrow, scarred.

"What is it?"

"I want to go to Sand Fox. To ride with him."

Indigo shook his head. "You heard the command."

"I must ride where the battle is. I must have blood for my lance."

Indigo hesitated, uncertain. He had decided that Stalking the Wolf was slowly going mad. Should he feed this madness or try to starve it? Finally he said, "Do what you want." With a whoop Stalking the Wolf turned his pony to race after the messenger. Indigo could only watch him go.

"It is best," Horse Warrior told Indigo as they drifted northward, staying close to the quick-running gray river. "My son Stalking the Wolf has terrible grief within his heart. Fighting can draw off the poison."

"Perhaps." Indigo guided his pony down into a shallow grassy gully where rosecrown and wild timothy flourished and a quick silver rill wove through the grass like a mercurial serpent. On the far side he resumed the conversation with his father-in-law.

"I have grief for Tantha too, Horse Warrior. Grief and anger. I wish to fight; I wish to drive the white man out. You must feel this as well, a terrible sorrow. Yet I do not want to slaughter children. I do not feel the need to be everywhere white blood is let."

"He loved her dearly." Horse Warrior shrugged beneath his blanket. "What if it had been my other daughter, Indigo? What if Amaya had been killed?"

What if? Indigo rode silently, the rain cool against his face, glossing the gray horse, screening the land around him. Would he become like Stalking the Wolf, a mad hunting thing? Perhaps. Perhaps Horse Warrior was correct. He knew this—he would not want to live without Amaya. Not now.

They divided into smaller groups and waited along the river in the rain and mist. For hour upon hour nothing happened while they sat silently, eyes alert, ears reaching for battle sounds. Then they heard it through the muffling rain: a distant pop-popping, a crackling concatenation which broke off into constant, nearly methodical shots fired individually, answered individually.

The battle did not last long. Either the whites had fled or they had been caught completely by surprise, cut down in the first savage barrage.

"Sit your ponies," Indigo told his men, and the word was passed along. "If they did escape, any of them, they may flee toward us." Though, Indigo knew, eastward would have been their preferred direction, toward Fort Laramie. But Sand Fox, anticipating that, would surely have had a force flanking the white soldiers on that side.

Indigo's war party had a brief part in the battle after all, brief and slightly ludicrous, slightly shameful.

The two soldiers, one with yellow stripes on his sleeves, burst from the willows and into the face of seventy waiting Cheyenne warriors. The man was young, pale, with bloodstained sleeves. Musket fire and arrows as numerous as the raindrops filled the air and the soldier fell, instantly dead. A dozen or more Cheyenne warriors leapt from their ponies to savage the body. Indigo looked at Horse Warrior. The older man was expressionless, pitiless. The white soldier had chosen to come here and fight. Now he was paying the penalty. To Indigo the scene was more that of a pack of dogs tearing a wounded antelope apart than an act of bravery. But these were young men, wanting a feather of valor, wanting to count coup, to be praised, and he praised them.

The second soldier died no less quickly. Hands on His Face had ridden to him, and while the horse soldier raised his rifle to fire, Hands on His Face had clubbed him down with his war ax, splitting his skull open. The rifle had discharged near enough to Hands on His Face to scorch his cheek and tattoo him with black powder grains. Hands on His Face waved off offers of resistance, scalped his man, and holding it high, danced in the rain over the bloody blue jacket.

Indigo waited another hour and let his men ride slowly toward the battle site, spread out across the land, combing the trees and brush for other survivors. They found none.

The sun had broken briefly through the clouds when

they came upon the battlefield. The dead white soldiers lay scattered across the field, many with their arms or legs cut off, all with their scalps taken. Sand Fox's warriors held new rifles aloft, packs of ammunition, bright sabers, handguns. Some, like Sand Fox himself, wore captured jackets. The army horses, those that had not been wounded or killed in the battle, had been gathered to one side. They were all of the same height, taller than the Indian mustangs by a hand, all of a uniform bay coloration.

The Cheyenne cheered each other, danced, laughed, and exchanged trophies. Except for one. Stalking the Wolf moved restlessly among the dead as if searching for something he could not find. Blood stained his leggings and shirt. Two fresh scalps hung from his lance. Indigo got down from his horse and walked for a while among the triumphant living, the silent dead.

It had begun to rain again, hard this time, when the Cheyenne war party moved out, still riding northward parallel to the river they took for their boundary.

They met the Sioux at the junction of the two great rivers, the Lodgepole and the North Platte. Sand Fox held up his hand, and the signal, passed on by others in the ranks, brought the army to a standstill. Indigo rode forward.

Stalking the Wolf was beside Sand Fox now. He seemed to have attached himself to the wild-eyed sachem. Both men glanced at Indigo with slight disparagement. He's told him about the white children Indigo thought, giving the possibility little import. He would have done it again.

The Sioux leaders came cautiously forward through the haze and driving rain. They were wearing paint. The man in front was of medium height, broad in the shoulders. There was a peculiar wave in his hair—very remarkable for an Indian. After that he had been called Curly all through his youth. As a young man he had witnessed the killing of an old Sioux chief named Conquering Bear by white soldiers on the Oregon Trail. It was a senseless shooting over the loss of a settler's cow. Watching the chief die had hardened Curly's heart forever to the whites.

He had left his family camp and gone up onto the

sacred bluffs beyond. There he had fasted, and when he had felt sleep coming on, tortured his body with sharp stones to keep himself awake. All day and night he walked along the bluffs, singing songs. His eyes burned and he grew weak. Another day passed and he waited for a message from the spirits, feeling unworthy, young, but desperate. On the third day he gave it up. He was sick and dizzy from lack of sleep and food. He tried to return to where his pony waited, hobbled on the long grass, but he fell. He lay against the earth in a delirium, and the dream came.

A man came riding across the sky on a yellow-spotted war pony, and around him arrows and lead balls flew, but he was unharmed. A storm darkened the day, thunder roared, and lightning scored the black, tumbling skies. The man rode on through the storm, heedless of danger. On his cheeks were magic zigzag marks of yellow, like the lightning which crackled around him. On his body were painted the marks of hailstones. Over his head a red-backed hawk swooped and screeched. The warrior's own people came toward him, stretching out their arms, calling out to him, making a great noise. Curly knew suddenly what the man was thinking; he felt the pride and the anguish—because he was the man in the dream.

When he awoke, his father and uncle were over him, scolding him. He paid them little mind. He had seen his vision. His name would no longer be Curly, but Crazy Horse, and he would be the destroyer of the whites, the protector of his people.

"I greet you," Sand Fox said.

"I greet you, Cheyenne brother," Crazy Horse said. His paint was fading in the rain, but the yellow lightning bolts on his cheeks were still visible. In his hair was a small red-backed hawk. "You ride far to the north on this day."

"This is the day we have chosen to follow war," Sand Fox said, and he spoke with some pride. A new scalp hung from the muzzle of his musket rifle. He was clad still in a blue soldier's coat.

Crazy Horse was expressionless. He looked past the ranks of Cheyenne to the south. "We have heard there are more white soldiers riding."

"No more," Sand Fox said.

"Red Cloud is riding. There is strong magic in the Sioux heart now," Crazy Horse said as if to himself. "Sitting Bull has seen the whites vanquished. Yesterday the *wasichu* Fort Smith was burned. It was burned by Red Cloud. The whites are falling back. Let us surrender no more land."

And then with a brief gesture, a formal raising of the hand, Crazy Horse turned his yellow-spotted war pony and led the Sioux northward again.

After a brief conference the Cheyenne turned south. There was no point in riding in the tracks of the Sioux. The Cheyenne warriors were ebullient. War was in the air, the sense of victory, the taste of it. The Sioux had waged successful war in the north and east. Their battle had gone well. The whites had lost a fort. Some of the young men who had not counted coup complained loudly that the war was over and they had not had a chance to fight.

Indigo rode in silence, watching the younger warriors cavort. Some waved weapons in the air, others performed tricks on horseback, clinging to their ponies' necks or standing on their backs.

"You are not joyful," Horse Warrior said to his son-in-law."

"I am pleased," Indigo said cautiously.

"Not so pleased as Sand Fox."

"Sand Fox thinks he has been part of a great victory."

"It was a victory. His victory."

"Yes." Indigo shrugged.

"You do not think it is over."

"I hope it is over. No, I don't believe it is. You and I have stood beside the long trail and seen the whites as numerous as ants flow past. We have counted until we lost count. Do you think the white soldiers will let them be killed as they cross our land?"

"They will have to stop crossing our land."

"Nothing can stop them. I do not know what they flee, these whites, what draws them to the far sea, but I know this: they will not be stopped, not by arrows or by guns."

"You are old before your time, Indigo," Horse Warrior said brightly. "Celebrate the day, do not look too far into the future! It is not good for a warrior to do that. Many times he sees his own death hovering."

Indigo smiled crookedly. Horse Warrior was right. When everyone around him was celebrating, why was he touched by this cold gloom? Perhaps it was only the weather, a need to be home again with his babies and Amaya, but Indigo was unsettled in heart, unsettled and apprehensive. Horse Warrior smiled again and Indigo blocked his concerns out of consciousness. He heeled his horse into a short run and let out a whoop as he rode forward in a brief race with Crooked Foot, who laughed as he clung to his quick, bloodstained pony.

She waited. The runner had come in an hour earlier, just before sunset, and he had reported that the war party was returning. Now Amaya stood with her shawl around her shoulders, the children beside her, watching the eastern horizon like so many other women in the Cheyenne camp, women who knew that each time a war party returned there was the chance that their man—husband, brother, son, or lover—might not ride with the living.

Gray Feather had come up to the rise to stand in the purple dusk, the cold wind lifting his thick gray hair. He carried himself erectly, this old council chief, but there were signs of illness in his face now. The eyes were still bright, but the cheeks had sunken, the lines around his mouth had deepened. When he placed his hand on Amaya's shoulder it trembled.

She glanced at Gray Feather and smiled; then she returned her gaze to the horizon, indistinct at this hour, the green of the hills and the purple of the skies forming a blurred, watery line.

She felt Gray Feather's hand tighten its grip briefly and then she too saw them. Small dark figures, only a few at first, tiny insects creeping toward them. And then there was an army still distant, small, the hundreds of them, taking on size, form, definition as they rode nearer through the twilight, their speed increasing, the sound they made growing to a roar as the horses trampled the long grass and the returning warriors raised a shout to the violet-hued, cloud-stained skies.

Amaya felt her muscles tighten, her heart quicken. She saw Indigo then, and it was all right. Her eyes were fixed on him; no, he wasn't wounded. Only then did she start looking for the others, for Horse Warrior and Stalking the Wolf, among the throng.

Men were swinging down from their ponies, dancing and leaping, some waving scalps, trophies, others hugging wives or children, mothers and fathers. It had been a good war.

The milling crowd had built around Amaya and she had lost sight of Indigo again. Now she saw him leading his horse through the near-darkness. He was erect, sound, but hardly exultant. Others might have felt like dancing; he obviously did not. There were, it seemed, qualifications to his joy.

He was before her, his hands on her shoulders. Then gently he drew her near.

"Let us go home," he said. Then he crouched and the children clambered over him, nearly knocking him over. Only then did he laugh and seem to share in the communal mood.

The first star was already probing the silky violet clouds when they reached their tipi. Inside it was warm. The children were excited. Dark Moon was playing with his father's bow.

"It went well?" Amaya asked.

"It went well."

"But you are troubled."

His eyes lifted. He didn't respond. How could he explain the way he felt? Victory was theirs, yet he felt apart from it, vaguely ashamed and more than a little apprehensive.

"There must be something done, Amaya. Something to secure peace."

"But we have peace if the whites have been driven out."

"Only until they return. Now is the time to make a true peace, while we are stronger. One day we may not be."

She knelt by the fire, stirring her pot as it warmed. She could see the concern in Indigo's face; she did not understand it, and yet in the back of her mind was a gnawing knowledge that he was right. Now was the time to make a true peace, to make a treaty, to give the wampum.

"What is to be done?" she asked.

"Nothing. No one is in the mood to listen to that sort of talk. Listen to them! They sing of victory, of pride and of strength. I am a war leader, Amaya. It is not my place to speak of peace and how it should be made."

"Gray Feather would speak for you."

"My father would not be heard." Indigo shook his head as if to clear it. "Perhaps I am turning into an old woman. Today I spared the enemy." He told her about the white children.

"What you did was right," Amaya said. "Children do not make war. What understanding can they have of the violence descending on them?"

"Stalking the Wolf wished to kill them. He told Sand Fox—I know this. And so I have an enemy."

"An enemy!" It seemed too strong a word.

"This man," Indigo said, "will brook no challenge to his power. He commanded us to kill all. I did not. In that sense I disobeyed. It could be brought up before a council."

"It won't be."

"No. It won't be."

Amaya knelt beside her husband, kissing his shoulder. "And soon Sand Fox will be gone. Our band will be alone again and all will be well."

Indigo turned, took her in his arms, and kissed her deeply. Together they toppled over onto the floor, and the children, laughing, giggling, rushed to them, eager to join in the game. They were tickled and drawn close, laughing, their hearts fluttering, and enveloped in the warmth of their parents' love. Outside the sounds of victory continued, but Indigo paid no attention. Nor did he sleep that night. He lay awake with Amaya in his arms until dawn quieted his uneasiness.

The war parties went out again. Three times that month the army led by Sand Fox rode to the boundary of the Cheyenne lands. Twice they met white armies. Both times they outnumbered the enemy to the extent that some of their forces were held back. Both times the white armies were overwhelmed. Each time the warriors returned, there were more horses for the tribe, more weapons, more blue jackets and caps on the Cheyenne.

The days were long while they were gone, the nights even longer. To Amaya it already seemed that this war was endless, brief as it had been, that her man would ride out time after time and there would never again be peace. Everything had changed, not externally, but in their hearts. Each woman looked with startled, anxious eyes to the east when a horseman approached. The children played at war, not at hunting. Hatchet and Remembers Long, Tantha's boys, did not play at war, they worked at becoming warriors, so that soon they were tiny braves, ready and eager to kill. They had gotten so rough that Dark Moon was not allowed to follow after them as they played.

And the old man was dying.

Amaya went to Gray Feather's lodge every day with food or a kind word, bringing the children, who delighted the old man. Gray Feather had Indigo's sister, Moon and Stars, and the frail Where the Waters Flow to attend him, but only Amaya seemed to be able to brighten his eyes.

"I know I am dying," he told her. He cut off her objection. "Why should I not say that? It is natural. We are given life; life ebbs. I have lived in my time; a man does not endure into another time. My strength was good. I hunted for my family, fought for my people; now my strength ebbs. I must be handled like a baby. So it must be; it is not good for a warrior, though, Amaya."

"You will regain your strength," she said, stroking his brow.

"Yes!" he agreed enthusiastically. "I will regain it, but not in this weary old body. When I walk the Hanging Road I will regain my strength. Then—up there—I will hunt again, and fight again and see my fathers. So what is bad about the dying? I have lived honorably. I have performed the rites, honored the spirits. Nothing is lost by dying except this husk of a body, which may dry up and blow away for all I care."

"I care about it, Father," Amaya said. "I am not ready to see it blow away."

"I am pleased by your words, Amaya. But it is not right for you to worry greatly about me. What is the sense in making my illness the center of your life? Look at that young man, at Dark Moon—yes, I am speaking of you, grandson—handsome, small. He needs forming while his strength grows. It is he who must fight now, he who must hunt. Indigo will teach him, he is a fine man; but it is the mother who forms a child—remember that, Amaya. A boy may be proud of his father, wish to follow him, but it is the mother who builds a man."

They spoke often and then one day Where the Waters Flow knelt before the lodge of Gray Feather, her hands filled with dirt, her old face smeared with it. It stuck in the deep lines of her face and made dark scars.

Amaya knew, but she asked anyway, "He is gone?"

Where the Waters Flow couldn't answer. She nodded her head, and Amaya went in, pausing to hug the old woman. Moon and Stars was beside Gray Feather's bed. Amaya got down beside her and they kept a silent vigil. He had said a man must live in his own time. Now that time was gone. He passed, an age passed, or so it seemed to Amaya then.

Indigo had not returned and so they held the ceremonies without him. The body, the husk of the old man in all of his finery, his hair braided and oiled, his white buffalo robe laid over him, was taken on a travois far out onto the plains, and there, while the gusting wind pushed scattered white clouds across the deep blue sky and a dozen wheeling, cawing black crows sailed overhead, Gray Feather was placed in the sturdy arms of a lone cottonwood tree to sleep the long sleep. Amaya stayed after the others were gone. She stood, a lone woman wrapped in a blanket, looking to the tree where the leaves rattled as the soul of Gray Feather escaped into the sky. The day darkened and still she stood until she heard, or felt, or sensed mysteriously the gasp of a *tasoom* breaking free of its last earthly bond, beginning the long journey through the clouds. Then it was over and there was nothing left to do or see. The husk was left to the wind and the sun and time.

Mother Nalin had all of the children—Amaya's and Tantha's. The camp was quiet. Amaya, lost in thought, walked through the oaks and cottonwoods at the perimeter of the camp, keeping the campfires in view but maintaining enough distance so that the only sound to reach her was the occasional barking of a camp dog.

She came suddenly upon the shaman. He was wearing only a breechclout. His body was painted weirdly. A single eye was painted on his chest, another in the middle of his forehead. His own eyes were open but unseeing. His throat worked silently as if he were swallowing rapidly, but he made no sound. Amaya started to turn away.

"No. Wait. You are the one," Sun Hawk said, coming out of his trance.

"I am sorry," Amaya apologized. "I was only walking—"

"No, you are the one." He walked toward her, looking into her eyes.

"What one?" Amaya asked, not understanding.

"Did I not tell you? I know too much, but the price of knowledge is fear. You too must know."

Amaya began to grow uncomfortable. What was the shaman trying to tell her? With her mind filled with grief and with worry about Indigo, she was overwhelmed by this sudden puzzling approach.

"I am sorry. I don't understand."

"No." Sun Hawk was near her now. The top of his head came only to Amaya's chin and he had to lean back to look up into her eyes. "I see you do not understand. But you will. And when you do, come to me, woman. You are the one." He started away and then stopped. "Your father," he said without facing her, "was a man with tattoos." And then the shaman was gone. He had a little medicine bag he had left in the clearing, and now he snatched that up and left, sifting through the shadows of the trees, becoming one of them himself.

Amaya stood there for a long minute watching after him. The stars glittered through the lacework of the branches overhead. She had no idea what Sun Hawk was talking about. None of it had made any sense.

Except the last of it. Her father *had* been a man with tattoos. How she knew this, she could not say, yet when she lay awake in the dead of night and tried to picture her mother and father, she always saw them as handsome people, her mother tall and beautiful, with proud, knowing eyes, her father as powerful, dark, his body wound with intricate purple tattoos. But Amaya had never mentioned that to anyone, not even to Indigo. Yet Sun Hawk knew, and she wondered.

At times when she lay awake or walked beneath the star-bright sky, or moved among the sun-dappled trees along the river or crept through the night forest, she had *felt* that there was knowledge beyond her, felt that there were ways of knowing that she could not quite grasp, secret ways just out of reach, just beyond comprehension. She would feel a touch like that of a cold hand, the breath of something vast and living, near, but when she turned, it would be gone. No amount of concentration seemed to bring it back, no amount of wishing ever opened the secret ways to her; yet Sun Hawk knew these ways, or seemed to. How else could he have known about her father, that faraway, long-ago man from the south? He *knew*. Amaya found the notion suddenly disturbing and she started quickly home, wishing for Indigo to lie beside her on this night and keep these strange doubts at bay with his sure touch, his strong embrace, his warm and gentle love.

When he did come home, he looked weary, drawn, aged. His gray horse was limping and his quiver was empty of arrows. That was the night that High Top Mountain and Long Sky Dreaming came to their lodge.

"Indigo," High Top Mountain said with a slight bow. "I apologize for keeping you from your bed, your supper, your wife. I know you have been warring and are weary."

"Your visit can be nothing but an honor," Indigo responded. "Please sit down. I will fill a pipe."

"Not at this time. There is no need."

Long Sky Running had seated himself. He was an ancient, wizened, cheerful man. His voice had grown thin and reedy with age.

"We have mourned your father's death, Indigo. He was a good man, a great leader."

"He was my father and I loved him," Indigo said simply.

Long Sky Running and High Top Mountain exchanged a look. There was a slight smile on Long Sky Running's face as if he was secretly pleased. Amaya noticed. She sat beside her husband, watching the faces of the old chiefs.

"I will tell you without borrowing time," High Top Mountain said. "Your father's death has left a gap in our council structure."

"Yes, I know that."

"We must have a fourth supreme chief; it is the law."

"One of the forty-four will be elevated to that position, will he not?" Indigo asked.

"No. It is you we want, Indigo. You the council wants."

"Me! I am a war leader, not a civil chief."

"So was your father once a war leader."

"But I am not even a council chief. I am young."

"Yes. Very young. But it is the time for a young man, perhaps. Every argument you may present has occurred to us, Indigo. Some have argued against you, some for you. Some are jealous, some are eager to put you in your father's office. None of that matters now. The vote was taken. The vote was favorable. We want you to give up your war leadership and take a seat in the council."

"As principal chief . . ." Indigo shook his head. One of the four men who guided all of the Cheyenne nation. It was too much of a burden, incredible in its ramifications and responsibilities.

"There are the three of us, the old three to balance you, Indigo, to guide you, to counsel with you, to be fathers to you. You will learn. You are stable, slow to anger, steadfast once you have decided. We want you. How will you have it?"

"I will have it as the council wishes. I am honored. I am pleased," Indigo, still astonished, said.

Amaya felt relief well up, vast, swelling relief. No more would Indigo ride into battle at the head of his war party. He was a civil chief now, and his life would be devoted to punishing lawbreakers, to considering the issues of peace and war rather than deciding them with his war ax. She felt vaguely ashamed of her feelings, as if they were not honorable, but she clung to them nevertheless.

When the old chiefs had gone, Indigo picked her up and hugged her. The children jumped around, cheering, tumbling, although they had no idea what had happened, only that it was good.

The days and weeks passed. Still they remained in the great camp, still the war parties went out, but after a time they found no more white settlers. Those who had been there had been killed or had withdrawn. The soldiers they expected to come never came. It was ended and the Cheyenne were preeminent on their own land once more.

With the coming of fall the ten tribes separated again, each departing for its home territory, where a last hunt would be held before the long looming winter camp.

Amaya found the day of departure cool. A low fog wound its way along the river. They were among the last to leave. The land where the lodges of the Cheyenne had been looked strangely mournful, empty. There were no leaves on the cottonwoods. The river flowed away gray and lonely.

"Homeward," Mother Nalin said. "I am glad too. It is time to return to our hills."

"How are they?" Amaya asked. Mother Nalin had the two boys with her, Hatchet and Remembers Long. They looked less like little boys than contentious midgets. Their faces were prematurely gaunt, their eyes bright. Hatchet especially seemed an old man waiting to arrive at his proper age. He carried a toy war ax—it was never out of his grip, seemingly. Stalking the Wolf fed them on blood and hatred.

"They are well enough," Mother Nalin said, but she was obviously unhappy with the state of affairs. Her grandchildren were growing up sullen and rebellious. Her love could not soften the shell that Stalking the Wolf's lessons in hatred had formed.

"Your children," Nalin said, "are lovely. Look at them, bright and active. Poor Akton, does she never smile?"

"Very little," Amaya said. It was something she had quit worrying about. For Akton the world was not an amusing place. If Hevatha was constantly dancing, cavorting, it was because it was her nature to do so. If Akton was silent and serious, that too was because it was natural. Perhaps it was because they were twins—the humor that should have been shared had gone to one side of Amaya's womb and Hevatha had absorbed it all. She didn't know.

She did know that what was happening to Hatchet and Remembers Long was not normal, was not right, and she determined to speak again to Indigo about it.

His answer was only a deep shrug. They rode northward side by side. Dark Moon was on the back of his father's horse, holding on precariously, his little legs swinging as he urged the stolid gray horse on.

"I can say nothing to Stalking the Wolf. When he returns—"

"He is gone again?"

"With Sand Fox," Indigo told her.

"Still looking for war, for a place to lay his vengeance?"

"Yes. Just that. I think he wishes to be killed."

They rode on in silence. The war was over, but some of them fought on. Where did they fight? Who? Or did they just ride the eternal plains hoping for battle, seeking phantom enemies. Indigo said that there were no whites this side of the Horn, that it would be a long while before any came back. They had heard of wagon trains to the south, heavily guarded, sometimes with army escorts, sometimes with many civilian scouts. Twice they had raided these wagon trains, but they were heavily armed, and with a new sort of weapon—one that fired many shots instead of one. Indigo had counted the puffs of smoke from one rifle during a raid, and he told Amaya there were fifteen in all.

"Possibly I missed one or two. I turned my head toward the shots when I heard the rifle speak like a drum, one shot after another."

All of that was far away. There was no war for those who were not insane. There was life to be lived, buffalo to hunt, bear and fox to be killed for their furs, winter lodges to build, meat to smoke, new clothes to sew, children to be nursed or dressed or fed or taught or amused, all of life to be done—these things must concern the people, not the taking of life.

They camped again among the hills near the Buffalo Camp. Luck was with them. The buffalo had arrived at their fall grazing grounds within the last few days, instinct and habit bringing them to meet their death as if they truly knew that was the purpose for their life. It was good. Their bellies would be full that winter.

There were four separate hunts before the tribe was supplied with all they needed for the winter—meat to smoke, hides to be made into clothing, blankets, tipis, medicine cases, caps, moccasins, mittens, leggings, coats and capes, dresses, belts, parfleches, hackamores, hobbles, picket ropes, lariats, travois hitches, snowshoes, and saddles; sinew to be made into thread, bow strings, feather wrappings, bow backing; horn to be formed skillfully into spoons and cups; bone to be used for knives, scraping tools, arrowheads, and awls; brains, fat, and liver to be used for the tanning of hides; the stomach to become cooking pots and water buckets. Every inch of the buffalo, from horn to tail—a handy fly switch—was used, save the heart, which was left on the plains to seed the next year's herd and the years after that so that the buffalo would always roam the wide plains where Manitou had put him.

When the hunts were over, the buffalo moved on southward and the Cheyenne watched them go. They watched until they could see only an indistinct dark stain against the grass to the south, and then they returned to their village, to their work, to preparations for the long winter.

Amaya waited awhile longer, uncertain why she did so. She watched the buffalo until they had vanished, until there was nothing but the yellowish grass, mile upon mile of it, reaching to meet the pale blue, arrow-straight horizon.

"They pass away," the voice behind her said.

She turned to find Sun Hawk there, wrapped in fur, although the day was not that cold. His eyes looked into Amaya's, but also past her, into the far distances. She could make nothing of his expression.

"They have gone, for now," Amaya said.

"Perhaps they will not come back."

"They always come back."

"They pass away," Sun Hawk said, completing his circle of logic. Amaya could only smile and lift one shoulder in a shrug.

They stood silently for a while, the slim, tall young

woman and the rotund shaman. They looked at nothing, at the buffalo that were no longer there, at the empty horizon.

"When will you dream?" the shaman asked.

"Dream? Tonight, perhaps, the night after." She laughed, but Sun Hawk was not laughing. The wind across the plains lifted a strand of Amaya's hair and drifted it across her face.

"When will you dream, Amaya?"

"I don't know what you are asking me," she said a little impatiently.

"You must! You must dream. I will tell you what I see. A woman who must dream. I have known this since I first saw you, when Tantha brought you back to us. You must dream because you have the ability to do so. You are exceptional."

"I am not!" Amaya said with a breathy laugh.

"You are, Amaya. I know this. But you have lived only half a life. You are trapped inside your own body without a dream. You are hidden away inside yourself, a small person within this skin you wear, waiting to be released, to grow. To dream is to escape. To dream is to create yourself and be created."

"I can't understand you," Amaya said. The conversation exhausted her. What was he telling her? To dream away her life?

"You must dream. When it is time, come to me and I will tell you how." Then his hand rested on her shoulder, a very unusual gesture for this man who lived apart, who prayed and suffered in private, who came for the rites and then was gone, who chanted his songs in the deep forest or in the dead of night. He was gone and Amaya stood watching him as the long winds blew.

She must dream.

8

Tᴛʜᴇ ᴡɪɴᴛᴇʀ ᴘᴀssᴇᴅ and the spring. They moved north-ward and the grass brightened and grew long. The buf-falo came as they always had and sheared the grass and then they were killed to give life to the Cheyenne. Win-ter came again, and another spring, and time was a comforting thing with the children growing tall and the love of Indigo and Amaya growing yet stronger. The springs were alive with flowers, heartleaf arnica and black-eyed Susans and rosecrown and timothy on the long plains, tended by white butterflies and bumblebees; in the hills the wild geranium grew in the shade, blue gentian and fleabane, scarlet trumpet and lupine be-neath the pines and in the mountain meadows where they sometimes hunted, sometimes roamed only to see what Manitou had constructed out of the mud of incipi-ence.

The mountains were strange and silent, shadow and sunlight, where the badger dug his burrow in the sunlit meadow and the cougar tracked, a flash of tawny mus-cle, and the doe led its fawn to the icy rills to drink, lifting water-silvered muzzles at the sound or scent of danger, where the silver-tipped, loose-skinned, loose-jointed, fat, ambling grizzly dwelled, all things moving from its path as it prowled among the cedars and blue spruce which stretched out for mile upon pristine mile, flowing up the flanks of the high mountains until trium-phantly the harsh gray snow-streaked rock above the timberline rose above them into the pale blue sky. At times it stormed and the wind rattled in the trees and shook the world as thunderclaps reverberated across the valleys and the meadow grass trembled; lightning would strike across the storm-darkened skies, arcing terribly from peak to peak and the scent of sulfur would fill the air as Manitou's quick calligraphy sketched enigmatic messages—warnings perhaps—across the sky.

"It is," Amaya said, "a place to dream."

Indigo lifted his head and looked at his wife, not knowing at first what she meant. Then his expression cleared. "I think so too. It is not far from here that I saw the snake."

"Where," she asked, "up there?"

She was looking to the gray-white crags above the timber, to the empty land where nothing grew, where nothing could long survive, where there was no clump of grass, no soil, no trees, and nothing which breathed.

"Yes," Indigo answered. "It is hardly of the world, is it? Forbidding, barren. It is a place for dreams. There a person walks the moon."

They discussed it no more that day, but the thought stayed in the back of Amaya's mind. Sun Hawk's words would return and she would wonder.

Three days later the man with no arm came to their camp.

They saw the blood-smeared horse wandering toward the river, moving erratically, stepping on its own reins. A rider clung to its back. He was Cheyenne, perhaps an Omissis. By the time they were able to lead his lame horse into the camp, he was nearly dead. He had time to tell them, "White soldiers. On the Horn. Very many." Then he was dead. His arm had been shattered and he had cut it off himself after binding it tightly with raw-hide. Too much blood had been lost for him to survive.

Indigo was grave, his expression severe and nearly angry. The warriors were crowded around him, demanding, begging, asking, shouting meaninglessly.

"What do we do?"

"Attack, Indigo."

"Let us ride."

"Please. Let us find out what has happened."

"Soldiers killed this man."

"Let us find out for ourselves."

"The dead man was not lying!" This was Stalking the

Wolf. Stalking the Wolf, who had become a crooked, secretive thing. He had returned from Sand Fox's camp to see his sons, to see if they were still poisoned, if the legacy of hate endured. He was gaunt now, his eyes standing out, appearing enormous in his sunken face. His cheeks were scarred, his forehead, his chest. His own knife had bitten his flesh a hundred times. The scars on his soul were deeper and more numerous.

"Let us find out what has happened," Indigo said stonily.

Stalking the Wolf stood glaring at his chief, his hands clenching and unclenching. "Sand Fox would be on his war pony's back by now."

"Then go to Sand Fox," Indigo said violently. Mockery formed on his brother-in-law's lips. Stalking the Wolf was no longer a man who thought. He only acted.

Indigo himself rode out, with Hands on His Face and a young warrior called Wing with him. The wounded scout had told them nothing except that there were soldiers on the Horn. Indigo meant to discover what was happening before any decisions were reached.

They found them at midmorning with the sun high in a hazy sky. A wagon train of white settlers, camped now, watering their oxen in the Horn. The powerful animals stood shoulder-deep in the river, bawling with satisfaction.

There were forty white soldiers with them. Indigo sat the hillrise watching the activity of the camp. None of the trio said a word. They had come back; the war must be fought again. The same war, over and over.

"It is no good," Indigo said under his breath. "There must be an agreement. The white leaders who send these people to die must understand that we cannot allow it."

At the camp of the Cheyenne they were met by a hundred eager men and boys. Stalking the Wolf's two children leapt up and down, weapons in their hands— not toy weapons, but the weapons of a man, although neither was taller than Indigo's shoulder.

"Well, what is it to be? Did you see them!" Stalking the Wolf was following Indigo, demanding answers before Indigo had even swung down from his gray horse.

"I saw them."

"Then it is war. Then we will fight!"

"We must council."

"Council and they will be gone. Why not call all the bands together," Stalking the Wolf mocked, "meet on the cottonwood island, smoke the pipe. By then even their dust will have dissipated."

"Stalking the Wolf," Indigo said. "You are my brother. We have suffered grief together, but I will tolerate no more of this. No more, understand me."

"I understand you. You are afraid. You have lost your courage. I saw you the day you lost your nerve—the day you let the whites live."

"Small children!"

"Sand Fox had given an opposing order."

"It was necessary that I disobey it," Indigo said in frustration.

Stalking the Wolf nodded. "Then understand this: there may be a time when I am forced to disobey one of your commands, Indigo." Then the warrior turned and walked away, his smirking boys with him.

"There will be war?" Amaya had come to him, bringing a water sack. She watched as Indigo drank, and then took the sack back, trying to read his eyes.

"There will be war. This time some of our men will not return. Forty white soldiers."

"Passing through or digging at the earth?"

"Passing through."

"Then perhaps you could delay war . . . speak against it."

"I could command it, but none of our people could respect me after that. I must let them go."

"And you . . . ?"

"No. You know I am no longer a war leader. I will not go. I do not wish to see it. We need another man."

"Not Stalking the Wolf?"

"No." Indigo would not have him as war leader. None had been chosen since Indigo became a civil chief. It was up to him to promote someone. "The man I want is his brother."

"Hands on His Face—but then Stalking the Wolf will be even more resentful."

"There's nothing to be done about that. I can't control

him anymore. He won't listen to Horse Warrior, to any of the elders. He listens to the singing in his blood."

"Indigo," she said as they walked back toward their tipi, where Indigo would dress before going to the council lodge with the elders, "what will happen now? We continue the war. Will the whites not strike for vengeance?"

"They will."

"Can't they be made to understand? Can't they see that more must die, and more, that the plains will be soaked with blood?"

"Who knows? How can we talk to them? How can we make a council?"

"Send a message."

"How? Who knows their tongue . . . ? You do!" He stopped and looked at Amaya in amazement. "You could write a letter to them. Perhaps if we spoke together, they could be made to understand."

"We must speak to them, Indigo. I feel this. If we do not, the war will never end. The generations of our children will still fight." She glanced across the clearing, seeing her tall, willowy daughters, girls already rapidly approaching womanhood. "I want them to have peace."

"We shall seek it."

"Then the warriors will not ride out this day."

"Today? Yes, they will. They must. The whites must first see that we have strength, then they will be willing to listen."

"If you oppose war . . ."

"The council will vote for war, and vote quickly. The warriors like Stalking the Wolf will not accept any other decision. There will be war—for now—and if we are successful, later there will be a good peace."

Then he kissed her and strode away, calling to Crooked Foot. Amaya watched him, his strong back, his confident manner. He spoke easily of war and peace as if he could control them with his will. How simple to say first we will have a little war and then a little peace. In many ways Indigo was still young.

"I only hope you are right, my chief. I only hope that some of what you wish can be done."

The warriors rode out two hours before sunset; it was

a time they favored. Shadows began to thicken in the
gullies, and twilight would come soon, confusing the
eyes of the soldiers. If they could, they would attack out
of the setting sun, further perplexing the whites. If the
attack had to be broken off, following darkness would
conceal the escaping Cheyenne.

But they expected no such rout on this day. There
were forty soldiers, a hundred Cheyenne. There would
be guns among the settlers, but few of them would be
experienced warriors.

At the head of the raiding party rode Hands on His
Face. His youthful leanness had given way to fleshy
strength. His hawk face tended toward an owl's now. He
was a reliable, courageous man. He had been told that
the job of war leader was his.

So had Stalking the Wolf been told. He rode glowering
beside his brother, behind him his two young sons.

"They must not enter the battle," Hands on His Face
had ordered.

"They must watch," Stalking the Wolf had said.

"They are children."

"They will be men. You were thirteen when you saw
your first battle, Hands on His Face. You went to the
enemy chief who was wounded and put your hands into
his blood then placed your handprints on his face. Or
does your name not remind you of that?"

"Your boys are younger than thirteen. Why do you
bring them?"

"So that they may learn. They will be great warriors.
They will kill all the whites."

"If they do not go mad," Hands on His Face said, and
he heeled his horse into a quicker pace, leaving his back
for Stalking the Wolf to scowl at.

They had circled to the west, and now, as the sun sank
low, flattening and reddening as it plummeted toward
the high mountains and its cradle in the great sea beyond,
the Cheyenne sat their war ponies, waiting. Some men
hurriedly applied their paint. There had been little time
in the camp.

"Will we be successful?" Hatchet asked his father.

"Of course," Stalking the Wolf said with a harsh and
bitter laugh. "This is Indigo's war, and has he not dreamed

of invincibility? Is not my brother Hands on His Face our leader?"

Hands on His Face turned his scarlet-and-black face away. His brother was not only teaching the boys to hate the whites, to love war, he was leaving them a legacy of hatred. All of his petty grudges and jealousies were being passed on to his sons. One day, Hands on His Face thought without rancor, they will hate me as well. How could it be otherwise?

His hand went up and his warriors raced to their horses. The whites could be seen now, sixteen wagons stretched out across the long grass, following the ruts other wagons had carved in the Bozeman Trail. Flanked out at its sides were dozens of blue soldiers, their gear clanking and gleaming in the sun, chains, sabers, canteens all making an incredible amount of noise. This was no silent army the whites fielded.

"The children are to be taken captive," Hands on His Face reminded the men beside him, and the word was passed. "Do not harm the women or the children."

Hands on His Face couldn't see Stalking the Wolf's scornful expression, but he didn't have to. Nor did he see the grimace Stalking the Wolf pulled for his boys, who smirked in concert. Nor the expression on the face of certain other warriors, like Wing and Eagle Lair and Mountain Wolf, who agreed with Stalking the Wolf. There would be no prisoners.

The sun was very low now, the hills going to purple and black, liquid shadow. Soon the wagons below would turn off the trail and make their camp. Hands on His Face waited for that moment, his eyes narrowed, his heart calm, thumping heavily, his hand tightly wrapped around his musket.

A soldier rode to the lead wagon and pointed toward the south, where a few scattered oaks grew. After another minute the lead wagon veered off toward the trees. Still Hands on His Face held his men back.

Another wagon turned from the trail, and another. The Cheyenne began to sift down through the little valley toward the flats below. They were as silent as the deep shadows, swifter, deadly. They reached the bottom of the canyon and fanned out across the land. Still they had not been seen, but as their ponies struggled up out of the bottom, a cry was sure to go up.

Hands on His Face urged his war pony on, up the sandy bank and onto the grasslands. There was no cry yet from the white camp, no shot, and he quickened his pace, glancing left and then right, seeing his warriors beside him, their weapons raised and ready. Still there was no shout of warning. The wagons of the whites grew large. Hands on His Face could see a woman and child walking between two halted wagons. Still there was no sound but the drumming of their horses' hooves, now running frantically, flat out, their manes blowing behind them, froth flecking their mouths.

A war cry ululated through the air. Hands on His Face raised his musket, waiting. The soldier had been leading two horses somewhere and he turned a pale, stricken face toward Hands on His Face. The Cheyenne shot him in the throat and the led horse reared up, racing off.

Hands on His Face had put his musket away beneath his leg. He had his bow and arrow out now, but he was through the camp before he had a chance to use them. Through the camp and turning his horse, hearing the sharp, near reports of gunfire, seeing the cloud of black smoke rising to hover over the wagons, hearing the screams, seeing the whites—men, women, children, soldiers—scatter and dive for cover, some of them firing guns on the run, others throwing their weapons down in panic.

From the rear of one wagon a gun fired six times, ten times, without being reloaded, and Hands on His Face scowled. What he would give for one of those weapons!

There wasn't time to dwell on that. He rode back through the camp again, the arrow notched, his bow-string taut. He saw a huge red-faced man in overalls and shot him, the arrow entering his chest, but the man managed to stagger on, turning with a pistol in his hand to fire two wild shots at Hands on His Face before he was out of the Cheyenne's sight.

The sun was dimming. The muzzle flashes of the weapons were bright tongues of yellow-red flame. A woman lay crumpled against the grass. Her scalp had been taken, and Hands on His Face felt anger surge in him. She could have been killed accidentally, but not scalped accidentally. He had given a command; if they did not obey him on this first raid, they never would.

His anger was swallowed up, drowned out by the activity and noise of the battle. Six blue soldiers had tipped over a wagon and were behind it now, firing their weapons with skill and patience. They did not all fire at once, so they could reload in turns. Hands on His Face turned his horse that way, yipping and whistling. He leapt the wagon, his horse's back hooves striking wood roughly, and managed to put an arrow to its mark as he landed. The soldier fell back, clutching his heart, but he was already dead. A bullet sang past Hands on His Face's head. Later he discovered that it had been near enough to clip a feather.

He was into shadow now, turning again, his horse exhausted and a little shy after hitting the wagon.

Hands on His Face held up and sat calmly, drawing his bow time and again, firing arrows into the knot of soldiers from behind. Two more soldiers had died before they even realized that the arrows were bringing death from behind their position. By then it was too late. Three guns could not hold back the horde of Cheyenne who rushed them afoot now and hacked them to pieces with war axes. Hands on His Face sat watching.

Fire blazed brightly against the sky. The first of the wagons had been set alight. In the trees shadowy figures flitted from shadow to shadow. Occasionally a lashing tongue of flame was visible, but the soldiers, caught unaware, were rapidly being slaughtered.

Hands on His Face watched a moment longer. Horse Warrior pursued a running soldier across the dark grass. The old man clubbed him down with his hatchet. There was still a little sun in the sky, or rather a memory of it—pale pink, orange, and gold woven in tapestry.

The war leader of the Cheyenne wanted to have the prisoners bound and gathered together by nightfall, and so he started his horse forward.

He saw Wing, tall, sullen, his lips slightly protuberant, and Wing smiled derisively, puzzling Hands on His Face. Eagle Lair and Mountain Wolf sat side by side on the grass, the bloodstained grass, going through a trunk they had found in the wagon.

"Where are the prisoners?" Hands on His Face asked. The two warriors looked up briefly, shrugged, and got back to their looting. Hands on His Face began to grow disturbed. Horse Warrior, as excited as a young man in his first battle, came in with a white scalp, waving it around. He was in the center of a group of warriors, telling his tale.

"Horse Warrior!"

He came to Hands on His Face, his gait betraying his age. "Yes, war leader?"

"Where are the prisoners?"

"I have seen none." Horse Warrior's face clouded. "I was out—"

"Yes, I know where you were!" Hands on His Face said sharply. "Where is Stalking the Wolf? Where is my brother?"

"I do not know," Horse Warrior said, stepping back to shake his head. The scalp leaked blood onto his foot. He shrugged and moved away, still walking backward until he spun and with a cry of joy returned to the celebrating men, some of whom were wearing white clothes, a lady's hat with a long feather, a derby hat.

Hands on His Face yanked his pony's head around and rode it into the oaks, his heart beating angrily, his mouth dry. He heard it then, from deep in the grove. A thumping, slow, muffled, methodical, and he walked his pony noiselessly that way. The world was dark but for the tips of the oaks, which still held golden fire. Then that light too was extinguished and there was only the pink of twilight, the purple of night in the east. The thumping continued.

There were dozens of them, across the ground in the deep shade of the night oaks, lying there without moving. The bodies of the whites; and there were women there and children. Among them went the Cheyenne boys, drumming. Their axes rose and fell and struck the dead, and the sound was like muffled drumming. The father of Hatchet and Remembers Long stood proudly, grimly aside, his arms folded while the boys mutilated the dead bodies of the white children, while they drummed out their hatred and made grotesque a love they had once felt, making it a dark and ugly ceremony of death.

"Stalking the Wolf!"

Hands on His Face's voice rang out, and the boys halted, turning to face their uncle, who walked his horse forward. "Brother, leader," Stalking the Wolf said.

"What are you doing?"

"What you see." Stalking the Wolf's hand gestured casually toward the dead bodies.

"This is not what you were commanded to do."

"It is what I have done."

Hands on His Face's lathered pony shuddered and he patted its neck distractedly. "To bring the boys here—I told you they were not to come to the battlefield, but to stay in the hills."

"But they are my sons."

Hands on His Face looked at the boys, standing there small and fierce, gore staining them and their weapons. "You are killing them, Stalking the Wolf. You are doing wrong."

"I do what I must."

"The law—"

For the first time Stalking the Wolf's voice rose with emotion. His chest heaved as he spoke. "I turned my back on the law when they . . . when she . . . it . . ." But he was unable to speak Tantha's name, to name the deed. "These are my sons. Her sons. They will revenge it!"

"You make animals of them," Hands on His Face said, and Hatchet threw his war ax. Hands on His Face saw it from the corner of his eye and jerked his head back a fraction of an inch, just enough so that the ax missed his face. It thudded harmlessly against the oak tree behind him. Hands on His Face sat looking at the three of them a moment longer, at the dark, hating eyes of the child, at the savage glee in the eyes of Stalking the Wolf. Then he mounted his horse and rode out of the woods, his heart driving itself against his rib cage as anger and pity and despair all collided within.

"We camp—" Horse Warrior began as he came out to meet Hands on His Face.

"We do not camp. We ride home," the war leader snapped.

"Tonight?" Horse Warrior was dismayed. He was weary. He was not so young as he used to be. Tonight was to have been for feasting on the white man's oxen, for sharing the spoils of war, not for a long, somewhat hazardous ride across the broken hills by starlight.

"Now," Hands on His Face said tersely. "Tonight."

All of their high spirits were gone by the morning, when they finally reached the home camp. The horses were lame with weariness, their heads hanging. The warriors on their back were trail-dusty, bloodstained, exhausted. From the camp came their women, children, and the old to greet them. There were only a few who raised their hands to the sky and began their songs of mourning. The victory of the Cheyenne had been nearly complete. Three men had died, that was all. Eighty whites had been killed.

Indigo came forward to greet his war leader, but Hands on His Face was not smiling.

"I must talk to you."

"Of course."

"At once," Hands on His Face said, and he got heavily down from his horse, staggering against it in fatigue. He waved away a helping hand and dropped his reins, leaving the horse to stand in its tracks, flanks heaving, legs braced unsteadily.

Amaya was watching from before the tipi. The girls peered out sleepily, wonderingly. Indigo strode up the pine slope, Hands on His Face, silent, steeped in anger, beside him.

"Go and play," Amaya told the girls.

"We are hungry, Mother," Akton complained.

"Then go see what Mother Nalin has in her pot."

Indigo and Hands on His Face were nearly there. Hands on His Face had heard Amaya's instructions. "Not to Mother Nalin's, Amaya. Send them to Moon and Stars or to Where the Waters Flow."

"But why, Hands on His Face?"

"Please. I will tell you and you will understand."

Amaya could see that something serious was working within the war leader, gnawing at him, and so she told the girls, "To the lodge of Moon and Stars, then, if you are hungry. If not, play in the small meadow."

"I want to go to Mother Nalin's," Akton said, a little whine edging her voice.

"Go," Amaya snapped, and Hevatha laughed at her sister. They stepped past Amaya, and it was Hevatha who got the swat. "Don't laugh at your sister." But she laughed again, scooted away from a second spank, and then the girls were gone, skipping down the slope.

"Come into my home," Indigo said.

Hands on His Face looked at his chief, then at Amaya, as if he had carried a great burden home, a burden which must be placed down. "Thank you." He entered and sat, refusing food and water. "I would choke on them," he said.

"The battle?" Indigo inquired without preliminaries, since Hands on His Face was in no mood for etiquette.

"We won a victory. A vast victory."

Indigo's face relaxed a little. "Then what troubles you, Hands on His Face?"

"Stalking the Wolf." The Cheyenne licked his lip dryly. "You will not like this, Indigo."

"Go ahead," Indigo said in measured tones.

"All right," Hands on His Face answered, and he related it all as he wiped his hands, face, and chest clean of war paint with a cloth Amaya had given him.

Indigo's face stiffened when Hands on His Face told of his brother's refusal to obey orders, and when he related the slaughter in the oaks, the participation of the young boys, Amaya and Indigo looked at each other almost helplessly.

"What did you do then? What did you tell him, Hands on His Face?"

"What could I tell him? It was done. He would have laughed at me."

"He is your own brother," Amaya said.

"Yes. He is my brother. But he will not accept me as leader. I must put aside my bonnet."

"No." Indigo placed a hand on the war leader's shoulder. "Don't be so hasty in this. You are war leader, but it

was my command, not yours he refused to follow. It was
me he wished to insult, not you. Shall I put aside my
bonnet?"

Hands on His Face looked at Indigo and shook his head
negatively. Then he made a small gesture as if to say:
What can we do?—and the tension, apparently nearly
unbearable, flowed out of him.

"I regret that this happened your first battle," Indigo
said. "No matter. I have faith in you, the elders have
faith in you. You must retain your position. As for Stalking the Wolf . . ."

"What *can* you do?" Amaya asked.

Her husband's mouth tightened. "I will ask him for an
explanation—but there can be no excuse for this. Who
was with him, Hands on His Face?"

The war leader gave him the names of those he thought
had participated in the massacre of the women and children: Mountain Wolf, Eagle Lair, Wing, and perhaps
Horn Cup. "They will tell you if they had a hand in
it—if they are like their leader, they are proud of it."

"Then I will ask them. It will be handled. You have
done your part, Hands on His Face, and done it well.
Stay now and eat with us."

"No. I wish only to sleep, Indigo," he said, rising.
Then, with a word of farewell, he dipped out through
the tent flap, letting a moment's harsh sunlight enter
and mark the floor, and he was gone.

"The children," Amaya said. "Those two boys of
Tantha's! It is filthy, Indigo. Stalking the Wolf has lost
his mind. What can he be thinking of, to raise them like
that?" She was incensed, animated.

Indigo sat thoughtfully brooding. He lifted his eyes.
"You have said it: he does not think. He hates. He has
indeed lost his mind."

"Those poor boys. Remember them, so chubby and
brown, happy with their mother . . ." Amaya remembered too well, and she forced the thought away. "What
will you do, Indigo?"

"What can I do? I will talk to him, and if he does not
give me his oath . . . he will have to be sent away."

"Banished?"

"Yes. Stalking the Wolf and his friends. Let them go to Sand Fox. *He* would have no objections to their behavior."

"That's it, isn't it?" Amaya asked. "He doesn't think you are fierce enough, that your war is large enough."

"That's it. In a way, I believe I caused this," Indigo said, and he recalled the two blond children he had let escape.

Amaya was behind him, her fingers rubbing his shoulder muscles. "You did not cause it. It has been in him like a serpent since Tantha's death."

"Perhaps I did not cause it. But I must end it. Now."

"End madness?"

"End the result of madness. End it or send him away."

"And the boys?"

Indigo shook his head heavily. "He may leave them with Nalin, as he did last time."

"But probably not. He thinks they are old enough to witness battles, if not to participate. That is obvious. He had them there yesterday . . ." Hacking at the dead bodies of children. It was with relief that she remembered Hands on His Face's warning. What tales would those boys have to tell over their breakfast bowls this morning? Grisly, filthy things for young boys like that to grow up on. And her daughters would have been there.

In the corner of the tent Dark Moon, who had been sleeping heavily, finally awoke, knuckling his eyes, looking around blearily before rising unsteadily and staggering toward his mother and father. "Is there something to eat?" he asked. Then he sat with his eyes closed, his head on his father's shoulder, and Amaya met Indigo's gaze. It must not happen to such as Dark Moon. The poison must not spread among the tribe. If the banishment of Stalking the Wolf meant that the boys had to go as well, perhaps it was best. A tragedy, but best for the tribe.

Indigo ate in silence, no more than Dark Moon did, and half as rapidly. Amaya watched her son, amazed again at the energy, the eagerness with which a child can face a new day. She herself felt heavy of heart. She did not envy Indigo his job.

Stalking the Wolf had been a brother to them, husband to her best friend. He had been a good husband, a good brother, a great warrior, now he was none of those. Stalking the Wolf continued to walk the earth, but all he had been, the soul and essence of Stalking the Wolf, was lost, scattered back along the war trail.

"I will go out now," Indigo said when he was through. Amaya didn't answer him. There was nothing useful to say. Indigo would speak to the council. No one would argue, not after Hands on His Face told his story. Then the man would be banished, cut off from the heart of the tribe, from its lifeblood, its nourishing unity. It was a terrible punishment; but not for Stalking the Wolf. He who needed nothing to nourish his hatred, which was all he lived for, who needed no friends, no family, but only blood. In the end, only the children were punished, and there was nothing to be done about that.

"If I go," Stalking the Wolf told Indigo, "others go with me."

"Then it will have to be that way."

Stalking the Wolf had been braiding his horse's mane. His thick, dark hands were amazingly nimble. Now he stopped and looked into Indigo's eyes.

"You are failing your people, Indigo. You drive off the warriors you will very soon need."

"I drive off no one. You separate yourself from the tribe when you refuse to obey our laws, my commands, those of the war leader."

Stalking the Wolf's smile was crooked, unrelated to the conversation apparently. His eyes too were distant. "What do you think will happen now, Indigo? Let me ask you that—what is happening?"

"I don't understand you."

Stalking the Wolf threw down the handful of thin rawhide strings he had been using to tie the braids. "You don't understand me? You, our chief? The wise one? I am speaking of the white men, the war."

"We will not see so many again."

"We will not? I say we shall. I say we shall see one, and then one with a hundred more. I say the only way to stop him is to cut off every head as it grows. I say the children must be given weapons, the women: they must be taught to hate and to kill everything that buds, everything the color white."

"And I say," Indigo answered, "that this is not the way a man behaves, not the way he wages war."

"Ah," Stalking the Wolf said with bitter sarcasm, "a warrior's pride, a man, a leader, a sage! These are different times, Indigo. If we do not slaughter them, they will slaughter us. We must take their blood first, kill them all, keep on killing, kill infants in the cribs. If we do not, then we will perish as a people."

"If we become what you describe, the Cheyenne deserve to perish."

Stalking the Wolf looked at Indigo without speaking for a long while. Then, turning his back deliberately, his scarred face held down and away from his brother, Indigo, he said, "I shall be gone in an hour. My friends go with me."

"To the camp of Sand Fox?"

"To his camp."

"The children, Stalking the Wolf, let them stay with their grandmother."

"No."

"Nalin will raise them with love, with care," Indigo said.

"That is not the way they will be raised. They will be warriors."

"They have never been children!"

"No." Stalking the Wolf, grinning as if he could not help himself, turned back to face Indigo. "Never children, and now it is too late. I will go. The boys go with me unless you wish to try to take them from me."

"No." Indigo shook his head. "I will not do that."

"Indigo—it is the times. It is the times that tear us apart, that make this trouble. We were brothers. Tell Hands on His Face that I bear no grudge, that ..." He shrugged and fell silent. Indigo walked away toward his lodge.

Amaya was waiting to meet him, Dark Moon standing beside her. Indigo was astonished to notice how tall the boy had become. How quickly they grow at that age.

"Did you tell him?"

"Yes."

"And he goes?"

"Yes."

Within the hour, as Stalking the Wolf had promised, the men who had chosen to follow him rode out. There were nearly twenty of them, more than Amaya would have imagined. More whose sympathies lay with the methods of Sand Fox and Stalking the Wolf, the slaughter of all, indiscriminate, total war.

"They ride!" The voice was high-pitched, cackling. Amaya saw Small Eyes then. Half-running, half-hobbling along beside the little paint pony which carried Hatchet and Remembers Long. "They ride away, little Cheyenne boys! Good Cheyenne blood. It is the Comanche woman who cuts them off from their people, who tells her husband to send away these good strong warriors, these boys of Cheyenne blood, while her own bastard Comanche children live as progeny of a chief."

"She is mad!" Indigo was furious. "What is this supposed to aid? The woman is divisive, irrational. I should have long since banished her as well."

"To die on the plains?"

Indigo looked into his wife's liquid, smiling eyes. Then he raised his gaze again to Small Eyes, who was still ranting, screaming things which became almost unintelligible as her anger possessed her.

"No." Indigo rubbed his chin. "Yet I wonder if there are others who feel as she does, who would not dare speak as she does."

"The council agreed with you. He disobeyed your order, that of Hands on His Face—he had to go."

"Perhaps there are many who feel the order was not wise."

"Those who felt that way are gone now. It is over. Do not dwell on it."

"No," he agreed, but he did dwell on it. He had weakened the tribe; he had driven his own brother-in-law away.

The whites came again. Word was brought to Indigo as he stood shirtless, watching his wife and children swim in the river. The rider, Arrow Song, swung down from his horse on the run and half-stumbled, regaining his balance to jog toward Indigo, waving a hand.

"What is it?"

"Soldiers," Arrow Song panted.

"On the Horn?"

"No, Indigo. Across it many miles. South of the big coulee. They ride this way."

"Toward our camp?" Indigo laughed at the folly.

"Yes. This way."

"They must not know that we are camped here."

"I think they know. They have Indian scouts. Crow scouts."

"How many soldiers, Arrow Song?" Indigo asked. The smile was gone from his face. Amaya had emerged from the water. She swept her wet hair back, and stood watching, her eyes concerned.

"Fifty, a hundred? Many, Indigo. Many."

"Alert the camp!" Indigo spoke rapidly. "Bring the warriors to the wooded point. Tell the women to take the children into the hills. Leave everything. The men are to take nothing but their weapons. The women a little sack of food if they have it ready. Now. Go now!" He actually shoved Arrow Song a little, and the scout, scrambling back to the horse he had left trembling at the verge of the pine forest, mounted and rode off.

"Indigo, husband—"

"You have heard? Go, then."

And Indigo was gone, trotting toward the camp. Amaya watched, then turned back toward the river, willing her voice to be calm and even.

"Come now. Akton, Hevatha. Dark Moon. We must go now."

"Already?" Dark Moon asked.

"Yes. Right now. Get out and dress yourself."

They splashed toward the shore, disturbing the bright silver of the river's surface. They climbed onto the oak-shaded shore and went to their clothes. Amaya meantime had been tying up her hair. "Hurry, children."

"Why must we hurry?" Dark Moon was cranky. He had his shirt on backwards. "What is happening, Mother?"

"Hurry," she repeated. They could hear sounds of activity from the village now. People calling to absent children. *The children.* If the whites came, what would their mood be? They knew about the slaughter of the wagon train. Perhaps they had actually followed Hands on His Face's tracks from there to this camp. Would they want revenge? Would not the Cheyenne?

"Hurry!"

The children were coming to her now, Hevatha tugging on a moccasin. They started in the direction of the camp, but Amaya, hesitating briefly, said, "No. This way, to the hills."

Now the children sensed her mood, the warning in her tone, and they did not argue, did not hesitate. They moved through the oaks until the land began to rise and the first of the great pines began to loom overhead, shading the sweet-smelling, sunny earth. Their moccasins were silent over the fallen pine needles. Here and there they saw other Cheyenne women, other children, slipping through the woods, climbing higher, higher, deliberately choosing the steepest routes, going over crags that no mounted soldier could surmount.

Amaya tugged, dragged, carried the children on. Her lungs were filled with fire, her head throbbed, her legs ached, but still she climbed. The higher they climbed, the safer they were.

Finally, exhausted, they halted on a white-streaked gray outcropping which thrust out from the surrounding pine forest and overlooked the miniature-appearing camp below. There were others on the rock, and below many more climbing toward it.

"Down," Amaya whispered, and the children, who had been standing, looking out across the plains beyond the hills, got down on their stomachs.

Amaya could see nothing. It was quiet and warm on the ledge, nearly peaceful. The wind swayed the tall pines. Squirrels climbed the trunks of the trees and bounded along the branches, the gray plumes of their tails held high. There were no birds singing.

Then, looking past the village toward the wooded point which sheltered the camp from the prevailing wind, Amaya saw a flash of color, a movement. The warriors had taken up a position behind the point. Another mile away she saw briefly an antlike procession riding into the great dry wash—another war party. Indigo would be in personal command of one of the groups on this day. Which one? Where was he?

Hours seemed to roll past. No one moved on the slopes now. All of the women and children had found a place to lie and watch and wait.

The lone horseman rode a dark pony toward the camp of the Cheyenne. He rode rapidly, clinging to the side of his horse. He approached within a quarter of a mile of the camp, coming just beyond the wooded point, and then he turned and rode away again, his dust casting a thin shadow against the yellow earth. He was a Crow warrior.

Amaya waited. Her breath was stilled, her pulse throbbing in her temple. She was gripping Dark Moon's hand, gripping it so tightly that he wriggled in discomfort until she realized what was happening and released him. Her children remained silent; all of the children were. The infants were being suckled to soothe and quiet them.

The first group of blue soldiers rounded the wooded point. Amaya stared in fascinated horror. They had come. They had finally followed her from the orphan school, from the fort at Laramie. It was absurd, she knew, but that was the thought that first entered her mind. They had come to take her again.

The soldiers fanned out at a hand command from their leader, a man with long yellow hair which could be clearly seen blowing in the wind even from this distance. Still Indigo did not strike. The soldiers approached the camp. From the ranks of the horsemen several riders broke free and rode challengingly through the camp, whooping and yelling. No one could hear their words. Still Indigo did not attack. There were no Cheyenne warriors visible on the point or in the coulee.

What was wrong? The soldiers rode through the camp, trampling tipis, destroying all in their path, meat racks, pots, water sacks.

Indigo did not attack.

Then Amaya saw the reason. Other white soldiers appeared from the north, forty more. They came in slowly, alertly, it seemed. They too knew something was wrong. Their scout had told them of many Cheyenne. They had found the camp but it was deserted. They must have suspected a trap, but they did not immediately withdraw. They wanted to war. They wanted Cheyenne blood!

The second group of soldiers had reached the first. Their leader broke off to talk to the other chief, the yellow-haired one. It was then that Amaya saw the color, the movement, the shadows. She heard the thunder and her entire body went rigid with fearful anticipation.

Up out of the coulee came one-half of the Cheyenne force—under Hands on His Face, she later learned—and the blue soldiers, their horses milling and rearing up, turned to face the attack. Already a white soldier had gone down, and then another, before Yellow Hair had lifted his long knife and his blue soldiers attacked, the two armies riding toward each other, unstoppable, frenzied, men willing death onto the plains. Dust obscured the charging horsemen, cries of pain, of triumph, of joy and fear filled the air, mingling, forming a jumbled, terrible, inhuman roar.

The armies collided and the guns began to fire, the dead to fall. From high on the mountain it all appeared absurd. Small creatures rushing here and there hitting each other with tiny sticks, blowing puffs of smoke at each other. But below there were the effortful grunts, the screams, the streaming crimson blood, the sight of friends going down before your eyes, brothers or cousins with arms lopped off, with cratered wounds in their faces, with entrails purple and obscene leaking from their bodies.

Amaya's heart bounded into her throat. From the wooded point the second contingent came, silent as a prairie wind. There was no warning, no war whoops to fill the air, only the painted, feathered wind, the sudden striking of the spiked war cloud whose lightning struck the whites before they had turned, appreciated the possibility of a trap.

The whites ran in confusion, fleeing northward and eastward, scattered in all directions, a headlong pell-mell flight for life. Once a bugler managed to pant a few breaths into his instrument and a few pitiful notes were sounded; but then he fell dead, strangling on his own blood.

Amaya stood. Everyone around her was standing, cheering. The blue soldiers ran and the pursuing Cheyenne struck them from their horses, killed them as they fell to the ground. It was a horrible, noble, disgusting, beautiful sight.

A dozen of the soldiers had regrouped and were riding away together under their yellow-haired leader. The army horses were much larger and faster than the Indian ponies and they rapidly escaped. The last barrage unleashed from the Indian muskets failed to hit anyone; the soldiers were already out of range.

The people were climbing down the hillside as rapidly as possible, yelling, singing songs of victory, cheering still, children screaming with exuberance. Amaya was with them, silent but ebullient. She carried Dark Moon on her hip as they reached the flats and emerged from the pines to come into the partly ruined camp.

The warriors were returning with the wounded, although some Cheyenne had stayed behind to strip the bodies and collect their scalps. Some of the women, those who had lost men to the whites, rushed out with sticks or knives to insult the bodies.

Indigo wore no paint. There hadn't been time. His gray horse carried him proudly through the camp, side-stepping, prancing. There was blood on the gray, but it was not Indigo's. Amaya rushed to him, the children in her wake.

"Now they will not come again," Amaya said as she waited for her man to swing down, then embraced his heated, excited body.

"They will not come. For a time." He held her near and stroked her sun-warmed hair. "In the morning we must begin to make ready."

"To make ready for what, Indigo?"

"To break camp."

"At this time of year? You said they will not be back."

"Not for a time. But they will be back. They have found our camp once, they will find it again. We are marked as enemies of the whites. It is Stalking the Wolf's doing. Killing the women and children has singled us out."

"This time of year . . . Indigo, it will begin to snow soon."

"It will begin to snow."

"Then we will travel south?"

"No." He shook his head and wiped the perspiration

from his eyes. "North. North to join the brother tribes, or the Sioux perhaps. We must find strength if we are to find security."

"If we must." Amaya looked into Indigo's eyes and for the first time she saw deep concern there, a concern he had perhaps been concealing from her. "I will begin to make ready." Her hand lingered on his arm a moment longer and then she turned away, hearing the sounds of victory cries mingled with the sobbing, the death songs, ancient sounds, the terrible eternal sounds.

Indigo was reliving the battle, wondering. The white chief had been too impulsive. What could have caused him to rush into their trap without having left a supporting column behind to reinforce him? You are a very impulsive man, Indigo thought. Brave, but I think more filled with pride than is good. It was something to remember.

With the dawn they were moving northward, out of the Buffalo Camp. As if in ominous warning the clouds stacked themselves against the northern horizon, gray, stolid, angry. The Cheyenne rode into the wind, into the storm, trying to avoid the larger, angrier storm which was building behind them. The whites continued to come. Their army continued to build, the trains to roll out onto the plains, the wagon trains to cross Cheyenne grass, the buffalo to be slaughtered by hunters, lone and peaceful Indians killed by whites who obviously thought of the Indian as being of no more worth, having no more intelligence than the bison that were left in dark, stinking mounds, slaughtered for their tongues and humps alone. They had struck back. The Sioux had struck back, violently enough at times to halt the tide of immigrants; but it was not enough to hold back the sea forever. They seemed to lack that strength in numbers, in armaments, at times in purpose. "Perhaps it is Sand Fox and Stalking the Wolf who are right," Indigo said at one despondent moment.

"You know they are not." Amaya, riding beside him, covered his hand with hers. "Perhaps it will end now. Perhaps you have given them enough of their own blood to taste."

"We are the ones being driven, Amaya."

"Only because you fear for your people, for your own young, your own old, Indigo."

"What is happening?" He looked around him at the long, cloud-shadowed land. "I don't understand this. There was nothing like it in my grandfather's time, in my father's. Where did they all come from? Where are they going? What do they want?"

Amaya had no good answer for him. Her husband was bitter and frustrated. He was right—his father had never faced such a situation, nor his grandfather. It was a unique time with no traditional answers, without protocol, without a precedent a chief could follow to find peace, a solution to the bloody puzzle.

They traveled only a little way that night, to the Bear Creek hills where the water flowing through the dark winding channel was already swollen with upcountry rain. It rushed past, muttering muted threats—slate gray, rippled with white froth. The sky was the same gray, the same occasional white, murmuring its own warnings.

Indigo was unsettled. Why, he didn't know. The whites couldn't have followed them. It would be folly, for they were far from any fort where reinforcements could be found.

Their tipis were set up hastily on the uneven ground along the dark slopes of the rolling hills. It had begun to rain before most of them were erected, and it rained throughout the night. Amaya felt the uneasiness of her husband and she slept only a little. She remembered Indigo's dream then, and it brought her a strange comfort—he could not be defeated. That was the promise of his dream. There was no defeat for Indigo, none for the Cheyenne. She snuggled close to him and slept, the rain driving down against their lodge.

They crossed Bear Creek the following morning in an icy rain which stippled the quick-running river and hammered the dark pines. A horse was lost crossing the creek, along with the goods it carried.

They were into the forest now, and they traveled through it for all of that day and into the next. Lightning struck the trees continually. There was always the smell of sulfur in the air, the sudden strike of lightning like an incandescent serpent, the fizzle of smoke and sparks and the lingering, sickening smell like the afterscent of gunpowder. Trees fell as the wind began to rumble through the forest, shaking the massive pines angrily, batting pine cones and heavy boughs from the trees. The boughs cracked off with a loud snap and crashed to the earth. Two women were struck by one.

It began to snow the next morning.

9

THE STORM WAS a howling wash of wind and heavy snow from out of the north. It blacked out the sky and set the naked pines to trembling. Whistling, crackling, thundering, it moved southward and the Cheyenne struggled on into the teeth of it.

"Why don't we camp here, set up our lodges among the pines?"

"No." Indigo was adamant. "We must move on."

"No one is following us. The white soldiers are beaten."

"We must move on," Indigo said, and they traveled northward again, staying within the forest verge where the wind was broken by the trees, where it would be more difficult to detect them in those rare, brief moments of clearing.

The snow continued to fall. Amaya was exhausted, but no more so than anyone else. The old stumbled forward, not understanding Indigo's insistence.

"Surely we have left them behind," Amaya said to her husband.

"Surely we will," Indigo said.

Then the old woman, Where the Waters Flow, fell and she could not get back up. She lay there panting in the snow, her breath steaming from her time-scored lips.

"What is this madness?" Small Eyes demanded. The words bubbled from her lips as her eyes raked Amaya and her husband angrily. "Why do we travel on?" Small Eyes turned, her arms outstretched, asking the warriors, the elders, "Why do we travel on? We should have stayed in the Buffalo Camp. What have we to fear? I tell you this Comanche woman is a witch and she has made her husband crazy!"

"I do not understand either," Horse Warrior said. "It is a sort of madness to run like this, Indigo."

"It is not madness to keep our people safe."

"There were only a few soldiers. Defeated!"

"We must travel on!" Indigo said obstinately. He looked ahead into the heart of the storm, which had frosted his eyelashes and placed a mantle of snow on his shoulders. The ponies stood, tails to the wind, knee-deep in the snow which swirled through the trees. They had gotten Where the Waters Flow to her feet and were patting her face, placing her on a travois, which she insisted she did not need.

Horse Warrior shook his head. "I am sorry, Indigo. This is far enough."

"We must go on!"

"That is not a matter you may decide on alone. No one of the council argued with you because we have faith in your leadership. I have no faith in this." A hand rose and fell in disgust. "No faith." Horse Warrior turned and walked away through the snow.

Indigo stood watching after the man. Amaya was beside him, holding his arm with one hand, with the other holding her shawl beneath her chin.

"Perhaps they are right, Indigo."

"No."

"What will you do?"

"Whatever they decide," he said. "But it is bad. I don't like it."

There was no one to side with Indigo. The council in a brief vote decided to make camp here, to wait out the storm and then decide which way to move. Indigo's pleas were ignored. As the storm ranted the Cheyenne set up their tents. Pots were set to boiling, the wind whipping the flames. Children were rushed inside and bundled in furs and extra blankets.

"I don't understand this, Mother," Hevatha complained. "People are angry. At whom—at me or at you and Father? First you tell us we must travel every day, and now we have stopped."

"The council wanted to stop. Your father wanted to travel north."

"Why?"

"The other Cheyenne clans are north, and Red Cloud's Sioux. Indigo wished to join them."

"Why?"

"There is safety in the north."

"Safety? From what? Soldiers? More soldiers?"

"More soldiers. So your father believes."

"What do you believe, Mother?"

"I believe Indigo." Amaya tucked the girls and Dark Moon into their beds. "They will see he is right. When the storm ends, we will travel north again, I know this."

"I'm still cold," Dark Moon complained, and she went to him to rumple his hair and kiss his forehead as she placed yet another fur over him. The wind shook the tent violently and whined in the trees.

"What makes the noise?" Dark Moon asked.

"That's only *mistai*," Hevatha said, "isn't it, Mother?"

"Yes. Just the playful little *mistai*. Snuggle in, now."

Amaya walked to the tent flap and looked out. The sky was dark and tumbling. Lightning stitched the fabric of the storm. Indigo was still not back. No doubt he was arguing with the council. That was a lost cause. She had seen the men's faces—like Horse Warrior, they refused to travel on.

Something small and hunched moved through the snow, a flitting ghostly thing, faceless in this weather, in the shifting shadows, but Amaya knew who it was—Small Eyes. Small Eyes, mad and constant, unforgiving.

Amaya went to her own bed and sat sewing, listening herself to the songs of the spirits in the trees, the loud hoarse laugh of the Thunderbird. It was hours before Indigo returned, silent, thoughtful, no longer angry. He crawled into bed with Amaya. The world was dark outside, only the small red fire in the center of the tent glowing, warm.

"Well?" she asked, helping him off with his jacket and hair shirt.

"We are staying."

"But your anger has seeped away."

"Yes. Can it be that I am right and everyone else

wrong? The storm is growing worse yet. The chances are that I am being foolish. Lie down with me, Amaya, and let us sleep the storm away."

It was still, cold. Amaya sat up abruptly, not knowing what was wrong. She had been sleeping, dreaming of know-not-what, and then suddenly she had come wide-awake. She listened, hearing nothing at first but the wind, the storm buffeting the world. She strained her ears, held her breath, and then she heard it—the uneasy mewling of Dark Moon in the corner. Likely he was too hot in that mound of furs.

She moved, and Indigo, sleeping restlessly, came awake as well. "What is it?" he asked.

"Nothing. Dark Moon is uncomfortable." She moved to the boy's bed. His eyes were open, staring up at her.

"What is the matter, Dark Moon? Are you too warm?"

"The *mistai*, Mother," he complained.

"What is it?" Indigo asked.

"Nothing. *Mistai.*"

"Are they tugging at your blankets?" Amaya asked the sleepy boy. "Whispering in your ears?" She smiled, continuing to stroke his forehead, erasing the furrows there.

"Wiggling all around. I don't like it."

Amaya's expression changed, set, hardened. "Let me see."

Indigo had gotten to his knees. He looked at Amaya without comprehension. Until she slowly peeled back the blankets and the furs which covered Dark Moon and found the huge rattlesnake lying across his legs.

Amaya could not move. Dark Moon lifted his head with curiosity. Indigo was quicker than the snake itself in striking. The war ax with its heavy steel blade was in his hand, rising and falling and the rattlesnake's head was severed. The snake lay writhing, coiling, flexing, and Dark Moon, seeing what his *mistai* had been, leaped to his mother's arms.

"I didn't think," Indigo said. "Where did it come from?" He looked at his ax in horror. "I just didn't think. All I knew was that Dark Moon was in danger."

"What is it?" Amaya asked. "Your face . . ."

"Don't you see? Don't you know, Amaya? My dream. I have broken my vow! I have killed the snake."

Amaya released Dark Moon and sat on her knees, watching the dismay on Indigo's face. He had killed a snake. His dream promise of invincibility was ended. Amaya saw the side of the tipi move and it was not the wind this time. Someone had stumbled into the tent. Barefoot, half-dressed, she leapt toward the entrance. The creature was trying to run away, but the snow was deep. Amaya launched herself through the air and dragged Small Eyes down by her heels.

"You dirty thing!" Amaya shrieked. "You tried to kill my boy as you tried to kill Hevatha."

"Yes!" Small Eyes answered. She was on her back, wriggling beneath Amaya's grip. "I wish I had! I swear I wish I had. I found the snake hibernating. I knew what it was good for. If I had had a hundred I would have put them in bed with your horrible Comanche children!"

Amaya was astride the old woman now. They had burrowed into the snow, and more snow cascaded down. No one had heard their fight above the storm. Amaya spat in the old woman's face and then was lifted to her feet by Indigo.

"Yah, yah! Comanche whore," Small Eyes screamed, wiping the snow from her face as she got to all fours and then rose unsteadily to stand in the snow, her eyes spiteful, vicious, mad.

Amaya leapt toward her again but Indigo pulled her back, holding both of her arms.

"Now," he said. "You will go. You are not of this clan! You are woman alone," Indigo said to Small Eyes.

"I go! To die while the Comanche lives with my people."

"Go or die here," Indigo said, and Amaya had never heard his voice like that. Small Eyes simply stared and then with a nod turned and shambled off through the snow.

"Will she go? Does she have to?"

"The council will make her go if she is still here in the morning. It is known that she is mad. I do not think she wants to wait for morning. I think she will go now."

"And die?"

"It is cold out here. Come. The children will wonder what has happened."

The storm surrounded them and the snow continued to fall. It snowed that night and the next morning and for three days afterward. Briefly then it cleared for one brilliant white afternoon, but they could see a second stalking giant, a second storm on the heels of the first, building in the north.

Scouts had been sent out at Indigo's insistence. To the south and east the land was deep in snow. No riders moved across the land, no blue-coated soldiers, or so the scouts reported.

"They will not ride through the storm. They will wait for spring if they wish to make war," Horse Warrior had said.

"I hope so." Indigo was momentarily silent. His eyes were on the far horizons.

"You worry too much, Indigo. It makes you a good leader, this concern for your people, but it is not good for your heart to continue to worry. The scouts have been out—no one comes—why worry longer?"

Why worry longer? He didn't know, but he was still worried. The memory of the snake haunted him and he cursed Small Eyes aloud from time to time. Dark Moon had already forgotten the snake. Perhaps he thought it was a dream. He and his sisters played in the snow while it was clear and warm and bright and then when the new storm blustered in from the north they returned complaining to the lodge.

The camp grew settled, more permanent accommodations were made. Drying racks and storage houses were built, and Indigo chafed under the immobility. He continued to send scouts out in all sorts of weather until finally he had to stop; it had become a joke to the council and the tribe. Indigo's soldiers never came, but he continued to look for them. The death of the snake had filled him with dread, some said. He thought he was bound to die now.

Small Eyes was gone for good—she had been seen stumping away through the deep snow, a heavy pack on her back, a steady stream of curses hurled against Amaya and her husband and her children flowing from her lips.

For Amaya the winter seemed endless. The children fretted, Indigo brooded. She was grateful for the occasional clear days when they could hunt or play, get into the air and see the sun once more. She would see Laughing Nose only occasionally, and Sun Hawk, who would always ask: "Is it time yet, Amaya? Time to dream?"

They found a white buffalo. Standing alone, an ancient, shaggy beast white against white in the snow. It watched them stolidly and then drifted away with the wind, taking its magic with it.

The nights grew longer, colder. Still, persistent winter would not withdraw. They stayed awake late now, telling the old tales, Amaya speaking intently, leaning forward to emphasize her points to the children, who watched with animated amusement. "You are Cheyenne," she would tell them, "and you must know what it means to be Cheyenne. I want you to know about the heroes and the spirits of the Cheyenne. Now sit quietly and I will tell you a story . . ."

The fire burned low, and Indigo, reclining on his bed, would stir occasionally to add fuel. The children, rapt and wide-eyed, listened to the stories of the ages.

"Long ago all of the world was water, and a being with no name drifted on its surface. Nothing else lived in the world but a few swimming birds, a duck, and some geese . . ." Indigo moved his head and sat as if listening to the storm. Amaya glanced at him, her eyebrows drawing together questioningly. He lifted a hand and she went on. "The being wanted to make land to walk upon so he called to the swan, 'You must dive down through the water and see if you can find earth on the bottom.'

"The swan tried . . ." This time Indigo leapt toward his weapons in the corner. He had reached his musket when the first shots started to explode like tiny thunderbolts in the night. Then the shots were nearer; someone hollered. They heard horses thundering through the camp and a bullet sang through their tipi, just missing Dark Moon, shattering a pot.

"Soldiers!" Indigo said. "Get out, get into the trees. Now! Take only a few blankets."

Hevatha started obediently toward the flap, but Amaya yanked her back. She crossed instead to the back of the tent, quickly slit the hides, and stepped through, Dark Moon on her back, the girls following.

It was chaos outside. Snow was falling, swirling down furiously from out of a dark sky. In the center of the camp a battle was raging, an unequal battle between just-awakened Cheyenne warriors, half-naked, armed with whatever weapons they had snatched up, and the white soldiers, mounted and alert. They rode full-bore through the camp, trampling kneeling Cheyenne men who tried to fight back or reload already discharged muskets. There were shouts, groans, the rush of wind, the drifting snow, the ghostly, charging horses, the bright lances of muzzle flashes, cries in two languages. Amaya was into the trees, the children with her.

The soldier loomed up before her. He was afoot, leading his lame horse. His rifle came up and he fired in panic. Amaya felt herself flung backward, the simultaneous searing pain in her temple. She was falling and Dark Moon with her. Then she struck her back against a pine and fell into the snow.

Her fingers moved, carving furrows in the snow. That was all that happened. She couldn't move otherwise. Her fingers scratched futilely at the snow. Blood—it seemed to be blood on the snow. Dark patches. Something . . . She couldn't think. She was lost temporarily in an odd, silent world.

The fury of the battle came back suddenly, strongly, the near firing of muskets loud, insistent. Amaya rolled over, getting to hands and knees, her hand trembling. Someone was tugging at her.

"Mother, Mother, Mother . . ." It was Dark Moon, and she wrapped him in her arms, holding him tightly. The soldier was gone. Others fought on in the camp, and beyond, in the snowfields. A yellow moon had broken through the ragged bank of clouds, flooding the battle scene with light. People lay twisted into inhuman forms. The body of a dead woman formed a brutal matrix. Two white soldiers lay together, clinging to each other in death.

Amaya's head suddenly cleared. "Where are the girls! Where are they, Dark Moon?"

His finger lifted and pointed. "They went there. To

find Father. To bring him to you. You were dead, but now you are all right again."

"Yes." She rose, her head ringing, her legs rubbery. She had to lean against the tree behind her, one hand on Dark Moon's shoulder. The moon was gone again. Muzzle flashes located the warriors. Their tipi, she noticed without caring, had been trampled into the snow.

"Where, Dark Moon? You must show me where they went," she said.

"There," he said, fear and uncertainty creeping into his words. "I told you, Mother—there. To the camp!"

Into the battle! Amaya felt her heart constrict and drop. What could she do now? Dark Moon couldn't be left alone. A musket, very near, exploded loudly. She saw the figure rushing toward her from out of the hazy, dim moonlight and stiffened briefly, then had to stifle a cry of joy.

"Akton?"

"Yes, Mother. But you are all right. We thought—"

"Yes, yes, but where is Hevatha! Please, Akton!"

"I don't know. There were too many people. It was too dark. I came back. We were looking for Father, and—"

"Which way did she go!" Amaya shook her daughter so hard that her head snapped back and forth. She stopped herself abruptly.

"I don't know, Mother. There." Akton could only shrug and Amaya could only hold her tight. It had gone dark again. The snow still fell. Crooked Foot appeared from nowhere. There was blood on his face.

"Quickly," he said. "Everyone must fall back. Into the timber. South, and keep going. Indigo's orders."

"I can't—my daughter."

"I saw her. With Mother Nalin. She knows. Quickly, now, Amaya," the brave panted. "There are more soldiers coming. Many more. You must withdraw. The Beaver Lake—go there. The men will fight a holding battle."

"All right. Yes." Amaya touched her head. She had lost her train of thought. The man before her wavered and changed forms.

"Are you all right?" Crooked Foot asked.

"Yes." She shook her head to try to clear it. Dark Moon was tugging at her arm.

"Go on, then. The Beaver Lake! We will be there tomorrow."

The gunshots began to build beyond the camp and Crooked Foot practically shoved Amaya away as he himself trotted back toward the camp.

"Mother!"

"Yes." She still held her head. Blood seeped through her fingers. "Hevatha?"

"She is with Nalin," Akton answered.

"Yes. All right." Amaya looked worriedly back toward the camp. "Let us hurry, then. Hurry!"

The gunfire was worse now. Hevatha felt her breast heaving with fear. Twice white soldiers had passed within a few feet of her, failing to see her as she stood pressed against a tree, only because of the night and the storm.

Now she could see more soldiers coming, cutting her off from the camp. Where was Indigo? Her mother was dead. She kept repeating that in her mind, wanting to drive the thought away, finding herself unable to. *Her mother was dead.*

Hevatha saw more soldiers, riding directly at her through the dark froth of snow. She withdrew into the trees, looking across her shoulder. Still they came, and she began to run. She tripped and fell. As she got up, her hand touched a dead body's face. She did not look to see who it was. She didn't want to know.

She scrambled to her feet and went on. The snow was very deep now and she knew that she had unintentionally left the shelter of the forest. That was no good—the white soldiers could see her there.

She turned toward the forest, or where the forest should have been, but she failed to discover it. Looking back now, and ahead, she could see nothing, no guns firing, no horsemen. Nor could she hear anything. The wind howled mockingly across the plains.

Hevatha hesitated. Which way? She didn't know. The storm was blowing from out of the north, so that if she walked away from it she would be going south. Into the arms of the soldiers? The soldiers that had killed her mother?

What was it my mother told me? "There is safety in

the north. The other Cheyenne are north. Indigo wishes to join them."

North. Hevatha stopped. The snow was to her knees. She was very cold. Indigo would take the people north. She would go north herself until she found other Cheyenne or Sioux. They would take her to her father then. She looked hesitantly south again, south, where war raged. Then, taking courage, she started north, a small wind-buffeted shadow moving through the storm.

She stumbled through a world of light and shadow, a cold and empty, limitless place where you could not think or breathe or exist. She fell and rose again. She staggered on, lurching into the storm, the vast whiteness swirling around her, separating her from reality until she no longer knew which way she walked, if she was among the cold and rumbling clouds or deep in the smothering snow with the earth somewhere far beneath her feet.

She fell again and lay there unmoving, in a white depthless pit where eternity clutched at her with cold, grasping fingers.

She lay still

And then they came from out of the whiteness: shadowy, substanceless figures who turned her face up to the endless storm and spoke among themselves in a strange Indian tongue like the whistling of the wind. They picked her up and laid her on a sledge. They covered her with a warm, heavy fur and she was content to lie there, to lie there and breathe in, to sink into the warmth of living.

The storm would not abate. Amaya hurried on—or they tried to hurry. The snow was very deep. They waded through it, seeing other faces only by chance. Their tracks crisscrossed the snow beneath the pines, but soon the new snow filled up the tracks. In the gullies they sometimes entered drifts up to their heads. The few women who had brought horses had to break the trail for those who followed, for those who were frail or carried children.

They had no way of knowing what was happening behind them. They had only their imagination, and it was best not to dwell on its creations.

They plodded on through the night, muscles knotted, aching, their blood frozen in their veins, their lungs filled with jagged chips of ice, their eyes aching from staring at the night and the storm, seeing nothing.

Amaya's eyelashes had ice on them. Her ears and nose had no feeling at all. If only there had been time to dress properly. She asked Dark Moon constantly, "Are you warm, are you all right?" as he clung to her back, his weight exhausting.

"Yes, Mother. Can we stop?" he would ask.

"No. Not today. Perhaps not tomorrow."

"Where are we going? Where is Father?"

She didn't answer. She had no answer. The storm was a carousing thing bringing war and death in its wake, and even now it could be that Indigo was dead. She knew that. You did not think about it too long or too hard. You walked on through the night and the snow.

Dawn brought a little clearing. It was a savage dawn, bleeding crimson against the tumbling clouds. Filaments of lightning gathered the clouds together, struck figures against the darker chambers and filled the air with the sharp sulfuric scent of skyfire. A pine had been struck by lightning in the night and had fallen directly in their path. A little girl had had her arm broken.

The sun briefly flourished at dawn and then withdrew behind the barricades of clouds again. The wind pushed the fleeing Cheyenne onward, whipping the snow from the trees, dropping it down their backs, lifting the lighter snow from the flats beyond, pushing it southward to drift and fog and swirl. They crossed the little creek at noon—or they thought it was noon. There was no sun to guess by. They climbed the snow-deep flank of the Beaver Hills and from there they could see the soldiers.

A hundred of them, more, traveling northward toward the Cheyenne camp.

"Mother," Akton whispered in fear. Amaya silenced her with a look. They could not be heard or seen—perhaps. It was best to take no chances. They saw the soldiers in long coats, their hats tied down with scarves, plod on into the face of the wind. The horses bucked through the heavy drifts. This army would be exhausted before it got where it was going.

But not too exhausted to kill.

Let Indigo be gone, Amaya said silently. Let them have withdrawn.

They moved on more quickly after that, but with heavier hearts. Beaver Lake, when they found it, was frozen solid. The snow-covered piny hills which folded gently to form a basin for the lake made a pretty view beneath the slowly clearing skies, but no one was in the mood to enjoy scenery. Their feet were blistered and raw, their muscles stiff. They had no shelters for that night, no winter camp, no food for the long months ahead. They did not know if their men walked this earth or had been driven from it by the white soldiers.

Amaya was with a smaller party which joined those who had come first on the northern bank of the lake where an unexpectedly deep canyon offered shelter from the wind which continued to blast and bluster and whine.

"First a shelter," Amaya told Akton. "It may snow again. You must help me. We'll make a lean-to out of pine boughs. Dark Moon, you look for dead wood for our fire—and watch out for your sister. When she gets here, tell her where we are!" Dark Moon was already running off up the snow-covered hillside. For a boy who had been exhausted, he had recovered quickly. Perhaps because the job was adventurous, something a "man" could do.

The pine boughs were heavy and difficult to cut—they had to use chipped stones held in their hands, and the work was tiring after the long forced march, but the weather held and they managed to make some progress. The first boughs were placed upright and then tied together. Amaya used rawhide strips cut from her skirt. The long, sloping roof would shed snow, and if the branches were interwoven properly, the lean-to would stay nearly dry in the worst weather. It wasn't as roomy or as comfortable as a tipi, of course, but it would keep the five of them warm for the time being.

Dark Moon had tired of dragging dead wood to the lean-to and had wandered off to look for Nalin. Inside the lean-to Amaya and Akton spread pine needles for their beds.

"It will be soft at least—and aromatic!" Amaya laughed. Their two blankets were spread over the pine needles.

Then Amaya went outside again, wondering what the others were going to do for food. They had several horses with them, but she thought the owners would not be ready to sacrifice them yet.

"And where is Dark Moon?" she asked. Akton, sagged just inside the lean-to, pointed down toward the lake, where other shelters were being completed. Amaya started that way, wondering if anyone had thought to send lookouts up onto the hill. The wind was cold, the sky cloudy with gaps of blue here and there. Amaya's head still ached. She touched the scabbed groove above her ear and winced.

"Moon and Stars!" Amaya called out.

The woman looked up from her work and lifted a hand. "Hello, Amaya. A bad time, is it not?"

"A bad time. Where is Mother Nalin?"

"Around the lake. You can't see it, there's a little cove." Moon and Stars pointed, and Amaya went on, looking for Dark Moon and Hevatha.

She found Dark Moon with Nalin, stuffing food into his face as rapidly as he could. Mother Nalin stood by smiling. "Hello, hello, Amaya," the old woman said. "You see—a hungry boy. A good thing I stopped to pack a sack, isn't it?"

"It seems so," Amaya said. Dark Moon only nodded, his mouth crammed full. "Where is Hevatha?"

"Hevatha? I don't know." Nalin shrugged.

"Did she go out to find wood? To look for us?"

"I don't know, Amaya. I don't know where she is."

"But she came south with you!" Amaya took Nalin's arm, squeezing it harder than she meant to. Her eyes were moving, fretful. She looked to the snowy slopes beyond Nalin's lean-to and then back to the old woman's face. "She came south with you."

"No. No, she didn't, Amaya."

"They told me . . . Oh, no!"

"She's not with you?" Nalin asked. Amaya just shook her head. "Where is Crooked Foot? He told me he had seen Hevatha with you."

"The night of the raid? Never. Once Akton was there—to ask for her father. It was all such a scramble.

Perhaps he mistook Akton for Hevatha. Then when he saw you, Akton had returned, and so—"

"She was never with you?"

"No."

Dark Moon had stopped eating, his fingers halfway to his mouth. He had never heard his mother's voice like this—broken, rasping. Her eyes drifted past him without seeing him.

"I have to go back," Amaya said faintly.

"You can't go back. You wouldn't make it."

"My daughter is back there!"

"Search the rest of the camp first, Amaya. Perhaps she is here."

"I know she isn't. I can feel this emptiness in me. I felt it all along but I didn't pay it heed."

"You can't go back anyway. She will be along. Probably she found Indigo at last."

"I have to go back."

Nalin saw panic setting in now, and took Amaya firmly by the shoulders. "There are soldiers back there, Amaya. Look to the north—it will snow again. What will you do there? How can you search with the whites around? Where will you go? Amaya, you have two other children. You cannot leave them."

"I have to do something!"

"Wait. Do that which is most difficult—be patient. Wait for Indigo to arrive. Perhaps by then Hevatha will be here. If not, council with your husband. At least one of you will be left with the children that way!"

"Yes." Amaya rubbed her head. It hadn't stopped aching, stopped ringing since the soldier's bullet had clipped her skull. Nalin was right. Everything she said was logical. But it didn't help to realize that. She stood for a long while looking northward, as if she could see past the hills. The wind was very cold and she realized at last that Nalin and Dark Moon were watching her uncomfortably.

"All right!" She managed a cheerful smile. "Let's go home, young man. Your belly is full at least." She reached out for Dark Moon and he came to her.

"Is Hevatha dead?" he asked as Amaya swung him

onto her back. She looked at Mother Nalin and saw the old woman turn away, her head down.

"No. Not Hevatha, not that funny girl." Amaya patted Dark Moon's leg and started back toward the tiny primitive shelter they had built, seeing the people, small and gray against the winter backdrop, huddled together watching nothing with hungry, sad eyes.

The warriors arrived in the morning.

They arrived singly at first, half-dressed, some badly injured. Two of the first five braves had frostbite on their feet or toes. One was dead of a bullet wound within fifteen minutes of arrival. He had lived long enough to tell his wife and children good-bye.

Later in the day the warriors arrived in groups. Few had their war ponies now—the soldiers had driven them off first. The Cheyenne were strung out across the snow-fields. Above them vast battlements of cloud rose into the sky.

Indigo was nearly the last man. Amaya stood waiting. Waiting for her husband and for the daughter who never came.

Indigo slid from the back of his gray horse to stand leaning against the animal. His eyes were red, his face drawn.

"Twenty-one men," he said before he had even embraced Amaya.

"Hevatha ..." Amaya's voice was hesitant, not wanting to know, but she needed to ask.

"What about her?"

"You did not see here there—dead?"

"Hevatha?" Indigo shook his head. "I don't understand you. She is here, is she not?"

"Gone. Indigo, she is gone!"

"We will find her."

"They say the soldiers are back there."

Indigo too looked northward. "They will not always be there. She is a clever girl. She can feed herself and find shelter."

"In this weather?"

"She will have seen us traveling south. She is probably trying to catch up even now. If she does have to shelter for the winter, we will see her in the spring. Where else would she go but to the Buffalo Camp?"

"If she lasts the winter. If she is not already dead."

"Then, Amaya, we can do nothing." His arm started to go around her but he did not complete the gesture. He touched her shoulder briefly and then staggered on, leaving Amaya to watch the white world to the north.

"What will we do now?" Amaya asked Indigo later.

"About Hevatha?"

"About everything." The low fire snapped and twisted in the wind. Indigo's face was bright with firelight, but deeply grooved around the mouth with worry.

"We will make war. So this cannot happen again, we will make war with all our strength."

"Is our strength enough?"

"It will have to be. This will not happen again. Not to my people!" Then Indigo threw down his bowl and rose to walk away from the small fire, to go out into the darkness and speak to the stars, to brood restlessly. Amaya picked up the bowl and turned it over, looking at it as if it held some small secret.

They traveled on, south and east. Twice they raided small settlements and brought away horses and blankets. Winter still raged. They made a camp on the Horn River, far above the water on the bluffs so that they could look out over the land for miles.

Others were drifting toward them, others who were being driven from the north, Omissis Cheyenne and Spotted Sioux. They came together naturally, seeking mutual protection in numbers. Sand Fox arrived on the Horn a month after Indigo and Amaya.

His party was painted for war. He had with him no women, no children but two—the children of Stalking the Wolf, who himself rode beside his rabid leader, Sand Fox. Stalking the Wolf was older, harder, his face yet more savagely scarred, his eyes haunted and deeply set. Many scalps decorated his leggings.

They lifted their hands and rode into the camp, greeting Indigo with neither dislike nor warmth.

"Have you been in the north?" Indigo asked. And

then, as always, he asked about his daughter. And as always, the answer was negative.

"We saw no living Indians, Red Cloud's great camp excepted. There Crazy Horse has brought his people. Sitting Bull speaks high magic. It is time for the whites to be driven from the land. Into the bowels of the earth, to be trampled over by our ponies."

"Yes," Indigo said, "it is time for war. If we cannot have peace, then we must be victorious in war. How are you, Stalking the Wolf, brother?"

"I fight. I live."

Indigo nodded. He looked to the boys, long stringy youths now with paint on their bodies. And one of them, Hatchet, had a scalp on the lance he carried.

"We must talk, Indigo. There is a reason for our arrival."

"All right. In my lodge. Please, get down."

Amaya was there and Stalking the Wolf greeted her without malice. The children were sent away and the men given sycamore tea.

"A man is coming, Indigo. He has something for us. Something we need badly."

"A man?" Indigo looked from one to the other, not understanding.

"A white man," Stalking the Wolf said. A smile curled the corner of his lip.

"A white man?"

"Yes. We must war, but now we are poor in horses, poor in arms. This man will help us. He has the guns that shoot many times."

"The rifles that fire without being reloaded!"

"Yes. So new the white soldiers do not have them."

"Then how—"

"The white government sent them to the Indian agencies to give to their 'tame' Indians. Those who live on their reservations so that they might hunt meat—what meat, I do not know, since the buffalo do not walk near the land the reservations are on."

"But we can get these rifles?"

"All of them. None are delivered to the agency Indians. Red Cloud has bought hundreds of them with furs. The agency man will sell them to us as well. He wants furs and gold."

"We have no gold."

"No matter." Sand Fox's eyes glinted. "No matter, Indigo. We shall have those rifles. And when we do, we shall drive the whites forever from our land. We need guns. We need the men to fire them. Will you make war?"

Indigo thought only a moment—after all, had they not been making war for years now? Not of their own choice, but war nevertheless.

"Yes. We are with you."

"Good. Will you come with us to talk to the Spotted Sioux?"

"If you want me to."

Indigo looked at Amaya, who had been watching, listening silently. There was worry etched on her face. He sent the others outside before he told her: "War has come, we must make it."

"What of peace?"

"I don't know," he said with some irritation. "Peace has never come to us. I do not know if there can be peace with the whites."

"We haven't yet asked for peace. Once we spoke of peace. Once we wanted to send a letter, to talk to them, to find out what they wanted of us—"

"But then they attacked us!"

"And Cheyenne people died. Now more will die."

"I know." He stood close, his eyes searching hers. "It is not the way I want things to be, but this is the way they are, Amaya."

"Ask first for peace."

"If I ask, I ask alone. Will Sand Fox ask? Will Stalking the Wolf?"

"I don't know what they will do, Indigo. I don't know what we *should* do. All I know is that more will die."

"Perhaps," Indigo said, "more will die through peace than through war," and then he was gone, leaving Amaya to wonder at his words.

She no longer knew what was best. She only knew that she was frightened. The world was growing dark and cold. Old friends were dying. Hevatha was lost. Dreams seemed to change to dust and blow away. If they fought, they died; if they made peace, their souls were lost. The winters were cold and the summers were too hot and the buffalo were leaving the hunting grounds or being left to die upon the parched earth. She no longer knew.

Indigo grew uncertain. His boyishness was fading, being overwhelmed by concerns he perhaps could not resolve. He had had no time to learn to be a statesman, a leader, a thoughtful patriarch. War had come and he had been thrust forward and at times Amaya thought that he was not the man for it. Reluctantly she thought that, but perhaps it was true.

And who was the man for it? Who won great victories on the plains? Who could form a lasting, just peace? They had no one to guide them, to use as an example. There were the "tame" Indians, the reservation Indians— and there were those slated to die.

The future was vast, vague, dark, like endless night settling, and at times she could not bear it.

She went out. Why, she did not know. She walked the long hillrise, seeking the silence of the forest. She walked nowhere, everywhere, and the skies went dark without her realizing it. She came upon him suddenly, but it was not completely unexpected. Somehow she had known.

Sun Hawk said, "You wish to dream?"

"Yes."

"In dreams there is sadness."

"I wish to dream."

"To know what will be can score the heart, Amaya."

She didn't answer, and when he turned to walk back to his small, smoky lodge, she walked in his tracks.

"Sit down." He offered her tea but she refused. She sat cross-legged on a blanket, watching the shaman, who was shirtless before the fire. His lodge was made of pine boughs. His buffalo tent had been lost in the north. "Is it time for a long journey, Amaya?"

"Yes. It is time."

"May I ask how you know that?"

"Yes. I know nothing, and so it is time. The need has come to me. The need to know about my daughter lost in the north, about the daughter and son who live with me, whose future is war and more war. I must know . . . *something.*"

"What you learn may be evil. It may be immensely sad."

"It may be joyous."

Sun Hawk shrugged and rose. "You have the right to dream," he said at last. "Everyone has the right. To know, to dream, to accept what lies beyond dreams."

"What lies beyond dreams?" she asked. He would not answer. Instead he told her what she must do.

"Go alone into the mountains. Take no food, nothing to drink. Take a mind that is clear. Start a small fire and on it place your prayers. Above all, do not sleep. Do what you must to stay awake, do not sleep."

There was more, and Amaya listened. Sun Hawk was intent, nearly anxious—why, she couldn't imagine. When she left his lodge, the entire conversation seemed to have no substance. It drifted away on four winds, meaning nothing at all. What was she thinking of—to dream?

It was dark. Stars like blue ice hung in the sky. The pines were dark, the snowfields gleaming. She returned home and told Indigo, "I must go."

"Go where?" he asked, astonished.

"I don't know. A part of me is rising, Indigo, a part of me that has nothing to do with you. Please see to the children."

"When will you be back?"

She was putting a blanket over Dark Moon. Now she straightened, snatched up her shawl, and answered softly, "Soon. I don't know." She kissed him and went out.

The stars cluttered the sky still, beaming and sparkling, crowding each other out of the hungry, many-eyed sky. Amaya walked up the long snowy slopes, her breath steaming from her lips, her head thrown back to breathe the cold air more deeply, her legs feeling strong again, long-striding, springy. The pines fell away and she came to a clearing where she could look back and see all of the star-glittering plains. It was not high enough—she went on.

The going became rocky, ice-sheathed, and treacherous. The cliffs began to glow with a dull sheen. Looking back across her shoulder, Amaya saw the full moon rising, a great yellow eye, a peaceful, comforting thing which dimmed the stars as it floated higher, paling, going silver.

She was breathing very hard when she found her way to the small hanging valley. In spring there would have been grass there and clusters of monkey flowers on the bluffs where water seeped, and gentian and lupine in the hollows and wild lilac in the sun, bobbing in the fresh warm breeze. Now it was an icy stronghold, dark and empty. The water which had run down the bluffs had frozen there, sheeting the walls of stone. The grass was dead. The snow had covered it, smothered it, and then been blown away by violent winter winds.

It was a place of dark beauty, silent and empty, forlorn and cold. Amaya built her fire. And then she waited. She prayed and waited, walking the stony ledge, watching the moon rise higher and begin to fall.

The night grew very cold. The blood stopped flowing in her veins and she could no longer feel her hands and feet. She walked back and forth, still praying, looking to the home of the spirits in the sky.

The fire went out and she started it again. A breeze began to grow and a red line appeared against the horizon. The night had gone. Amaya's stomach was hollow, constricted. Her limbs were like logs tied to her body.

I should go home. The girls will want to eat.

She felt foolish, thin, weak, helpless, small, and imprisoned. Imprisoned in her body, in her eyeless soul, in her heart that had not learned many things, but only—achingly—wanted to, and the things she wanted to learn were not of the earth in a man's arms, in a baby's cry, in the flowing of her milk, the toil and breath and struggle of life.

She sat on the ledge and watched the sun grow, brighten, fade. She was very tired. Her eyelids began to droop. She collected a bed of sharp flinty rocks like large arrowheads and she sat upon them, taking smaller stone slivers to wedge between her toes painfully.

She was very tired.

She rose and walked the valley, pinching herself, scolding herself. The fire was nearly out again, and so she fueled it. She prayed and fasted and the day drifted away, becoming purple dusk, and in the solitude of quiet dusk her eyes once closed and she nearly fell over asleep. Amaya railed at herself; that would not do. She had to know . . . something. That bothered her. She prayed, but for what? She asked for something from the spirits, but it was indefinable.

She crouched by the fire and watched the tiny writhing flames, the weave and twist of them, golden and red and deep violet and orange. She tried to sort out the colors, to understand the meanings of the colors. It had gotten very dark again but the moon had not risen. It had gotten dark and there were no stars.

She started to rise but her legs refused and she toppled onto her side, her hair across her face, a round stone wedged against her hip, the fire wavering before her eyes, a distant night creature calling.

The wind began. Moaning, creeping across the world, a whirling, softly touching, receding, prodding wind which found its way into the valley and reached for Amaya, taking hold of her legs, her neck, shaking her.

"Is it time?" something asked, and she sat up, not wanting to look into the wind, not wanting to surrender, for it had come to take her, she knew that.

"The Sky Maiden," the same voice said. "Fallen to its stony cradle."

She sat up, rubbed her eyes, and stared at the fire, which had become a fountain of sparks, golden and leaping, forming clusters of brilliant, evanescent flowers. They became smoke rising like cold and empty prayers to the starless sky. The wind took Amaya from her cradle and thrust her skyward, and she drifted through the soft, too-comforting world beyond the stars.

"Haven't I lived this way before?" she asked, and the universe echoed with the words, which returned to her ears as laughter. She was suddenly falling. Falling again, always falling. The snowstorm gathered around her, coalescing into brittle white stone which broke apart as it met the earth.

She rose and walked the broad and sunny land, seeing the yellow heads of the flowers turn toward her as the gentle southern breeze turned the long grass. Larks sang in the deep grass, and far off, antelope leapt high against the blue sky.

On the distant hilltop darkened by cloud shadows a man and a woman stood watching. The woman was tall and proud, extremely beautiful. The man beside her was tattooed from his neck to his feet. They lifted hands of greeting to her and then vanished in the mists.

Then a man came to her and they fell naked into the grass and he lay looking at her, wondering at her difference, wanting to enter her and find her secrets, and she pulled him down, smelling the sun warmth of the grass, of his hair, of his body. Tiny white butterflies danced overhead.

They rose and walked the land. It was good. On the hillrise the old woman watched and Amaya realized that the old woman was her, proud, content.

They walked and became warriors and the field was littered with dark, bloated dead. Half buffalo, half man. All dead. Amaya could not cry; she was a warrior.

"I am weary," her companion said. "Weary."

"You must go on."

"On your back. Only if you will carry me."

And so she carried him, her legs sinking into the earth as if it were deep snow. She thought for a moment the man was Dark Moon, but he was so large it couldn't have been. Still there were more bodies.

"I am weary," the man on her back said. His feet dragged the ground. The wind came and he was gone and the dead were gone. There was only Amaya. The land was long and she went to the river to swim.

He stood there. Poised on the low-hanging branch of a tree. The river glittered. Dragonflies hummed low across the water. He was a youth, a Cheyenne boy with his arms held high. He started to dive, crouching slightly, his face rapt, bright with the reflected light off the river. She knew him but had never met him. She wanted him to hurry. She rushed forward to tell him that it was important, necessary, that the plains were already dark with the dead.

But he was gone.

The water was still. She waited but he did not come to the surface of the river. He had never dived. A moment, a gesture begun, a necessary fulfillment left uncompleted.

She blinked and he was gone and the woman alone

walked the high, sunny plains. A woman alone and the man who had been waiting in the grass called out to her and she returned, laughing, the wind lifting her loose hair.

She fell into his arms and it was good. He put her on the grass and entered her. She could feel the flexing of his body, the tensing of muscle and tendon, see the blood rushing through the vessels on his throat, at his temples. Her hands felt the sun-warmed flesh of his back. The thrust and urgency of him overwhelmed her so that she could hardly breathe until the sun went down and he stopped, the night cooling his body, his breathing slowing as she stroked him, a child to be held and pampered.

They rose at dawn and watched the buffalo return to the plains. The children went with them. They lay in the grass and watched the tiny white flowers, smaller than the pupils of his watching eyes.

They watched the flowers and as a child laughed, they fell asleep, waking to find the gray hair on each other's heads. Their life had passed in a dream, or they dreamed now—they were not sure which. It had been happy; the buffalo came; the spring with its warmth and new grass.

And then the man was gone somewhere; she blinked and he was gone; she blinked and the Cheyenne boy was there, crouching slightly, face rapt, waiting to dive into the river, but he would not.

She stepped toward him and fell.

The ground was hard, cold, the land dark, the skies bright with far-dancing stars. Amaya sat up, her head ringing. She thought for a moment that the white man had shot her in the head. Dazed, she held her temple and looked around. It was cold in the tiny valley. The wind was raw and wintry. She tried to stand but fell. She was very weak. The second time she made it to her feet.

It was coming on to dawn. The horizon glowed softly with deep bloodred. A new dawn? The same dawn?

"I am the same."

It was an odd thing to say. She had expected to be the same. Why should she not be? The dream rushed back then in fragments and sections, tumbling over her, staggering her with the jumble of images: the dead, the living, the diver, the empty skies. There was a meaning beyond thought among all, but it would not come then. Not then, but soon.

She walked down the mountain slope, going very cautiously, and when she reached the village she went into her tent to lie beside Indigo, who said nothing, who put his arm around her and stroked her hair.

That evening the white man came. He was not alone. Two half-breed Sioux Indians were with him. He looked confident and pleased; the half-breeds looked very wary.

They rode in a spring wagon which jolted and rocked across the miserable camp of the war-torn Cheyenne. Indigo said, "I must go down now."

"I will come too."

Indigo looked at his wife with curiosity. "All right. It may not go well."

"What do you mean?" Amaya picked up her shawl and ducked out of the tent. She walked with Indigo toward the creek, which still flowed onto the frozen lake, making strange, monstrous shapes where, frustrated in its passage, it eddied and sought new outlets, freezing en route.

"Sand Fox and Stalking the Wolf."

"Yes?" Amaya anticipated more answer, but Indigo offered none.

They walked through the oaks to the clearing where the wagon had been halted. Sand Fox was there with Stalking the Wolf. Beside them was a warrior Amaya had only seen but did not know from Sand Fox's band, and Wing, who rode always with Stalking the Wolf now. There were others in the woods, but the white was not aware of it.

"So this is the other man," the white said. He spoke the Cheyenne tongue, but not well. He was small, round in the belly, red-haired. His hands were thick and freckled. The other Cheyenne glanced at Indigo and at Amaya. Stalking the Wolf didn't seem to like her being there, but nothing was said.

"Here, try this one out, big chief." The white man gave Indigo a rifle. The Cheyenne leader examined it closely, working the lever which ejected spent cartridges and placed new ones in the breech.

"You have bullets?" Indigo asked.

"Of course, big chief, but I got to hold them back until we've made our deal."

"How," Amaya said in English, "do we know the rifles work without trying them? Give him the bullets he's asked for." She didn't like the man. He was dirty. He had no loyalty to his people. He was rude and probably very wealthy. Where had he gotten these guns? They said from the reservation Indians, who needed them to hunt game.

"Sure, lady." He turned his head, gestured, and one of his half-breeds tossed him a green box of cartridges, which the white man gave to Indigo. Sand Fox's eyes glittered.

Indigo loaded five cartridges into the gun, put it to his shoulder, and fired twice, clipping a branch from a tree. Sand Fox asked, "All the others are the same?"

"Sure, big chief."

"You have plenty of bullets?"

"A hundred rounds for each."

Sand Fox nodded. He stretched out a hand and Indigo gave him the rifle. Before Amaya could blink, the Cheyenne war leader had turned the gun on the white man. The first shot tore away his throat and hurled the gun-runner back against his wagon. He sagged to the earth in a pool of his own blood. Sand Fox switched his sights to one of the half-breeds. He had started running, running wildly for the shelter of the woods. Sand Fox shot him in the back, shattering his spine. He dropped like a rag doll to the earth. He missed the second half-breed, and the rifle's hammer snapped down on an empty chamber. No matter. There was a scream moments later. There had been other watchers in the woods.

"So!" Sand Fox smiled and handed the rifle back to Indigo. "It is good."

"It is good," Indigo said, but he seemed uncertain. He held the rifle as if it were a strange object never seen before. When Sand Fox gave him a box of bullets he held them in the same way. From the woods and from the camp other warriors came. They whooped and leapt across the clearing as Sand Fox and Wing threw down the shiny new weapons from the wagon.

"Come," Indigo said, "let us go home again."

"Yes." Amaya did not like what had been done either.

"I am weary, Amaya," he told her, and her head jerked up. Echoes from deep in the chambers of her mind, or from the dark forest around her, swept over her. *I am weary.*

He was weary and she must carry him. *Weary.* She had stopped without realizing it. Now Indigo peered closely at her. "What is it, Amaya? Is something wrong?"

"No, Indigo." She shook her head, put her arm around his waist, and leaned her head against the strong shoulder. "Nothing is wrong."

Behind them the cheers went on, growing louder. Now there was a fire, brilliant against the night and snow. The white man's wagon was burning. The war fires were stirring again.

10

THE WORLD WAS in chaos. In the north the Sioux battled, winning a little ground, a little time. The Cheyenne struck hard, their forces rolling back the tide of settlers, their soldier guards. Then more soldiers came and the ammunition for the new rifles ran low and the Cheyenne withdrew. Nothing was gained but death for too many.

There was no word of Hevatha. Amaya sent inquiries to all the tribes of the north. She had not been seen. There was nothing left to do but mourn her.

Indigo grew unhappy. "We fight and the young men die. We must fight and so we do not even hunt. When we do hunt, we find the buffalo few. When we return, sometimes there is no village. Sometimes those we love have been killed. What sort of war is this? I see my friends grow bitter; they become war lovers. There is a rot at the heart of our culture like a tree infected. Stalking the Wolf breeds children who must kill. Where is the end to it? I see this, Amaya—more blood, starvation, hatred. And there is nothing at all to be done about it. Nothing." His head hung. Firelight caused moving shadows to flow across his face.

"I will go," Amaya said abruptly.

"Go where, Amaya?"

"Do you not wish to seek peace, to ask the whites what they want?"

"You can't go! Are you mad?"

"Isn't that what you want?"

"Yes." Indigo admitted it as if the idea stunned him. "I want my people to live as they have. Not to war so that war will never pass away."

"So they will." Amaya got to her knees beside Indigo. Taking his face in her hands, she lifted it. "I know this. I have had a dream, Indigo. Of sunlit plains and long herds of buffalo, of joy and love."

"I will council—"

"Not now, not yet. Let me find out first what they want. Perhaps it will come to nothing."

"Will you be safe?"

"I think so."

"Where will you go?" he asked anxiously.

"Fort Laramie. I think I know the way," she remarked ironically.

They discussed it the night long, but Amaya had already made up her mind. She had done so even before speaking to Indigo. Long ago she had decided that peace must be made, an honorable peace. It was necessary to know what the whites wanted. Perhaps small concessions could be made.

She rode across the long plains. The grass was new and bright. Here and there were still patches of snow. She thought of her daughters, walking the long plains, finding a man as they had in her dream, living the life of the Cheyenne, being happy in the endless way, suffering occasional sorrow, but living within the heart of the tribe as she had, hunting, praying, celebrating.

The low dark forms on the horizon gradually rose from the plains and Amaya's mouth tightened. She forced away her anger. She could do her people no good if she let emotions dictate her course. To the right was the town, much larger now. To the left the old fort. Did they still have an Indian orphan school? Was that despicable Reverend Quill still here?

She felt suddenly inadequate. Whom could she talk to, what could she say? Would they listen or throw her in jail, perhaps kill her? She scolded herself. Indigo was weary, the people weary.

She rode directly to the main gate, and since it was open, she rode through. There were soldiers lounging here and there along the plank walks in front of the buildings. At one building they drank from brown bottles, some glancing up, but paying no particular attention. There were all sorts of people at the fort—civilian teamsters with huge freight wagons filled with supplies, farmers in overalls and big hats, buffalo hunters in buckskins, carrying long rifles, bearded and lean. There were Indians there as well. Amaya saw Crow and Arikara. They saw her as well, these Indian scouts, and they knew if the whites did not that a high-ranking Cheyenne woman was among them, not a woman from off a reservation, a quiet, meek little thing, but a woman from the warrior tribes.

Amaya hadn't read English for a time, but she had forgotten none of it. She walked her horse to the post commander's office and got down, looking at the sign there: MAJOR HAROLD STAGGS, COMMANDER.

She went up the steps and into the small room beyond the door.

"Hey, get out of here, woman!" A big red-faced man rose from behind a small desk. "No squaw woman here, understand? You go."

"I wish to see Major Staggs."

"You do, do you?" The man walked toward her. He took her by the shoulders and turned her. "You wait till he rides by the reservation, squaw, then you will see him."

"Damn you!" Amaya spun angrily away. "I am here to try to prevent war, maybe to prevent your death, and you make of this a game. I am Amaya, the wife of Indigo. I am Cheyenne!"

"What is this, Sergeant Percy?"

The man in the inner doorway spoke with a drawl. There were broken veins across his nose and cheeks; his eyes were red and pouched.

"Sorry, sir. Woman trying to bust in here."

"Did she say she was Cheyenne?"

"I am Cheyenne," Amaya said. "The wife of Indigo. You know that name. And the name of Sand Fox and Stalking the Wolf."

"You come to speak for them?" Staggs's eyes narrowed in amusement.

"I have come to speak! Someone must speak. Time is running out. There can be only blood and then more blood."

Major Harry Staggs had a thin cigar. He lit it slowly

and blew out the match. "If it's Indian blood," he said coldly, "then it's all for the best. Get her out, Percy!"

"Yes, sir! Lock her up?"

"What for? Just get her out of here. Probably one of Pierce's schemes anyway."

Then the major turned and slammed his office door. The big sergeant propelled Amaya toward the door. She twisted in his arms and asked over her shoulder, "Please, the major said 'Pierce.' Did he mean Andy Pierce?"

"You know he did. Go on, now." Amaya was outside, the sergeant blocking the doorway.

"Andy Pierce is here?" Amaya asked. "Where? Please tell me."

"He's down on the reservation. That's where he lives. Now, get off this post before something happens to you." The sergeant leveled a stubby warning finger and tramped back inside, leaving Amaya to stand beneath the awning on a plank walk, turning slowly away to look toward her horse, where two Crow scouts wearing German silver conchas stood watching back.

She walked to her horse and mounted. The Crow were standing so near that her foot brushed one of them. Amaya ignored them and their comments muttered in their own tongue, and rode toward the gate.

It was no trouble to find the reservation across the river, but she could find no buildings. An Arapaho man stood inside a split-rail fence leaning on the handle of a hoe. Behind him was a cornfield, or what was supposed to be one. Crooked furrows scored the dry earth where here and there brown plants a few inches high sprouted out of the sides of the rows.

"Where is Andy Pierce?" Amaya asked in English. There was no answer immediately. The Arapaho looked at her and knew she was a free Indian. Perhaps he was ashamed. He let the hoe drop from his hands and finally pointed up the road. He stood watching her as she rode toward the white house beyond the trees.

There were hogs here and there, a cow or two, but Amaya saw no horses. There were tipis and the old log barracks and a few buildings of brick, one of which said "Indian School" on the front of it. Children sat in front of the school, staring at her with dark eyes. There was anger there, anger which had no outlet, which one day would find one.

Some of the homes were only shacks thrown together out of old packing crates, and Amaya sucked in her breath in anger. Trash littered the ground, old tins and empty boxes, rusting farm implements.

The small white house at the end of the road was newly painted. Behind it was a small garden, neatly planted. Corn and squash flourished there. A man in a straw hat, a half-breed, was working in the garden. Amaya got down and tied her horse to the rail before the house. An old Indian in a blanket sat on the porch watching.

Amaya mounted the steps and entered the house.

"Yes?"

The woman behind the desk was Indian, but she wore a white dress. She looked impatiently at Amaya.

"I want to see Andy Pierce."

"All right. Will you wait, please? You may sit." She spoke very slowly to Amaya, making a pushing gesture with her hands as she told her to sit.

The secretary waited until Amaya did sit, then went into an inner office. Amaya looked around at the white walls, the war lance and Mandan shield on the wall, the painting of a Pawnee in full regalia to the left. There was a window through which Amaya could see a ball game she didn't understand being played on a dusty field.

The door opened and the secretary returned.

"Mr. Pierce will see you now." A faint perfunctory smile followed.

Amaya rose and walked to the door. She went in, stopping just beyond the door. Andy Pierce was bent over his work, scratching away with a steel pen. He wore spectacles which magnified his green eyes. His freckled face was a little rounder, his reddish hair a little thinner. He looked up and his eyes grew wider yet. He dropped the pen, smiled hesitantly, rose and took off his spectacles, peering more intently at her.

"Is it you, really?"

"It is me, Andy Pierce." Amaya walked forward a step. Pierce stretched out his hands but Amaya did not take them, and they fell awkwardly to his sides.

"Please sit down . . . I can't believe you're here. I can't guess why you would be."

Amaya sat in a wooden chair—a little rigidly, he noticed. A cool breeze blew through the open windows. They heard an Indian boy yell out on the ball field.

"I have come to you because I don't know whom else to ask."

"Yes?" Pierce sat and leaned back, steepling his fingers.

"People are dying, Andy Pierce. The Cheyenne wish to know what the whites want, what the price of peace is. I want to talk to someone who can tell me."

"Good God! You're serious?" Pierce came upright suddenly.

"Of course."

"But this is wonderful. The Cheyenne seek peace?"

"We ask what the price is, Andy Pierce. Perhaps then we will seek it."

"I understand. . . . Have you spoken with Major Staggs?"

"I was thrown out of his office."

"That sounds like Harry, unfortunately. Do you remember him at all? He used to drink and rake hell. His younger follies have turned to vices—they have aged him, I'm afraid, and lessened his acuity."

"Does he fight?" Amaya wanted to know.

"Harry? Oh, yes, indeed!" Andy laughed humorlessly. "Fighting is salvation for a soldier like Staggs. He dreams of greater things, other promotions, but they'll never come. His superiors must know his weaknesses."

"Whiskey."

"Among others. Yes, whiskey. It's a shame. I liked Harry Staggs once." Pierce cocked his head and lifted one shoulder in a crooked shrug.

"Then whom do I talk to?"

"There's no one here, I'm afraid."

"No one who can speak of peace!" She was incredulous.

"No. Someone from Washington would have to come out. Someone from the BIA and someone from the War Department, I expect. Perhaps Congress would—"

Amaya laughed harshly. "And how many of these people must come to make a war?"

"That, Major Staggs makes alone. He and this other

flamboyant jackass, Custer. I'm sorry, Amaya. You know how it must be with councils."

"Yes. But I cannot give this up like this. Someone must speak, someone must decide if we wish to continue the killing."

"Can you guarantee the Cheyenne will not fight until this is resolved?" Andy asked hopefully.

"No. I cannot speak for the war leaders."

"You can make no assurances?"

"No more than you can—I only know we must seek to understand each other before it is too late."

"If only you could promise an armistice . . ." Pierce went to look out the window. His waistline, Amaya noticed with a smile, had expanded a little.

"Even if I could speak for my husband, I could not speak for men like Sand Fox."

"You are married, then. Of course, you would be." Pierce turned from the window. "What is his name?"

"Indigo."

Pierce only nodded, returning to his desk. "We must do what we can. You're right, Amaya. Will you help me?"

"How?"

"I am going to draft a letter to my superiors. Copies will be sent to the army and the Congress, to the president. I want you to help me word this, to word it very carefully. I want the Sioux and the Cheyenne to come into Fort Laramie or to meet us on some neutral ground. I want to find a way to peace, as you do."

"Is there a way?"

"I don't know." Andy smiled. "Let's hope so. Now, then . . ." He took paper from his desk drawer and dipped his pen in his inkwell, and as Amaya watched, he began drafting his letter.

It would take weeks, perhaps months before any answer could arrive. Amaya stayed on the reservation; there was no point in traveling home. She also nurtured a suspicion that if she did leave, she would be followed to the new camp.

She lived in a barracks with other unmarried, widowed, or separated women. She entered it that first day with Pierce and was gripped immediately by a sort of tangible

horror which seemed to reach out and seize her heart.
She must have shown her emotions on her face.

"You can leave whenever you want," Pierce said.

"This is all right."

"You fear the place, don't you?"

"It is white," Amaya said; but there was more to it
than that. It reminded her too strongly of the past, the
past which had seemed an imprisonment with no promise of release. She was not in the same building, but it
might have been the one where she and Tantha lived,
where she had slept the long, hopeless nights away,
dreaming of the land of the Cheyenne, thinking she
could never reach it.

The women who lived there now were the same as
before. Their faces were blank, purposely blank. Their
souls were dark, their eyes searching yet unexpectant.
Some waited and watched for ghosts; others slept their
lives away.

The fields Amaya was shown were all much the same
as the one the Arapaho had been tending the day of her
arrival. Andy Pierce put a foot up on the rail of the fence
and stared at the stunted corn.

"I had hoped they would take to this. Now I see they
won't."

"How could you expect it?"

"I don't know. The Indian used to grow corn."

"Yes, the Cheyenne did. Now we have 'lost the corn,'
as the saying goes. Do you know how that happened,
Andy Pierce? The Sioux and Cheyenne used to live to
the east. Then the whites came. Then they gave up the
corn and took to the horse and became buffalo hunters.
Now the whites come and give them back the corn—it is
an insult to a warrior."

"Yes." Pierce was thoughtful. "I suppose it is."

"But you will continue to make them grow corn?"

"It's not my decision, Amaya. This idea has been pop-
ular with reformers and progressives since Jefferson.
The idea of making the Indian white, to fit him to our
culture. The seed is shipped, the iron tools. I am told to
give them a place to plant corn, and the corn is indiffer-
ently, carelessly, angrily planted. The corn does not grow,
so more seed is sent."

"You sound angry, Andy Pierce."

"Don't you think a white man can become angry at injustice or foolishness? We aren't all warriors, Amaya."

"You were."

"No longer. No longer."

They walked and spoke. The river, the Platte, was narrow and bright in the sun. "James Dawes is dead. He retired and, I think, brooded himself to death. His son came through here one summer and told me. I was sad to hear it."

"I think he was a friend of the Indian."

"Amaya." He stopped and started to take her shoulders before halting. "I am a friend of the Indian too. Please believe me."

"Show me one friend," she said, more sharply than she intended. "One Indian who calls you friend."

"Pandtha, who works in my office—"

"Works for you."

"And her brother, Broken Antler, who maintains the garden and grounds—"

"Works for you."

"You? You, Amaya. Are you at least my friend?"

"Come," she said, "let us walk on." She felt vaguely ashamed, for she thought that Andy Pierce, like many men who are too sincere, had no friend anywhere, white or Indian.

It was four weeks before the letter came. Andy caught Amaya as she watched a lacrosse game, a torrent of dust and noise, waving sticks on the ball field. He arrived breathless. "It came. It's been agreed to. There will be a peace conference!"

He waved the letter under her nose so that she couldn't read it and then sheepishly handed it over so that Amaya could look the words over herself. She nodded briskly, with satisfaction. "Then . . . has Major Staggs heard of this?"

"He will have gotten a simultaneous dispatch, yes. Amaya, you really believe there will be a good peace, don't you?"

"There will be a peace. I know this from a dream. There first will be a battle and then long summers. My daughters walking the plains with a strong, good man, an Indian man. A Cheyenne! And the buffalo will be hunted but they will return. I saw this; I know this."

She saw the way Pierce was watching her, with deep interest, with a hint of amusement, but more than anything with fondness, and she broke off quickly.

"You would not understand," she said hastily.

"I would not understand what it is to dream?" Pierce smiled and then the smile fell away. A sadness had settled on him. She still thought so little of him. Still she would not even consent to friendship. "Believe me, I understand what it is to dream. I have always been a dreamer."

He turned then and walked away, and Amaya watched him before she spun and with a tight expression began watching the lacrosse game once more.

She left under cover of darkness. It was to be another six weeks before the men from Washington arrived. The paper had said nothing about ceasing hostilities before that time. Amaya still feared being followed and so she did not ride due west, but crossed the North Platte as the moon rose, drawing a silver band across the water, turning north to ride for a mile or so through the oaks which clustered along the river's edge. Then she turned south again. Reaching the deepest part of the oak woods, she dismounted and squatted down patiently to wait.

She waited. The wind was soft, like the breathing of the night. The river slid away, moon-bright and silky. Her eyes were drawn suddenly to the shadows moving northward. Patient, plodding shadows, one with the dark woods. And then the moon caught the German silver conchas and Amaya smiled wryly, bitterly.

She remained absolutely still, her hand over the muzzle of her horse so that it would not blow when it smelled others of its kind. She waited and they passed by, within twenty feet of her, following her tracks by moonlight.

She let them go, and when they were out of sight she mounted her horse again and rode to the river's edge, then swiftly southward along the sandy beach until she recrossed the river and was gone onto the western plains, leaving the Crow scouts far behind.

It was three days to the Pine Camp. All seemed to be

well as she rode in and swung down. Dark Moon had seen her from a distance and now he ran to her, throwing down the toy bow he had been playing with.

"Is everything all right?" she asked him, holding him up with one arm, rumpling his hair with her free hand.

"Yes. Akton pinched me!" he said quite seriously. Amaya laughed.

The horse herd to the south of the pine ridge was greatly increased. Amaya asked Dark Moon, "Is someone here?"

"Sand Fox," he told her, snatching up his tiny bow as they walked past it. "Uncle Stalking the Wolf and his boys—I don't like Hatchet, he hits me. Why do I have a baby's name when he has a man's? No one else—just them."

He stopped only because he ran out of breath, Amaya thought. She spanked him once affectionately and he ran off to play. The new lodges, made from the first hunt of the year, were just now going up. Amaya had not been there to tend to such work. Nor would she be for a while if things went as she hoped. There was time for that sort of work later.

Indigo was at the lake. Not fishing, not swimming, only watching the rippling of the water, the shifting lights that played across its surface. He turned toward her, his eyes deep and soft.

"Amaya!" He held out his arms and his blanket fell away. She held her husband, feeling the need in him, a need for all sorts of support, for something Indigo could not define himself—the need for her to perhaps replace a dream that had withered.

"The whites wish to council," Amaya said, and she pulled the letter from her dress. Indigo took it, peering at the mysterious characters.

"What does it say?"

"That representatives of the United States government wish to meet under a covenant of truce to discuss means of negotiating a lasting peace upon the plains with those Sioux and Cheyenne tribes which have been engaged in hostilities against the United States."

"What do we do?"

"You are council chief, Indigo."

"I do not know the whites. Do you trust them?"

"No," Amaya said after a minute, "not at all. I trust them to meet with us and speak, yes."

"You do not think it would be a trap?"

"No."

"Will the Sioux go?"

"I don't know, they have already refused one peace proposal. Whether they go or not, Indigo, we must. We must at least talk! To talk is not to surrender. To talk is to explain who we are, how we feel, what must be done to satisfy us. In return perhaps they will tell us what they wish, and it may not be so complicated as we fear."

"They may not have land this side of the Horn," Indigo said strongly. "I have always said that."

"All right. Tell them that."

"Perhaps it could be allowed for them to cross our land," he added uncertainly.

"All right, then we may have means of bargaining."

"Perhaps they will misunderstand me. You must go with me, Amaya, so that I make no mistake."

"I am going, Indigo. I am going so that there can be no mistake."

It took time to gather the leaders of the Cheyenne nation. Some refused to come. Long Sky Dreaming was too old to travel, and bowed out. High Top Mountain with three young war leaders came to the camp of Indigo. Sand Fox was not wanted, not invited, but he insisted on going.

"Perhaps it is right," Amaya said. "He is the warlike one. He is the one they must convince."

At any rate they could not refuse the war leader, nor Stalking the Wolf, who rode with him. The party in all was less than fifty Cheyenne dignitaries. Three days before the white leaders from Washington were due to arrive at Laramie, they rode out of the Pine Camp, leaving it in Hands on His Face's charge. Laughing Nose was there to see them off. He told Amaya, "Please stay away. No one will ever miss you," and he ran backward alongside her horse for nearly half a mile.

Then Laughing Nose was gone, the camp was gone, and the world became a sober place. Ahead there was a chance for peace, a chance to stop the bloodshed before her daughter and son, her friends, were touched by it. There was an equal, perhaps greater chance, of failure. Looking at the faces of the men she rode with, Amaya sensed that their mood was not optimistic.

"A long way from the Arrowpoint, is it not?" High Top Mountain asked as he and Amaya rode side by side across the wide land.

"A long way," she agreed with the old chief.

"Do you have memories of that time, Amaya?"

"Yes, of course."

"And I. That was a peace meeting, but to have peace with Quahadi was worse than to have war with him. He brought many enemies with him. The man wished to use the Cheyenne."

"That is so."

"What of the whites, Amaya? Do they wish to use the Cheyenne?"

"It may be. I do not know."

"And you do not trust them."

"No." She told him briefly of the Crow scouts. "The army even then, I believe, wished to follow me to our new camp. I have met this Major Staggs, the commander at Laramie. Whiskey has made him reckless and moody. He is also bitter over lost promotions. He sees war as a salvation."

"Yes," High Top Mountain said. His eyes had drifted to Sand Fox. "I understand that. But he will have no voice in this peace?"

"Perhaps a small one, but no more."

"That is good. A warrior must make his war; the council must make the peace. That is the way it must be."

The following morning they arrived. The Cheyenne party halted on a hillrise a mile west of Laramie and they simply sat and stared. Most of them had never seen a white town. It wasn't what they expected. It was much larger than they had thought, for one thing, the fort more ominous, solid. They could see blue soldiers on the ramparts, more within.

They rode in slowly. The Sioux did not seem to be there yet, if they were coming at all. From the reservation, Indians ran to watch the Cheyenne ride in, the wind shifting their war bonnets' feathers, their faces dark, immobile, proud, their backs straight.

A party of whites was coming out of the fort now, and High Top Mountain held the Cheyenne back. Three men in uniform, three in suits, all mounted, rode slowly toward them. Amaya could identify only two of the whites.

"The man in uniform on the left—that is Major Staggs. The one without a hat is the Indian agent, Andrew Pierce. It is he we can trust if any of them can be trusted."

Indigo asked, "Do you trust him completely?"

"I trust no white completely," she answered, and the response was well-received by those around her. It was through Amaya, of course, that all negotiations would have to be funneled. Her translations would be influenced by what she believed to be implicit in the white words.

Now Amaya recognized the officer in the middle, corpulent, wearing a star on his shoulders. It was Charles Lord, once post commander at Laramie himself. The other officer also wore stars. He was a huge man with a white mustache. The other civilians were of two distinct types. The one was tall, lean, pale, nearly effeminate. He had spent little time in the sun. This, they would discover, was William DeQuincy from the BIA in Washington, Andy Pierce's superior. The other man, although in civilian clothes, had the cut of a soldier, the confident, stiff manner, the tan of a Western man. He was Senator George Tufts, former brigadier general in the Civil War.

High Top Mountain looked at the whites as they slowly approached, measuring them. Then he glanced at Indigo and Amaya—he did not like what he saw.

"Welcome." This was Senator Tufts. He lifted his hand and High Top Mountain returned the strained gesture. "My name is George Tufts. You are the supreme Cheyenne chief?" he asked, indicating immediately that he had no idea how the Cheyenne government was organized.

"This is High Top Mountain," Amaya said. "He is a principal chief. This is Indigo, another principal chief." Amaya saw Andy Pierce's eyes grow thoughtful, run over Indigo's face and lean body. "I am the wife of

Indigo, Amaya. I will speak to the council chiefs for you."

"Well said," Tufts said patronizingly. He then proceeded to introduce the others. Major Staggs looked restless and hung-over, DeQuincy completely ill-at-ease. Lord actually looked bored with things. He had gone on to Washington and apparently now found Laramie lacking.

Amaya introduced Wing, and High Top Mountain's subchief, Hour of Thunder, then Stalking the Wolf and Sand Fox. The eyes of Staggs, red and weary, suddenly became alert as he looked at Sand Fox, small, dark, cunning, and the badly scarred, twisted features of Stalking the Wolf. He said something in a very low voice to General Lord.

The Cheyenne camp was made adjacent to the reservation. Amaya took Indigo for a walk through it. He shook his head as he looked at the corn, the weeds, the faces of despair.

"They have traded their birthright," he said, and for a long time they continued to walk in silence. Then, he said, "So, this is where you lived. It is strange to walk the ground where you have walked in other years. How differently you must see things."

And she did. She saw Tantha and Little Dove and the Quills. Yes, and Andy Pierce, who had been so young, his face freckled and funny, alien; she saw the sober, kind Dawes, who had failed so miserably. "We must not fail, Indigo," she said as they stopped beneath an oak to watch the sunset.

"We will not," he laughed. He turned. They both did, and watched the red sky beyond the outstretched arms of the great oak. The long-running sky, infinite, beautiful, unmarred. A dog barked on the reservation and they looked that way, seeing the collection of ramshackle houses, the leaning sheds, the rusting tools. Silently they walked away, out onto the long grass where the Cheyenne had made their camp.

In the morning they counciled with the white leaders. Since Indigo and High Top Mountain refused to go into the fort, the meeting was held inside a great white canvas tent with a wooden floor outside the walls of Laramie. The Sioux, they were told, had refused to come.

"Of course they shall come to our point of view in time," Major Staggs said rather mysteriously. He smelled of bay rum and licorice. The senator sat at the head of the table, but it was General Lord who spoke.

"We welcome the Cheyenne to our table," Lord said, smiling. He paused to allow Amaya to translate. "I trust we can find a solution to our mutual problems. High Top Mountain? Would you care to speak first and tell us what it is the Cheyenne require?"

The old chief looked right and then left along the table. He stood then with dignity but with some trouble. Indigo braced his elbow as he rose. High Top Mountain looked at the whites one by one. Then he began, speaking slowly, but with clear emphasis.

"The land where you have made your camp is Cheyenne land. It was given to us by Manitou. I can show you where it is written down on a sacred buffalo hide. The water you drink is ours, sweet and cold. This, Manitou gave us. When your hunters go onto the plains to hunt, it is our buffalo they kill. When you wish to cut timber, our trees are cut down. When your people wish to dig in the earth, they are digging into the breast of our mother." High Top Mountain touched his fingertips to his breast. His face, lined, serene, hid a multitude of rising emotions.

"When our land is crossed, the travelers cut furrows in the grass and burn the grass and kill the game that live upon it. When we come and chase them away, then the white soldiers come to punish us! To punish us," he repeated, shaking his head. "I want to say this: the land is ours. You have taken much. You may have no more."

Senator Tufts responded as High Top Mountain seated himself. "Much of what you say is true," he admitted offhandedly, hurriedly. "But what of the people who wish to cross your land to Oregon? Many have been killed. Women and children. We can't allow that."

Sand Fox was seething. His head hung forward much as Amaya had seen in the great council meeting on Cottonwood Island. The tendons on his throat bulged and leapt.

Indigo answered the senator. "Perhaps these people could cross our land." Sand Fox was glowering at Indigo now. "If we could make peace. If they would not kill our buffalo. If they would not settle there and plant their corn."

"I don't see how we could promise that," General Lord muttered. "People are going to do what they're going to do."

"How can we not?" Andy Pierce asked, speaking up for the first time. "What the Cheyenne say is true. It seems a sound foundation for a just peace if we could agree to hold western expansion to this point as far as permanent settlements go. Then the Cheyenne, if I understand, would be willing to entertain the thought of allowing settlers bound for Oregon and California to cross their land unmolested."

"And that, sir, leaves us with a nation divided by a thousand miles of hostile territory," General Lord snapped.

"That has nothing to do with the Cheyenne. This expansionism is a government policy which has always failed to take into consideration the fact that we *do* have borders with sovereign nations like the Cheyenne and Sioux!"

"I don't think this is the time to discuss politics," the general said brusquely.

"I think," William DeQuincy said in a nervous voice, "we are getting away from the issues, gentlemen. Mr. Pierce, it is certainly not the BIA's function to criticize Congress and the president."

"It's not my intention to criticize anyone, sir, but only to clarify certain points so that we may find a meeting of the minds."

"I think you exceed your prerogative," DeQuincy said. "These small internal dissensions need not be discussed at a bargaining table." DeQuincy spoke very rapidly, sotto voce; nevertheless Amaya got most of the exchange and translated it.

Indigo asked Amaya, "What is the point of contention? I don't understand."

"Everyone but Pierce assumes we have no right to our land and our own form of government, our own way of life," Amaya said bitterly.

High Top Mountain had been leaning toward her, listening. "Tell them we want peace." She did. "Tell them this . . ." He glanced at Sand Fox. "We will allow white settlements as far as the Horn, which they call the North Platte. Tell them that whites bound for the far sea may cross our land—"

"High Top Mountain!" Sand Fox exploded. He got to his feet angrily. The old chief motioned to him and he sat again to stare at the tent wall, silently fuming.

"They may cross unmolested if they do not hunt the buffalo. Along with the Sioux we forbid their crossing to the Black Hills to hunt for this gold Custer has promised them. These are our concessions. I can go no further." High Top Mountain looked to Indigo. He was in agreement. They could go no further and maintain their pride. This much was a disgrace in the eyes of some, like Sand Fox and Stalking the Wolf.

"This is preposterous!" General Lord said. "I appreciate the fact that we must have points to bargain from, but what you are offering, sir, is preposterous. First: Mr. DeQuincy, you had better explain what has been decided."

"Certainly . . ." Caught off-guard, DeQuincy stuttered, searched for something he never found in his pockets, and goggling at the Cheyenne leaders like a frightened schoolboy, told them, "The BIA under congressional injunction has created a program for the peaceful resettlement of the recalcitrant plains tribes—"

"What are you talking about?" Amaya demanded.

"What? Oh . . . the BIA has created a program—"

"You are not answering me. What are you talking about?" Amaya was standing now, not translating any of this. She leaned across the table, her eyes scoring DeQuincy.

"My dear young woman, please control yourself," Tufts said. Andy Pierce was looking into space, shaking his head. Staggs looked bored and thirsty. Indigo touched Amaya's arm questioningly.

"It is best for everyone concerned," DeQuincy went on, "that is . . . we have already considered the situation."

"You want us moved to a reservation?"

"Why, yes!" DeQuincy tugged at his long nose. "I am sure you would find life here very congenial, much easier than having to eke out a living on the plains. The government means to supply you with farm tools, with seed, with meat—you have seen, I am sure, how the peaceful Indians live here in government-built houses. There are schools to teach you and a church where you . . ."

DeQuincy spoke on. Amaya turned to High Top Mountain, who knew only that she was angry. "There can be no peace unless we surrender completely," she told the old Cheyenne. "We must give up our land, our ways, our dreams, our faith, our freedom and our pride, our language—and then the white man will make peace with us."

High Top Mountain was shocked into speechlessness momentarily. His cheeks actually flushed with rising pride, with indignation. Sand Fox looked vindicated, Indigo shattered.

"This can't be so, Amaya," High Top Mountain said. "What sort of travesty is this? This cannot be what the whites offer us for peace. Unless they do not wish peace at all, unless they want to see their own blood on the plains. Ask them again, Amaya. Be sure that this is what they mean, for it is something we can never accept, never, if the last Cheyenne must die."

"He wants to know," Amaya said, speaking very carefully, "if this is your position, one you cannot withdraw from. He wants to know if this is to be the only road to peace?" Amaya's voice trembled a little. Andy Pierce was looking at his fisted hands resting on the table.

"It is the policy of the United States government . . ." DeQuincy had finally found the piece of paper he had been looking for. "By a resolution adopted unanimously by the Congress of the United States, 13 February . . ."

Amaya heard no more. High Top Mountain had risen, and now he swept toward the door, the feathers of his great bonnet brushing the floor. Indigo was behind him, and Sand Fox, smirking and triumphant. General Lord had gotten to his feet with Tufts, who was sputtering, "Wait just a minute now. If you walk out on this conference, you'll live to regret it, you great bloody savage!"

"And you," Amaya said before exiting, "may also live to regret this day, Senator. You, after all, are the one who must explain the bloodshed that will follow."

She looked once at Andy Pierce, who could do nothing,

say nothing, and then she went out into the cool, open air where Indigo waited.

"There has to be a way," he said in wonder.

"The only way is the reservation."

"Then there is no way."

"No," Amaya said. "There is no way, not at this moment. But the time for peace will come, and it will be a good peace, now that they know we will not accept a bad peace."

"You believe this, Amaya?"

"With all my heart. I must believe it. I have dreamed of peace for my daughters, Indigo. I have dreamed that they will walk this land, our land, and be happy, be Cheyenne. Yes, I believe it. What are we to do? No longer believe in Cheyenne dreams?"

"You are right. Why would they want to war? They know we will fight. They brought us here to try to make fools of us, to try to threaten us. Now they will have to go to this Washington and make their report, tell the men there that the Cheyenne are not fools, that they wish to live free. Then there will be peace."

They rode now into a deep sandy coulee where willow and blackthorn grew. In the coulee bottom Sand Fox waited.

"What is it?" Indigo asked, looking around.

"Crow scouts behind us. Stalking the Wolf has turned back. When you ride from the coulee, do not ride toward the camp."

Indigo nodded his understanding and agreement. His horse labored up the far slope of the coulee, Amaya following. They rejoined the others, who were strung out now across the plain, angling southward, away from their camp. Sand Fox was no longer with them.

The war leader and Stalking the Wolf did not catch up with them again until night camp. "One dead, one has run away. I think we should ride tonight."

"High Top Mountain?"

The old man was exhausted, but he nodded his head. "I think we must. They intend to war, these whites. The peace conference was a charade, an ultimatum they tried to press home. The only surprise is that they didn't try to capture us while we were at the fort."

"That may have been the plan," Indigo said, "but we left abruptly."

"Your wife took us there," Sand Fox said. "Ask her if it was a trap." He was wiping the Crow blood from his scalping knife.

"Don't make a fool of yourself," Indigo said angrily, and for a moment Sand Fox tensed. He knew what sort of warrior Indigo had been, however. He shrugged his veiled accusation away.

"I will never speak to them again. Never see a white man but I shall work for his death," Sand Fox vowed.

"Don't be rash," High Top Mountain advised. "There may come a time when you will have to do otherwise."

"No time will come. I will die first."

Stalking the Wolf, who wore German silver conchas in his hair, nodded his agreement. "They meant to put us on a reservation, and failing that, to arrest us. Failing at both, they sent scouts to follow us to our camp."

Amaya followed the conversation with grim, compressed lips, narrowed eyes, angrily flared nostrils. They were right—she knew this in her heart. Hadn't the Crow scouts been sent to follow her before?

"The whites mean there to be no peace unless it is a peace which buries us," Amaya said softly, and the men turned their heads and stared at her in silent surprise. Finally Stalking the Wolf rose and put his bloody hand on her shoulder.

"This woman sees. You must apologize, Sand Fox. Amaya knows now what you and I have known all along. The only peace the whites will assent to is one that leads to slavery or death for the Cheyenne!"

Indigo hadn't spoken, nor had High Top Mountain. The war leaders seemed to have taken charge. They were angry, and even Amaya shared their anger. There was nothing for Indigo to say. What was it High Top Mountain had remarked? The councils must discuss peace; the war leaders must fight the wars. Now, it seemed, the time of the war leaders had come.

11

THE CAMP HAD to be moved and so the tents were folded, the travois loaded, the children prepared. Northward— they would go northward to where the tribes of the Cheyenne and the Sioux were massing, where no white army would dare to come.

Sand Fox had refused to join them. He and Stalking the Wolf with their small, experienced army vowed to stand their ground if the whites came. They had ridden out the morning before Amaya and Indigo led their people from the camp. With the rising sun on their right shoulder, they went away from a war that could not be avoided but must be delayed.

They left the long grass behind as they rode north toward the Rosebud, which they had chosen as their temporary camp. The hills were a dry, dusty brown dotted with sage. Occasional Spanish dagger grew here, and now and then at great intervals a lone oak. The draws sheltered chokecherry and scrub juniper, prairie pea vines and lavender-tipped thistles. Along the dry watercourses gray willows clustered together.

"I don't like this land, Mother," Dark Moon complained. He had galloped up to her in a cloud of dust—he was getting to be quite a horseman—and then walked his pony sullenly, silently beside hers. "Is the Rosebud green?"

"They say it is. I have never seen it."

"I want to swim, to see green trees."

"You will see them," Amaya assured him.

"Why can't we go right to Red Cloud's camp? I want to see the Sioux boys."

"Your father has to talk to them first, to send envoys, to see what our course must be."

"If we are going to war with the Sioux?" Dark Moon asked.

"Who told you that?"

"Everyone knows the Sioux are at war. Everyone knows we are going away so that we won't have to fight."

"Everyone knows everything; no one knows anything," Amaya commented to herself. Dark Moon was close to the truth, however. The rumors had been drifting down from the north, carried by fleeing Pawnee and Omaha Indians. Red Cloud and Crazy Horse were ready to make their long-awaited big war. The whites had heard too, and the yellow-haired one, Custer, had been given a great army to stand against the Sioux.

The Cheyenne feared pursuit from the south, but they were not yet ready to throw themselves into the situation developing around the Sioux. Indigo talked constantly of peace, but no one knew whom they might talk to, when, where. They made their camp on the Rosebud, but many bags were kept packed; many sacks filled with provisions were kept near at hand.

It was a bad time, the worst of times. There was no peace and no war. They did not know if they were in conflict with the whites. They knew nothing except that war was building in the north, the great cataclysm they had been anticipating, expecting. Sitting Bull had sung his songs and viewed his portents and declared the time to be right. Now they only waited, in their great camp at Greasy Grass, for more allies to join the true cause.

But Indigo vacillated. To join the Sioux was to commit the people totally to war—now and to the end of time. How many would die? How many children, women, helpless old? To wait was perhaps to invite disaster. They lived from day to day not knowing if morning would bring war or flight.

The rider came in from the north, dusty, gaunt, his horse foundering. He swung down on the run and ran to Indigo's tipi. The Cheyenne chief was just stepping out into the sun.

"Wing!"

"It is over," Wing gasped. "Much blood ... Come. Quickly."

Amaya was there, and Horse Warrior. Wing was calling for a fresh pony. He waved his arms wildly and shoved away anyone who tried to help him, even when he slumped to the ground from exhaustion.

Indigo's gray pony was finally brought at his command, and Amaya's little roan. A fresh horse was given to Wing, who clambered aboard and started northward. They rode for mile after empty mile in the heat of midday, seeing nothing but the brown plains, the back of Wing. The sun heeled over and started to sink, and still they rode. They found the dead in the hour before dusk.

Amaya reined in sharply, turning her pony's head. It snapped at its hackamore and reared, whickering. She walked it forward, Indigo beside her. They knew them all, the dead across the earth.

Sand Fox was there, a dozen bullets in his body. And Eagle Lair, and Stalking the Wolf. They got down to look at him, at their brother. He had been scalped, perhaps by the Crow scouts. A silver concha lay near his bloody hand.

The boys were at his feet. Hatchet and Remembers Long, struck down as if they had been men—and they had been in their hearts: their boyhoods had been stolen from them.

"Where are the others?" Indigo asked Wing.

"I am the others," Wing answered. He stood staring across the field strewn with the dead. "I was scouting to the south. When I came back, it was over."

His eyes were empty, staring into vast distances. Amaya shook her head. She knew what the warrior felt. She too had once come back to a war-ravaged camp to find the dead. Death is the way of life; it cannot be feared or despised. Yet when it comes and settles and eliminates all that one knew and loved, when it is so indiscriminate as this, when it is carried like a disease by man, it is not bearable.

A shadow passed across Amaya and she looked to the sky. There were a hundred vultures there, perhaps more.

"Come," Indigo said, "we can do nothing."

"They must be buried!" Wing cried.

"They cannot be, Wing. There are far too many."

"Then I shall stay."

"Come with us. Don't be foolish."

There was no time to stop him. His knife was at his own throat, and with a little half-smile he opened the arteries there. He fell, covered with blood in seconds. They rushed to him, a little cry escaping Amaya's lips. Wing was writhing on the dry earth, blood pulsing more weakly now from the opened arteries. And then it stopped, and after a time the twitching stopped. The blue flies which swarmed over the battlefield walked on Wing's unfeeling eyes. Indigo and Amaya turned and walked away.

It was silent, apparently peaceful along the Rosebud when they returned. Indigo sent out more scouts, summoned the elders and told them what had happened.

"And now what can we do?" Horse Warrior asked.

"Nothing. What has happened cannot be undone. The whites knew Sand Fox, knew Stalking the Wolf. They were punished. They do not know where we are. They have no reason to attack this camp."

"We must ride north," Horse Warrior said.

"There is a white army to the north!"

"Red Cloud is there."

"And perhaps he soon will not be. Perhaps he too will be defeated."

"Can we sit, Indigo, and wait to be defeated as well?"

"We will refuse to enter battle. If the soldiers come, we will be warned."

"And we will run?"

"Yes," Indigo said emphatically.

"Again?"

"If we must, to the far mountains."

"I don't like this. Ever since you killed the snake, we have been running. It is our way to fight, Indigo, not to run."

"Yes," he answered. "It was our way. It was the way of Sand Fox."

No one slept well that night. Indigo did not sleep at all. Amaya knew he could find no answer. He was troubled and there was no resolution. He rolled to her in the dead of night and his body worked against hers. He clung to her thighs and breasts, needing all the comfort she could give him, but when it was over she could do no more and he lay there staring skyward, Amaya lying beside him, breathing softly.

The man at the tent flap appeared with shadowy stealth. Indigo was instantly aware of his presence. He reached first for his war club and then relaxed. It was Hands on His Face.

Amaya too was awake. She saw Hands on His Face crook a finger, and Indigo nodded, dressing quickly. Amaya reached for her dress. "Rest, Amaya," he told her, but she shook her head.

Outside the stars were brilliant. The river slid past, muttering and whispering. The village slept.

"What is it?" Indigo asked.

"A prisoner. A white," Hands on His Face replied. As they walked hurriedly out of the camp toward the willows below the village, Hands on His Face spoke. "He came from the south. Right toward the camp. He is not a soldier. No one knew what to do, what he is saying."

Andy Pierce looked a little the worse for wear. He had a bruise on the right cheekbone, blood trickling down across his brow from a cut in his scalp. The sleeve of his jacket had been torn at the shoulder seam. He looked up, and recognizing Amaya, attempted a smile. He was pale and shaken.

"This is the one from Laramie, is it not?" Indigo asked. "The Indian agent?"

"Yes. Pierce is his name." She crouched to look at his head. Her breasts rose and fell heavily, and she sucked in her breath through clenched teeth. "What are you doing here?" she demanded, standing to tower over him.

"I have to talk to you both. Someone does. May I stand up?" He did so shakily. "I suppose I'll get fired for this. Maybe locked up, I don't know. You are supposed to have been informed, but no one bothered."

"Are you going to say something, Andy Pierce?" Amaya asked.

"Sorry. The bump on the head, I expect. The army is going to move against you."

"When!"

"I don't know. Tonight, tomorrow, a week."

"But why?" Rapidly she turned and translated for Indigo, who hunched forward tensely, staring at the white man in the darkness.

"Because that is the new policy. The Sioux are allied with the northern Cheyenne. Since it is impossible to tell which Cheyenne are not preparing to make war against the United States and which are . . ." Andy took a deep breath, wincing and holding his side as he did so. ". . . all Cheyenne and Sioux who are not living on a reservation are going to be presumed to be hostile."

"We are not making war!"

"Not now, perhaps, but as I've said, they can't guess the intentions of every small clan."

"They could have asked!"

"They would not have believed you, Amaya," Pierce said emotionally. "Anyway, the reasons don't matter any longer. It is simply a matter of fact that the army is going to treat every Cheyenne not living on the reservation as hostile!"

Pierce stood there, running his fingers through his hair as Amaya told Indigo what had been said. The warriors around them listened intently, their dark eyes shifting to Pierce's face occasionally. Indigo said something in a very low, sad voice and shook his head.

"He wants you to go now. Quickly, before someone grows angry with you."

"Someone like Indigo?" Pierce asked with an ironic smile.

"Perhaps." Amaya's voice briefly softened. "Thank you for coming. Please go. Your white face is a provocation."

"I'll go. Amaya . . . they're very serious about this. If you don't take your people to the reservation, they'll make their war." But she didn't answer, and Pierce could only turn, looking around futilely for his hat, and walk to where his horse was being held by a Cheyenne brave. At a sign from Indigo, the watching warriors drifted away into the trees.

"And so," Indigo said as Amaya walked to him—they were alone but for the river, the stars—"they leave us no choice in the end. Die or live as slaves."

"The reservation is worse than slavery," Amaya said.

"What can we do?" His voice was soft; a quiet anguish colored his words. He asked the question again, in a whisper, looking to the stars.

"The children must live," Amaya said.

"The reservation!" He was shocked that she could come to that conclusion, though privately he already had.

"What is it but another camp? We shall go for now; later we will leave. Perhaps the whites will leave. The war may be won by the northern tribes."

"We can always leave."

"Of course."

"That is perhaps what the whites mean," Indigo said, grasping the point anxiously, "that they want us to be there until the war is decided, so that the innocent are not involved."

"Perhaps," Amaya said, and then she spoke no more. Her throat was filled with a silent, welling sob and a tear broke free and ran down her cheek hotly. Angrily she thumbed it away and turned her back on her husband, the night, the river, the lies.

"Hurry, hurry!" Amaya urged. Akton looked up at her mother and sighed. The sun had been up only an hour, but they had been working for nearly three. They had had no breakfast.

"Where are we going?" Akton asked wearily. "Why do we have to hurry so?"

"To a new camp, that is all. Have you gotten our baskets?"

Mother Nalin came by, frail, white-haired, bent. She had been physically ill after hearing about Hatchet and Remembers Long. "Little boys, young boys. Tantha's babies," she had repeated endlessly. "I am happy we are not going to fight. I am happy! Will I need my iron pot, Amaya, or will they give me another on the reservation?"

"Take it along. Then perhaps you will have two."

Nalin seemed not to hear. She stared past Amaya, still seeing her grandsons in her mind. Amaya got back to work, hurrying the children, folding the tent herself. Indigo came by once, but they did not speak. He was ashamed, apparently, ashamed of his inability to extricate his people from this disgrace.

By noon they were on the move, following the river north. The dogs ran yapping happily through the willows, the only signs of Cheyenne joy, of animation. Even the children were silent and somber. They knew that this was something different, unprecedented—to go to the white man's camp.

They detoured far around the battleground where Stalking the Wolf and Sand Fox had died. Still it was well marked by the constant cloud of vultures which shadowed the earth. Hands on His Face killed a coyote which carried a human hand in its mouth.

The day was dry, the sky clear. The Cheyenne party went on quickly, nearly rushing toward the reservation, still far distant, fleeing war. Amaya watched her children anxiously, as if they could be struck down at this distance by the guns of battle.

Scouts rode ahead many miles but reported nothing when they returned. No one spoke. It was dusty, dry. The wind picked up the dust they made and cast it skyward in a long horse's tail. At night they camped again along the Rosebud. Their cooking was done before the sun went down. There were no fires at night.

Indigo was haunted by the possibility of battle, a battle which would embrace his family, his people. He blamed himself.

"I killed the snake, and this began. I was faithless to my dream."

Amaya said nothing; she only hoped that they would reach the reservation soon. They had to know what they faced, not try to guess, to rush toward and flee from know-not-what.

If his dream is bad, mine is good, she reasoned. And hers was of a free life on the plains, of a fine Cheyenne man and a healthy, free woman living life in the traditional way, proud and happy upon Manitou's land. *That* was the truth of her dream, and Indigo's despondency could not darken that truth, nor Sun Hawk's remembered words: "In dreams there may be immense sadness. The dreamer knows, but the price of knowing is fear."

That meant nothing. Sun Hawk must have had his

own obscure reasons for trying to frighten Amaya. Her dream had been joyous and she would cling to it! The joyous is vision beyond hope. She must carry her dream as a constantly recalled resource. In the joyous there is shelter from despair. She would not let joy slip away from her! She would dream. She rolled to Indigo in the night, throwing her leg over his, placing her ear to his chest, listening to the troubled beating of his heart.

In the night they came.

There was a brief warning, a moment's sharp cry.

"No!" Amaya sprang to her feet. Not again! It couldn't be happening again. She rushed to the tent flap, saw the charging cavalry, and was yanked back inside by Indigo, who was bringing his rifle to his shoulder, firing three times in a mad fury. A soldier bounced to the ground and was trampled by the night charge.

Guns were everywhere, flame and powder smoke. Lodges burned. Someone screamed; a horse rolled head over heels and lay thrashing.

"Get out of here!" Indigo yelled at the top of his lungs. His eyes were white, round, mad in the night. She didn't want to go. She wanted to pick up his war club and throw herself into the battle, to crush the skull of one invading soldier.

"Get out!"

The children were clinging to her legs, and that decided it. Amaya took them out the back of the tent, yelling to Indigo, "Kill them! Kill them all!"

Outside, flames danced against the sky. Horse soldiers were everywhere. A volley of twenty rifles fired at once sounded from the hillrise to the left of the camp. The white soldiers were shooting blindly into the lodges, killing everyone inside.

Someone was suddenly before her. Someone who knew her name. Mother Nalin, but she had no face! A bullet had chipped away cheekbone and flesh. An eye had been damaged. It goggled at Amaya. She put an arm around Nalin and tried to hurry on, but the old woman couldn't stay on her feet. Amaya got her into the tangled gray willows and then had to leave her lying on the ground. Her children came first.

The willows had been set afire. Flame swept toward

them, and behind them the guns roared. By the light of
the great fire she saw the commander of the whites,
thirty feet from her, on the other side of the willows—
Staggs, bathed in firelight, soaking in battle glory.

"Mother!" Akton yelled, and Amaya grabbed her hand,
racing on, dragging both the children—toward the fire,
not away from it. Others were running away, and as they
emerged from the burning willows they were shot down
by the waiting soldiers. Age, sex, fitness, made no difference. The guns kicked and a Cheyenne went down. They
lay in a row, half-burned by the fire, dead or dying. An
officer with a pistol walked among them, finishing the
wounded, the babies in arms.

All of this Amaya saw in a few wild moments as she
plunged through the willows. The brush tore at her face,
her hands. The children wriggled and tried frantically to
yank free, but nothing this side of death could break her
grip.

The flames formed a wall twenty feet high. Crackling,
swiftly moving flames which twisted into the black sky
and burned the few Cheyenne who tried to hide in the
willows and let the fire pass.

"Mother!" Dark Moon screamed. She ignored him and
rushed on. They could no longer hear the guns, only the
popping, snarling crackling of the lashing flames.

There it was suddenly, dark and shallow, narrow and
slow-running—the creek making its way through the
willows—and Amaya plunged into it, dragging the children with her as the sea of flame raced past them. They
lay facedown in the water, feeling the heat of the fire
against their backs. The river was colored by the flames,
becoming liquid fire, but cool fire, saving fire. They held
their breath until they could no longer, and then Amaya
lifted her head and blinked, wiping her eyes, staring
through the smoke at the still-living flames which swept
northward before the driving wind.

"Come," she whispered, and they went on a little way.
The burned willows crowded around them, black and
ragged. Here and there, spot fires burned, hissing and
fizzling. The river, heavy with ash, drifted past, and she
sat, this Cheyenne woman, there in nature's ruin, the
children under her arms, staring at the end of time.

The soldiers had not gone in the morning. Amaya could hear them among the rubble of the razed camp, searching for prizes, for trophies of bravery, perhaps for scalps, holy things to mock, the prize possessions of the dead to laugh over. Dark Moon did not move. His eyes were open but he was as still as if he had been asleep. Akton moved too much, fidgeting, her heart urging her to run away, to fight, when her mind would allow her to do neither.

The sun rose high and Amaya heard the leaders of the soldiers call to them, ordering them to mount, to ride away, as if they could ever ride away, as if the plains could be cleansed of them, as if they were not everywhere killing.

The soldiers did leave, but Amaya did not move. Not for hour upon hour. They might be back; how did she know? Dark Moon got to his knees and whispered into her ear, "Are we all the Cheyenne who live? Are the others all dead?"

She hugged him tighter and shook her head. Of course not—others had made their escape. The warriors had fought their way out of the trap. *They could not all be dead. Not Mother Winona and Beskath and Uncle Foxfoot and Crooked Arm . . .*

"What is the matter, Mother? Mother, are you all right?"

She was flat on her back, staring up at the dazzling, empty sky through the web of blackened willow branches. The children were over her.

"Yes." Amaya sat up, touching the old bullet wound at her temple. She was dizzy, sick to her stomach. She shook her head.

"What is it? Are you hurt?"

"No." Amaya attempted a smile. "I'm all right. I fainted!" She sat up with the children trying to help. "I'm going to the camp now. I want to see where everyone has gone."

"We'll—"

"You'll wait here, promise me, Akton!"

"I promise, Mother."

She got unsteadily to her feet and started forward, the fire-blackened twigs scratching at her, painting her with dark scars. Why had she fainted? Was she all right? Her vision wavered and dimmed. She did not want to see!

She did not want to know. She did not want to believe that existence could be so cruel, that this could happen twice in a person's lifetime, that they could be dead, all dead, all!

She crept to the edge of the willows and crouched, staring at the ruined camp, at the still-smoldering tipis, the crushed baskets, the broken jars, the shattered lances.

At the dead.

Emptiness like an ache in the universe gaped before her and rose to engulf her as she walked forward, finding them. Laughing Nose: the bullet that killed him had gone in his chest, not his back. He had not been contrary at the last moment. Mother Nalin still lay there, her body savaged. Hands on His Face had been riddled with bullets. The old man, Horse Warrior, her second father, was there, facedown in the scorched dust. Where the Waters Flow had been stabbed with a saber. A horse had ridden over Moon and Stars. Amaya passed the dead baby without looking, without naming it.

Death was there, and silence, and long memory, floating past like relics on the wind. Now and then anger flashed hotly, a brief echoic flare. Whispered thoughts pushed her onward. The ashes underfoot were still warm. She saw the shattered weapons, a rag-and-straw doll, shards of cups drunk around a Cheyenne campfire.

Indigo had died a warrior's death.

She got down on her knees and rested her hand on his back. His face was twisted away, and she did not wish to see it. They had shot him many times. In his hand was his war club. What had been in his heart, in his mind, those last fierce moments? Had he thought of her, of the children, or had there been only anger, despair for a lost effort?

How long she remained there on her knees, she did not know. It seemed it had started to rain, for there were spots of water on Indigo's back. Amaya wiped the tears from her eyes and stood.

She stood for a long while, her numbed mind refusing to decide, to tell her what to do now. The children must be saved. There was nothing else of any importance at this point. She suddenly came to a decision, and walked swiftly back to where Akton and Dark Moon waited.

"Come now, we must be going."

"Where are the others?" Akton asked.

"Gone ahead."

"Ahead? Where are we going?"

"To the only place we are allowed to go on living. To the fort. To the reservation. Hurry now, hurry."

Andy Pierce pushed away his papers and rose, rubbing his eyes. Why he worked on, he didn't know. The resignation paper, signed, dated, was on his desk. They could have that in the morning. Word of the Rosebud massacre had reached him.

Staggs had been cheerful about the whole thing: "They were traveling north to join Red Cloud. We cut off those reinforcements, by God!"

"Where are the prisoners, Harry?"

"What?" Staggs gulped a glass of whiskey. His hand was shaking, Pierce noticed. "There were no prisoners."

"Not one?"

"Fought to the last man." Harry Staggs finished his whiskey, sat down, and started tugging off his boots.

"The women and children?" Pierce asked.

"Why, they must have taken to the hills, Andy. I didn't see any."

"It'll come out, Harry."

"What are you talking about?" Staggs asked mildly. When he repeated the question, it was with heat. He came to his feet and banged a fist on his desk. "Just what in bloody hell are you intimating, Pierce!"

"I think you know. It'll come out, Staggs. Soldiers talk."

"Maybe so." Staggs's mood changed completely. He sat behind his desk, small, hunched, wolfish. "You think only the redskins should be allowed to butcher innocent women and children? You forget that wagon train along the Horn last year?"

"I haven't forgotten."

"Well, they chose the tactics, didn't they! They decided how it was going to be!"

Andy Pierce had just turned and walked away. Staggs

had railed, but Pierce hadn't heard any more. He had walked to the office, tried to finish up his work, signed a letter of resignation, and sat there staring at it. What was he accomplishing, what had he accomplished? It was hard to remember what misplaced idealism had caused him to take up the standard. Having seen James Dawes, a more experienced and probably more competent man, broken on the rack of bureaucracy, he should have had enough sense to see that there was nothing anyone could do to ease the Indian's burden. To bring him onto this reservation and hand him a hoe was essentially the same as cutting his throat. He and Staggs seemed to be working toward the same end—the extinction of the Indian and his culture.

Angrily Pierce walked out of his office. It was dark outside. When he went out to stand on the porch, he could see only a few late fires burning, a few lanterns from the town across the river.

Had they been waiting there, in the darkness?

As he looked out across the reservation, the lone, shambling horse came toward him. On its back were a woman and two children. The younger child slept. The horse shuffled to a stop and stood, its flanks heaving with exhaustion, head down.

"My God, Amaya!"

"We have come, Andy Pierce."

He managed to catch her before she fell, to help the three of them down and into his office, where he started a fire and brewed tea. The boy had fallen asleep again on a rug. The girl was trying to sleep, but Pierce could see her twitching, see her eyes flutter. Amaya sat in a rocking chair, her eyes staring at nothing, the firelight revealing the hollowness of her cheeks, the strain on her face. She spoke as if to herself.

"It was a mistake, you see. I dreamed, but my dream was of the past, not of the future. It was I who walked the peaceful valleys, I who wed the strong young Cheyenne, I who saw the buffalo walk the long plains . . . not her. Not my beautiful daughter. Not her and others like her. It was a mistake. I have had my dreams; I cannot dream for her. And my dream has ended."

She sat there awhile longer, silently, her breast rising

and falling softly until Andy Pierce thought she was asleep, but she wasn't. The dark eyes, fire-bright, far-seeing, looked into the distances, knowing something he could only guess at, reliving a lost and broken dream.

12

AMAYA LOOKED UP from her sweeping to find Andy Pierce in the doorway of her cottage. He had his hat in his hand and a serious look on his face. There was, Amaya noticed, gray coloring his hair at the temples.

"Good morning, Amaya."

"Good morning." She hurriedly finished her sweeping and put the straw broom away. She came to the doorway then, and Pierce's eyes watched her, admiring the litheness of her, the dignity she retained. Her elkskin dress was beaded with an eagle motif, her graying hair was braided and tied with rawhide thongs. She was still Cheyenne, would be Cheyenne to the end of her days.

"I had hoped you would walk with me, if you have the time."

"For a special reason?"

"No."

If only she would smile again, Andy thought. If only once her grief would show, but it never had, not in all this time.

Pierce himself had remained. How could he have left after Amaya came back? He stayed and was as ineffective as ever. He tried, but that was not enough. The war had gone on. Custer had been defeated and the reservation Indians walked in quiet pride for a time. Then the tide turned again and the Sioux were crushed by Crook in one battle after another, and still more battered, weary people trudged onto the reservation.

"I saw Akton singing with the choir at the school. She looks lovely," Pierce said.

"Yes."

That was all the reply she made. They were walking toward the river, sun-bright, silvery. The oaks cast mottled shade across the earth.

"She is quite a young lady now."

"She is," Amaya said.

Akton, who wore white-made dresses, who had been well-educated, who had taken to the ways of the Americans. "Why not, Mother?" she had said many times. "This is the present. I can't live in the past! What will happen to us all if we refuse to adapt? *That* is truly the death of the Cheyenne."

Amaya hadn't argued with the girl. Perhaps she was right. Who knew? She and Dark Moon, who had had his hair cropped and called himself by a white name and wore knickers like the boys in town, who spoke of becoming an engineer for the railroad which whistled and thundered its way through Laramie and out onto the plains where once the buffalo had walked.

Pierce had stopped. He placed one foot behind him against the trunk of a massive white oak and stood studying her face, the fine appealing lines of it.

"There is still time for us," he said.

"There is time. Who knows when there will be no more time?"

"Time for us to be . . . together, I meant, Amaya."

"I know what you meant, Andy Pierce."

"We could marry. We should marry. We belong together, Amaya."

There was a pause before she answered. "We do not. You are white. I am Cheyenne."

"Does that always have to be there? Does that always have to be a barrier, Amaya?"

"Yes," she replied. "Yes, it does. What you wish cannot be."

She turned away toward the river, and after a while she heard his footsteps receding, the dry oak leaves crackling as he walked heavily away.

Yes, she thought, there would always be that barrier. Times changed, apparently, but the heart did not change so readily. Time changed and the river ended but the heart went on mourning.

She turned and walked along the river, her hands

behind her back, her head bowed. It was quiet and still.
A slight haunted breeze drifted through the oaks, carrying faraway memories.

Amaya heard the shout of joy and she looked up. The
white boy, naked, lean, young, stood on the low-hanging
branch of the oak tree, and as she watched, his body
arced through the air and knifed into the silver surface
of the water. She waited and after a moment he emerged,
laughing, wiping back his pale hair, calling out to a
friend.

Then there was nothing more to see and Amaya turned,
walking homeward.

Sweeping Sagas from SIGNET